CW01177473

ROXXY
TO THE RESCUE

ROXXY
TO THE RESCUE

ROB RONIN

ILLUSTRATED BY
KIM RONIN

Copyright © 2024 Rob Ronin | www.RoxxyDog.com

All rights reserved. Except as permitted under the U.S. Copyright Act of 1976, no part of this publication may be reproduced, distributed, or transmitted in any form, or by any means, or stored in a database or retrieval system, with the prior written permission of the publisher, except for the use of brief quotations in a book review.

For information about this title or to order other books and/or electronic media, contact the publisher.

Cover and interior design by The Book Cover Whisperer: OpenBookDesign.biz

979-8-9916527-0-4 Hardcover
979-8-9916527-1-1 Paperback
979-8-9916527-2-8 eBook

Printed in the United States of America

FIRST EDITION

To Kim, always and forever.

To the many four-footed rescues that brightened our hearts and enlivened our household over the years.

And to Roxxy's alter ego, Ginger.
Who's a good dog?

Acknowledgments

I am grateful for my endlessly beautiful wife, Kim, who not only created the original artwork for Roxxy, but who helped me with a critical plotpoint when I was struggling at the beginning of the project.

Special thanks to my friend, Theresa Hamilton, who found Roxxy's alter ego, Ginger, when the stray pup was living behind a pile of rocks next to a parking lot. Ginger appeared and walked next to Theresa, who was strolling during a break at work. Being a cat person (nobody's perfect), Theresa attempted to avoid eye contact, but Ginger was relentless. The rest is history. I ended up with Ginger, Ginger ended up with me, and every day brings the certainty for me that I got the best of the deal. Ginger sends a tailwag to Fairy Godmother Theresa.

Thanks also to my many friends who provided encouragement while I was writing Roxxy. You know who you are, and I am grateful. A special shoutout to Rich Waycaster, who offered invaluable feedback near the end of the project. Rich could teach Roxxy a few things about saving the day.

Sincere gratitude to my editor, Cyndi Sandusky, for her many contributions, not the least of which included identifying where I had Fall-blooming plants blossoming in the Spring, Spring-blooming plants blossoming in the Fall, insect-eating birds consuming seeds, and seed-eating birds gobbling insects. Sheesh! What happened to artistic license? In any case, thank you Cyndi for making me a better writer and a more astute observer of nature's wonders.

Many thanks as well to Christine Horner at Open Book Design. I benefited from her brilliant design skills, her flexibility when flexibility was called for, and her practicality by reminding me that art directors don't tell writers how to write, and writers would do well to reciprocate. Christine is a rockstar.

Any inaccuracies contained in the manuscript are my responsibility alone.

CHAPTER 1

"Being adorable is exhausting."

"Stop stalling," growled Max, scruff bunched across his shoulders. "I want a rematch."

"I bet you do," replied Roxxy. "Loser."

"Ancient history. This time—"

"Itch," she announced, rolling over and pressing her back into the family room's beige carpet. All four legs waved in the air as her hips swiveled one way and shoulders the other in an enthusiastic wriggle. *Ahhh.*

"Don't think you're getting off that easy," huffed Max, dropping to the floor and resting his chin on hefty paws. "I'll wait."

"You do that."

Roxxy stopped mid-wriggle and cocked an ear. The rattle of pots and pans came from the kitchen at the back of the house. The family's humans—Bill and Carol—were preparing dinner, which meant the evening meal for the canines would soon follow. Roxxy's nose twitched, sifting scents. Bill could usually be relied upon to slip a bit of savory roast beef or chicken into the dog bowls to supplement the kibble. So far, the only food prep smells were the disappointing and pungent aromas of peeled onions and crushed garlic.

"Still waiting," huffed Max.

"And annoying." Roxxy wondered if all brothers were such a pain. Max was obsessed with taking the alpha-sib position from her. She could understand it. He was far bigger and would be dominant if not for her quickness. Their sister, Lulu, had never shown any interest in the role, commenting, "That alpha stuff is old fashioned. We don't need to *organize*. The only scary thing around here is the vacuum cleaner."

Roxxy snorted. She and her littermates were as different in temperament as they were in physical appearance. They definitely put the "mixed" in mixed breed.

She amped up her wriggling.

"Chigger bite?" asked Max, his cinnamon eyes narrowing with interest. "Or seizure?"

"Hysterical," replied Roxxy, putting a little more oomph into the motion to reach a particularly troublesome spot in the middle of her back.

"Bee?"

She ignored him. Like most scratching, the process became satisfying even after the itch disappeared. Her back tingled from the friction with the carpet.

"Are you going to make me guess? Poison ivy?"

"Hornet."

Max's scruff relaxed. "Sorry, Sis. Those things are no joke. Where did it sting you?"

She went still but kept her back pressed against the carpet. "Take a wild guess."

"Where in the *yard*?"

"Near the vegetable garden. Got me while I was chasing that carrot-loving rabbit. What a cliché."

Max's ears shot upright, creating short, triangular fins on either side of his head. "He outran *you*? Hard to believe."

Her tail—leading a life of its own as usual—swept back and forth at the implied compliment, producing a whispery *swish* as it brushed the low-pile Berber. "I just wanted to warn him off. Besides, what would I do with a live rabbit?"

"Eat him?"

Roxxy shuddered. "Can you imagine the mess? Give me a nice bowl of kibble any day."

She rolled to her stomach and gathered in a length of brown rope with a knot at each end. The tough material was her favorite chewy. Real hemp. *Not* the red and white cotton that started out tightly woven but soon deteriorated into a soggy mess that left strands wedged between her teeth. Yuck.

"Roxx, let's get back to that rematch." Max's gaze flattened into a challenging stare.

Her jaws worked busily to cover the chewy with enough spit to claim it as her own—at least until one of the other dogs had a go. That was the problem with five canines under one roof. You had to share everything, and if you weren't a fast eater, forget about it. Still, at nine months old, she was grateful to live in her birth home with her littermates, even if her parents lectured them daily about being *good dogs*. Loyal, obedient, blah, blah, blah. Honestly, was a concept ever more overrated? Bill and Carol were the only humans in the household. Roxxy heard more *swishing*. The pair were the best personal assistants a dog could ask for. *So* adorable, especially when they acted like they were in charge.

Roxxy knew she had a good setup. Her only source of irritation—well, besides the family cat, but that was another story—was the big-boned, rangy, wire-haired brute on the opposite side of the room. Max sat Sphinx-like between two rectangles of yellow sunlight slanting across the carpet. Ropy muscles stood out beneath his black-and-tan coat. He was older than her by seven minutes but acted like it was seven years and often provided an abundance of unwelcome advice, such as encouraging her to take a turn fetching Bill's house slippers. Not in this lifetime. She could understand *chewing* on shoes, but fetching them for a human who was perfectly capable of doing the task? Please.

She bit deep into the hemp and gave it a good shake, enjoying the way her teeth slid between the tough fibers.

"Afraid I'll win this time?" asked Max.

Roxxy laid a furry paw on the chewy and gnawed a knot, tasting undertones of dried straw and hay. All the alpha-sib matches had gone the same. Max would charge. She'd dodge. He'd trip over those gigantic paws and go down like a water buffalo on roller skates. She'd zip in and place her jaws lightly on his throat, and he'd go limp like tradition dictated. Match over. She'd return to her normal duties of napping and... well, more napping.

"Roxxy," Max prompted.

Her nose twitched as a breeze stirred the linen curtains framing the south-facing windows. She wished Bill had planted the herb garden a little farther from the house. Basil and cilantro were a double whammy. Too strong, and—

"I'm tired of waiting!" snapped Max, lips fluttering in a snarl.

Roxxy blinked. She knew he wouldn't really *hurt* her, but he was creeping her out with all the aggressive posturing. Maybe she should concede the alpha-sib position. What difference would it make? The only changes would be Max getting first dibs on treats and the primo napping spots. She sighed. And he would feel even more entitled to offer commentary on how she should mind their parents and stay out of trouble.

Roxxy worked her teeth free of the damp hemp and gathered her legs beneath her.

"*Get ready!*" A strip of fur rippled down the length of Max's spine. "*You had your chance!*"

The barking bounced off the walls, sending a framed photo rattling against the wire and nail keeping it in place.

Roxxy's eyes settled on Max's front paws as he leaned forward to spring.

"For goodness—pipe down in there!" came Carol's voice from the kitchen.

A second later, Bill's baritone followed. "Quiet, Max. It's not like you to bark in the house."

Max's ears fell in submission.

"Serves you right," said Roxxy, flicking her foreleg to send the chewy bumping across the carpet.

She stood and stretched, pleased that Carol and Bill had put Max in his place, but her satisfaction disappeared when she caught a glimpse of her reflection in the fireplace's glass doors. She looked as intimidating as a throw pillow. Her shoulders barely reached knee high to an adult human, and her compact body was no bigger than a gym bag. Blond curls swirled in every direction, making her look like she'd just stepped out of a wind tunnel. Fortunately, she was plenty sturdy under all that wavy fur. She was a better leaper than Max or even their dad, despite having shorter legs. The problem was she resembled a cuddler instead of a scrapper…and truth be told, she did enjoy a good snuggle with her housemates. Except the family cat, of course. She wasn't insane.

Roxxy sighed, wishing her reflection suggested less *pushover* and more *give me that chewy or I'll thump you with it*. The tip of each furry ear flopped forward in a neat fold to give her a perky, good-natured appearance. Her shortish muzzle, courtesy of a distant pug ancestor, ended in a black button of a nose. Chestnut eyes peeked through a fringe of blond bangs. She noticed that her tail, coated with a double layer of blond shag, was drooping. *Great,* she thought. The thing was like carrying a sign to announce your inner feelings to the world. *I hate my looks!*

Worst of all, she was the only dog in the house cursed with an underbite. Even when her mouth was closed, the row of tiny bottom teeth peeked out at the front. Bill and Carol seemed incapable of going a day without gushing, "Who's got the cutest *wittle* underbite in the *whooooole wiiiiiide* world? *You* do! *You're* the cutest *wittle* doggy!"

Why did two perfectly reasonable humans turn into babbling—

The thought brought her up short. There hadn't been much baby talk or high-pitched cooing from Bill and Carol lately. In fact, both had been acting strangely. One minute distracted, the next caressing the ears and rubbing the bellies of Roxxy and her littermates. Come to think of it, her parents had seemed a bit off as well. The "good dog" lectures had become more frequent and intense. But why? Everybody in the household was healthy—her nose would've detected any illness. There was plenty to eat, and the water bowls were always full. What could be wrong?

Frustrated by the mystery, she took her irritation out on the oaf at hand. "Max, you annoyed Carol and Bill. They *never* get mad."

"I didn't mean—"

Roxxy interrupted, "In case you haven't been keeping track, we're practically adults! Try showing a little dignity."

She went silent as her nose registered a savory scent. She shoved her face into the carpet. Was a morsel of corn chip goodness buried deep in the fibers? Hard to be sure. She took a massive breath. A tiny crumb flew up her nostril and disappeared down her windpipe. The ensuing bout of sneezing/coughing/hiccupping left her spent and dizzy.

"What was that about dignity?" asked Max.

Roxxy sat up tall, placing her eye-level with Max's breastbone. "I wasn't the one who barked loud enough that Carol and Bill heard it from the other end of the house!"

"They know I'm a *good dog*!"

"Dumb and obedient?" Roxxy gave a double blink of amusement. Max had clearly fallen for their parents' propaganda.

She couldn't see the point of following all those rules. Don't chew on the curtains. Don't bother the cat. Don't raid the picnic basket when no one is looking. Her eyes went out of focus. If only she'd been quick enough to get *both* drumsticks. You had to hand it to Bill. The man could fry a chicken.

"You're drooling," observed Max.

Her pink tongue cleaned up the corners of her mouth. "Am not. Maxey, be a *good dog* and run along, but wake me when it's dinner time." She dismissed him by wrinkling her muzzle.

Like all canines, Roxxy used her whole body to talk. Tiny variations in ear flicks could communicate *great to see you*, *drop that chew toy and back away*, or any number of things depending on the angle and depth of the movement. And tail twitches? Too big a subject to even get into.

Max growled, "I'm not going anywhere. Besides, I can't believe you're telling *me* to be good? You're a born troublemaker. You drive Bill and Carol crazy."

"Don't be so dramatic," she replied.

"You ate a *chair*!" exclaimed Max.

"Only the leg. And I didn't *eat* it. Just chewed."

Her mouth tingled as she recalled the earthy richness of the mahogany. She wondered if all antiques were so tasty. Hmmm…there were three chairs left in the dining room, not to mention the table.

Max scolded, "I know that look. Don't even think about it! Bill and Carol are the best people ever. You should learn to behave."

Roxxy shared Max's opinion about Bill and Carol. The pair *worked like humans*—an old canine expression—to provide a wonderful home for the dogs. Roxxy fulfilled her end of the bargain by being on-call for petting, and she handled chores such as napping and making sure her food bowl was squeaky clean. She felt sorry for humans. It must be terrible to be burdened with those opposable thumbs that produced computers and cell phones. From the way humans stayed glued to the screens, the gadgets must require constant attention. Some of their inventions were wonderful, for sure. Crunchy nuggets of kibble? Sheer genius.

Roxxy was constantly amazed at how people could be so clever in some ways but clueless in others. For instance, humans had never figured out that canines understood people-speech. Even *good dogs* didn't let on they knew more than basics like "sit" and "stay." Otherwise, humans would never give them a moment's peace. "Don't shed in the house." "Keep the gophers out of the garden." "Give yourself a bath." People might even expect dogs to get a *job*. The thought was so disturbing, Roxxy gave herself a vigorous head-to-tail/tail-to-head shake.

Mood and fur pleasantly adjusted, she hopped onto the sofa and turned in a series of tight circles before collapsing. Nap time.

Max yapped, "I'm serious about you staying out of trouble! You—"

"Indoor voice." She snuggled deeper into the cushion.

Max fell silent and cocked an ear. When no rebuke came from the kitchen, he continued quietly, "Carol was really upset when you destroyed that chair leg."

"She forgave me."

"Only because you can do that, uh…that *thing*."

"This?"

Roxxy's ears tilted back to a half-mast position of submission. She batted long lashes, sending bangs atremble while gazing out soulfully from behind the fleecy blond curtain. She threw in a whimper as a promise that she would never again misbehave.

Max grumbled. "Bill and Carol melt when you do that."

"They fall for it every time," agreed Roxxy with a snort, ears lifting perkily. "You've got to love humans and their wacky sense of optimism."

"What about that alpha match?" asked Max. He began gnawing on the ropy chew toy.

"I need a nap. Being adorable is exhausting. Not that you'd know."

She folded her tail tight around her. The room darkened as she placed the feathery tip across her eyes.

"Come on, Roxx. All I need is another chance."

"Hmmm?" The call of a mourning dove drifted through the window. *Hooo-oh, hoo, hoo, hoo…hooo-oh, hoo, hoo, hoo.* Roxxy imagined the ash-gray creature settling on a cozy nest, keeping her chicks warm, and …

A burring snore filled the room.

"Sis!"

Roxxy's eyes flew open. *"Dinner?!?"*

"You were snoring. I want that alpha match."

"You woke me for *that*?" She sprang off the sofa and stumbled when a rear paw landed on a red rubber ball the size of an apple.

She examined the offending object. *Worst chew toy ever.* The sphere was hollow and had a hole where a treat could be deposited. Determined gnawing was required to extract the goodie. *Typical.* What was it with humans and making everything so difficult? They could simply hand over the treat and add a little context, like "Nice going on being so cute."

She lashed out with her back leg like a mule, sending the ball arcing through the air to land on the armchair next to the sofa.

"Ouch!"

Roxxy craned her neck to get a look at the chair's seat. The ball rested against her sister's flank. Lulu, the middle sib, was four minutes older than Roxxy and three younger than Max.

Roxxy was convinced that her sister was the prettiest dog in the world. Lulu had the conformation of a small beagle. Her white coat was striking in contrast to her ebony ears, paws, and inch-long black tip at the end of her tail. And Lulu *wasn't* cursed with an underbite.

"Sorry for waking you, Sis," apologized Roxxy. "It was Max's fault."

"Figures," Lulu replied as she rose and shook.

Roxxy watched with envy as a white cloud swirled around her sister. Lulu had a shedding ability that produced results like a feather pillow fluffed with a chain saw. Carol vacuumed daily in a self-proclaimed effort to "keep the place from looking like a hair factory." Roxxy snorted. The woman clearly loved a challenge.

Lulu jumped from the chair and landed lightly on the carpet. "Roxx, why is our goofball brother bothering you?"

Max protested, "Hey! I haven't done anything!"

Roxxy huffed, "Lulu, don't believe him. He wants an alpha-sib rematch."

"Not *again*." Lulu eyed Max. "You always lose and spend the rest of the day pouting. What makes you think this time will be different?"

"Growth spurt. I'm a lot bigger now."

Roxxy silently agreed. Max had always been bigger than her, but now his body had fulfilled the promise of those gargantuan paws. He was a hefty forty-five pounds, if not more. Far bigger than her own thirty. He'd probably add another twenty-five by the time he reached full adult size, while she'd put on another ten pounds at best.

Lulu said, "Roxx, he *is* freakishly large."

"That's what I mean," agreed Max, short tail bobbing. The movement stopped. "Wait, what?"

Lulu continued to Roxxy, "Maybe it's time to admit that you're overmatched."

"I don't know about *freakish*," Max objected.

"Lulu, you really believe he can beat me?" Roxxy asked.

"I was thinking *rugged*, or maybe *imposing*."

"Shut *up*, Max!" Roxxy and Lulu chorused.

Max pleaded, "Give me a chance. As the big brother, it's my duty to teach my little sisters important life lessons."

Lulu snorted. "I've got to hear this."

Roxxy said darkly, "Somehow, I think most of these lessons are going to be directed at me."

"Well, yeah," said Max. "Lulu, you're level-headed and you make good decisions."

Lulu frowned. "You make me sound boring."

"You're not boring. You're, uh, *normal*. Roxxy, on the other paw, has never encountered a bad decision she didn't like."

Roxxy growled. "Give me an example."

"I already did. Eating furniture."

"Give me *another* example!"

"The alpha-sib issue. You beat me in the past by being quicker, but that only goes so far. I'm a *lot* larger now. I'd never forgive myself if you took on a big dog and got hurt. You've got to learn your limits. We can even skip the match if you'll concede."

She blinked. Maybe she'd been wrong to peg Max as a sore loser after their previous matches. What if he'd been disappointed in himself for failing to fulfill his—so-called—big-brother duties? Still, she didn't like the idea of him thinking she needed to be taught a lesson...although he *did* seem to have her best interests at heart. The air behind her stirred. Stupid tail. It was making it hard for her to stay mad at him.

Lulu said, "Roxx, I think Max is right. You should concede. Besides, who cares if he's gotten too big for you to beat? He'll never come close to being an adorable fluff ball like you."

Roxxy grumbled, "I wish Bill had never called me that. Makes me sound like a cat toy."

She paused, ear twitching as she picked up the *snick-snick-snick-snick-snick-snick* of a knife blade hitting a chopping board in the kitchen. Bill did all the cooking, and Carol took care of all the other household chores. Roxxy sighed. They really were well-trained humans. She hoped Bill was putting aside some pot roast to mix with the kibble for dinner. Maybe she would forgive him for burdening her with the fluff ball description.

Lulu wagged her tail. "Roxxy, fluff ball sounds cute! I'd kill for those blond curls."

Max snorted. "But we've forgotten Roxxy's best feature."

"Bad idea, Max," warned Lulu.

"Why? Bill and Carol love that cute *wittle* underbite."

Roxxy's eyes narrowed. "Mention my underbite one more time, and your new name will be Tripod."

"Don't be so sensitive. Let's get back to you conceding."

"Concede *this*!" She darted forward and nipped him hard on the ear.

"Owww!"

She pulled back and dropped into a springy crouch. He'd definitely grown, but she was still way faster. Plus, he was unaware she had another advantage. She'd noticed early in their matches that his front paws kneaded the carpet when he was about to spring. That habit allowed her to sidestep his charges and pivot back to plow into his flank. The second he thudded to the floor, she would be on him.

"What are you waiting for?" she taunted. "I thought you wanted a rematch. Having second thoughts?"

Max's toes flexed, making small indentations in the carpet.

Roxxy's body hummed with anticipation. All distractions faded—Lulu's concerned panting, the ticking of the walnut clock on the mantel above the fireplace, the spicy scent of a neighbor's freshly mown grass. She readied herself for Max's charge.

Any second now…

"Thought so," said Max, toes going still.

"What?" she asked, trying not to sound disappointed.

"Come off it. I know you know that I know."

"You're babbling," she growled.

Max gave his toes a quick flex. "I figured it out."

"Stop gloating, Max!" yapped Lulu.

Roxxy threw her sister a grateful look—and knew instantly she'd made a mistake. Max charged. There was no time for her to dodge left or right. Her legs uncoiled, and she shot straight up like a fur-covered rocket. Max zoomed through the space she'd occupied an instant before, his airstream ruffling the curls on her belly.

"Take that, half-wit!" she yipped triumphantly, pleased she'd leaped over his charge, but at the last second his thick tail struck solidly against her right rear paw.

Ceiling and floor spun end over end as she tumbled in a midair flip. She tucked in her legs and managed to stick the landing by sheer luck, but she was facing away from Max. She whirled, expecting to see him in a tangle of limbs after tripping over his snowshoe paws.

"Half-wit?" snarled Max, poised in a ready crouch. "I've had it with the name-calling!"

Roxxy's nose twitched at the scent of real anger—a smell like a metal pan left too long on a hot burner. *Uh oh.*

Lulu croaked, "Roxx, stop messing around and concede."

"Too late," Max growled. His wide jaws snapped up the rope chew toy from the floor. He released it with a twist of his muscled neck. The hemp smashed into the end table beside the couch. The lamp atop the table rocked without toppling. The brass base clicked against the polished maple surface before settling back in place.

Roxxy heard her heart thudding in the sudden silence.

Lulu squeaked, "C-calm down, Max."

The scruff rose across Max's shoulders. "Stay out of this, Lulu! Roxxy and I are going to settle this once and for all!"

Roxxy gulped and took a step back. A try for another step ended when her rump smacked into the upholstered surface of an ottoman.

"Trapped, huh?" asked Max, lips skinning back in a snarl.

Roxxy looked left and right. Furniture formed a barrier on both sides. Her gaze returned to Max. A froth of saliva glistened on his teeth.

Trapped, she acknowledged with a shiver.

AXEL

"Next delivery?" asked Ethan.

"You know the schedule," replied Axel. "I just dropped off a batch. Three weeks until the next group."

"My buyer wants them as soon as possible, which means *I* want them as soon as possible."

"The problems of a middleman," said Axel. "Breaks my heart. Counting cash and avoiding risk. You've got it tough."

"I'm in charge, Ax. This isn't a partnership anymore. You work *for me*."

Axel gripped the cell phone tighter. The current working relationship with Ethan was less satisfying than the one they'd had as cellmates in the state penitentiary. The other cons had called them Hustle and Muscle.

Ethan had devised schemes for smuggling and bookmaking.

Axel's specialty had been collections.

"Well?" prompted Ethan.

"The schedule is set."

"The schedule's what I say it is."

"I haven't even started gathering the next batch."

"Then stop whining and get a move on."

Axel's free hand curled into a fist. Ethan had gotten early release and had had an operation up and running by the time Axel made parole. A year in, Axel still couldn't believe there was so much money in stealing—

"How soon?" repeated Ethan.

Axel leaned against the warped door frame. At a towering six-five and a hefty two-fifty, his solid bulk sent a shiver through the metal jamb. The entry to the makeshift warehouse was the best place to capture the breeze that kicked up every afternoon. Lifting his chin, he inhaled the cool air laced with a heavy dose of pine sap. The wind quickened, and the building surrounding the doorway ominously groaned. Old rivets strained to hold the corrugated panels together.

Axel shrugged. The place might be a dump, but the location was ideal—a thirty-minute drive from Asheville and surrounded by low mountains covered in dense forest inhabited only by wildlife. The isolated structure perched atop one of the elevations and was only accessible by a rutted gravel road twisting up the mountainside. The walls were rusting but solid enough to deaden the sounds that echoed from within when he was accumulating a shipment.

Movement caught the corner of Axel's eye. A dragonfly cruised closer in a flight path of angular fits and starts. The insect stopped and hovered within a yard of his face. The elongated emerald body glowed in the sunlight. Iridescent wings beat in a silvery blur and generated a faint hum as the creature remained in place, as if suspended from a string.

Axel spat.

The soaked dragonfly windmilled backward and tumbled to the gravel parking pad. Wings heaved, but the coating of goo bound them to the stones.

"You awake?" prompted Ethan.

"Savoring the joys of nature."

"Savor on your own time. How soon can you deliver?"

Axel shifted his weight to the other side of the doorway. A screw popped free from the overhead sill and pinged off the cracked cement stoop. Even money as to whether the Outpost would collapse before the short-term lease ended in a month. Outpost was the term he used for whatever remote building was serving as his warehouse when putting together a shipment. The present structure was a barn-like, windowless rectangle with no air conditioning or heat, but it had electricity and running water. A crusted drain rested in the middle of the cement floor.

The corners of Axel's mouth turned down when he thought of the Outpost he'd used before the current one. It had been an abandoned tobacco farm near Tryon. He'd rented the place solely because of the large, enclosed shed that had once been used to dry harvested leaves. All had gone fine until the property's well dried up after a month. After that, he'd had to haul water in forty-gallon jugs. He'd kept the shipment alive until it was ready to transport, but there hadn't been enough water to rinse out the cages. And the smell? Never again.

Axel noticed the dragonfly lifting a wing free. His jaw worked. The insect disappeared beneath a yellow-streaked blob.

"Stop stalling and answer," snapped Ethan.

"I already did," replied Axel, dragging the back of his hand across his mouth. "The whole point of a schedule is to follow it."

He scanned the forest beyond the parking pad. Hikers sometimes wandered off the trails winding through the Appalachians. A well-placed kick would send them on their way. No serious damage, but enough to get the message across.

"Let's try this one more time," said Ethan. "The schedule's whatever I say it is. Got it?"

The breeze quickened, whistling past Axel as it funneled through the doorway. He hooked a finger in the neck of his black t-shirt and pulled. Air slid across his chest but did nothing to cool the flush creeping from breastbone to chin. On the shirtfront, the image of a grinning white skull stretched as if baring its teeth.

A flash of light caught his eye. The dragonfly's silver wings moved in determined flutters. The creature was struggling out of the yellow glop like a dinosaur dragging itself from a tar pit. Only a thinning strand kept it grounded.

"Answer me," insisted Ethan. "Unless you're too dumb to understand the question."

Axel bit his bottom lip to prevent a curse from escaping. He winced as his teeth broke the skin and the taste of iron settled on the tip of his tongue. A forefinger wiped the blood from his lip and smeared it on the front of the t-shirt, giving the skull a red eyebrow. He turned to go inside the Outpost but stopped and looked back.

The filament parted that held the dragonfly. The creature rose in a blur of silver wings.

Axel stomped.

Mood improved, he raked the sole of the boot across the threshold and entered the building. A series of sneezes brought him to a halt. He squeezed his nose between thumb and forefinger. A glance up revealed streaks of black mold coating wooden rafters. The old beams did double duty by supporting the low-pitched corrugated ceiling and providing braces to suspend boxy fluorescent light fixtures from chains. He'd never gotten around to replacing the bulbs in the rear of the building. That area was useless to him. Broken wooden crates, old tractor parts, and other assorted junk. The front part of the interior was a different story. Bright fluorescent lights glinted off the tops of the wire cages, throwing grids of shadows on the empty interiors. Axel's nose wrinkled, and he looked at the stains snaking across the cement. Might be time for some bleach.

"One last chance," said Ethan flatly.

"I'm dumb, remember? Takes me awhile to think things through."

"Okay. I was wrong. You're a bright guy, Axel. A regular genius. When can you get the shipment here?"

"Tell you what I'll do, Ethan. I'll bring a partial—"

"Forget it. I want a full order, and I want it in two weeks."

"No way. I told you about the flyers going up all over Asheville. I need to let things cool down."

"Has anybody connected the dots?"

"What are you talking about?"

"Cops, Axel. Are any of the flyers posted by the local PD? You know, call if you see anyone suspicious, that kind of thing?"

"What difference does it make?" Axel grimaced.

He should've thought of that himself.

"Churn and burn, baby! The flyers don't mean anything unless the cops are involved."

Axel changed the subject. "We haven't talked money."

"The price is set."

"Not for a rush job."

"Don't go there, Axel."

"An extra thousand, or you can gather the shipment yourself." Axel waited, but the only sound was the rumble of flexing sheet metal as the wind picked up outside.

"Done," rasped Ethan.

"I'm glad we could work it out. No hard…" Axel's voice trailed off.

The phone's screen was blank except for the time—5:17 p.m. He smiled. Let the twerp sulk. Ethan had no idea what was in store for him after the next delivery.

CHAPTER 2

"I hope you've learned your lesson."

"Roxx," Lulu pleaded. "You've *got* to concede."

"I'm not afraid of this oat!" squeaked Roxxy in a high yip. She swallowed. "I mean, *oaf*!"

Her tail curled between her back legs. She sent it a silent rebuke. *Traitor!*

"Yeah," growled Max. "You look really confident."

"I can still beat you"—Roxxy lifted her mutinous tail and ordered it to remain upright—"and I don't need tricks to do it."

"We'll see about that." Max's hackles rose.

Lulu stomped her front paw. "Roxx, I wish you'd listen for once. Max isn't the slow, clumsy dolt he used to be."

"Right." He frowned. "Wait, what?"

"Pipe down," Lulu ordered. "I'm trying to talk some sense into Roxxy."

Max choked.

"This isn't funny. She's too hard-headed for her own good."

"Don't you think I know that?" Max shot back. "That's why I'm doing this!"

Roxxy studied her brother. His hackles were now smooth, and the hard light in his eyes had softened. *He's concerned about me!*

"Lulu," said Max. "Roxxy *has* to learn to back down when she's outmatched. Every dog does. I don't want her to think she's invincible."

"There's got to be another way besides these stupid alpha matches!"

"Fine!" retorted Max. "Let's hear *your* idea."

Roxxy tuned out the byplay between her sibs. Her mind raced as she tried to think of something new that would give her an edge over Max. Maybe provoke him into doing something foolish? And the sooner the better. The minute he finished explaining himself to Lulu, he'd launch another charge.

Think, Roxxy ordered herself. Dinnertime was approaching, and Max would want to finish the match before then. The rectangles of sunlight had stretched far enough across the room to include the ottoman in front of the comfy chair where Lulu had napped. Roxxy squinted. Atop the flat surface of the round footrest, strands of gray-cream-black fur were visible in the slanting afternoon rays. *Yes!*

"Maxey," said Roxxy, interrupting the heated discussion still going on between her sibs. "Let me get this straight. You're saying you've gotten so big that I don't stand a chance against you?"

"Finally!" Max's short tail flicked back and forth in a relieved wag. "I'm glad you finally get it."

Roxxy lowered one ear to feign confusion. "Well, if you're so big and tough, why did you let Muffy chase you out of the kitchen last night?"

Max's cinnamon eyes hardened to teak, and his lips fluttered in a snarl.

Roxxy gulped. Maybe provoking him wasn't such a good idea. She knew he wouldn't like being reminded that Muffy, the family cat, scared the living daylights out of him, but she hadn't expected him to turn feral. Roxxy realized she should've chosen a less touchy subject. None of the household's dogs could figure out why Bill and Carol kept the feline around, but that was humans for you, sentimental to a fault. Roxxy's parents had long ago established a peaceful and respectful coexistence with Muffy and had ordered their offspring not to pester the black/orange/buff tabby. The cat, for her part, ignored the young canines if they kept their distance.

Max growled, "I leave Muffy alone because Momma and Poppa told us to."

"Please." Roxxy snorted dismissively. "That cat *owns* you."

"You're just jealous because *you* don't have enough sense to avoid her."

Roxxy frowned.

Max had a point. She wished she *could* restrain herself from tangling with the mangy tabby, but the walking hair ball strutted around the house like she owned it, flowing from room to room with her nose in the air. Worst of all, Roxxy often found herself the object of Muffy's attention. The cat would perch on the window ledge in the family room, emerald eyes aglow as they followed Roxxy's efforts to wrestle a chewy away from Max. Roxxy was sure the feline's expression was a smirk of contempt. When Roxxy couldn't stand the scrutiny any longer, she'd charge Muffy, and a whirlwind battle would ensue. The spirited clashes were over in seconds and included more hisses and growls than actual clawing and biting. The encounters usually ended with Muffy landing the deciding blow. Roxxy brushed a paw across her nose. The scratch was healing nicely.

Max snorted. "Muffy got you good, didn't she?"

Roxxy took a breath to reply but paused as an aroma wafted through the doorway to the hall. *Yessss!* From the smell, pan drippings and beef stock were reducing nicely. Bill must be in the last stage of making the gravy for the pot roast…juicy, juicy pot roast…

"Sis?" asked Lulu. "What's with the trance?"

"Uh, sorry." Roxxy turned her attention to Max. "I apologize for insulting you."

"Narrow it down."

"For saying you were terrified of Muffy." Roxxy paused for a beat. "You can't help it. She's a *scary* kitty-cat."

"I am *not!*" blurted Max. "I mean, *she* is not. Uh, I'm not scared of her. Got it?"

"Sure." Roxxy glanced past his shoulder. "Hi, Muff."

Max spun.

Roxxy reached full speed by her second stride. She lowered her shoulder and slammed full force into the soft flesh behind his rib cage.

"*Ooof!*" Max rolled halfway across the room before coming to rest on his back, limbs flailing weakly in the air.

The pads of Roxxy's paws slid across the carpet and sent her well past her dazed brother. A flick of the tail helped her turn. *Take that, Maxey!* She was only a pounce away from clamping her jaws lightly on his exposed throat to end the match. Her legs bunched to leap…but she hesitated. The stunned goof looked so pitiful lying there like an overturned beetle. He'd be disappointed at being defeated, believing he'd failed once again to fulfill his big-brotherly duties. Well, it was too late for her to forfeit this match, but she decided to concede if he challenged her to any future ones. Seeing him beaten was causing that stupid tail of hers to start drooping again.

Roxxy leaped, focusing on the wiry curls covering Max's throat. She was almost on him when he twisted and his powerful back legs lashed out, smashing into her chest. Air left her lungs in a *whoosh*! She hurtled backward, tumbling end over end. Her spine slammed into the floor, and her efforts to suck in air were thwarted by a paralyzed diaphragm. She willed her body to get up and *fight*, but it had other ideas. The most prevalent was *try to remember how to breathe*. Her eyes cut to the fireplace.

The glass front showed a blond rag mop lying in a tangled heap. The only thing worse than being a fluff ball was resembling a *limp* fluff ball.

"Roxx, you'll be okay in a second," Max huffed as he rolled upright. "You just got the breath knocked out of you. I guess you've figured out I was pretending to be helpless." He chuckled. "I'm not the idiot you think I am."

"Okay," she wheezed. "What kind of idiot are you?"

"I'll give you credit. The way you distracted me by bringing up Muffy was pretty clever." He padded toward her. "But like I said when we started, I've gotten too big for you to handle. I hope you've learned your lesson."

"Are you going to finish this or not?" she grunted, tilting her head back and waiting.

Fair was fair. She would concede when his teeth touched her throat. Her ear twitched at the welcome distraction of *snick-snick-snick-snick-snick-snick* coming through the doorway. Bill was continuing his efforts at the chopping board in the kitchen. She frowned. What was that accompanying scent? *Ugh*, rosemary. Not her favorite, but gravy was gravy.

"Sorry, Sis," said Max as he neared, "but this really is for your own—"

"Big bully!" barked Lulu, leaping in front of Max. Her black eyes shone like onyx and the snow-white fur bristled down her back. "You should be ashamed of yourself! You could have *hurt* Roxxy."

"You know I'd never injure her on purpose. I love the little pest."

"Then *act* like it instead of flinging her halfway across the room. I'm starting to wonder if there are any brains in that thick skull of yours."

Max took an involuntary step back. Everyone in the family knew Lulu was slow to anger, but when the switch was flipped, she was a force to be reckoned with.

"I said I was sorry," mumbled Max, ears tilting down.

"And don't call Roxxy a little pest. Try being more sensitive!" Lulu paused for breath. "Blockhead!"

"Okay, okay, I didn't *murder* her. And if you're so concerned about name-calling, cut out the blockhead remarks!"

"I'll stop calling you that the minute you stop acting like one. *Think*, Max! How would you feel if you'd really hurt Roxxy?"

"You know I'd feel terrible." His short tail drooped. The setting sun angled through the window and highlighted the black curls forming a saddle pattern across his otherwise tan coat. "She's cute as a button when she's not driving me crazy. I can't wait to see what she's going to get into next."

"That's better." Lulu touched noses with him to show he was forgiven. "Just remember to be careful."

"I get it, but I'm telling you, Roxxy's a lot tougher than you think. She—" He looked around the room. "Hey, where did she go?"

Roxxy peeked around the edge of the sofa. Her sibs' argument had provided the perfect distraction to allow her to slip away unnoticed. She suppressed a snort of amusement. They faced away from her, paws shifting as they stared at the place where she had lain temporarily winded after the double-leg kick from Max.

Roxxy felt her tail lift high in anticipation. *That's more like it!* A single leap and she could land on Max's back and drive him to the floor. Let's see how he feels with *his* breath knocked out. She'd roll him over and finish the match before he knew what hit him. Her claws dug into the Berber as she readied herself…but she hesitated yet again as a wave of affection swept over her. Max was a softie at heart, and describing her as cute as a button had been sweet. Not to mention, well, let's face it, *accurate*. Should she announce her presence so they could have a good chuckle about her sneaking away?

A second later her curls flattened in the wind stream of an arching leap. She arrowed over Max's hindquarters and dropped toward his broad back.

The "little pest" comment had been completely uncalled for.

CHAPTER 3

"Why was that guy trying to steal you?"

Steel-gray wings folded as the male nuthatch settled into an upside-down perch on the curved bottom of an oak branch. The early fall breeze seemed determined to dislodge him from the towering tree. His tiny claws sank deeper into the rough bark, and he trilled an annoyed "Wheet-wheet-wheet-wheet-*wheet*! Wheet-wheet-wheet-wheet-*wheet*!" The gust subsided, and he preened his russet chest feathers with a jet-black beak as sharp as a knitting needle.

Far below, in the milder current near the ground, fleecy fur stirred on Roxxy's belly. She slept on her back with paws pointing toward the sky, nestled in a favorite patch of cushiony clover the same vibrant green as the nearby basil plants. Her legs jerked as she dreamed of evading Max in a game of tag.

A scent penetrated her slumber. Her nose twitched in response to the nutty aroma of acorns combined with the dry musk of an animal that spent all its time outdoors.

She awoke fully. Her legs stiffened, but she remained on her back, turning only her head to stare into the shining black eyes of a young squirrel. He sat on his haunches only six inches away. The white belly fur glowed against his otherwise gray coat. Tiny paws absently turned an acorn.

Roxxy frowned. Was that an amused glint in the rodent's gaze? She had to be imagining things. Normally, the bushy-tailed creatures were wary of her and kept a respectful distance, scampering up a tree if she came too close. She liked observing them as they leaped acrobatically from branch to branch. In her opinion, squirrels were largely inoffensive, unlike cats, who had *no* redeeming qualities.

She huffed to notify the little animal that it was time to move along. He stayed put and raised the acorn to his mouth, snapping off the ribbed crown with prominent front teeth. She growled, but the sound was muted by the crunching that came as he bit into the bronze nutmeat and chewed. Was the gleam in his eyes growing brighter?

A flip brought her upright, sending grass clippings flying. The squirrel dropped the acorn as if it were on fire. He whirled and darted toward the oak's trunk. She charged after him but adjusted her stride to ensure she wouldn't catch him. Squirrel innards? *Yuck!*

Roxxy snapped at the rodent's streaming tail as he leaped for the oak. He emitted a high-pitched *eeeekk* while somehow levitating six feet up the trunk, landing with a rattle of claws on bark. She skidded to a stop and ran her tongue over the grass to dislodge a few wisps of feathery gray fur from her mouth. The squirrel squatted on a branch and pulled his tail forward, eyes widening as he examined the tiny patch of plucked strands on the tip. A chatter of outrage spilled forth.

"You got off easy!" she yapped, turning away with an insolent flick of her *intact* tail.

Squirrel situation well under control, another nap was in order. Indoors this time. A little shuteye on the family-room sofa would be perfect. A glance at the sun indicated she'd have an hour or so of undisturbed peace before her sibs and parents returned from the dog park with Bill and Carol.

Roxxy shuddered. She didn't understand the appeal of dog parks. Was there anything worse than charging around with a bunch of slobbery strangers? Her regular exercise routine was plenty satisfying. A nice game of keep-away with Max and Lulu or a dash along the fence line with her friend Toby, the squat, thick-chested basset next door. Toby believed himself to be as fast as a greyhound, but his actual speed was more akin to an elephant wearing snowshoes. Roxxy would stay in second gear so they could run together as they raced—Toby's racing was more of an enthusiastic lumber—along the chain-link fence separating their yards. When finished, they'd settle down on their respective sides for a long chat. One of her favorite pastimes was watching Toby and his person, Kimberly. The girl was a second grader and frequently had her friends over for play dates in the back yard. Toby would throw himself into the mix when the kids engaged in a game of tag. The group usually ended up in a tangled pile on the lawn, with Toby groaning blissfully as the children caressed his big floppy ears.

Roxxy's other next-door neighbor, Leo, wasn't much for playing, but the tiny Pomeranian knew all the neighborhood gossip and was good company. He was small enough to squeeze through a slight gap at the bottom of the fence that separated their properties. She looked forward to his daily visits. The pencil-thin legs carried his bushy, coppery form in springy bounces as he pranced across the yard to join her as she chatted with Toby.

She decided to do a quick patrol before going inside for her nap. A trot brought her to the far corner of the sprawling back yard. The perspective gave her a good view of the rear of her home—a comfortable, two-story brick structure. The ground fell away from the house in a gentle slope. Well-kept flower beds blazed with early fall colors—spikes of scarlet celosia, clusters of purple asters with yellow centers, heaps of orange chrysanthemums, and an array of other plants showcasing various shapes and hues. Both Bill and Carol were avid gardeners—and good cooks.

Finished with her quick patrol, Roxxy followed the grass path that curved along a bed of red spider lilies. The lacy tendrils swayed in the breeze and reminded her unpleasantly of the insects they were named for. She picked up her pace. The course ahead was so familiar she could picture it without trying. The path would deposit her at the steps leading to the rear deck. Once atop the pine planks, she could access the pet entry located at the base of the back door. A push through the heavy plastic flap and a trot across the kitchen would take her to the laundry room. She'd automatically do a quick inspection of the food bowls lined neatly in a row, although her parents and sibs never left even a speck of kibble. Greedy guts.

She froze with a paw poised above the deck's bottom step. *What was that sound?* Being careful to keep the rest of her body still, she swiveled both ears toward Leo's property. Footfalls crunched on the gravel path connecting his front yard to the back. The rhythmic, stony rustle grew louder. Slowly, she turned her head. A man strode along the walkway. Her bangs twitched in a frown. Leo had said earlier that he and his person, Helen, would be absent all afternoon. They had a spa day planned, which meant a mani-pedi for the woman and a clip-shampoo-blowout for Leo.

Roxxy's chestnut eyes widened as she studied the huge man skulking around the Pom's property.

She hadn't realized humans came in that size. His shadow stretched out behind him, as long and black as an open grave. Wraparound sunglasses gave the broad-featured face an oddly blank expression. The clipboard he carried looked small in his huge hand. A pair of heavy canvas gloves were tucked inside the front of a wide belt next to a square, sharp-edged iron buckle. The khaki shirt bore a smear of yellow just below the top button. The pants were the same light tan, but more wrinkled. Heavy work boots kicked up gravel, the stones pinging off the plastic edging along the path. A baseball-style cap with a creased brim was clamped upon his head. No hair showed where the hat ended. *Was he bald?* The cap's front design depicted a pair of metal-framed towers connected by cables, wide at the base and narrow at the top.

Roxxy lifted her nose with little hope. The breeze bent the curls along her back toward the man, putting her upwind. Too bad. Analyzing his scent would've revealed all the essentials—the kinds of pets he had, what he'd eaten for lunch, whether he had any treats in his pocket, and, most importantly, what kind of mood he was in. She jerked in surprise as a cardinal burst from the holly nearest the man. A swing of his clipboard caught a scarlet tail feather. The bird pinwheeled. Roxxy held her breath, but the nimble creature righted itself and shot into the cloudless sky.

A curse drew Roxxy's attention. The man pivoted in place, the dark glasses tracking the bird's flight path. A tiny red image shone in each lens. He raised his hand and pointed an index finger at the cardinal. His thumb lifted like the hammer of a gun being cocked.

"Pow," said the man as his thumb snapped forward.

With the stranger's attention focused on the cardinal, Roxxy decided to get closer to the guy. She dashed to the fence that separated her yard from Leo's and hunkered behind a pile of fertilizer bags stacked against the chain-link fence. The reek of pungent chemicals threatened to make her sneeze. She swept a paw across her muzzle to stifle the urge and edged around the pile for a one-eyed view.

The man squatted in front of a gray metal box fastened to the brick wall of Leo's house. The middle of the fixture had a round white center containing tiny letters and numbers. Roxxy had no problem deciphering human speech, but writing? Forget about it! All those wiggling lines were a total mystery.

The stranger wiped a palm over the clear dome covering the center of the box. His khaki shirt stretched tight across his broad back as he leaned closer for a better look. He went perfectly still.

Roxxy wondered what was so interesting, but the question remained unanswered as the man rose. One knee popped with the sharp report of a pecan in a nutcracker.

Taking no chances, she withdrew behind the pile and was pleased to find a sliver of space between two bags that would allow her to continue to see the stranger, although she was beginning to lose interest in his presence. He was huge but otherwise unnoteworthy—just a human going about one of the many inexplicable jobs they engaged in.

She stifled a yawn and watched through the tiny gap as he turned to face her yard. He stretched, extending long arms. The clipboard remained clutched in one hand. He seemed so relaxed, she almost missed the way his head swiveled in a slow, flat arc, scanning the surroundings.

Did the movement pause when his gaze passed over the bags that concealed her? Before she could be sure, he turned away and proceeded along the path beside Leo's house. The man halted at the rear, peeking around the corner and examining the back yard.

Seconds dragged past before the man's shoulders slumped, and he muttered, "No luck."

Roxxy shrugged. The guy's behavior was a little odd, but he didn't appear to be up to any type of mischief. He hadn't tried to force open a door or window.

Concerns about the stranger dismissed, she rolled over to expose her belly to the sun. Why not just stay outside for her nap? The sun was so nice…so warm…so…

She woke to the chattering of a squirrel. A glance at a limb of the big oak revealed the culprit. Might have known! It was the same little beast she'd chased earlier. His tail flicked up and down, beating the air, and his widened black eyes were fixed on something behind her. What was he—?

Roxxy felt a gloved hand scrabble at her collar. The nylon went tight as a finger slipped beneath. She corkscrewed, wrenching free from the grip and spinning away. A bounce to her paws brought her face to face with the stranger. He was leaning over the fence, waist balanced atop the chain links. His arm was so long that it easily reached past the fertilizer bags. His lips were pulled back in a grimace that exposed blocky yellow teeth.

She backpedaled well out of his reach but stayed close enough to get a good whiff if the direction of the wind changed. Once she had his scent, she'd recognize him anywhere—regardless of the dark glasses or the cap with brim pulled low.

"Come here, pooch." The stranger clenched his teeth as he straightened. "I just want to pet you."

He dropped the clipboard and pulled a square of folded burlap from his back pocket. A hard flick of his wrist transformed the material into a large sack with a drawstring.

Roxxy tilted her head and studied the bag. The burlap billowed as the wind began to swirl. *What's that for?* Her fixation was so complete that she barely registered the man reaching into his front pocket with his free hand to extract a compact metal canister.

"You've got to love the dumb ones," remarked the stranger, chuckling.

Dumb ones? Who does he think he's talking—?

The thought cut off as a sibilant *hisssss* filled the air. A ribbon of neon-orange liquid streamed from the canister's nozzle and shot toward her, expanding into a tight cone. The harsh, peppery odor reached her an instant before the substance did. She exploded into a backward arcing somersault. The spray splashed the grass where she'd been an instant before.

She landed facing him, balancing on all four paws. Her mouth opened wide to release an outraged protest. "*RAHR! RA—*"

Her jaws clamped shut mid-bark as she rolled right, dodging another acrid burst. The man cursed and swung the canister to follow her as she came upright. She backed away, juking from side to side all the while. Sunlight glinted on the rounded container in his hand. The contents spewed forth, missing her by the width of a dewclaw. The stench burned her nostrils, but the fear was receding. Every second she avoided the awful stuff buoyed her spirits.

"*RAHR! RAHR! RAHR! RAHR! RAHR!*" she thundered, still backpedaling.

The man grinned. "I saw you in the reflection of that dome covering the electric meter. The plastic is just like glass."

Roxxy continued to bark and move, but a thought niggled at the back of her mind.

Why is this creep so chatty? It's almost like he's trying to keep me focused on him while—

She went down hard as her rear paws tangled in a coiled hose attached to a garden spigot. She fought to free herself, legs churning, but the effort only wrapped the green bonds tighter.

"Dumber than I thought."

The spray from the canister left a glistening orange path on the lawn as it swept toward her.

Hissssss…sputter…hiss…sput, sput…hiss…sput…

She stared dazedly as a final drop of liquid trickled from the nozzle. The man shook the canister and pressed the tab on top, but nothing came out. A red flush spread across the hard planes of his face, and a short, sawtooth outline of a vein pulsed beneath the skin of his temple.

"*RAHR! RAHR! RAHR! RAHR! RAHR!*" she bellowed, glad for the chain-link fence between them. *Thought you had me, didn't you?*

"Guess I'll have to do this the hard way." The man's gloved hands tightened on a horizontal metal tube connecting two of the fence's support posts. He swung a leg to clear the barrier, but a boot heel caught on a twisted tine at the top. The chain links rattled as he jerked free and landed nimbly on her side of the fence.

She swallowed. *I wish I'd gone to that stupid dog park!* Her efforts to free herself from the hose had left her trussed like a chicken.

"Don't move," said the man, beginning to laugh. "I'll be right there."

The stranger's guffaws morphed into a rattling cough that sounded like gravel hitting the bottom of a metal bucket. He cleared his throat, and a wad of yellow phlegm arced toward her but fell short.

Panic overtook her as the man approached. She kicked harder, and the hose inched up her flank like a boa constrictor.

The man removed the sack from where he'd tucked it into his belt. Wind caught the burlap and spread the top wide.

She stared. *Is he going to…to…to put me in that thing!*

"*AAAWWHHOOOOOO! AAWWHHOOOOOO! AAWWHHOOOOOO!*"

The man froze. His dark glasses pointed at a spot well past her.

"*AAAWWHHOOOOOO! AAWWHHOOOOOO! AAWWHHOOOOOO!*"

Roxxy twisted to follow the human's gaze. *Toby!* The big-boned basset stood stiff-legged just outside the fence on the opposite side of the property. Brown and white fur stood upright down the length of his spine. His massive head tilted back, sending the ears swinging like pendulums.

"*AAAWWHHOOOOOO! AAWWHHOOOOOO! AAWWHHOOOOOO!*"

Roxxy looked back at the man in time to see him flinch. Toby's bellowing was like the pounding of a kettle drum echoing off the surrounding houses. One of the residents would surely come out to see about the racket.

"RAHR! RAHR! RAHR! RAHR! RAHR!" she barked exultantly. "*Tell him, Toby!*"

"He's leaving, Roxx," Toby bellowed, pointing his chin toward Leo's property.

She turned just as the man hopped back over the fence. A glimpse of his profile revealed the skin and marched up the gravel path alongside the Pom's house. The long-legged strides were quick but controlled as the human marched toward the street. Casual observers wouldn't think anything amiss if they didn't notice the stiff gait or the scarlet hue suffusing the skin across the back of his neck.

Roxxy's eyes stayed glued to the man as he stepped off the curb in front of Leo's house and yanked open the door of a pickup truck so rusted that the original color was indiscernible. She caught a glimpse of the interior as he threw open the door. The vehicle's seat sagged under his weight. The engine coughed to life, sending oily exhaust from the tailpipe. The pickup lurched forward.

BANG! BANG!

Roxxy's ears clamped to the sides of her head as the double backfire split the air.

"Caw!"

She looked up as a crow lifted from a nearby pine, wings glistening blue-black in the sunlight.

"Caw!" screeched the bird, annoyed at having its morning disturbed.

Roxxy nodded. *You don't know the half of it.*

She glanced at the road. The truck was no longer there but hadn't gone far. She could detect the rattle of the old engine coming from the next street over. Her ears lifted at the distinctive sound. The motor produced a steady *ping...ping...ping.*

When that noise grew too faint to hear, she turned her attention to the lawn where the orange liquid had struck. The substance had dried and left an acrid, brownish residue.

"Get over here and tell me what's going on!" Toby demanded.

"I'm coming!" She untangled herself from the hose—a much easier task when a maniac wasn't coming for her—and gave herself a rippling head-to-tail shake that rattled her teeth. The shake felt so good she started another one.

"Hurry up!" Toby stomped on the ground with a platter-like paw. "Why was that guy trying to steal you?"

She paused in mid-shake as the question registered. For the life of her, she couldn't think of an answer.

CHAPTER 4

"That would explain the sack."

Roxxy dashed across the yard as she took the most direct route to Toby. She was midway through a perennial flower bed before she remembered her parents had ordered her to avoid trampling the early Fall blooms. *Too late now!* Mulch scattered behind her as she dug in for a powerful leap, clearing a mound of purple asters. The hurdles continued as she jumped a cluster of orange-and-red marigolds, soared above a yellow clump of black-eyed Susans, and cleared a stand of spiky pink snapdragons. She was congratulating herself on her nimble paw-work when her momentum carried her through a mound of chrysanthemums. The shape disintegrated, and a shower of scarlet and orange petals followed in her slipstream like confetti in a windstorm.

She sighed resignedly and slid to a halt next to the fence.

"Impressive," Toby huffed. "I've never seen a plant actually explode."

"You think Carol will notice?" Roxxy touched noses with her friend through the chain-link fence. The basset was five years her senior, and she valued his opinion.

Toby flicked an ear in amusement.

"I don't think Carol will mind much. You've got that adorable vibe working for you. But—" A snarl fluttered his lips. "Let's change the subject and talk about that big guy. When did he show up?"

"Just a few minutes ago. He was snooping around Leo's place. I checked the man out but thought he was harmless. I guess he spotted me watching him. Or maybe he was looking for me. Anyway, I drifted off to sleep behind some bags of fertilizer next to the fence." She glanced around the yard, but the squirrel that had woken her was nowhere in sight. "The man almost grabbed me, but I managed to slip out of his grip."

"I saw the sack and that canister in his hand. He came prepared." Toby's wrinkly forehead buckled. "Has to be a dog thief."

"What did you call him?" The muscles in Roxxy's legs suddenly wouldn't support her. She sank onto a scattering of oak leaves that crackled as her weight settled. "Dog thief? You really think he was trying to *steal* me?"

"Yeah," responded Toby dryly. "That would explain the sack."

"B-b-but why would a human do something like that?"

Toby's ears drooped. "Roxx, *our* people are wonderful, but not all humans are like that. Some are crueler than you can imagine. Luck was on your side today."

Her gaze went to the base of the oak. She could use her paws to rake together a pile of acorns. How many could she gather if she put her mind to it?

"Everything okay?" asked Toby.

"Thanks to you. Sounding the alarm saved me." Roxxy's tail thumped the ground.

"You'd have done the same for me."

"But not as well. I've got a bark. You've got a bellow."

Roxxy shook herself. It was still hard to believe she'd had an encounter with a dog thief. She scanned Leo's yard. The oversize footsteps along the gravel path were the only sign that the stranger had been there. Even the cardinal had returned to its perch on the holly and was preening scarlet feathers as if never interrupted.

"I'm just glad the man didn't grab you," said Toby. He tilted his head and one of his big ears swung toward Leo's property. "With all the commotion, I'm surprised the annoying Pom didn't charge out of his dog door and start yapping his head off. Twenty seconds of that and the guy would run screaming."

"Leo's very proud of his yapping ability." said Roxxy, eyes twinkling.

"He certainly practices enough. His yammering reminds me of a woodpecker trying to drill through a rain gutter, only less pleasant. Speaking of the little runt, we better warn him. The dog thief could come back."

"Why would you care?" Roxxy asked, trying to hide the snort of amusement that was burbling up. "I thought Leo gets on your nerves."

"Who said I care?" replied Toby, shuffling his big paws. "I'm just concerned about his person, Helen. She's a nice lady. If anything happened to Leo, she'd be devastated."

"No need to be concerned for either of them. I saw Leo early this morning. He and Helen are having a spa day."

"Figures."

"Don't start." Roxxy sighed. Her two next-door neighbors couldn't be more different. The big-boned, rough-and-tumble basset followed his bulbous nose wherever it took him—through mud puddles, into banks of thorny rose bushes, or hot on the trail of a skunk. Leo, on the other paw, was a tiny, ornamental creature who avoided any activity that might mar his perfectly round mane or tawny coat. "Leo's a lot spunkier than you give him credit for."

"Spunky? He likes *bubble* baths. No self-respecting dog would ever—"

"*Yap, yap, yap!*"

Roxxy pivoted toward the opposite side of the property, where Leo was squeezing through the small gap at the bottom of the chain-link fence dividing their yards.

Toby huffed. "Speak of the devil."

"Be nice," she admonished. "You should try harder to get along with Leo."

"Why? So we can swap grooming tips?"

She watched the Pom emerge from the tight passage. His coat glowed from the daily attention provided by Helen. The widow-lady was in her sixties and used an assortment of combs and brushes to keep the Pom well coiffed.

Leo called out, "I'll be there in a second!"

"I can hardly wait," Toby grumbled, just loud enough for Roxxy to hear. He squinted at the Pom. "At least his stupid mane got squished."

Roxxy had to admit the mane—Leo's proudest feature—was a little worse for wear. The gap under the chain-link fence had left it looking like a deflated basketball. Normally, his mane was perfectly coiffed. Helen took special care to blow-dry, tease, and spray the bushy mass until it was a spherical masterpiece.

"The vain little gerbil," said Toby. "Serves him right. His mane will never be the same, and…"

Leo gave himself a vigorous, all-over-body shake, and the globe sprang back to full glory.

Roxxy glanced at the basset. "You were saying?"

"Forget it," he conceded. "That thing's indestructible."

She chuckled and watched Leo approach. Tiny paws curled inward with each measured, prancing step. His head was held high and proud, and his black eyes twinkled. She was certain he was putting on a show to annoy Toby.

"Hi, Roxx," said Leo, tail wagging as he arrived. "Great to see you."

"You too," she replied, leaning to touch noses with him. "How's it going?"

"Really good." His tail went still, and he looked past Roxxy to the figure on the other side of the fence. "Toby."

"Leo."

The Pom cocked his head to the side. "What did you roll in?" His nose wrinkled. "And when did it die?"

Roxxy groaned. *Here we go.*

"Hounds," Toby grated, "have a pleasant, *earthy* scent."

"As in landfill."

"At least I look like a *dog*, rather than a rat with a bad perm."

"A dog? You look like a cinder block with legs."

"Enough!" Roxxy added a growl to show she meant it.

A nearby chipmunk gave a startled squeak and darted down its burrow's narrow entry.

Toby protested, "Leo started it."

"Did not!"

"Did!"

"Cut it out!" she snapped. "Both of you apologize."

"Roxxy, I'm sorry," Toby muttered.

The Pom nodded. "Yeah, me too, Roxx. I didn't mean to make you mad."

"Don't apologize to me. To each other!"

"Never!" Toby's jowls quivered.

"Not in this lifetime!" blurted Leo. "I'd rather be dewormed."

"I can arrange that," the basset said darkly.

"Leo, let's start with you." Roxxy tossed her head to shoo away a monarch butterfly trying to land on her nose. Sunlight shone through the insect's wings. Sharp black lines divided the orange panels like stained glass. "Say you're sorry for the cinder block remark."

"Uh, Toby, I'm sorry you're built like a cinder block."

The fur bristled down the basset's back.

"I mean," Leo added, "I'm sorry I *called* you a cinder block."

"Your turn, Toby," Roxxy prompted.

"My turn for what?"

"To apologize to Leo for saying he looks like a rat with a perm."

"I should apologize to the rat."

"Toby! Say something nice."

"Let me think…uh, Leo, I'm sorry for the rodent remark."

"And?" Roxxy prompted.

"Well…let's see…your mane's truly outstanding. You must be the envy of Poms everywhere."

"I wouldn't go *quite* that far." Leo tilted his chin up to show the furry sphere to its best advantage. "But my mane does have a certain majesty."

Roxxy let one ear droop while lifting the other in the canine equivalent of a human eyeroll.

"And Toby," Leo continued, "your aroma is less, uh, *pungent* than usual. My gag reflex hasn't kicked in even once."

"Too kind." The basset's features contorted as if he'd accidentally swallowed a bee. "Old pal."

"My pleasure." A shudder rippled down Leo's glossy coat. "Good buddy."

"You guys are doing great," Roxxy interjected. "Keep going."

"*More?*" asked the Pom, panic-stricken. "You've got to be kidding."

"Yeah, Roxx," Toby agreed. "I think I pulled a muscle coming up with that compliment about the rodent's mane."

She snorted so loudly her friends jumped, and the chipmunk, who had cautiously ventured out of his burrow, darted back down the tunnel. A giggling fit overcame her. She rolled onto her back and wiggled side to side, all four legs churning as she pawed the air. From her upside-down position, she saw Toby and Leo exchange startled looks. Their expressions fueled more giggling that eventually left her breathless in a string of hiccups.

"What," Toby demanded, "is so funny?"

"Watching you guys trying to be nice to each other." She wheezed. "Priceless."

"I'm *so* glad we could amuse you," Leo said. "It's what we live for."

She began giggling again. "But please, I can't take anymore. Go back to bickering."

"Thank goodness," sighed the Pom. He turned to Toby. "Can you move a little further downwind? My eyes are watering."

"I think that's from all the hair spray in your mane," replied the basset, stretching out on the lawn and clearly glad to have returned to familiar territory. "The fumes are affecting your brain."

"You should give grooming a try. Ever heard of a brush?" Leo's eyes swept over Toby, whose coat sported a variety of leaves and twigs from a recent patrol through the bird sanctuary that bordered the back of their properties. "Or a yard rake?"

"H-h-how dare you!" Toby sat up and the fur bristled along his back. "Kimberly brushes me every day! Are you saying she *neglects* me?"

Roxxy tensed, hoping Leo would have the good sense to avoid criticizing Toby's blond-haired, blue-eyed, six-year-old person. The basset was smitten with Kimberly. He slept at the girl's feet in a big canopied bed every night. Kimberly was just as devoted to the wrinkly hound. Roxxy often saw her brushing Toby on the rear deck after breakfast and before dinner. However, he liked rambling in the bird sanctuary that backed up to their properties, and his coat at midday often sported enough twigs and leaves to fill a wheelbarrow.

Roxxy held her breath as she waited for Leo's reply. If he said something to disparage Toby's person, there was no telling how the basset would react.

"Kimberly *is* a doll," confirmed the Pom. His flanks rippled in a shrug. "Too bad she's saddled with a walking garbage heap."

"Rodent! I ought to—"

"*Enough!*" Roxxy barked. "Both of you stop arguing!"

"He started it," Leo mumbled.

"Did not!"

"Did!"

Roxxy growled. "We are *not* going through this again. Leo, I need to tell you something important."

Before she could continue, a mournful honking drew her attention overhead. A V-shaped formation of Canada geese flew southward. The birds' sweeping gray wings and arrow-straight necks conveyed a relentless intent to reach their destination. Roxxy silently wished them well on their journey.

"Come on, Roxx," demanded Leo, his black eyes glowing. "Give."

"Okay. A little while ago, there was a guy poking around at your place. He was obviously looking for something. When he didn't find it, he tried to pepper-spray me."

"*What?*"

She quickly recounted the whole story and concluded by adding, "All of us need to be on the lookout for the creep. He might come back."

"You bet!" Leo shuddered. "I don't like the thought of that sack."

The basset huffed in agreement. "You can't be too careful. I think—"

"You three seem to be enjoying each other's company."

Roxxy's tail responded with an automatic wag to the friendly human voice. She focused on the source and saw a short, thin boy of eleven or so, standing on Toby's rear deck. A breeze tugged at carelessly combed auburn hair, and sunlight picked out golden flecks in the greenish-brown eyes studying her and her friends. The kid carefully closed the back door as if not wanting it to bang shut. *Teen*, she decided, revising his age upward to thirteen or fourteen after studying his face more closely. His features had lost the soft edges of childhood, and dark crescents hung beneath his eyes.

Roxxy's nose quaked, picking up a lingering hint of bacon and eggs, minty toothpaste, a woodsy rather than floral-scented shampoo, and a freshly laundered t-shirt depicting a superhero shooting a web from the wrist of a blue-and-red costume.

Her thoughts were interrupted when Leo said, "Enjoying each other's company? Can't the boy see that Toby's here?"

"How about I dig under the fence," replied the basset agreeably, "and turn you into a pawprint?"

"I'm ignoring you both," said Roxxy. "In fact, consider that a policy statement moving forward." She pointed her chin toward the boy. "Toby, who's that?"

"Jason. I've known him forever. Doesn't usually carry treats, but he's great at petting and ear-scratching. Marcy—"

"Who?" asked Leo.

"Kimberly's mom. I talk about Marcy all the time. Don't you ever listen?"

"What?"

"I said—" Toby caught himself and glared. "You never get tired of that one, do you?"

"It's a classic," replied Leo.

"I'll show you a classic! I'll—"

"Toby," prompted Roxxy. "The boy?"

"Jason's the son of Marcy's best friend, Susan."

"I've never seen him before."

Toby shrugged. "Susan hardly ever comes over."

"I thought you said she and Marcy are best friends."

"Marcy usually visits Susan instead of the other way around."

"When," huffed Leo, "did we decide that any of this is important? And why didn't I get a vote?"

"I'm interested in Jason," said Roxxy mildly, but her chestnut eyes took on a bronze glint. "Problem with that?"

Leo swallowed. "Fascinating human." He turned to Toby. "Let's hear more about Jason."

"Not much to add," replied the basset with a snort. "Besides, I thought we were boring you."

"Focus, you two," said Roxxy. She ducked as a grasshopper whizzed past. She'd once snagged one of the spiky insects in mid-flight. Took her all day to get the taste out of her mouth. "Toby," she asked, "why does the kid look so…I don't know…tired, for sure, and maybe worried?"

"I think he's just stressed with school. He started tenth grade a couple of weeks ago."

"You're kidding!" exclaimed Leo. "The kid's a runt."

"Look who's talking!"

"Guys," said Roxxy.

"Sorry, Roxx," said Toby. "Anyway, I heard Susan telling Marcy that she's worried about Jason,"

"Why?"

"He's only thirteen, but he's skipped a couple of grades. He might feel out of place with all those bigger kids."

"Here he comes," said Leo.

"Hey, Jason!" bellowed Toby in a canine greeting as the boy approached the fence. "How's it going?"

"Keep it down, big guy," whispered Jason, squatting to scratch underneath the basset's chin. "You know how my mom is. She'll have a fit if she catches me with you."

"Why," Leo asked, "is the kid fawning over that smelly hound instead of doing something useful? Like looking for a firehose."

"Eat your heart out," said Toby, leaning into Jason's petting.

Roxxy agreed with Leo—at least about Toby hogging the attention. She sat and waved her front paw in the *shake hands* gesture Bill had taught her. A pitiful whine followed.

"No fair!" protested Toby.

"Deal with it," she huffed under her breath, then put a little more pleading into the whine directed at the boy. She widened her eyes into a gaze of soulful longing.

"What a cutie!" Jason poked a finger through the chain links and crooked it beneath her still raised paw. "You're a curly fluff ball, aren't you?"

She sighed, wondering if there was a conspiracy.

"And look at that adorable underbite!"

"Roxx, forgive the kid," Leo encouraged. "He's lightheaded from inhaling all those basset fumes. It's a wonder he's still conscious."

"You overbred and overgroomed gerbil! I ought to—"

"Hush." Jason glanced from Leo to Toby. "Why are you two barking at each other? If you don't quiet down, my mom's going to make me go inside." A lock of auburn hair fell across the boy's eyes, and he swept it back.

He nodded at Roxxy, and the comma of hair fell again.

"Look at this little angel. You should be good like her." He edged closer to the fence. "Come here, girl. Press against the chain links so I can scratch behind your ears."

"Everybody's getting petted but me," grumbled Leo. "What am I? A yard ornament?"

Roxxy leaned her flank against the diagonal wire grid. Jason's fingers caressed the delicate area behind a furry ear. A rhythmic thrumming filled the air that was somewhere between a prolonged grunt and a deep sigh.

"I'd swear she's purring," commented Toby.

Leo nodded.

"Either that or she's having an asthma attack. Helen has an inhaler she uses during allergy season. I'd go get it"—he lifted a hind paw and brushed a yellow leaf from his mane—"if I was the kind of moron who fetched."

"I *like* a good game of fetch," huffed Toby.

"Precisely."

"Both of you pipe down," murmured Roxxy. "You're ruining the vibe."

She pressed harder against the fence. Jason obligingly increased the pressure of his kneading fingers.

"*Don't let it bite you!*" The panicked shout sent a flock of yellow-and-gray cedar waxwings erupting into the sky from a nearby maple. It also propelled Jason to his feet like a jack-in-the-box.

Roxxy whirled toward Toby's house. A small-boned woman stood on the deck, staring at her with widened eyes the same color as Jason's. The female wore jeans and a long-sleeved, forest-green, pullover sweater. Delicate hands clutched the railing. The knuckles shone white against the brown stain of the wood.

Roxxy shivered. The skin over the woman's high cheekbones was pulled so tight that her face had a skull-like appearance.

"I'm fine, Mom." Jason swept a hand in Roxxy's direction. "Don't worry. She's very friendly."

The woman's mouth moved, but no words came out. Roxxy cocked an ear. The faint *click-click-click-click* of chattering teeth could be heard despite the shifting of overhead leaves in the breeze.

"J-Jason," stuttered the woman. "I've t-told you to keep away from dogs, p-particularly strange ones."

"I know a dog-hater when I see one," Leo blurted out. "I'm out of here!"

He dashed for the far side of the yard and the gap in the fence that was passage to home.

"Roxx, that's Susan," huffed Toby, remaining otherwise still. "And Leo's right...well, sort of. I don't know if she hates dogs or if she's just scared of us, but even I make her nervous, and she's known me since I was a puppy."

Roxxy flicked her tail in acknowledgment, but most of her attention was on Jason, who had crossed the yard and was ascending the deck's steps in a weary trudge. The rubber soles of his sneakers rasped upon the treads.

The boy stopped next to the woman and put a hand on her arm, but the gesture was shaken off.

Roxxy squirmed under the woman's stare.

Toby's brow wrinkled. "This is getting creepy. Susan's never looked at *me* that way. I wonder why you're freaking her out."

"No idea. People usually adore me. It's sort of my thing."

She shifted nervously. The grass pricked the webbing between her toes.

"Mom," said Jason, awkwardly embracing the woman who still faced Roxxy. "I didn't mean to upset you. I just came outside because I got bored waiting for you and Aunt Marcy to finish talking. It's been nearly an hour since we got here."

The female's fingers peeled away from the railing. She turned to embrace the boy.

"I'm sorry, honey. Marcy and I lose track of everything when we get together. I should have left you at home." She paused and drew in a breath. "But Jason, you've got to learn to stay away from strange dogs." She gestured in Roxxy's direction. "That one has its *teeth* bared."

Roxxy groaned. *Stupid underbite!*

"Mom, that dog isn't baring her teeth. It's just the way she looks."

"Are you suddenly the world's expert on dogs?"

"I'll stay away from her. Uh, did you and Aunt Marcy have a nice visit? I know you enjoy getting together with her."

"Don't change the subject."

"*Okay*, Mom."

"And don't get snippy."

"How many *don'ts* are we going to cover? Should I make a list?"

A tinkly sound floated on the wind, and Roxxy realized Susan was laughing. Dimples appeared that were identical to Jason's.

"Don't be funny," said the woman. "Add that one in. Makes it hard for me to stay annoyed."

She ruffled the boy's hair and kissed him on the forehead.

Jason squirmed and said good-naturedly, "I'm not a little kid anymore."

Susan sighed. "I know, but you'll always be *my* kid."

"Deal. But can we go home now? I want one of your custom BLTs. You make the best sandwiches in town."

"You got it."

"With extra 'B' and some pickles?"

The tinkling sound returned.

"All the 'B' you want. You're my growing boy."

Roxxy was so pleased by the affectionate byplay that she let out a joyous, "*Yip-yip-yip-yip-yip-yip!*" She sucked in a breath for another happy outburst but froze when Susan whirled toward her.

Roxxy's mouth went dry.

The woman's face was once again a rigid mask.

Jason cast an anxious glance between Roxxy and Susan.

"Mom," he said urgently, "don't let that dog bother you. She's harmless. Let's say goodbye to Aunt Marcy and get going. I'm starved." He tugged at his mother's sleeve.

"Don't herd me," snapped Susan. "And don't be fooled by that mongrel. There's no such thing as a *harmless* dog. They can *all* bite."

"Mom, that little dog wouldn't hurt—"

Susan poked a manicured fingernail at Jason's chest.

"Stay away from that animal. Understood?"

"Sure, Mom, sure," placated Jason, lifting his hands in surrender. "I won't go near her again."

"See that you don't!" Susan pivoted and stalked inside the house.

The boy moved to follow.

"Jason!" barked Roxxy.

He turned, and her tail did its thing as their gazes locked. His dimples showed, and he lifted a hand to wave, but before the movement was completed, an arm clad in forest green yanked him inside. His tennis shoe caught the jamb. He was still in an off-balance stumble as Roxxy watched him disappear.

The door slammed so loudly that it almost drowned out the plaintive whimpering that echoed across the yard.

AXEL

"*Hunh, hunh, hunh, hunh, hunh, hunh, hunh, hunh.*"

"What's that racket?"

"Hang on, Ethan," said Axel, eyeing the burlap sack on the old worktable.

The gyrations of the unit inside sent the bag on a wobbly path across the scarred surface. The table had once been used to repair carburetors and fuel pumps for heavy equipment. Dried machine oil was embedded in the blackened wood. The fumes hung thick and heavy above the surface, like the stink hovering over roadkill. A small refrigerator hummed noisily next to the table.

Axel grinned as the heaving bag moved inexorably onward. Another inch, and…

"*Yelp!*"

The sack tipped off the edge. *Thump!* Dust rose from the concrete floor of the Outpost.

"*Hunh, hunh, hunh, hunh, hunh, hunh, hunh, hunh.*"

The sack writhed and flopped.

"*Hunh, hunh, hunh, hunh, hunh, hunh, hunh, hunh.*"

Enough was enough.

"Shut up!" roared Axel, forgetting the cell phone wedged between his ear and shoulder.

"You still unclear on the chain of command?"

Axel shifted the device to a better position. "What? Uh, sorry, Ethan. I didn't mean you."

"Somebody there with you? Nah, even you're not that dumb."

Axel ground his teeth. *Just a few more days…*

"Well?"

"Lay off. There's nobody here but me and the units. I just brought in a new one, and it hasn't settled yet. Gimme a minute."

"*Hunh, hunh, hunh, hunh, hunh, hunh, hunh, hunh.*"

Axel placed the phone on the table. The sack had fallen between the refrigerator and a low metal toolbox resting beside the closed door.

"*Hunh, hunh, hunh, hunh, hunh, hunh, hunh, hunh.*"

Axel lifted the bag from the floor and snapped the container in the same hard, quick motion as someone popping a towel. The whimpering cut off.

He put his mouth close to the burlap and felt the rough material against his lips. "Finally getting it?"

Axel knew if Ethan found out he talked to the units he'd never hear the end of it. The good news was that Ethan didn't know, and the better news was that soon it wouldn't matter *what* Ethan thought. Axel shrugged. He liked having little chats with the units to let them know who was in charge. Perk of the job.

He carried the limp sack along the rows of cages. The panting occupants watched him out of the corners of their eyes. The toe of his boot sent a yellow-handled screwdriver clattering off the front of a cage and spinning away. He cursed. No time to look for it now. He should've put the thing back in the toolbox after he'd tightened the hinges on the cage doors. *Getting careless*...like when he'd let the unit with the underbite get away. The mutt had been amazingly quick, but that was no excuse. Next time, he'd bring a full can of the juice.

He reached an empty cage and deftly opened the latch. A tug with his teeth loosened the slipknot on the sack. The black-and-brown Yorkie landed hard on the plastic panel lining the bottom. Its panicky eyes bulged as it skittered into a rear corner and cringed. The units in the enclosures nearby began to whimper, but a glare from Axel silenced them. He nodded.

They all learned.

He retraced his steps and picked up the phone. "Sorry, Ethan."

"Took you long enough."

"What am I keeping you from? Figuring out ways to take advantage of old partners?"

"Axel."

The word hung heavy, made more so by the silence that followed.

"Okay," said Axel, yielding. "No offense."

The empty sack hit the surface of the worktable and sent up a cloud of mold spores from the oily wood. Axel's eyes watered, and he pinched the bridge of his nose to stifle a sneeze.

"Like I said, no offense. I'm a little edgy. Brought in a unit, and it kept making noise. I had to"—he paused, searching for the right phrase—"use a firm hand."

The words were barely out of his mouth when he gave a blat of laughter, expecting Ethan to join in, but there was no response.

Axel's knuckles whitened as his free hand gripped the side of the table. "You still there, Ethan?"

"Yeah. Did it occur to you that my buyer won't accept a broken unit?"

"The mutt's not—"

"*Unit!*"

"Yeah, yeah, *unit*! It's not damaged...well, at least not permanently."

"What's the status with the shipment?"

"Right on schedule, but..." Axel paused, intentionally making Ethan wait.

He shook an unfiltered cigarette from the pack, lit up, and inhaled deeply. The tip glowed bright orange, and an inch of the paper tube disappeared in a satisfying hiss. Smoke rushed into his lungs.

He held the fumes for a second before exhaling. "Last time we talked I asked for an extra grand to put together a rush shipment."

"And I agreed. So what?"

"I thought it over. I want to change it to three grand above the regular price."

"You're dreaming."

"I'm taking all the risks. Call it a hazardous duty bonus"

"Your *regular* pay is for taking risks. Besides, my margin's too slim as it is."

"Spare me." Axel lifted the top of the toolbox with the toe of his boot.

He squinted. Adjustable wrenches and pliers lay in a careless jumble. No way to tell if he had a replacement for the screwdriver.

He let the toolbox clang shut. "You can afford it. That lab must be paying you plenty for—"

"Open line. How many times do I have to tell you?"

"You want the shipment or not?"

"I'll add five hundred to the grand we settled on before, which makes fifteen hundred for your so-called hazardous duty bonus. That's it."

"A bonus of twenty-five hundred sounds better."

"Two thou. Final offer."

Axel smiled. The renegotiation was a ploy to keep Ethan focused on the payout instead of...other possibilities. Interesting, though. If Ethan was willing to go two thou above the regular price for a shipment, he must be cleaning up.

"Well?" demanded Ethan.

"You drive a hard bargain, but I'll go along."

"That's big of you. Now get to work."

"You're the boss." Axel pressed the button to end the call.

He blew out a stream of smoke. Beneath the gray swirl, a cockroach explored an empty food bowl in a cage occupied by a shivering sheltie mix. The insect's shiny black carapace was reflected in the curved aluminum sides of the dish. Axel shrugged. Time to wrap it up for the day. He set his feet to yank open the warped front door but stopped. *Speaking of careless.* He walked to the pen where he'd deposited the Yorkie and unlatched the wire door. A quick grab caught the dog by the throat and pulled it forward. A gasping *SQUAWK* echoed up to the ceiling rafters. The animal's limbs flailed as Axel removed the collar with practiced ease and flung the mutt back inside the cage.

Axel stood and examined the short length of red nylon with a black clasp. Two tags dangled from a metal ring. One was bright yellow and contained the vaccination info. The other was stainless steel and glowed brightly under the overhead lighting. "Izzy" was stamped on the metal, along with a phone number. An underhand throw sent the collar clattering into a trash can in the corner.

He grinned. That made it official. "Izzy" was history, and "Unit 16" was ready to go.

CHAPTER 5

"But she's a cat."

Roxxy's claws dug into the lawn as she juked left-right-left without breaking stride. Behind, Max matched her, his big paws pounding like the hooves of a Clydesdale. Drops of slobber flew from his mouth. Roxxy glanced over her shoulder, and their eyes locked. Her eyes grew round with alarm.

"Got you!" woofed Max as he pounced.

Roxxy snorted. Widening her eyes worked every time.

She leaned into a hard turn and barreled through a white dandelion standing in her way. A cloud of tiny seedpods followed her slipstream as she angled away from the trajectory of Max's leap. Her front legs stiffened as she stopped dead and watched him sail past. A satisfying *thump* sounded when he belly-flopped on the lawn. His momentum carried him into a stand of purple coneflowers. A single wobbly stalk remained upright in his wake.

"I think you missed one, Maxey." Roxxy stopped and raked a hind paw through her feathery blond fur. A breeze toppled the remaining coneflower over. "My mistake. You got them all."

"Don't gloat." He blew out a big breath to dislodge a mouthful of colorful petals.

The breeze quickened and swept across Max. Roxxy sifted through the scents wafting off him by quaking her nostrils—rapidly wrinkling her nose in a series of short inhalations. Quaking was better than a deep breath for identifying subtle smells. She easily picked up the heavy, sweet aroma of honeysuckle mixed with the grape-like musk of kudzu. Nothing surprising. Max often explored the tangled vines that poked through the chain-link fence separating their property from the bird sanctuary behind. She wished he was out there right this minute instead of prattling on about being a good dog. Her parents were bad enough.

Max continued, "I almost caught you that time."

"Uh huh. Right up until you face-planted." She squinted at the sun. Almost dinnertime. The prospect of a crunchy bowl of kibble brought a tingly sensation to her jaws.

I wonder... She pointed her nose toward the sky and sniffed. *Yes! Roast chicken!*

Her small pink tongue made a pass across her muzzle. There was just enough time for a quick nap before Bill and Carol dished up the grub. She huffed contentedly as she imagined the pair bustling around the kitchen. Her tail wagged with satisfaction. Once you had humans properly trained, they were pretty much maintenance free.

A trot carried her to a patch of clover that offered a perfect napping spot. She turned around five times in a tight circle, reversed course for an additional five turns, and then changed direction and completed another set of circles before collapsing bonelessly. The spicy aroma of crushed greenery surrounded her.

"Have you ever thought about lying down like a normal dog?" Max asked, settling beside her.

"Since when are you an expert on normal?"

"He's got a point, Roxx," Lulu interjected. She was sprawled nearby on her own patch of clover. "You go down like a hippo hit with a tranquilizer dart."

"I know how to get comfy," acknowledged Roxxy.

Max frowned. "You know what I don't understand?"

"Everything?"

"That was too easy, Max," Lulu chided.

"What I don't understand about *Roxxy*," he plowed on, "is how a canine who's too lazy to go to the dog park—"

She shuddered. "Please."

"Can be as fast and agile as a jackrabbit."

"The answer's obvious," Lulu interjected. "Roxx conserves her energy for when she needs it."

"Thanks, Sis. I—" Roxxy cocked an ear as the plastic flap of the dog door clacked against the frame.

Her father, Jake, came out first, followed by her mother, Molly. The duo crossed the deck and descended the steps side by side. Roxxy smiled in the usual canine fashion, tilting her ears back and opening her mouth so the corners curled upward. Her mom and dad were looking good. Jake was a larger version of Max. The only significant difference in their appearance was that her father's wiry, short-haired coat was all tan, while Max was adorned with a saddle of tight black curls across his back and shoulders. Roxxy was particularly proud of her mother's markings. Molly had black ears and paws—like Lulu's—but instead of a snow-white coat, Molly's fur was fleecy and golden like Roxxy's. Molly's nose was pug-like, but unlike Roxxy, she had not she been afflicted with the dreaded underbite.

Life was so unfair!

Roxxy and her sibs trotted over to meet their parents. The group settled themselves on a patch of lawn close to the fence that separated their yard from Toby's.

Roxxy's nose quaked, picking up the scent of meatloaf wafting from the open kitchen window in the basset's home. Her tail thumped. She was pleased for her friend, certain that Kimberly would slip him tidbits at the dinner table.

"All right, you three," Jake began, studying his offspring. "It's time for another lesson on how to be a good family dog."

Roxxy's tail went still. "Not *that* again. It's almost dinnertime!" Her eyes crossed as she examined a red ladybug that had landed on her nose. A quake of her nostrils sent it on its way.

"*If* you pay attention for a change, this won't take long. Besides"—Jake cocked his head—"if anyone needs this lesson, it's you. I don't want another incident like last week."

"I'm not sure what you mean," replied Roxxy, batting her eyes and making sure the lashes sent her bangs atremble.

Jake snorted. "That only works on humans."

"Fine," she grumbled. "What incident?"

"Digging up the rose bed near the back fence."

"But that's where the soil is softest." She caught herself before adding *only an idiot would dig where the dirt is hard.*

A glance at the area in question revealed that Bill had repaired the damage. Well, mostly. A yellow rosebush had a definite tilt to it.

She turned back to her parents. "And I like that mulchy feeling between my toes."

"*That* attitude," huffed Molly, "is why we're having another lesson in how to be a good dog. Let's start by you listing the qualities."

"Why me?"

Molly stared at her fixedly in the canine equivalent of a human tapping a foot.

"Okay, okay." Roxxy chewed meditatively on a dewclaw. "Let's see… be faithful, comforting, uh…" She spat out a bit of sheath and cut her eyes to Lulu. "Jump in when you feel like it."

"Protective. And *your* specialty"—Lulu playfully nipped Roxxy's ear—"obedient."

Roxxy giggled and pawed her sister's shoulder. "How could I forget *that* one?"

"You two stop kidding around," Molly admonished. "Especially you, Roxxy. It's important to take this seriously. Learning to be a good family dog is the key to ensuring that you'll always be with humans who love you and who…who…" Molly shivered. Shadows darkened her usually bright eyes.

Roxxy and her sibs jumped up, bumping into each other as they crowded around their mother, sniffing to determine what was wrong. Roxxy ran her nose along Molly's flank, identifying the pleasant scents of rosemary and thyme. Her mother must have passed through the herb garden earlier in the day. But sickness? There wasn't even a hint.

"Momma," Roxxy paused to twitch an ear toward their home. "We've *got* wonderful humans! There's nothing for you to worry about!"

Molly whimpered.

"What's *wrong*?" Roxxy rubbed her muzzle against her mother's.

"Nothing, sweetie." Molly sucked in a deep breath. "Just be a good girl."

"I promise. I'll be faithful, comforting, protective, and…" She frowned. "Uh…obligated?"

"*Obedient*," corrected Max.

"Right. That's what I meant. I'll be the most obli—*obedient* dog anybody's ever seen. Well…I'll try."

"I know you will," replied Molly, lifting her chin in acknowledgment. "You can do anything you put your mind to."

"We're still talking about Roxxy, right?" asked Max.

"Shut *up*, Max!" Roxxy and Lulu snapped in unison.

"And never forget," added Jake. "While all the qualities of a good family dog are important, the most essential is to protect everyone in the household."

"Wait a minute," said Roxxy as a horrifying thought occurred. "Even Muffy?"

She craned her neck to survey the yard. The gray-cream-black tabby was—fortunately—nowhere to be seen. Not surprising, really. The hair ball spent most of her time inside the house, lounging on whatever windowsill was getting the most sun, which was just fine with Roxxy. She could do without the feline dragging her lazy carcass into the back yard.

"Even Muffy," confirmed Jake.

"But she's a *cat*!" said Roxxy indignantly.

Jake turned to Molly. "Hon, you want to take this one?"

"Why stop with felines?" asked Roxxy before her mother could weigh in. "What about the mouse living behind the baseboard in the laundry room? Is *that* creature part of the household? Where does it end?"

"You owe me, Jake."

"You're the best, Moll."

"Well?" Roxxy looked from one parent to the other. "I get why it's important to protect humans and dogs, but cats? No way."

"Young lady," said Molly. "Muffy's a family member like we are. She's not some random feline who trespasses on our property and deserves to be run off."

Roxxy seized the opportunity. "Like Cuddles, Momma?"

"Exactly." The fur rose along Molly's spine. "I can't stand the way that mangy mouser sneaks into our yard and uses it for a litter box. What is it with cats, anyway? Somebody needs to teach them—"

"Hon?" Jake interrupted gently. "We were talking about Muffy. Member of the household?"

"Uh, right," replied Molly. She shook herself. "Roxxy, do I have your attention?"

"Yes, Momma."

"You are a good family dog. Muffy is a member of the household. Your job is to protect her."

"But she's a *cat*," said Roxxy.

Molly turned to Jake. "I'm tagging out."

"Can't say I blame you. I've seen lampposts easier to reason with."

"I'm right *here*," huffed Roxxy.

"So you are," Jake conceded. "The humans in our household love Muffy. They would be very sad if anything happened to her. Do you want that to happen?"

Roxxy scratched behind an ear while staring into the middle distance.

"Well?" huffed Jake.

"I'm thinking."

"*ROXXY!*"

"But Poppa, have you seen the way that arrogant hair ball struts around the house? I won't let her get away with it."

"How's that working out?"

Roxxy rubbed the thin scab on her muzzle. The feline was quick. No doubt about that.

She sighed. "Point taken."

Her parents remained quiet, presumably letting the lesson sink in. She had been so preoccupied with rebutting the ridiculous demand to protect

Muffy—as if the sharp-clawed cat *needed* protecting—she hadn't noticed the shadows lengthening in the yard. Her eyes drifted to the horizon. Only the tiny upper crescent of sun remained visible, sitting like a molten cap on a distant hill. A scattering of low-hanging stars pricked the purpling sky above. One burned more brightly than the rest and drew her eye.

"Roxxy!" Jake barked sharply. "Are you listening to me?"

She blinked. *Well, no.*

Her coat rippled as an evening chill took hold. Might as well pretend to go along with her parents' demands. What harm would it do? There was nothing to protect Muffy *from.*

Besides, continuing to argue might put off dinner. "All right, Poppa, if you want me to protect the hair ball, I—"

A dazzling radiance replaced the surrounding twilight for an instant, outlining every leaf and blade of grass in stark relief. Roxxy's gaze whipped back to the horizon. She fully expected to see a dwindling halo of fire surrounding the star she'd noticed before, but it hadn't changed. Or had it? Was its light somehow warmer?

"Roxxy," prompted Jake. "You were saying?"

"Huh?" Her body tingled in a way that reminded her of the time she'd licked an electrical socket in the family room.

She huffed. "Wasn't that *amazing*?"

"Wasn't *what* amazing?" asked Jake gruffly. "And don't try to change the subject. Did you hear what your mother and I said about protecting Muffy?"

Roxxy twitched an ear in annoyance. "Forget that stupid cat. Didn't you see the—"

"The only thing I see," Molly snapped, "is that you're trying to get out of admitting Muffy's a family member, just like we are."

Roxxy frowned.

Was it possible they really hadn't seen it?

Jake demanded, "Well? Are we getting through to you?"

"Uh, sure, Poppa."

The back door's oiled hinges made only a whisper of sound, but all the dogs turned. Bill was framed in the light from the kitchen.

He grinned and yelled, "Dinner!"

Roxxy's parents and sibs bolted for the house. She remained in place, staring at the low-hanging star sparkling just above the horizon.

AXEL

Tat-a-tat-tat, tat-a-tat-tat…tat-a-tat-tat, tat-a-tat-tat…tat-a-tat-tat.
Axel's thumbs beat out a staccato rhythm on the steering wheel. The pickup was parked in an inconspicuous slot at the back row of a strip mall lot. The L-shaped configuration of businesses included a payday loan shop, a tanning salon, and an assortment of other low-rent enterprises. A grocery store was doing the most trade. The windows were plastered with ads written in red marker on butcher paper featuring chicken legs, paper towels, and a variety of other items. The ad that had caught Axel's attention featured two-for-one bags of off-brand dog kibble.

Tat-a-tat-tat, tat-a-tat-tat…tat-a-tat-tat, tat-a-tat-tat…tat-a-tat-tat.
The noise stopped as Axel spotted the blinking of a yellow turn signal. A massive Buick slowed on the main road and negotiated the entrance to the lot like a tanker approaching dry dock. Axel suspected the old car had been burgundy when new, but the paint had faded to dull reddish brown. The driver was an ancient guy with humped shoulders. He leaned

forward, staring goggle-eyed through the windshield like a goldfish peering from a bowl.

Axel's eyes narrowed as he spotted the car's other occupant. A glossy black dachshund had its front paws propped against the driver's narrow shoulder. The russet tip of the dog's tail blurred in a wag.

The geezer's wrinkled cheeks creased in a happy smile as the dachshund's small pink tongue licked an earlobe that was oversize in a profile shrunken with age.

Axel felt a warm glow as he watched the byplay. The sleek little dog would bring top dollar.

The Buick eased into a handicap parking space. Axel adjusted his dark glasses to compensate for the rays slanting beneath the bottom edge of the sun visor. A second later, a refrigerated panel truck rumbled in front of his parking spot and slowed, throwing him into shadow and blocking his view. He cursed and slid a hand around the cool metal of the door handle, ready to hop out and send the driver on his way, but the big truck moved on. Axel again had a clear view.

The geezer was still in the car, caressing the mutt's ears with a liver-spotted hand.

Axel grunted. *How long is this lovefest going to last?*

Finally, the old man unfastened his seat belt, and the Buick's windows slid down to create gaps of about four inches to provide plenty of ventilation for the dog, but not enough space for it to jump out. Axel nodded. The supermarket allowed service dogs inside but not pets. Temperatures were cool enough that most dog owners felt they could safely leave Fido in a well-ventilated car for a few minutes while they went inside to pick up a couple of items.

Axel grinned. *Welcome to the real world.*

The dachshund's owner clambered out of the Buick and opened a rear door. Several tugs on an aluminum walker brought it only partway free. The stoop-shouldered man paused and bent forward with hands on knees. His thin chest heaved.

Axel's grin faded. *Get a move on!* A red haze filled the corners of his vision. Without realizing what he was doing, he raised a hand and brought it down. *Smack!* A seam split in the old vinyl seat, and yellow foam rubber bulged along the opening.

Axel turned his head at the sound of a startled gasp and looked into the wide blue eyes of a twenty-something woman standing beside his truck. He cursed without bothering to keep his voice down and was pleased to see her shocked expression morph into fear as the blood drained from her face. The toddler on her hip began to wail.

Axel held the woman's eyes while his features slackened and erased any vestige of human expression. She whirled and hurried toward the entrance of the grocery store. The soles of her flip-flops slapped the asphalt with each rapid step. The child bounced in her arms, and she raised a palm to steady its head.

Axel turned his attention back to the Buick. The old guy had the walker open and was reaching through the gap in the driver-side window to caress the dachshund's ears. The dog stuck its narrow muzzle through the opening and licked the man's nose. The geezer smiled and pressed his forehead against the dog's.

Axel muttered in disgust. "Saying goodbye and don't even know it."

CHAPTER 6

"This just gets better and better."

"No way." Roxxy flopped onto the cool hardwood floor of the front hallway.

Her body went limp as she settled into the deadweight sprawl that announced she was immovable.

Jake sighed as he looked at his mate. "I'm getting too old for this."

"Who isn't?" Molly turned to Roxxy. "Don't 'no way' *us*, missy. Get up this minute. Carol's taking you to the vet for a checkup."

Roxxy didn't answer. Was there any way out of this? The front door was closed—and off limits in any case because the area beyond wasn't fenced. The only potential escape route was to the rear of the house and the dog door in the kitchen. Her parents would eventually corner her in the back yard, and Jake would sit on her until Carol showed up with a leash, but that was better than lying there like a throw rug.

Too bad her parents had eliminated the possibility of her reaching the kitchen. They were strategically positioned to block her path. Sneaks! Her eyes narrowed. Was it possible to squeeze *between* them? She weighed the odds. Her father loomed impressively, but her mother was the real problem. Molly was nearly as nimble as Roxxy herself. To make matters worse, a grandfather clock stood against the wall, further narrowing the passage. The mechanism ticked loudly in the silence, and the narrow pendulum swung with hypnotic precision in the tall frame. She'd once stared at it so long that she'd thrown up in a pair of Bill's hiking boots. His fault, of course, for leaving them in the hallway.

"Why aren't you getting up?" asked Molly.

"I'm considering my options."

"Your only option is a trip to the vet's office!"

"There's nothing wrong with me. Why do I have to go when Max and Lulu get to stay home?" She glared at her siblings, who sat on their haunches behind Jake and Molly watching the proceedings with undisguised interest.

Lulu bumped Max with a shoulder. "What do you think?"

"I'll bet the afternoon treat that she weasels out of going. Nobody does uncooperative like Roxxy."

"Good point." Lulu raised a coal-black paw and scratched an ear of the same color. "I'll take that bet, but I want odds. Two to one in my favor?"

"You're on," said Max.

Roxxy huffed irritably. "When did my life become a wagering event?"

"Max and Lulu, pipe down!" Molly snapped. "As for you, Roxxy, on your paws this instant! You're going to the vet, and that's all there is to it. When I gave birth, you were the weakest and sickliest pup in the litter."

"That was *nine months* ago! I'm fine now!"

"Dr. Amy hasn't seen you in a while, and she wants to make sure you're okay."

"I *hate* going to the vet!" protested Roxxy.

"We all hate it. We're *dogs*!"

Air trickled past the weather stripping on the bottom of the front door. Roxxy's tail thumped the floor. Somebody in the neighborhood was smoking a brisket. Was there a possibility some might come her way? *Unlikely.* Her tail went still.

"Pay attention!" Molly snapped.

As if on cue, Carol appeared at the end of the hall. She asked in a chipper tone that put Roxxy's teeth on edge, "What's all the barking about?"

Roxxy stayed glued to the floor while her parents and sibs ran to greet the woman. *Suck-ups!*

Carol reached down and petted each of the dogs swirling around her legs. She straightened and cocked an eyebrow at Roxxy.

"I've seen that determined sprawl before, and it won't work. Besides"—the woman smiled—"you should cheer up. You'll have company on your trip to the vet."

Roxxy grunted with satisfaction as the other dogs exchanged uneasy looks.

Serves them right.

Her misery-loves-company feelings were reinforced when Carol disappeared into the laundry room, where the pet paraphernalia was stored. Roxxy anticipated the woman returning with a handful of leashes.

Those hopes were dashed when Carol reappeared toting a cat carrier. Muffy crouched inside, her ears laid back and emerald eyes ablaze.

"*You're* going?" Roxxy woofed, outraged.

"What gave it away, genius?" hissed Muffy.

"Just wait until we get back, you moth-eaten—"

"Roxxy," Carol said. "Stop bothering Muffy and fetch your leash from the basket. We're going to be late."

Car keys jingled as Carol pulled them from her shoulder bag.

Roxxy closed her eyes. *I'm one with the hardwood. I'm—*
"Up!" barked Molly.
—I'm immovable. I'm—
"Any time now," Carol said, tapping her foot.
—outnumbered.

Roxxy trudged to the laundry room and nosed through the leashes in the low wicker container. She found hers and took one end in her teeth. She dragged it into the hall. The length of woven pink nylon trailed between her paws and behind her as she proceeded at the slowest possible pace she could without generating a rebuke from her mother or Carol.

Max snorted. "Hey, Sis, maybe you can bond with Muffy at the vet's office."

Roxxy opened her mouth to snap a reply—and dropped the leash. Her paws tangled in its length, and she face-planted.

Muffy's satisfied purr echoed from the carrier.

Roxxy staggered upright.

This just gets better and better.

Roxxy squirmed, but the strong arms in the short-sleeved blue smock held her securely. She gave a huff of grudging respect. This vet tech knew her business.

"You *could* walk instead of throwing yourself on the floor and making me carry you," said Patty, chuckling.

Fat chance. Roxxy amped up the squirming.

No self-respecting dog would ever go willingly to a vet's exam room. She'd rather be dragged or carried, thank you very much. And if carried, she would make every effort to get free and dash back to the reception area.

The thought of the check-in area set her jaws atingle. A couch was located across from the counter where pet owners signed in. The piece of furniture was long and had deep cushions, and the frame was supported by short tapered oak legs. On her last visit, she had managed to crawl far enough under it to sink her teeth into a rear support leg. She had learned a few new words when Carol knelt on the floor and wriggled in to pry her teeth loose.

Good times!

Unfortunately, she knew there was no escaping Patty's grip. Prior visits had shown the vet tech to be a worthy adversary. Unlike most humans, Patty never fell for the eye-batting routine. She was also an experienced dog wrangler, and Roxxy had never found a way to slip from her grasp. Still, what was life without a challenge?

Roxxy torqued her body and tried to slither to the floor.

"Settle down, you rascal. You're worse than usual."

She went still and waited.

"That's better. You—*ewww!*"

Roxxy tried to pinpoint the flavor. *Cherry? Why didn't they make bacon-flavored lip gloss?*

"You got me," acknowledged Patty, wiping her mouth on her shoulder. A smear of pink adorned the blue fabric. "Be glad you're so darn cute."

As they neared the end of the hall, a teenage girl wearing the light-green smock of a kennel assistant—a position that Roxxy knew was well below the status of a vet tech like Patty—walked out of an exam room. The girl's slender arms cradled an agitated feline.

"Oh, look!" exclaimed Patty. "There's your housemate."

Roxxy's eyes narrowed. Sure enough, Muffy was the hair ball in question. The cat's twitching whiskers and lashing tail indicated the feline had undergone the indignity of a thorough exam.

"What are you looking at?" hissed the tabby as they passed.

"Did the *wittle kitty* get poked and prodded?"

"At least I went first."

"So what?"

"Now it's your turn. I'll be sunning myself in an outdoor kennel while Dr. Amy goes over you from head to tail."

Roxxy was working on a snappy reply when Patty made an abrupt turn into the exam room that Muffy had exited.

"*Yelp!*" Roxxy rubbed a paw across the ear that had clipped the doorjamb.

"Sorry, sweetie. I cut the corner a little close."

Could the day get any worse?

"Hold still," the vet demanded in a stern tone, belied by twinkling green eyes. "You're impossible."

Roxxy tried to jump from the table, but her paw pads slipped on the stainless-steel surface, and she pitched forward and bumped her chin. An arm clamped around her middle and hauled her upright.

"That must have smarted," observed Dr. Amy, continuing the exam without missing a beat.

Roxxy grunted.

Great to have the opinion of a professional.

The vet chuckled. "Just about finished."

Carol, who was standing near the exam table in case an extra pair of hands was needed, said, "She's being pretty good."

"For Roxxy," agreed Dr. Amy.

Roxxy made the mistake of taking a deep breath. The acrid smells of antiseptic cleaning products and medicinal sprays—not to mention the lingering odor of cat—hit the back of her throat. She gagged.

"One last thing. Hold still."

"*Yelp!*"

"Sorry," apologized the vet, reading the thermometer.

Roxxy pulled her tail free of the woman's hand. *Would the injustices never end?*

"Temperature's fine." Dr. Amy turned to Carol and winked. "And I think Roxxy's had enough of my exam."

"Really?" replied Carol, chuckling. "What makes you think so?"

"I detect a beady stare behind those blond bangs. Is she always such a handful?"

"Let's just say she has a lot of personality."

"That's one way of putting it."

A beat of silence ensued, and then both women dissolved in laughter.

Roxxy lifted her chin in what she hoped conveyed an aloof dignity. She gave herself a head-to-tail/tail-to-head shake.

"She is adorable, though," Dr. Amy said as she wiped her eyes.

"Isn't she?"

Roxxy nudged the vet's elbow. The human took the hint and handed over one of the beef-flavored biscuits that usually followed the exam. Roxxy eyed the treat and decided to accept it daintily.

"Watch my fingers!"

Well, maybe not as daintily as planned.

Savory goodness filled her mouth. Her jaws applied pressure. The treat held its shape for a tantalizing second before crumbling with a satisfying *crunch*! Chewing busily, she realized Carol and the vet were talking.

"The pups aren't really *pups* anymore," said Dr. Amy. "Nine months old, if I'm not mistaken. What are you and Bill planning?"

Roxxy tuned out the conversation. The crumbs between her teeth were priority one. She probed her back molars with her tongue.

"It's hard," replied Carol. "We love them so much. I think we'll wait to hear about his transfer before deciding."

"When is—" The vet's voice cut off as the door opened, and a current of air from the corridor stirred Roxxy's curls.

"Sorry, Doc," apologized Kaitlyn, the office receptionist. The young woman brushed a strand of pale red hair from a cheek dotted with freckles. "Mr. Jacobs just called, and he's frantic. Says he left Wiggle in the car yesterday while he went inside the grocery store. The pooch somehow got out and disappeared. I told him we haven't heard anything, but..."

The receptionist paused and gave a slight tilt of the head toward Carol.

"It's okay," said the vet.

"With Wiggle, that makes six dogs in our practice that have gone missing in the past couple of months."

"Have we gotten any replies from the email I sent out last week?"

"Several. From local clinics and some from as far away as Hendersonville. It seems a lot of dogs have disappeared. I was going to talk to you this afternoon. I think...I think you may be right and somebody's taking them."

Dr. Amy raised a palm. "We'll talk about it later."

The door clicked closed.

Carol cocked an eyebrow. "What was that all about?"

"I'm not certain, but I think we have a dog thief operating in the area."

"Dog thief?" Carol blinked. "That's...that's *horrible*! I've never heard of anything like that."

Roxxy's tongue made a pass over her muzzle to check for biscuit crumbs. Long shot, but better safe than sorry.

"Most people haven't, but I checked online, and it's not as uncommon as you'd think. A criminal will come into a community and steal dogs, making sure not to take too many from a single neighborhood or a particular part of town. The thieves don't want the disappearances to look organized and draw the attention of the police." Dr. Amy frowned. "Most owners think the pets have run away."

"Why would someone steal dogs?" Carol pulled Roxxy close. "It doesn't make any sense."

"Unfortunately, it does. A lot of money can be made if the thief has the right connections."

"I still don't—"

"The dogs get sold to labs. Second-rate ones."

Roxxy grunted as Carol's embrace tightened.

"That's *worse* than horrible…to take a pet from a loving family and…and…"

The vet nodded. "I feel the same way. I'm calling the police as soon I hear back from the clinics I've contacted. The more info I have, the better. The authorities may take some convincing to accept that a dog thief is in the area."

Carol straightened. "I just thought of something. Why doesn't the thief adopt from shelters? There would be a steady supply."

"Not cost effective," replied the vet, shaking her head. Light glinted off her round spectacles. "Most shelters charge enough to cover the cost of spaying or neutering. Plus, there's a lot of paperwork with the adoption process. A dog thief would have a hard time staying under the radar."

"I hope the police take you seriously when you call them."

"Me too."

Carol blew out a breath. "On a cheerier note, are you and Lou still planning to come over to the house for dinner on Saturday? It's been weeks since we've gotten together. I'll make lasagna, and we can open that bottle of Chianti you like."

"Best offer I've had in a while. Walk back with me to the office, and I'll double-check my calendar. I've got a few minutes before my next appointment. We can chat a bit."

A knock sounded.

"Yes?" asked Dr. Amy.

Patty entered. She crooked an arm, and the outline of a slim bicep was visible beneath the blue smock. She grinned at Dr. Amy and indicated

Roxxy with a tilt of the head. "I'm ready for round two with the little she-devil. Are you finished with her?"

Roxxy sighed. Hard to live down a rep.

"Thankfully." Dr. Amy chuckled while scratching Roxxy behind the ears. "Would you put her in a kennel while Carol and I go to my office?"

"Is it okay if she keeps Muffy company? We're short on space."

The vet looked at Carol.

"Sure. Sometimes they squabble, but I think they're really pals."

Roxxy's chestnut eyes softened as she studied Carol. *So innocent.*

CHAPTER 7

"Good luck with that."

The corners of Muffy's lips curled into a sleepy grin. The sunshine on her flank was pleasantly warm after the refrigerated air of the vet's office. With a twist of her tail, she rolled over, allowing the rays to bake the other side. A purr tickled the back of her throat. Roxxy would be well into her exam by now. She could imagine the surly expression on the fluff ball's cute button-nosed face as Dr. Amy checked her over.

Claws slid from their sheaths as Muffy stretched to her full length. Each kennel had an indoor and outdoor section. Both areas were approximately eight feet by eight feet. Muffy favored the exterior space, accessed from inside by a pet door—fairly good size to allow bigger animals to pass through—set into the rear wall of the building.

Lazily, she gazed through the chain-link fence that comprised the rear wall of the kennel. The enclosures ran along the back of the building, so there were no traffic sounds to disturb her. A strip of well-worn grass separated the kennel from the wooded area beyond. The grass was currently being watered by automatic sprinklers. Moisture hung suspended in a canopy and shone with the bluish-green iridescence of dragonfly wings. Only the soothing *chuff-chuff-chuff* of the sprinklers disturbed the stillness. Even the animals in the adjoining enclosures were lulled into silence.

A contented purr buzzed in Muffy's chest. *Nice and quiet.*

Muffy rolled over, putting her back against the locked exterior gate. The metal was pleasantly warm against her spine. The entry allowed humans to access the space from outside for cleaning purposes. The enclosure's side walls were plywood, providing privacy from the adjacent kennels. Very civilized, as far as Muffy was concerned. The last thing she wanted was some goofy Lab barking at her, or worse yet, some pedigreed Siamese telling her his life story. She sighed contentedly.

All in all, a sweet setup.

Her ear flicked as a black-and-white warbler sang from the top of a pine. "*Weezee-weezee-weezee! Weezee-weezee-weezee!*"

The sound reminded her of the blue squeaky toy Roxxy sometimes gnawed on. Muffy snorted. She hated to admit it, but Roxxy's company was far more entertaining than the average dog's. Jake and Molly were commendably civil. Muffy had long ago reached a truce with the pair, and they all coexisted in the same house without rancor. Likewise, she'd never had problems with Max or Lulu. The two young dogs were intimidated by her haughty demeanor…and her claws.

But Roxxy…

Muffy's purr built, resonating loudly in rhythm to the sound of the sprinklers. She was careful to conceal her feelings for Roxxy. Namely that the little beast was a constant source of entertainment! The purr took on a bittersweet note. Roxxy wasn't so little anymore. The pooch was solid and about the size of a smallish cocker spaniel—assuming it came covered in blond shag carpet! Muffy's tail curled in amusement. As cute as Roxxy was, the scamp's attitude was even more special.

Muffy recalled the first time Roxxy had charged her. The little puppy had waddled forward with so much determination that it'd taken all Muffy's willpower to hold back a purr of approval. Sidestepping the rag mop had been easy. The best part was when Roxxy had plowed into the kitchen counter, dislodging a bag of flour that tumbled off and left the munchkin covered from nose to tail in snowy-white powder.

Movement drew Muffy's attention. A large garden spider crawled beneath the chain-link fence and paused on the concrete floor. The oval yellow body bore an oblong black center anchored by four precise dots at the corners. The two legs closest to the head lifted and probed the air. Apparently satisfied with its surroundings, it glided to a plywood side wall and ascended to the ceiling where it clung effortlessly upside-down.

Muffy yawned. The creature was too far away for her to spring up and take a swipe at it. Better to save her strength for Roxxy's appearance. Her whiskers twitched in a sleepy grin. She sometimes felt guilty for affecting an arrogant attitude to taunt the fluff ball, but she couldn't help herself. The canine was so darn cute when she got mad! Blond scruff bunched along the pooch's back, and her chestnut eyes sparkled with outrage. *Adorable!* Muffy's purr deepened. Roxxy would be shocked to find out her *supposed* arch nemesis was so fond of her. The purr faltered. She'd have to tell Roxxy how she really felt before—

Muffy's ears tilted toward the pet door. Was that a paw-scrape? Hard to tell with the lawn sprinklers still going. Her tail lashed the floor in anticipation. Roxxy would probably come charging through to try and surprise her. In fact…*yes!* The bottom of the opaque plastic began to swing upward.

Muffy's purr thrummed. The only thing that could make her sweet setup better was a nice tussle with her housemate.

"Time to go," said Patty, hefting Roxxy off the stainless-steel table.

Roxxy snuggled against the smock's crisp fabric as Patty carried her from the exam room. The cotton was pleasantly warm from the woman's body heat. Roxxy enjoyed the ride as they proceeded down a side corridor, heading toward the rear of the building and the kennels. Roxxy twisted and shoved her muzzle into a pocket of the smock's top.

"Subtle," said Patty, producing the biscuit. "Chew, don't gulp."

Roxxy gulped.

Patty rolled her eyes. "Why do I bother?"

One furry ear lifted while the other tilted downward. *Why, indeed?*

They had almost reached the kennel area when Patty stopped without warning. Roxxy saw a teenage boy rushing down the hall toward them, massaging his shoulder. He wore the green smock of a kennel assistant and had a narrow-eyed, petulant expression.

The teen edged against the wall to avoid running into Patty and grumbled, "This job doesn't pay me enough. That big boxer almost pulled me off my feet."

"*Yelp!*" exclaimed Roxxy, taken by surprise when Patty stepped in front of the boy, forcing him to stop.

The woman ordered, "Hold on a minute, Larry."

"Why?"

"I want to offer some constructive advice."

"You're not my boss."

"Maybe not directly," replied Patty agreeably. "But I'm a licensed vet tech, and I have more experience and training than you do."

"Listen, I—"

"Here's the deal, Larry. You need to focus more on doing a good job and less on whining. We don't want any more mix-ups like the one from last week. That corgi needed stitches."

The boy's face reddened. "When I put the corgi in the indoor section, I didn't know there was a Doberman on the other side of the pet door." His lip lifted in a sneer. "I can't see through walls."

"You can *read*, right? The clipboard on the kennel door had a notation showing the space was occupied by the Dobie. If you had taken time to look, you would have—"

"I'm run ragged."

"—known the kennel was already occupied." Patty frowned. "Come to think of it, have you been looking at the clipboards today and making notes when you need to?"

"Uh, yeah," muttered the boy, trying to ease by.

Roxxy's stomach lurched as Patty sidestepped to cut him off.

"Larry, tell me the truth. We need to be careful, or—"

"Whatever," interrupted the boy, attempting to pass on Patty's other side.

The woman again sidestepped to stop his progress, but Larry's move was a feint, and he juked around her.

Roxxy flicked an ear in approval. *Nice move!*

"That kid's a problem," grumbled Patty under her breath as she resumed her stride down the corridor. "I'll talk to Dr. Amy."

Roxxy stopped squirming as they neared the door that led to the kennels. What had Muffy said earlier? Something about lounging in the sun? Roxxy's breathing quickened in anticipation as a plan formed. As soon as Patty deposited her in the indoor part of the kennel, she would burst through the flap to the outside section and scare the arrogant hair ball.

"What's with the panting all of a sudden?" asked Patty.

Still lying on her side, Muffy watched the plastic flap swing ever so slowly toward her. The breeze was at her back, so she couldn't yet pick up her housemate's scent—a combination of spicy clover, citrusy blond coat, and clean, woodsy paws and skin. Muffy stretched, savoring the last moments of peace and quiet. The respite had been nice, but truth be told, she couldn't wait for the fluff ball to shove through the flap and liven things up. Muffy forced herself to stop purring. No need to let the scamp know—

Slap!

The hinged flap smacked into the wall above.

Muffy stared.

A lantern-jawed brindled head filled the open pet door. Rubbery black nostrils quaked. Mud-colored eyes swept the area and settled on her. The frame of the opening creaked as muscled shoulders lodged for an instant, but a determined push by the boxer brought him into the enclosure. Sturdy legs unfolded, and he rose up, up, *up* to loom before her.

Muffy flinched at the brute's scent—oily coat, liver-scented breath, and predator funk oozing at the sight of easy prey. The reek hit her like a tsunami and pinned her to the concrete like a swimmer against the ocean floor.

The sweet setup had become a death trap.

"Whew!" Patty deposited Roxxy into the indoor section of the kennel and latched the gate. "Next time I'm leashing you and making you walk."

Roxxy snorted. *Good luck with that.*

She gave herself a thorough shake. The fluorescent lights from the narrow hallway shone through the chain-link gate and cast a diamond-shaped grid over her and the floor. She glanced at the pet door dividing inside from outside, but the heavy plastic flap was too thick to see through.

"That's done," said Patty, making a note on a clipboard attached to the outside of the gate by a length of brown twine. "As for you," the woman continued while pointing a stubby finger at Roxxy. "Don't pester Muffy. She must be lounging outside."

Roxxy sat primly and tilted her ears back in submission.

"Nice try"—Patty's eyes crinkled at the corners—"but I'm a professional."

Roxxy shrugged. *Worth a shot.*

She listened to the soft cadence of rubber-soled shoes and a burble that sounded like a chuckle as the woman walked away. When the heavy door at the end of the hall closed with a metal click, she whirled and lowered her head in anticipation of plowing through the plastic flap to the outside section at a dead run.

Oh yeah, this was going to be fun!

MUFFY CAME UPRIGHT AS if jerked by the strings of a puppeteer. A desperate backpedal sent her rump smacking into the chain-link fence separating the kennel from the grassy area beyond. Wire mesh pressed into her haunches even as terror rattled her thoughts like marbles shaken in a can. The boxer was large enough to have a Great Dane somewhere in his lineage. Or a Clydesdale. His *head* was larger than her whole body. What she couldn't figure out was why he'd just been standing there for the last few minutes, stiff-legged and staring. He could've already ripped her to shreds. Was he cat-friendly—or at least cat-tolerant? A lot of dogs were. Maybe if she stayed perfectly still, and…

The brute's eyes changed from muddy brown to near black and as hard as hickory. Muffy gulped. He'd been as shocked to find her in the enclosure as she'd been to see him. But now? Saliva appeared at the corners of his mouth and dripped to the floor in glistening strands. The rubbery lips skinned back, revealing yellow teeth that could crush her skull like an eggshell.

"RORRFFFF! RORRFFFF! RORRFFFF! RORRFFFF! RORRFFFF!"

Roxxy's head snapped up. Thoughts of charging outside and surprising Muffy shriveled and died. The sound pounding through the flap reminded Roxxy of a garbage disposal chewing through a teaspoon. Unfortunately, *this* sound reverberated with a menace that could only be made by a living creature—and a huge one at that. She crept to a far corner, taking care to keep her nails from clicking on the cement. Her eyes fixed on the flap. What kind of animal was on the other side?

Muffy felt the chain-link fence give a fraction under the pressure of her hindquarters, but the barrier was anchored too well to provide an escape path. She jerked as the spider appeared in the airspace between her and the boxer, descending from the ceiling on a silver filament. The dog stumbled backward. Muffy's eyes widened in disbelief. The beast is scared of spiders! The insect settled on the floor and scurried toward the fence. She watched with envy as the yellow-and-black body passed through the wire mesh and disappeared from view.

The scuff of a paw pad drew her attention. The boxer had fully recovered from his momentary fright. Mottled black and brown fur bristled down the length of his spine. The muscled chest swelled, and his weight shifted forward in attack mode.

His head thrust forward, jaws snapping viciously. "*RORRFFFF! RORRFFFF! RORRFFFF! RORRFFFF! RORRFFFF!*"

The spittle blinded her as she waited helplessly for the attack.

Roxxy's mind stuttered. Is th-th-that a *dog*? It must have a chest the size of an orange crate! She tucked her tail between her legs and swallowed a whimper.

Muffy blinked the slobber from her eyes. What was he waiting for? They both knew she had no chance against him. He was too big and the space too small. Her eyes widened as his pink-and-black tongue—as large as a washcloth—swept across his muzzle with a smack.

Her flanks rippled in a shiver. *Licking his chops…*

Seconds passed.

Curiosity ate away at the edges of her panic. *Why* wasn't he attacking? She looked into his eyes, and the predatory glitter provided the answer. He was enjoying watching her squirm. Her claws slid from their sheaths. *Toying with me?* A hiss burbled from her throat like steam whistling from a teakettle.

Roxxy's ears shot up. She'd forgotten about Muffy! The pieces fell into place. Her idiot feline housemate and a dog—a *big* dog—had somehow ended up together in the kennel's outside section. Roxxy's tags jingled against the concrete as she rested her chin on the floor and covered her eyes with her paws. Red streaks of the afterimage of fluorescent lights blossomed on the underside of her lids. Too bad she couldn't do something to help Muffy, but the dog with the booming bark had to be an eighty-pounder. It would tear her apart if she got in its way. She flattened her ears. Any second now, the sound of Muffy being mauled would come past the plastic flap. Too bad about the feline. The household wouldn't be the same without—

Household?

The most important duty of a good family dog is to protect the members of its household.

CHAPTER 8

"Being a good dog is highly overrated."

The boxer charged. Muffy lunged sideways, freeing her stiffened tail from the chain-link fence. The dog slammed into the barrier, and the wire rattled as if hit by a baseball bat. He spun toward her, but before he could attack, she rose on hind legs and raked his blocky head with her claws. He burbled a yelp-growl as he stumbled back. She wanted to follow, but her limbs were too watery. The best she could do was take gulping breaths and watch the parallel streaks of blood that welled on either side of the black muzzle. As the crimson lines grew thicker, she promised herself to do as much damage as possible before the end came. She arched her back, and she readied herself for the next charge, but the brute surprised her. He stayed still and swiped a foreleg across his face, his forehead buckling as he stared at the red smear coating his dewclaw and paw. She stayed as still as possible. Would the injuries be enough to discourage him from coming after her again? The boxer shook. Spittle arced from his rubbery lips and darkened the plywood side walls.

Muffy waited. Would he back off, or—?

The dog sprang. She gave ground, claws flashing in the sunlight as she fought to keep him at bay. He barreled forward with face scrunched to protect his eyes. The yellow teeth clacked inches from her face, driving her across the enclosure. A hollow thump sounded when her back slammed into plywood. An iron nail tore free above and bounced off the concrete beside her.

"RORRFFFF! RORRFFFF! RORRFFFF! RORRFFFF! RORRFFFF!"

The boxer's triumphant cry blew her whiskers back. She hissed defiantly and raised a paw to deliver a final slash. His gaping maw opened to engulf her.

Thunk!

Muffy's eyes widened as a blond projectile bounced off the boxer's flank like a tennis ball caroming off a backboard. The big dog staggered. His snapping jaws missed her head and closed on the whiskers along her right cheek. They tore free as he stumbled and crashed into the wall beside her. Another nail fell and ricocheted off the floor to disappear outside.

Muffy darted to the opposite side of the enclosure while licking away the blood filling the empty pores along her muzzle. A disbelieving grunt drew her attention. The boxer had righted himself and was staring slack-jawed at the unmoving heap of curls that had interrupted his attack. The blond mound lay sprawled in the middle of the floor.

The boxer shook his head as if to clear it. His rubbery lips flapped against his jaw. The sound was like sheets snapping on a clothesline in the wind. When his contortions were finished, his gaze again fixed on the still form.

Muffy felt a fleeting instant of kinship with the brute. The object of his attention was no stranger to her, but she found its presence equally hard to believe. The pile stirred. Chestnut eyes blinked open and peered blearily from beneath a swirl of bangs.

"I always knew"—Roxxy muttered through a wince—"being a good dog was highly overrated."

"Get out of here *now!*" hissed Muffy. "There's nothing you can—"

The glint of teeth offered a second's warning. She ducked under the boxer's bite and rose to rake his face. Her claws sent scarlet droplets arcing through the air. The big dog muscled past the onslaught, jaws snapping. She dodged and weaved, but her muscles were leaden with exhaustion. Only minutes had passed since he'd come through the pet door, but it felt like weeks.

A *clack* sounded as teeth came together, and a tuft of fur disappeared from the tip of her left ear. She ignored the pain and lashed out with a paw. The blow missed and sent her lurching to the side, just in time to see Roxxy appear above the boxer's hindquarters. Muffy blinked. Her housemate hung suspended at the top of an impossibly high arc. Sunlight turned her blond curls into spun gold. Gravity asserted itself, and the glowing object plummeted squarely onto the boxer's back. The big dog staggered but remained upright.

Muffy's left ear—the part still attached to her head—twitched in astonishment. Roxxy's teeth were anchored in the scruff of the bigger dog's neck. Not only that…her housemate's stocky little body was flattened along the length of the boxer's spine. Furry limbs draped across the beast's shoulders and hindquarters. The boxer appeared to be wearing a curly saddle.

"RORRFFFF! RORRFFFF! RORRFFFF! RORRFFFF! RORRFFFF!"

The big dog's torso rippled in a violent shake. Muffy expected Roxxy to go flying, but the small jaws somehow remained clenched. The boxer growled and spun like a Brahma bull at a rodeo, sending his passenger's tail streaming out behind them.

"RORRFFFF! RORRFFFF! RORRFFFF! RORRFFFF! RORRFFFF!"

The boxer threw himself on the concrete and rolled. His full weight crashed into Roxxy again and again. He came upright and shook as if trying to shed water. Roxxy went flying and pancaked into a plywood wall like a hay bale hitting the side of a barn. Muffy felt the impact through her paws. The limp dog slid to the floor and lay still.

The boxer bared his teeth and charged Roxxy. Muffy leaped and landed lightly between her dazed housemate and the attacker. She unsheathed her claws and delivered a series of right-left-right slashes that stopped the drooling brute in his tracks. Edging sideways with each blow, she led him away from Roxxy's unconscious form. She staggered as a swipe missed and the boxer rammed his blocky head into her chest. Air exploded from her lungs. A backward tumble landed her next to the chain-link fence. She tried to stand, but it was no use. A glance into the savage dog's eyes revealed her reflection—a slumped bundle of gray/cream/black fur, bedraggled and beaten.

The boxer bent his legs to pounce, but before he could leap, his flanks heaved in a burst of violent coughing. "*Acchhht, acchhht, acchhht!*"

Red mist flew from the black nostrils. Muffy cringed as the warm spray coated her fur, but she was pleased his bleeding muzzle was buying her time. He sucked in red drops with each breath through his nose. The wounds were far from fatal, but they were clearly aggravating. Her momentary sense of satisfaction evaporated when the dog cleared his airways with a *whuff*. The big tongue appeared and swept his muzzle. A hickory-hard gaze settled on her.

Muffy shivered as the nerve-jangling terror returned. She used the last of her strength to lever herself upright. Her haunches pressed into the chain-link fence for support. A weak hiss was all she could manage as the boxer leaned forward, and his hot breath buffeted her.

"Oh my—*THOR, NO!*"

Muffy turned. A scarlet-faced woman—*Patty*, her shocked brain supplied—stood outside the kennel, fumbling with a set of keys to unlock the gate.

"*THOR, STAY! STAY!*"

Muffy turned back to find the boxer standing almost on top of her. His eyes were wild, and he was well past listening to a human's command. She knew with a sick certainty he'd finish her before Patty could open the gate and intervene.

"*THOR, NO!*" The woman slammed her palms against the chain-link fence. "*EYES ON ME! EYES ON ME!*"

"*RORRFFFF!*" The boxer's weight shifted forward.

From behind, Muffy heard Patty trying keys in the lock.

"*THOR, N—DARN!*"

A *clink* sounded that could only be a set of keys landing in the grass. Helplessly, Muffy watched the boxer lean in for the bite that would finish her. He took a half step forward…but suddenly stopped dead.

"*YELP!*" cried the boxer.

Muffy gaped, unable to comprehend why the dog had paused his attack.

The boxer's rubbery lips fluttered in what she first thought was a snarl but then realized was a grimace of pain. But from what? Her scratches hadn't done *that* much damage.

"*YELP!*" The big dog repeated. His blocky head turned to look over his shoulder.

Muffy crouched and peered past the long legs to determine what had drawn the boxer's attention.

I should've known…

Roxxy sprawled on the floor behind the bigger canine. Her lips were drawn back from her muzzle and her teeth were buried in the hock of the boxer's right rear leg. She growled weakly, "Thath *my* cath you're trying to kill, tho lay off." She paused before adding, "Thimwit."

Muffy heard a key turn in a lock.

"Finally!" said Patty. "Do *not* move, Thor!"

A rubber sole brushed Muffy's ear as the woman leaped over her and grabbed the boxer by the collar. He tossed his head and began to struggle.

Patty half-screamed, *"DO NOT MOVE!"*

The tone of command finally registered. The boxer's docked ears drooped.

"Bad dog!" said Patty, giving the collar a shake. "Bad, *bad* dog!"

Muffy hissed. *You think?*

"Thor, you come with me, and no more nonsense! And Muffy," the woman's voice softened. "Everything's okay now. I'll be right back after I get him sorted out."

Start with a tranquilizer dart.

"I don't blame you for hissing." Patty turned her attention to the boxer and pulled him toward the gate. "Come *on*! Why are you making me drag you? What's keeping you—"

The woman's voice died as she peered past the tall dog to see why he was moving so slowly. Her jaw dropped.

"I...I didn't see you back there, Roxxy. You can let go now. You"— Patty cleared her throat—"you did your part."

Roxxy's jaws unclenched, and her chin hit the floor with a soft *thock*.

"YARRR!" yowled Muffy in alarm.

"Roxxy!" exclaimed Patty. "Are you okay?"

Muffy's heart thudded as the woman reached down with her free hand and gently shook the unconscious form. Roxxy's limbs flopped lifelessly.

Patty straightened, dabbing her eyes with a sleeve.

"Sometimes the strain is just too much when a young dog…" She shook her head. "I've got to get Dr. Amy!"

The vet tech dragged the boxer from the enclosure and marched him toward the front of the building.

Muffy dashed to Roxxy and brushed what was left of her whiskers along her housemate's face, but there was no response.

"Don't you *dare* die on me."

Desperately, she tried to think of something that might rouse the unconscious dog. She glanced at the drying brick-red droplets that spattered the concrete.

"Look at that, Roxx! We taught that boxer not to fool with *us*."

No response.

"And…and who named that idiot *Thor*? That's moronic, even for a dog. Uh, sorry. Now stop messing around and wake *up*!" She paused, waiting for Roxxy to show some sign of life, but the blond form remained still. Even her *curls* were limp.

"Come on!" Muffy commanded. "Open your eyes! I'll never hear the end of it if you…if you—"

She froze, remembering an old trick for rousing newborn kittens struggling for their first breaths. Vigorous licking followed as her tongue scraped lightly over Roxxy's button nose. There was no response.

Muffy paused and wailed, "I've *got* to do something!"

"For a start," groaned Roxxy, chestnut eyes fluttering open. "Stop slobbering all over me."

A vibrating purr filled the enclosure.

CHAPTER 9

"Who'd do something that terrible?"

"Be still," said Dr. Amy.
"Yip!" Roxxy shifted on the stainless-steel surface that was warming slowly under her weight.

"Ribs, huh? I thought so."

"Broken?" asked Patty.

"No, thankfully." The vet's tone hardened. "Did you tell Larry to go home?"

"I did. He seemed genuinely sorry for putting Thor in with Muffy."

"He'd better be."

"Yip!"

"Sorry, sweetie. We're almost done."

Roxxy tried to pull away, but the vet trapped her chin in a palm. "Hold still."

The beam of a penlight made her squint.

"I know this isn't fun for you, but I want to make sure you don't have a concussion."

Roxxy blew out an exasperated breath. Her face was so close to the vet's that a fringe of dark bangs fluttered. Roxxy's nose quaked. Minty toothpaste…but an underlying hint of a savory breakfast of bacon and eggs. Wasn't bacon the best thing in the world? Roxxy imagined crunching down on a crispy strip.

The sound of thumping echoed off the exam table.

Patty commented, "Doc, look at that tail wag. She really loves you."

Roxxy raised one ear and lowered the other. *Humans.*

"It's mutual," said the vet, slipping the penlight into the breast pocket of her white coat. She leaned forward to brush her cheek against the side of Roxxy's face. "No concussion, sweetie. You somehow managed to survive this fiasco with no more than a few bruises. You—we—were really lucky."

"Lucky?" said Carol, voice shaking.

"Sorry," said Dr. Amy, turning to look at the figure standing stiffly at the end of the table. "I was so focused on the exam, I forgot you were—"

"Seems like you've forgotten a lot, such as how to keep your patients safe."

Roxxy shifted uncomfortably. Weren't Carol and Dr. Amy supposed to be friends? The scent of anger coming off Carol was like the smell of an overheated light socket. What was going on? Even more perplexing, why was Carol clutching Muffy to her chest as if the hair ball were a priceless treasure instead of…well, a *cat*?

The feline suddenly leaped from Carol's arms and landed nimbly on the table despite a bandaged paw. Roxxy groaned. *What now?* Before she knew what was happening, Muffy's twitching nose began sweeping across her body. The final straw was the tickle of tattered whiskers caressing her face.

Roxxy recoiled. "Did that boxer step on your head?"

"Feeling better?"

"What's it to you?"

"I'm a *cat*, stupid. Curiosity."

"Take it somewhere else." Roxxy wriggled away to flee the inspection. She settled in a new spot and waited for the metal to warm beneath her.

"Be careful! You're going to fall off the edge," growled Muffy. "Do you have a death wish?"

"I don't need *you* looking out for me."

"You can use all the help you can get. Too bad there aren't service animals for animals. You need full-time supervision. Think about it."

"I'd rather think about inviting that moron Thor to the house so you two can have a playdate."

"Both of you settle down," ordered Carol. She turned to the vet. "Muffy and Roxxy were almost mauled! How could you let that happen?"

"You're right." The vet straightened her shoulders. "I take full responsibility, and I feel terrible. I probably should've fired Larry weeks ago."

"Not *probably*!" Carol said. "Anybody careless enough—no, *stupid* enough—to put a boxer in an enclosure with a cat shouldn't be allowed *near* a vet's office." She pointed a trembling index finger. The encircling thin silver ring glinted under the fluorescent light. A clear manicured nail tapped the blue thread sewn over the breast pocket of the vet's white coat. "That says *Doctor* Amy, right? You're supposed to keep animals safe, not endanger their lives."

Roxxy's eyes widened. *Go Carol!*

The vet lifted her palms in surrender. "I just never imagined—I'm *truly* sorry."

Silence hung for a moment.

Carol's hand fell back to her side. "Well, I guess I should be grateful

Roxxy and Muffy came through it pretty well. Plus"—the corner of her mouth twitched—"you're a dear friend, so there's that."

"Thank you." Dr. Amy rubbed her hands across her face and slumped against the counter.

An ink pen rolled over the lip and clattered to the floor. Patty bent and picked it up.

The vet nodded her thanks and turned back to Carol. "I still feel bad about what happened."

"Just make sure that—"

The door opened, and an elderly man pushed through. His aluminum walker smacked into the corner of the counter opposite the table.

The office receptionist was close behind. "Mr. Jacobs, you can't just barge into an exam room."

"Doc, there you are!" the man said as his rheumy eyes settled on the vet. "I'm sorry, but I have to see you."

"Kaitlyn," Dr. Amy said to the receptionist. "I'll take it from here. You can go back out front."

"Doc, I don't know what to do," Jacobs blurted out as soon as the door closed. "Wiggle somehow got out of the car when I went to get groceries. She hasn't been seen since. I've phoned all the shelters."

He paused and sucked in a wheezing breath.

"One of her tags has your office number on it. Kaitlyn told me nobody's called, but I had to check with you." He dragged a frayed shirt cuff across his eyes. "Wiggle means everything to me."

"I'm so sorry, Mr. Jacobs," the vet replied as she laid a hand on his thin arm. "But we haven't received any calls about Wiggle. I promise we'll let you know the minute we do."

The man nodded jerkily, and a tear worked its way down his wrinkled cheek. Roxxy whined softly.

The vet bit her lip. "I…I don't want to alarm you, but I think it's best if you're aware of all the possibilities."

"I don't understand."

"There's a likelihood that someone in the area has been stealing pets."

Jacobs gasped. The walker thudded against the exam table as he staggered.

Carol put an arm around his shoulders. "That doesn't mean *your* dog was stolen or that the police won't find her if she was."

"Who'd *do* something that terrible?" His Adam's apple bobbed in his skinny neck. "If Wiggle's in the hands of—"

"Wiggle needs you to be strong," Carol interrupted. "You have to be in good shape to take care of her when you get her back."

Jacobs nodded. "You're right. Thank you for reminding me, young lady."

"No one's called me a young lady in years." Carol's cheeks dimpled. "Thank you."

The man's lips trembled as he made the effort to smile.

"I'm sorry I blundered in here and interrupted things." He paused and looked at the exam table for the first time. "What have we here?" He adjusted his weight, and the rubber tips of the walker squeaked against the tile.

Roxxy rolled upright and waved her front paw in a shaking hands gesture, ignoring the ache in her side. She refrained from throwing in some eye-batting and bang-trembling. The guy looked kind of frail. Hitting him with all her cuteness at once might be too much. Being adorable carried certain responsibilities. Her tail acted on its own as usual, creating a *swishing* sound as it brushed side to side on the table's surface.

"Oh my," Jacobs murmured as his watery blue eyes studied her. "She's an angel."

Roxxy ignored Muffy's amused purr but made a note to get back at the hair ball later. Well, maybe after that bandaged paw healed. Fair was fair.

"What kind of dog is she?" asked Jacobs, reaching out a gnarled hand to fondle Roxxy's ears.

"Mutt." Carol grinned. "But I think she falls into the category of a spuggle."

Jacobs cocked an eyebrow that was as white and fluffy as an albino caterpillar.

Carol explained. "Spaniel-pug-beagle combined with who knows what."

The man's delighted laugh morphed into a cough that rattled the glass fronts on the surrounding cabinets. Carol patted him gently on the back.

"Her name?" he wheezed.

"Roxxy."

"Suits her." Jacobs leaned forward, keeping his weight balanced on the walker with one hand while extending the other to shake Roxxy's waving paw. "Adorable underbite. And look at that perky expression. I bet she's a handful."

Carol gave—in Roxxy's opinion—a very unladylike snort.

"Really?" Jacobs asked with a chuckle.

"Really."

"Meow!"

"If I didn't know better, I'd swear that cat was agreeing with you."

"What the hair ball needs to do," Roxxy growled, glaring at the feline, "is put a sock in it."

Muffy flicked her tail. "You fight off one boxer, and suddenly you're giving orders? Get over yourself."

Jacobs's rheumy eyes flicked between the pair. "They don't seem to, uh, get along very well."

Carol chewed her lip. "I used to think the same thing." She shrugged. "Now I'm not so sure."

"Well, your little pooch is adorable."

"Thank you." Carol placed her palm on Jacobs's shoulder. "I'm very sorry about Wiggle. I hope you find her soon."

"I appreciate that. She's so beautiful. Shiny black coat except for a patch of brown on her chest that's the perfect image of a bow tie." His shaky hand brushed a tear away from his cheek. "I'll be lost without her."

"Then we'd better get busy."

"Busy?"

"Absolutely," Carol confirmed in the determined tone Roxxy usually associated with pronouncements like *Everybody out so I can vacuum.* "I'll help you make flyers with Wiggle's photo. We'll put them in shop windows all over town."

"You'd do that?" the old man asked.

"Of course. We dog lovers have to stick together."

Dr. Amy added, "Mr. Jacobs, I promise that I'll be in touch if I find out any information about Wiggle."

The old man nodded and placed a trembling hand on the edge of the table.

Roxxy licked the knobby knuckles.

"That tickles," Jacobs said, making no move to take his gnarled hand away. He looked at Carol. "I don't mind her licking, but I hope I'm not teaching her a bad habit."

"Don't worry. That's the only kind she has."

The humans' laughter and the hair ball's snort were so distracting that Roxxy stopped licking, but her eyes remained fixed on Jacobs's hand. Splotchy brown spots covered most of his paper-thin skin. Below, a network of faded purple veins stretched across bones as fragile as a sparrow's.

She resumed licking.

You don't see a hand this beautiful every day.

AXEL

The sun baked the top of the truck, turning the cab into an oven. Axel tugged at the neck of his damp t-shirt, peeling the black cotton away like a second skin. Wasn't early fall supposed to be cool? At least he had a decent vantage point. The pickup was in a far corner of the parking lot with a good view of the rows of vehicles at the entrance to the mega-chain pet store. The place carried everything from goldfish to iguanas, and puppies, of course. Not that puppies were any use to him. Not sturdy enough, according to Ethan, for what the buyer planned to use them for. Still, a pet store parking lot was a good hunting ground. Where there were puppies, there was dog food, and where there was dog food, there was usually a well-meaning owner dumb enough to leave a mutt unattended in the car.

Tat-a-tat-tat, tat-a-tat-tat…tat-a-tat-tat, tat-a-tat-tat…tat-a-tat-tat… tat-a-tat-TAT.

The drumming on the steering wheel grew more insistent with each repetition. Two hours of waiting was beginning to feel like two days.

He'd arrived just before ten, hoping an early bird shopper would leave an unattended unit in a vehicle. His stomach grumbled. Nearly noon and no luck. Fifteen more minutes and he'd give up and hit a drive-through.

Tat-a-tat-tat, tat-a-tat-tat…tat-a-tat-tat, tat-a-tat-tat…tat-a-tat-tat… tat-a-tat-TAT.

Axel dug a pack of unfiltered cigarettes from his jeans pocket and opened a stainless-steel lighter with a flick of the wrist. The ball of his thumb rolled across the ridged flint wheel. Yellow flame appeared. He lit up and took a deep drag. A third of the cigarette disappeared in a sizzling hiss. Twin streams of gray smoke flowed from his nostrils and swirled against the inside of the windshield. He worked the tip of his tongue between the space in his two front teeth and spat out the window. The brown flake stuck against the side mirror.

He waved to clear the smoke and peered through the windshield. A small red Toyota made a hard right into the lot, tires protesting with a brief screech. A heavyset woman in her early twenties parked the compact and lowered the windows a hand's width before turning off the engine.

Axel grinned. *Bingo!*

He flicked the cigarette out the window and leaned forward. The woman locked the car with a chirp of a key fob and walked to the passenger side. A brown-and-white shih tzu popped up and balanced its front paws against the base of the slightly open window. A gold bow secured a furry topknot.

The dog's owner reached through the narrow gap and scratched the dog's well-brushed cheeks while cooing in a singsong voice. "It's warm today, Mac-Mac, so I'll only be a minute. Be good, and Mommy will buy you a special treat."

"Save your money," said Axel under his breath, watching the woman stride briskly toward the store.

The soles of her flip-flops slapped the asphalt and echoed across the lot. His pulse quickened as the automatic doors closed behind her. He extended a hand to turn the key in the ignition.

"Hot day, isn't it?"

Axel turned so fast that cartilage popped in his neck.

"Hey, sorry. Didn't mean to startle you."

The speaker was a young guy, bent at the waist and peering through the passenger-side window. He hooked a thumb toward the front end of the truck.

"Just wondering if you were having engine trouble."

Axel relaxed as he took in the security guard's earnest expression, acne scars, and pencil-thin neck.

Not a real cop.

How old was this skinny punk? Twenty? Axel fought not to laugh. The kid's oversize uniform shirt was buttoned at the collar, giving him the appearance of a turtle poking its head out of its shell.

"Sir?" the guard prompted. "Engine problems?"

Axel grinned. "Nah, just waiting on my girlfriend. She's supposed to meet me here. We're going to buy a kitten."

"Is that why you've been here so long?"

The grin slid from Axel's face. "You've been watching me?"

"N-No, sir," stammered the guard, taking a step back. "I mean, I've been keeping an eye on the parking lot. We...the company I work for, we—"

"Yeah?" interrupted Axel, his good humor returning as the punk squirmed.

"Well, the company I work for does outside security for this mall and a bunch of others around town. We've had reports about dogs going missing from cars. It's possible someone is stealing them, but I can't believe it. How could a human being sink so low?" His nose wrinkled as if he'd whiffed a carton of curdled milk. "Anyway, we've put on extra patrols, and we're checking when we notice an occupied vehicle that stays in a lot for a long time. Are you planning to—"

"Guess I've been stood up," interrupted Axel. "Got to go."

The guard's mouth was still moving, but Axel ignored the words. The engine coughed to life. He stomped on the accelerator and the truck shot forward, issuing the usual double backfire. A glance in the rearview mirror showed the guard holding the ridge of his hand across his forehead while squinting at the license plate. No worries. A carefully applied smear of mud made the numbers unreadable. The real problem—Axel downshifted as he turned onto the busy thoroughfare in front of the strip mall—was that people were wondering why so many dogs had disappeared from cars in parking lots.

He depressed the clutch and maneuvered the gearshift with his palm. The transmission slipped for an instant before catching with a grinding noise. The truck settled into third gear, blowing past a slow-moving city bus. An ad for a car dealership was plastered down the length of the lumbering vehicle. A gleaming black pickup was pictured—oversize tires, a long cargo bed, and a massive chrome grill. Just the kind of truck he'd buy after he delivered the next shipment and took care of Ethan.

The wind streaming into the cab dried the neck of his t-shirt but lifted an empty potato chip bag from the seat. He made a grab and missed. The bag sailed out the passenger-side window and landed in the gutter. Cursing, he leaned over and turned the window's crank handle to close it. Getting stopped for littering would be a disaster. A cop would run his record, and he'd be back in the joint in no time. He couldn't remember the last time he'd checked in with his parole officer.

Axel realized he was grinding his teeth. He worked his jaw from side to side.

Best to avoid strip mall parking lots for a few days.

Well, there were plenty of mutts to be found in the residential neighborhoods around town. In fact, he knew just where to start. The corners of his mouth drew back in what casual observers might've considered a smile—if they ignored his eyes.

CHAPTER 10

"What were you thinking?"

"Don't...drool...all...over...it!" Roxxy called out between gasps as she raced after Max, who was well ahead and clutching a red rubber ball in his mouth.

Grass clippings arced from beneath his back paws and showered her. She choked on a blade of emerald St. Augustine while making a series of hard cuts to follow his zigzag course. A wince creased the corners of her eyes. The injuries sustained in the encounter with the lunatic boxer were almost healed, but sudden movements could still cause a twinge.

"You okay, Roxx?" panted Lulu from a few strides behind.

"Fine, Sis!" To prove the point, Roxxy put on a burst of speed and sliced in front of Max. He tripped and slid face-first across the lawn, but his jaws remained clamped around the ball.

Lulu woofed, "Good one, Roxx!"

"Sit on him before he gets up! I'll pull the ball out of his mouth."

"Gladly!"

Lulu planted her hindquarters on Max's head and leaned back, pinning him to the ground.

"Outh!" he exclaimed around the ball in his jaws.

Roxxy leaned down and bit into the sphere, careful not to clash teeth with him. She threw herself backward in a series of hard yanks, but the pads of her paws couldn't gain traction on the smooth lawn.

"Hurry up, Roxx!" urged Lulu. "The big goof keeps squirming. He'll throw me off any second!"

"Um thying!"

"Try harder!"

"Max, you're doing great!" yapped Leo. "Don't let go!"

"Hang in there, Maxey-boy!" echoed Toby, twitching an ear to dislodge a housefly. "Don't let those girls push you around!"

Roxxy continued to pull while cutting her eyes to the spectators. The Pom was in their yard and close to the fence dividing their property from Toby's. The basset was on the other side of the chain-link fence and within a few feet of Leo. In Roxxy's opinion, each looked insufferably comfortable stretched out on their respective patches of springy green clover. Leo hadn't wanted to join the game of keep-away for fear of messing up his mane. Toby was happy to watch from his property.

In Roxxy's opinion, the duo seemed annoyingly pro-Max as they observed her failing efforts to take possession of the ball.

"Max, keep those jaws clamped!" barked Toby.

"Right!" agreed Leo. "Win one for the guys!"

He paused and snapped at the housefly trying to take up residence on his mane.

Roxxy and Lulu made eye contact. A blond tail flicked. A black ear lifted. Roxxy put all her weight into a yank while Lulu simultaneously shifted pressure to Max's neck. A *gacking* noise filled the air. Roxxy snatched the ball from Max's limp jaws and immediately dropped the slobbery thing. *Yuck!* Next time, she'd sit on Max while Lulu pulled.

"Good try, Max!" yipped Leo.

Toby added, "You almost won!"

Roxxy glared at the cheering squad. "Max weighs more than me and Lulu *combined*. The big oaf doesn't need your help." A thought occurred to her. "Besides, since when do you two agree on anything?"

Toby and Leo looked at each other with widened eyes.

The Pom recovered first. "I was rooting for Max first. You copied me!"

"Why would I copy a runt who could get lost in one of my paw prints?" asked Toby. "Besides, I always root for Max when he's taking on his sisters. The poor kid is outclassed."

"Thanks, Toby," huffed Max. "I appreciate—wait, what?"

Leo glared at the basset. "Don't insult poor Maxey. It's not his fault Roxxy and Lulu always outsmart him."

"I wouldn't say *outsmart*," Max muttered. "Maybe *outmaneuver*, or—"

"Pipe down, kid!" Leo and Toby snapped in unison.

"Agreeing once again," observed Roxxy, eyes twinkling. "How sweet."

Before the outraged duo could respond, the plastic flap on the dog door slapped against the frame, drawing all the canines' attention.

Roxxy watched as her father emerged from the family home and trotted down the deck steps. His claws clicked a steady cadence on the pine.

She frowned. *What's he carrying in his jaws? Looks like...*her ears drooped. The tattered remains of an emerald-green cashmere scarf fluttered in the wind as he approached.

Max stood so quickly a nearby chipmunk gave a startled squeak and disappeared down its burrow. "Roxx, how *could* you?"

"Maxey's right," added Lulu. Her black ears tilted forward. "What were you thinking?"

"Who said I did anything?" protested Roxxy, but her mutinous tail curled between her legs in what amounted to a confession of guilt. *Stupid thing!*

"Good luck, Roxx," huffed Leo. "From the look on Jake's face, you're going to need it." He dashed across the lawn and squeezed through the little gap in the fence to return to his own yard.

Toby rose and shook, ears slapping the sides of his head.

"I'd better go as well. Roxx, just tell the truth and hope for the best." He paused. "On second thought, make up a *really* good story."

"Why," Roxxy asked indignantly, "does everyone assume *I* tore the scarf to shreds?"

Max stared at her. "You're kidding, right?"

A shadow swallowed her. She tilted her head back and looked up. Sometimes she forgot just how big her father was. This wasn't one of those times.

He *loomed*. His cinnamon eyes—usually so warm and loving—narrowed into slivers of flint. The mangled garment dropped from his jaws. "Well?"

She thought for a moment. "Moths?"

Max choked down a laugh while Lulu sighed.

The flint glittered. "Try again."

She stomped her paw in frustration, just missing a fuzzy yellow caterpillar. "Carol shouldn't have left the scarf draped over a chair where I could get to it!"

"I stand corrected," replied Jake stonily. "You're not to blame. This is all Carol's fault."

Roxxy winced, knowing where this was heading.

A low growl vibrated beneath Jake's words. "Carol should have better judgment? Is that what you're saying? The person who, five years ago, found your mother when she was a stray and took her in? That Carol?

The human who found *me* a few months later lying helpless on the side of the road with a broken leg and rushed me to the vet?"

"Poppa, I—"

"Is *that* the Carol you're talking about?"

"Well, uh…" Roxxy's throat went dry.

"You're saying Carol *deserved* to have her scarf chewed up because she forgot to put it in a drawer?"

Roxxy pawed the garment. *What was it about cashmere?* Mouthfeel, she decided. The material slid so naturally between the teeth.

"*Speak!*" roared Jake.

Roxxy flinched. Blaming Carol wasn't getting her anywhere. The woman was undeniably wonderful. Was there another strategy? Hmm… how about countering outrage with outrage? That might—

"*Roxxxxy!*"

"Poppa, why make such a big deal about a silly old scarf? Carol's got tons of them."

Jake flicked an ear as if expecting the tactic. "I'll tell you what the *big deal* is. Do you know where Carol got that particular scarf?"

Roxxy groaned. *This just gets better and better.* She had a sinking feeling the item hadn't been acquired at a yard sale. "Where?"

"Bill gave it to her as a birthday present."

"You've *got* to be kidding," blurted Roxxy, her guilt momentarily superseded by outrage that the fates were conspiring against her. "What's next? Bill *knitted* it? The yarn was dyed to match Carol's eyes? I mean, come *on*, Poppa, I thought the scarf was a regular…well, *scarf*."

The flicker of amusement came and went so quickly in Jake's eyes that Roxxy couldn't be sure she'd actually seen it. Besides, Max and Lulu's shocked gasps had distracted her.

Better get it over with.

She sat up straight. "Let's hear it, Poppa. Tell me I've been a bad dog."

Instead, Jake woofed tiredly. "There are chew toys scattered all over the house and back yard. The whole *point* of having them is to give you something to gnaw on."

"I *try* to be good!"

Roxxy dropped her eyes to the scarf fluttering on the lawn, held in place by Jake's paw. The fabric *was* the same emerald as Carol's eyes…and the identical shade of a jade pendant she wore on special occasions. Roxxy remembered how beautiful the scarf had been when it was tied loosely around the woman's neck with the pendant peeking between the folds.

Bill must have gone to a lot of trouble to find a scarf that was exactly the right color.

"I *do* try." Roxxy whispered. "I really do."

"She really does, Poppa," ventured Lulu. "Roxxy's just, well…"

"Hopeless," supplied Max helpfully.

Roxxy rounded on her brother. "You big lummox! I ought to—"

"Enough!" Jake roared.

The ears of all three younger dogs tilted back in submission.

"Roxxy, I'm going to bury this…this *mess* someplace where Carol won't find it. I don't want her to know what you've done."

"How would she know it was me?"

Jake raised one ear and lowered the other.

"Okay," acknowledged Roxxy.

"And *please* try and be a good dog. It's important that you learn to behave so that…so that things work out well."

He rose and took the scarf between his teeth.

The tip of Roxxy's tail lay limply on the ground as she watched her father trot to the farthest corner of the yard. She was determined to take this lesson to heart. *No* chewing on birthday presents!

Her tail rose and assumed its usual upward jaunty curl.

Fortunately, her father hadn't said anything about anniversary gifts.

Carol and Bill had recently exchanged presents, and he had received a scrumptious-looking pair of leather loafers. Surely chewing on shoes wouldn't interfere with things working out well.

She frowned. *What things?*

CHAPTER 11

"We've got a problem."

Late-afternoon sunlight lengthened Jake's shadow as he did one of his regular patrols along the chain-link perimeter of the back yard. Molly and the kids were having a pre-dinner nap inside the house. Dry leaves crunched under his paws, but the yard was otherwise still. The peaceful break was welcome. His three offspring—well, mostly Roxxy if he was being honest—ensured there was never a dull moment. His nose quaked as he neared a rear corner of the lot. He sniffed the usual scents. Rabbits, wild sage, honeysuckle, and…and …

Jake stopped dead. He pointed his muzzle into the wind, but the current shifted before he could be sure if he'd actually detected the feral scent of a predator. The tail on his shadow bobbed in an uncertain shrug. He snorted. *You and me both.*

Finished with his patrol, he trotted toward the house, being mindful to skirt the herb garden. His back paw came down on a cilantro stem that had toppled and lay on the lawn. The rangy plant had bolted in a final growth spurt for the season. A pungent, spicy smell flooded his nostrils. *Yuck!* How can humans eat that stuff?

"Jake!"

He turned toward the source of the deep woof. Toby stood outside the fence separating their properties. Jake's tail wagged in greeting. The basset was a good-natured sort, and Jake was grateful Toby and Roxxy had become friends. With any luck, some of the hound's common sense would rub off on the willful troublemaker. Jake glanced at the spot in the far corner of the yard where he'd buried the mangled scarf. His tail slowed. Roxxy *had* to settle down before—

"We've got a problem," barked Toby.

Jake chided himself for not noticing his neighbor's stiff posture and raised hackles. His breath caught when he spotted the slit below Toby's left eye oozing blood. A little higher and the wound would have left the basset blind on that side.

"What happened, buddy?"

"Snatcher."

Jake shivered as he recalled the faint scent that had come and gone with the change in the wind's direction. *I wasn't imagining things.* Still, he had to ask.

"Toby, are you sure it was Snatcher and not some other fox?"

"Positive."

"I thought he was gone for good."

"Me too, but he's back." Toby wiped a thick foreleg across the side of his face, smearing red over his muzzle. The slit immediately refilled with blood.

"Sorry he nailed you."

"Could've been worse. I was upwind, and he took me completely by surprise."

"Where did it happen?"

"I pushed through the yew hedge on the far side of the yard. As soon as my head cleared, I saw a flash of teeth and pulled back just in time. If I'd been a second slower, Snatcher would have taken out my eye. Thank goodness he turned and ran."

"He knows he can't handle you in a stand-up fight."

"If I used my weight to pin him, he'd be in trouble. But..."

"Yeah, he could do a lot of damage in the meantime." Jake watched as a crimson bead detached itself from the wound and trickled to the corner of Toby's mouth. "Better get that taken care of."

The basset licked away the drop. "Jake, it's not me I'm worried about."

"I don't...wait a minute. Y-you don't think *she'd* have so little sense as to take on Snatcher, do you? That fox would rip her to shreds. He'd—"

"Who are you trying to convince? Me or you?"

Jake whirled, so intent on reaching the dog door into the kitchen that he forgot to avoid the herb garden. His chest crushed a stand of lavender, unleashing an explosion of floral scent. Tendrils of mint and rosemary pulled at his legs. He fought through, ripping plants free from the ground. A shower of soil flew from the web-like roots. All went unnoticed.

Roxxy!

"WHAT'S GOING ON?" HUFFED Lulu, leaning close to Roxxy. "And why does Poppa smell like potpourri?"

"Beats me." Roxxy stifled a yawn.

She'd been woken up from a perfectly good nap and ordered outside for a family meeting. Ugh! Didn't her parents know it was almost dinnertime? Where were their priorities? She snuggled deeper into the clover patch near the big oak and waited, pleasantly sandwiched between Max and Lulu. Hard to beat sibs for body warmth.

"What do you think Momma and Poppa want?" whispered Max.

"Probably just another stu—uh, *silly* lesson on how to be a good family dog." Roxxy flicked a paw to dislodge a ground beetle trying to burrow between her toes. The insect's hard black carapace glinted in the dying sunlight as it tumbled away. "Momma and Poppa are obsessed."

Max snorted. "You can use all the instruction you can get."

"Thanks, oaf, but I wish I was still napping. I was dreaming about juicy pot roast." Her tongue ran across her muzzle. "With gravy."

"Stop thinking about food. Something important is up."

Roxxy's eyes widened. "What's more important than pot roast with gravy?"

"I think Max is right," Lulu said. "Take a look at Momma and Poppa."

She did so.

Molly sat with her hindquarters perched on the lawn as if she was prepared to spring upright at any second. Jake lay on his stomach, gnawing savagely at a dewclaw. The wiry fur bristled along his back.

And both of her parents were staring directly at her!

She blurted instinctively, "I didn't do it!"

"Didn't do what?" asked Jake, licking the grass to remove a bit of dewclaw from his tongue.

"Whatever you called the meeting for. It wasn't me."

"Roxxy, you're not in trouble. Unless"—Molly frowned—"you've done something we don't know about."

"Of course not, Momma." She batted her eyes, projecting an air of wounded innocence.

She'd been very good about refraining from chewing on scarves or birthday presents. But the walnut legs on the chest of drawers in the spare bedroom? Her jaws tingled. Different story.

Molly sighed. "Roxx, that innocent look's a dead giveaway. What have you been up to?"

"Hon," Jake huffed before Roxxy could respond. "We've got something more important to talk about."

"Right." Molly flicked an ear in agreement. "Go ahead."

Jake's eyes swept his offspring before settling again on Roxxy.

"Listen closely. There's a red fox named Snatcher roaming around the neighborhood. He's been in the area before, and he is absolutely the most vicious animal I've ever come across. Stay as far away from him as possible. In fact, until he's moved on, none of you can go outside unless your mother or I are with you."

"That's ridiculous!" Roxxy's claws curled into the lawn.

Why was she still being treated like a *puppy*! She glanced to either side, hoping to see some support from Max or Lulu, but both had their ears tilted back submissively.

"Roxxy, you heard your father," snapped Molly. "You stay in the house unless he or I accompany you outside. Period."

"I don't need a babysitter. I can take care of myself, even if I do run into Snagger."

"*Snatcher!*" barked Jake. A startled mockingbird shot from a nearby holly in a blur of gray-black wings. "Listen to me, Roxxy! You still have some growing to do before you reach full size. And trust me, Snatcher's no ordinary fox. You wouldn't stand a chance against him. He's big and lightning fast. He *survives* by killing."

"But *I'm* quick," Roxxy protested as a breeze stirred a nearby group of dandelion balls.

A cloud of white seedpods drifted past, but a few caught in her blond coat.

She impatiently shook them off. "You've said so yourself."

"I have," Jake agreed. "But you're not a killer."

"I—"

"Take a look at the open field behind our property."

"Why?"

"Do it."

Grudgingly, she studied the expanse beyond the back fence. Water oaks and cottonwoods anchored a sprawling field thick with goldenrod and green sedge. Isolated clumps of sunflowers and purple coneflowers wafted in the breeze. She'd heard Carol describe the area as a green belt set aside by the neighborhood developer to offer a haven for birds and other wildlife.

"Okay, I looked at it." Roxxy gave a double ear flick of impatience. Hanging in the air was an unspoken *"satisfied?"*

Jake growled. "You need to take this seriously. I saw Snatcher dart into that field and pounce on a rabbit before it had time to blink. One twist of Snatcher's head"—Jake mimicked the movement—"and the rabbit's neck snapped like a twig."

"*I'm* no rabbit. You've always said a fox won't take on a dog unless it's a puppy or tiny like Leo. I don't think—"

"That's right," Molly said. "You *don't* think. *Or* listen. Your father said Snatcher's no ordinary fox. He's bigger and faster than most of his kind, and he *hates* dogs. Thinks we're a bunch of softies who wouldn't last ten minutes in the wild."

Roxxy felt Snatcher had a point—to a degree. When it came to securing her own food, she was pretty hopeless. She might be capable of tearing open a bag of kibble in a pinch, but that was about it. But *softie*?

She growled. "I'll show that moth-eaten fox that I'm no—"

"*STAY AWAY FROM HIM!*" Jake's bellow blew her curls back. "*DO YOU UNDERSTAND?*"

"Yes, Poppa." She swallowed to moisten her suddenly dry mouth. "I promise."

"You'd better!"

"Question?" she ventured.

"Go ahead."

"If Snatcher's as dangerous as you say—don't get upset, I believe you—he could kill Leo as easily as a rabbit." A horrible image flitted through her mind. "Snatcher could *eat* Leo."

"I've already thought of that," replied Jake, glancing at Pom's home. "I'll warn Leo the fox is back in the area. He's smart enough to be *very* careful until Snatcher moves to another territory. It's you I'm worried about."

"I'll be good," she promised.

"Roxxy," said Molly. "Let's get back to the earlier topic."

"What's that, Momma?"

"You were professing your innocence, even though you hadn't been accused of anything."

"Me?"

"You." Molly's eyes narrowed. "How much damage are we talking about?"

CHAPTER 12

"You got him good."

Roxxy rested her chin on the family-room carpet and wondered if it was possible to *die* of boredom. The house was quiet—Bill and Carol were out running some errands, and her sibs and parents were sprawled around her, dead asleep. Ordinarily, she'd also be snoozing, but the order she'd received yesterday to avoid venturing outside alone until further notice was making her fidgety.

Her nose twitched as a breeze made its way down the chimney. A dry, smoky scent came from the well-swept fireplace, where remnants of ash stirred in the corners. *What was that other smell funneling down?* Her nose shifted from twitching to the more efficient quaking.

Hmm…some kind of heavy engine exhaust. Unusual for this time of day. The UPS van normally showed up later. Might be a truck driven by a contractor. Some of those things belched fumes that made her eyes water.

She gnawed on the twisted hemp of a chewy. How long was she supposed to stay inside like some helpless puppy? A week? A month? *Forever?* What could possibly go wrong if she snuck out and made a solo patrol of the back yard?

The thought was barely finished before she moved past the family room and down the hallway. A quick trip across the kitchen brought her to the dog door. She took a deep breath and eased through. Once past, her tail caught the thick piece of plastic before it could drop. Ever so gently, she lowered it into place and allowed herself a soft snort of satisfaction.

Ninja spuggle!

A frown sent her bangs aquiver. Could Snatcher be as dangerous as her father described? She pointed her nose skyward and inhaled, sifting scents. The wind came from the direction of Toby's property. The aroma of his oily coat was strong, even though he was nowhere to be seen. Probably inside with Kimberly.

Roxxy trotted down the steps of the deck, cataloging other smells as she went—congealed grease droppings from outdoor grills, decomposing vegetables in compost bins, and the funky aroma of trash containers next to neighboring houses. The trash bins were particularly interesting because—

"Urrp!" squealed Roxxy as she rocketed into a straight-up vertical hop that would have done credit to a well-oiled pogo stick.

She gazed down from the apex of the leap. The two-foot striped garter snake she'd trod on an instant before was now slithering away impossibly fast, parting the grass as easily as if navigating the surface of a stream. By the time Roxxy touched down, the creepy thing had disappeared beneath a pile of oak leaves. She shook out her front right paw. The feel of the snake's surprisingly firm flesh still registered against the pad. Yuck, yuck, *yuck*!

Her ears perked up as the flap of Leo's dog door rattled against the frame. She turned to see her friend walk listlessly onto his back deck. He paused and lifted his nose into the air just as she had. She almost barked a greeting but caught herself, imagining the lecture she'd receive if she woke her parents and they found her in the back yard.

A dash took her to the chain-link fence separating her yard from the Pom's. Part of her mind registered the chattering of a squirrel, the slamming of a vehicle door somewhere on the street out front, and the smell of fertilizer coming from the garden shed, but she was too mesmerized by Leo's appearance to take much notice. Was that a…?

"Hi, Roxx," said Leo, arriving at the spot where she waited.

"How's it going?" She touched noses with him through the chain links. When she pulled back, her gaze settled on the middle of his forehead. "Nice day, huh?"

"Don't pretend," he grumbled.

"Pretend?"

"That you don't see it."

"See what?" She was getting a crick in her neck from the effort to keep her gaze from drifting upward.

"You're going to hurt yourself."

"Not sure what you mean."

"The *bow*," growled Leo. "The gold one. Stop pretending it's not there."

"Hardly noticed it. *Ip!*" The suppressed snort morphed into a case of hiccups. "The bow is very—*ip!*—uh, decorative. The color sets off the highlights in your coat. *Ip!* How did Helen find one so—*ip!*—big? And sparkly?"

"No idea. I think it came off a parade float. Have you ever seen anything so hideous?"

"Nonsense," she said stoutly, thankful the hiccups had stopped. "Bows are very, uh—"

"Idiotic."

"*Festive* is the word I was searching for." She giggled before she could stop herself. "Toby will love it."

Leo winced. "I hadn't thought of that."

"Sorry," said Roxxy. "I shouldn't have brought it up."

"No, thanks for the warning."

The Pom sat. A hind paw moved in a blur as he raked the golden ribbon from his mane and left it in a glittering pile on the green grass.

"Better?" Roxxy asked.

"Much. I feel like a dog again." He sighed. "I adore Helen, but sometimes she's mental. A *bow*?"

"Couldn't you wiggle away from her when she was tying it on?"

"Sure, but I love making her happy. She's so sweet that—"

A stream of neon-orange liquid splashed against the side of Leo's face, turning the tawny fur into a garish shade of pumpkin. Roxxy sat stunned as her friend's small body contorted. He collapsed, choking and writhing on the grass. Tiny front paws wiped his muzzle, but it did nothing to stop the ragged gasps.

The acrid odor brought her out of the trance. *Pepper spray!*

A hiss from a canister alerted her that another blast was on its way. Leo was already down, so why—

MOVE!

She obeyed her mind's command and ducked.

The ribbon of fluid passed between the grid of chain links and sizzled past her head. She flung herself into a sideways roll as the next blast came. Another miss! She surged upright. A new stream of the smelly stuff bounced off the rounded fence post in front of her, creating an orange spatter that she avoided by taking a step back.

Now's my chance! One good bark would waken her parent and sibs. Air filled her lungs, but an errant drop of the spatter was sucked in with the breath. Fire seared the back of her throat. She convulsed, flopping in place like a goldfish thrown from a shattered bowl.

"Two for two."

Her twitching body went still. *I know that voice!*

She struggled upright in time to see a familiar figure edge from behind the dense holly next to Leo's house. The man's crouching form straightened to its full height. He was even larger than she remembered.

He was hiding there the whole time!

Roxxy threw back her head and tried to bark, but no sound got past her swollen windpipe. The man ignored her and moved toward Leo. The human stopped when his pant leg caught on one of the holly's low-hanging branches. He jerked it free, sending a spray of red berries rolling across the side yard.

She watched helplessly as his pace quickened. *Squish-squish-squish* accompanied his long strides as berries were pulverized under heavy work boots. He stopped next to Leo, who was rubbing his face against the grass in a futile effort to remove the pepper spray embedded in his fur.

The man pulled a tightly folded square from his back pocket. A flick of his wrist unfurled a burlap sack with a *snap*. He bent and grabbed the Pom by the scruff. A meaty fist held the wriggling dog over the open bag, but the human paused. His head swiveled.

Roxxy found herself pinned by a stare. She inspected her reflection in the black lenses of the sunglasses—a stiff-legged form with jaws opening and closing in an ineffectual effort to bark.

The man grinned at her and jiggled the sack.

"Thanks for keeping your buddy occupied. I couldn't have nailed him without you."

Still holding her eyes, he uncurled his fingers from Leo's scruff.

Roxxy cringed as her friend dropped toward the open sack, but as the Pom came level with the drawstring top, he corkscrewed and bit the hand holding the burlap container.

"Arrrgh!"

The man dropped the sack as his face crumpled in pain.

Leo dangled from the man's hand, teeth sunk into the webbing between thumb and index finger. With a swift, violent motion, the man's muscular arm twisted, sending Leo pinwheeling through the air like a tawny rag doll. The Pom collided with the gravel path that ran along the side yard, his momentum carrying him in a tumbling motion toward the house's foundation. His collar tags jingled as his head bounced off the bricks. He rose groggily and vomited half-digested kibble.

"Unit," said the man, pulling an oil-streaked rag from his pocket and tying it around his bitten hand. "You're going to pay for that."

Roxxy's eyes widened as the human moved quicker than anyone that big had a right to. He slid in front of Leo and pinned the dog against the side of the house.

She tried again to bark, but the effort sent her into a coughing fit. The man made a grab for Leo. Her friend gamely dodged. The process repeated itself, with the Pom skipping side to side. The human cursed. A sawtooth vein pulsed in his temple.

Roxxy stomped her paw to draw the stranger's attention, but he didn't turn. Could she do *anything* to help? She eyed the five-foot fence. *Way too high to jump.* She was known in the family as an amazing leaper, but she wouldn't have a chance of clearing such a tall barrier. Her gaze traveled to the tiny opening Leo customarily used to enter her yard. The gap was too small for her, and she didn't have time to dig her way under.

"Stand *still*, unit!"

The man made another grab for Leo. Her friend managed to duck, but his pencil-thin legs were wobbling, on the verge of collapse. Roxxy could no longer hear the man's cursing because of her own wheezing pant. Out of desperation, she scanned the length of chain-link fence, searching for anything that would help her get over—or under—the barrier. Her eyes slid past a wheelbarrow parked midway down the yard—and snapped back. The carrier was within a few feet of the fence and piled with sacks of fertilizer.

Maybe…

She dashed to the opposite side of the property and made a tight turn to charge back, slaloming past the rose garden and a perennial flower bed as she gained speed. A leap lifted her atop the sacks in the wheelbarrow, and she continued without pause, pushing off with her rear paws. Unexpectedly, her claws tore through the heavy paper. Beads of fertilizer clattered against the plastic interior of the wheelbarrow. Her momentum faltered, but she bunched her rear legs and *pushed*!

She wheezed a gasp as she soared upward.

I knew I was a good leaper. But this?

She cleared the chain-link fence with room to spare. The ground rushed up. She landed in a rolling tumble and bounced upright. *Not bad!* Her tail rose high, but the elation over the jump evaporated at the sound of a strangled yelp.

Leo hung limply; his neck encircled by the man's thick fingers.

"Got you!"

Whitened knuckles applied pressure. The Pom uttered a croaking squawk and went still.

"Thought you'd get away, did you?"

The man shoved Leo into the sack. The drawstring closed with a hiss of finality.

Roxxy's ears slid back in defeat. Jumping the fence had been useless! She'd planned to nip at his heels and distract him so Leo could get away, but she was too late.

"And you?" The man pointed a finger at her. "Next time."

She edged back a step even though she was well out of range of the pepper spray. A shiver ran through her as she watched him pivot and stalk away. Sweat shone on the shaved scalp at the base of the baseball-style cap. The sack hung from one hand, held casually, as if it contained nothing more important than trash.

When the man reached the front corner of the house, she looked past him and saw the rusted pickup truck parked on the street next to a yellow fire hydrant. She swallowed and turned away. There was obviously nothing she could do to stop the man. Poor Leo! What would happen to him? She forced herself to focus on the chain-link fence. How was she going to return to her back yard? There was no cart on this side to—

Her ears twitched at the almost inaudible sound. What...*whimpering*! She looked over her shoulder.

"Shut it," hissed the man.

He raised the sack and delivered an open-handed slap that sent it swinging. A high-pitched yip came from within.

The human laughed. "You'll learn."

Rip-rip-rip-rip-rip-rip-rip-rip-rip. Her back claws tore chunks of grass from the lawn in a rapid-fire cadence. The man must've heard her because he whirled, mouth dropping open in a perfect O.

She leaped, curls flattening in the wind stream. Her jaws opened to bite down on the sack and pull it from his grip, but he moved with startling speed for such a big person. The snap of a pants cuff warned her of the kick. She corkscrewed in midair, and the blow grazed an ear. In desperation, she bit the laces of the boot while sailing past. The taste of leather filled her mouth as she pulled the man with her. Both spun out of control. She landed hard, and breath exploded from her lungs. A thud signaled the human crashing next to her. The sack containing Leo tumbled across the grass.

A ragged curse drew her attention. The man was on his back but trying to lever himself upright. The sunglasses were askew, and the skin stretched taut across his face was as shiny and purple as an eggplant. Rage wafted off him like heat rising from freshly poured asphalt.

She threw a glance at the sack lying well out of his reach. The burlap sides heaved. A tiny paw pushed through the tightened drawstring, but the opening was too small for Leo to escape. How could she stop the man from retrieving the sack and driving away? A grunt drew her attention. *Speak of the devil.* The human had his feet under him and was preparing to stand. She leaped and clamped her jaws on a pants leg. A hard yank put him on his back again. She pulled every time he started to rise. Her eyes crossed from the effort.

"Got a good grip?"

The pleased tone startled her. She had been concentrating so fiercely on keeping her jaws clamped shut that she'd blocked out everything else.

Once glance was enough. She gulped and tasted the detergent that had been used to launder the pants. The man's free leg was cocked with knee drawn to chest, ready to unleash a stomp and crush her head.

Her jaws opened to release the grip, but her teeth snagged. Her legs churned as she tried to backpedal away. Paw pads slid uselessly over the grass as the attempt failed.

The sole of a heavy work boot drove toward her face. Her eyes closed reflexively.

"*Argh!*"

She cracked a lid and peeked out. The man's hand was clamped to his bloody ear.

"Take *that*," wheezed Leo, staggering away.

She stared in wonderment. Her friend's small sharp teeth were smeared with red. He'd somehow worked his way out of the bag while she'd kept the man on his back.

"*Bit* me? Bit *me*?" The human took his hand away from his ear and stared at his bloody palm.

Roxxy worked her teeth free of the jeans material and dashed to Leo, who had inexplicably stopped within range of the pepper spray. Fortunately, the big man was preoccupied with staunching the blood flowing from his ear, but that could change at any moment.

"Come on!" She bumped the Pom with her shoulder. "Let's go."

"That man put me in a *sack*!" growled the Pom, leaning forward as if preparing to dash back in for another chomp.

"And he will again if we don't get out of here!"

Leo's teeth skinned back from his upper lip. "I can get in one more bite before he—"

"Don't even *think* about it!" She took his rhinestone collar between her jaws and gave it a jerk. "*Come on!*"

Leo hesitated before giving an ear flick of consent. "Right."

She released him.

"Thanks, Roxx."

"My pleasure," she replied while briefly touching noses with him. His bloody muzzle smelled of copper. "What are friends for? Let's get away from this creep."

She and Leo didn't stop until they were deep into the side yard where crushed holly berries littered the pathway. They edged close to the shrub. The Pom stood with head drooping, wheezing from the run.

Roxxy looked over her shoulder. The man nearly stumbled as he rose to his feet, but he steadied himself and clamped a dirty handkerchief to the side of his wounded ear. She gave a grunt of satisfaction. His head swiveled to her, and he stared with such malice that it took all her will to continue facing him.

A door slammed in a neighboring house.

The man snatched the empty sack from the ground and strode

hurriedly toward the truck. *Swish-swish-swish* sounded as the limp burlap brushed his thigh.

"Glad we've seen the end of *him*," said Roxxy. She nudged Leo. "You got him good."

"I wish I'd bitten his ear *off*."

The human threw the sack in the bed of the pickup and wrenched the driver's door open. A second later, the engine revved to life and backfired twice as the vehicle sped away, trailing a cloud of blue exhaust.

Roxxy's nose quaked as she recognized the smell she'd detected earlier, wafting down the flue of the chimney. *Clever.* The man had arrived early and found a good hiding spot. She snorted. *But not clever enough!*

"I need water," said the Pom. "And a treat, a bath, and some serious petting. I'll even let Helen tie another bow in my mane." He paused before adding, "What's gotten into you?"

"Me?" asked Roxxy, voice muffled by the air rushing past as she whirled in a series of circles like a blond dervish.

Now that the danger was past, she was too exhilarated to remain still. The series of turns carried her halfway to the fence dividing their properties.

Dizzy but jubilant, she plopped onto the grass and gushed, "We showed that creep! I bet he'll think twice before messing with *us* again!"

"He's not a creep…he's a *m-m-monster*! He almost *g-got* me!" yapped Leo.

Roxxy sobered instantly. She should have recognized that her friend was traumatized. "I know it was awful for you, but everything's fine now. I promise."

"If you say so," replied the Pom. A holly berry dropped from a branch that overhung the spot where he stood. The red orb lodged in his mane. He shook, sending it into the shadowy depths of the shrub.

"Feeling better?" she asked.

"Getting there. I—"

A reddish-brown streak sprang from the holly, sending berries scattering in a scarlet fan. Needle-sharp teeth glistened in the sunlight as they descended on Leo's neck.

CHAPTER 13

"Is it impossible for you to stay out of trouble?"

This can't be happening...

Roxxy flinched, expecting to see the snapping jaws crush Leo's neck, but the Pom flattened himself on the ground. The fox's teeth closed on a mouthful of bushy mane. Snatcher—her mind was finally catching up with what she was seeing—hoisted Leo and shook him like a rat. Her friend's high-pitched squeal tore at her heart.

Snatcher's head torqued in a vicious twist, and Leo went limp and silent. The predator's narrow jaws worked as he gathered in more mane and secured his grip.

Roxxy stood very still, doing her best to remain invisible, even though the fox appeared to pay her no more attention than he would a beetle. Despite her father's warning, she was startled by Snatcher's size. He was nearly her height, and his coat twitched from the flexing of underlying bands of muscle. Narrow strips of bare skin were visible on his chest and shoulders. The brick-red coat and battle scars gave him the appearance of a rusting metal sculpture—sharp, dangerous angles. The oddest feature was his tail—a bushy black tube almost as thick as his torso—jutting straight out behind him.

The wind shifted, and Roxxy's nose wrinkled at the feral scent of old blood embedded in the fur around the fox's mouth. Some ancestral part of her mind recognized that only a diet of raw flesh could produce such a smell.

Snatcher's triangular head swung toward her. She felt herself shrink under his gaze. The vertical black pupils were elongated slits surrounded by amber. The eyes were measuring and merciless.

Her parents' concerns now made sense. Killing was as natural to the fox as chowing down on a bowl of kibble was for her. She was out of her league.

Snatcher issued a *chuff* of warning that came out muffled by the prey clamped between his jaws.

Roxxy realized she was standing between the fox and the area where he likely kept a den—the nature sanctuary bordering the rear of the properties on her side of the street. The undeveloped acreage was matted with towering purple loosestrife, thorny blackberry vines, and various native plants, offering the perfect habitat for pheasants and other ground-nesting birds. Plenty of prey for the fox! Why did he have to hunt a little dog beloved by its owner?

A growl of impatience rumbled from Snatcher's chest.

Roxxy shuffled aside. Her tail folded between her legs, and she hunched her shoulders in a posture of utter submission.

Snatcher grunted contemptuously. He trotted toward the woodsy area that comprised the nature preserve behind the lots on Roxxy's side of the street. Once there, he would quickly disappear in the tall brush.

She watched the fox depart. Leo's limp form swung side to side in time with the fox's loose-limbed, effortless stride. A breeze detached a clump of the Pom's mane and sent it rolling across the lawn. Roxxy watched it catch in the waxy leaves of a camellia. The patch of tawny fur fluttered as if marking the last passage of the little dog.

The fox was nearing the nature preserve when Roxxy's tail lifted and curled over her back. Her eyes narrowed as she studied the small white patch of fur on each of Snatcher's haunches.

Wait…wait…now!

She sprang, paws thudding on the lawn to make as much noise as possible. Snatcher whirled to face her. A wheeze of challenge escaped her throat—would the effects of the pepper spray *ever* wear off?

Snatcher lunged and snapped. Leo's limp form fell from his jaws and landed with a soft *plop* on the lawn. Roxxy jerked left to dodge Snatcher's bite. He pivoted to follow, but she made an impossibly tight turn and threw her shoulder into his flank with all her weight. He went down, and she tripped over him. They tumbled together in a tangle of limbs and gnashing teeth, but neither landed a bite. Their path carried them into the base of a lilac azalea that sent them rolling in different directions.

Thock!

Lights burst at the corners of her vision. Vaguely, she was aware that she'd stopped moving. A root dug into her stomach, and her head rested against the smooth bark at the base of a maple tree. An alarm sounded somewhere deep in her brain, but she couldn't pinpoint the reason. *And why was a fox limping toward her?* He seemed to be favoring one rear leg, but there wasn't anything wrong with the razor-sharp teeth exposed by his fluttering upper lips. When he reached her, he paused. Hot drops of saliva dripped onto her face as he said in a low, hissing growl, "*Bad* doggy. I'll show you what happens to—*OOOOOMPH!*"

Roxxy blinked as a mottled cream-gray-black blur thudded into the fox's flank...precisely where she'd smashed it a moment before. Snatcher staggered away as his attacker did a perfect backflip and landed on four white paws.

"Uh, hi Muffy."

Roxxy's head cleared as she squirmed under the feline's gimlet glare.

"If we get out of this alive," spat the cat, "I'll murder you myself. Is it *impossible* for you to stay out of trouble?"

"Who says I'm in trouble?" Roxxy lurched upright. "I was just catching my breath."

"Funny time to do it," hissed Muffy, "with Snatcher about to rip your throat out." Her tail lashed the ground. "What now?"

"Let me think."

"By all means. Maybe it'll become a habit."

Roxxy ignored the jibe. Snatcher had returned to where he'd dropped Leo and was sniffing the Pom with a carnivore's anticipation. The fox nosed the dog over and licked the soft belly experimentally.

Muffy meowed. "You're trembling."

"I-I can't come up with any ideas."

"It's time for you to admit that we're no match for Snatcher."

Roxxy flicked away an acorn digging into the pad of a paw. "You're right. The two of us can't stop him."

"Well...I didn't expect you to agree so easily," replied the feline, a hint of disappointment in her tone. "But at least you're being reasonable."

"Thanks. I'll keep the fox busy while you head inside and get Poppa and Momma."

"*What?*"

"What *what*? I'm agreeing with you. The two of us alone can't stop Snatcher. That's why we need Poppa and Momma's help. I'm still too wheezy to bark loud enough for them to hear." Roxxy pointed her chin at the fox. "I'll keep him busy until you get back."

"How?"

"I, uh, can temporarily block his path."

"With what? Your mangled corpse?"

"The cat's right," said Snatcher, his voice somewhere between a sibilant feline hiss and a gravelly canine huff. He stepped over Leo and faced them. "The Pom's mine. As for you two? Leave or die."

"Go get help!" Roxxy threw a shoulder into Muffy, surprised at the lightness of the feline's frame. The hair ball had always seemed so… substantial, dominating the space around her.

Roxxy gulped. If Snatcher got his jaws on the cat, she'd be dead in an instant.

"Get going, Muff," Roxxy implored. "Hurry!"

"I'm staying if you are," growled the feline, nimbly recovering her balance. "I'd never hear the end of it if you got killed."

"But—"

"Let's spread out." Leaves rustled under the cat's white paws as she sidled to a spot that would allow her to nail Snatcher's flank. "We'll hit this idiot from two angles. If we make things difficult enough for him, maybe he'll run and leave Leo behind."

Roxxy took a position on the fox's opposite flank.

"This should be fun," said Snatcher, pointy ears folding back against his head. "A couple of *house pets*? I'll rip you both to shreds." His legs bent to assume a fighting crouch. "I'll—*yip!*"

Roxxy's heart leaped as she remembered the limp she'd spotted earlier.

"Well, look at that," she said. "I'll bet your leg's still hurting from our tussle. Torn muscle, maybe?"

"There's nothing wrong with my teeth." The fox emphasized his point by thrusting his head forward and snapping his jaws. *Clack!*

"True," said Muffy. "But you don't want that leg injury to get any worse. Better leave while you can."

"I'm taking my prey with me."

Roxxy's hackles rose. "Leo stays."

"What's a Leo?"

She suspected Snatcher was mocking her but answered anyway. "The Pom."

"Oh. *It* belongs to me. Hunter's right." He glanced at Muffy. "*You* should understand."

"I do."

"Then let me pass."

The feline sighed. "Not up to me." She tilted her head toward Roxxy. "*Her* call."

Snatcher's ears stood upright. "Wait a minute. You're putting your life in the hands of a dog? What kind of cat *are* you?"

"I know, right? But she grows on you."

"I don't see that happening." Snatcher's lips fluttered in a wet snarl. "In fact, I see me gutting you!"

Roxxy swallowed. His teeth reminded her of the serrated edges of the steel saw Bill used to prune tree branches.

"Get ready, Roxx!" warned Muffy in a low hiss. "As soon as he goes for one of us, the other has to come in low and fast! Try for that injured leg!"

Roxxy was only half listening. Behind Snatcher, Leo stood on wobbly, pencil-thin legs. A wave of relief passed over her. She'd been afraid that being shaken by the fox might have broken her friend's neck.

The Pom's black, glassy eyes stared blankly, and his once proud mane was a ragged mess. The small patch of lawn where he'd lain was mostly flattened, but now that he was standing, the green blades were popping up.

Roxxy willed her friend to sneak away while he had the chance. Instead, he did what all dogs do to clear their thoughts—he shook.

Snatcher whirled on three legs and lunged. Leo threw himself backward. The predator's teeth closed on nothing but air.

Leo's reprieve was short-lived. His paw pads slipped on the grass, and his rear end hit the ground.

Snatcher's jaws darted for the Pom's head, but the fox froze in mid-attack. His eyes took on a vacant look of puzzlement. The expression suddenly morphed into a rictus of pain.

"*Rarwww!*"

Roxxy's teeth sank deeper into the rear haunch that had been presented to her when Snatcher turned on Leo.

Take that!

She bit harder. Coppery blood spurted into her mouth.

Snatcher torqued his rear in a violent shake.

She went flying and landed hard on her flank.

"Roxx!" barked Leo.

She stared frozen in disbelief. Snatcher was *hopping* toward her on his three good legs. Grass clippings scattered each time his paws lifted in unison. His flanks rose and fell with panting breaths. She gagged at the rank scent of decaying meat. His bobbing shadow was almost upon her prone form when Muffy flashed between them and delivered a swipe across his pointy muzzle.

"*RARWWW!*" roared the fox, stopping to wipe a paw over his face.

"Way to go, Muf—" began Roxxy.

"*MOVE!*" spat the cat over her shoulder. "*Idiot!*"

Roxxy blinked. Good idea! She raced after her streaking housemate, taking care to avoid tripping over the knobby roots of a maple.

"*RARWWW!*"

Snatcher was following in a surprisingly fast hobble. She wondered whether he could keep it up and was validated when his body suddenly tilted. He toppled like a cart whose wheel had come off. His shoulder smashed into a slim metal pole holding up a cylindrical bird feeder. The impact sent the seed-filled tube dancing. Black-oil sunflower seeds flew from the feeder openings and rained down on the fox's red-brown pelt.

"RARWWW! RARWWW! RARWWW!" Snatcher screamed as he tried—and failed—to stand.

Roxxy stood rigid, watching from well away. She was grateful she hadn't been mauled by the—she leaped straight up, rubbing a paw over the side of her face to get rid of the tickly sensation. She landed and huffed irritably, "Keep your whiskers off me! And don't sneak up beside me like that."

"Teach you to stay alert," said Muffy, watching Snatcher struggle to stand upright.

"I'm plenty alert. A near-death experience will do that." Roxxy paused. "But...well...thanks for keeping Snatcher off me."

"Had nothing to do with you. I don't like foxes. They remind me of dogs." Muffy yawned. "Smarter, though."

"Interesting. They remind me of cats." Roxxy scratched behind an ear. "But not as creepy."

"Draw?"

"Draw," agreed Roxxy. "What are we going to do about Snatcher?"

The fox lay panting, seemingly exhausted by his efforts to rise.

"He's in bad shape," purred Muffy, green eyes aglow.

"But still dangerous if we get too close. Plus"—Roxxy frowned—"he may not be as hurt as he seems."

"You're learning, fluff ball."

Before Roxxy could reply, Leo settled on her other side.

"Any more surprises?" asked the Pom sourly. "Bears? Wolverines? Serial killers? I'm never leaving the house again."

"Can't say I blame you." Roxxy gave his ear a friendly nip. "But other than your mane looking the worse for wear, you seem okay."

"Are you kidding? I've been pepper sprayed, stuffed in a sack, and shaken in the jaws of that...that *creature* who wanted to turn me into his dinner. I'm a lot of things, but *okay* isn't one of them!" He cleared his throat. "But I want to thank you. I wouldn't be alive if not for you."

"And Muffy."

"Of course! Did you see the way that beautiful tabby tore into Snatcher? I think I'll convince her to be my bodyguard." He lifted a paw and fluffed his mane. "You know, turn on the old charm."

"We have enough problems without your charm making an appearance."

"I'll ignore that," said Leo.

He leaned past Roxxy. "Muffy, you were amazing out there. A whirlwind of feline ferocity. Lethal yet graceful. Would you consider being my—"

"Save your breath, Pom."

"But—"

"I've coughed up hair balls bigger than you."

"Tough crowd," muttered Leo.

"Let's focus," growled Roxxy.

Snatcher rose on his three good legs. He held the injured limb slightly cocked and tucked against his side.

"What are you looking at?" snarled the fox, hopping closer. "I can still take the three of you!"

"If you could get close enough," agreed Roxxy, measuring the distance between them. "But you can't. That leg's in pretty bad shape. Any more damage, and you won't be able to hunt. And no hunting"—she bobbed her tail in a shrug—"no surviving."

"You'd better be worried about yourself," snarled Snatcher as he charged forward. "I'll— *RARWWW!*"

Roxxy watched coldly as his wounded leg buckled and he fell sideways. His flank struck a garden gnome sporting glossy blue shorts, orange suspenders, and a banana-yellow shirt. The tip of the figure's peaked white hat dug into the fox's side.

"RARWWW! RARWWW! RARWWW!"

Grass flew as Snatcher scrabbled at the turf.

Roxxy waited until the thrashing ended. "What's it going to be?"

He rolled clumsily upright, grimacing when the paw of his injured leg skimmed the ground. His bushy tail hung limply behind him, and his ears sagged in defeat.

He growled, "The Pom wouldn't have made much of a meal anyway."

"You miserable—"

"Hush, Leo," interrupted Roxxy. "Let's clear a path so Snatcher can leave."

The Pom—encouraged by a shoulder nudge from Muffy—moved well to one side. The cat followed. Roxxy sidled in the opposite direction.

Snatcher hobbled through the opening in a three-legged shuffle.

Roxxy released a pent-up breath as he entered the field beyond the property's back border and disappeared into a mounded thicket of butterfly bushes. A scattering of tiny purple petals was the only sign of the fox's passage.

"I wish," grumbled Leo, "that we'd finished him off."

"Bold talk for a snack," purred Muffy.

"When you put it like that…"

"Leo," said Roxxy. "Snatcher's leg will never be the same. He'll be able to scavenge enough to survive, but his days of terrorizing the neighborhood are over."

"I guess you're right." The Pom's voice brightened. "He'll only be dangerous to animals who are really clueless."

"Just when I thought you were safe," purred Muffy.

Ten minutes later, Roxxy trudged up the steps of the deck. Returning to her back yard had been far more complicated than getting out. There was no wheelbarrow on Leo's side of the fence to provide a platform to jump from. Fortunately, there *was* a large wheeled bin for household trash near the chain-link fence that would serve the same purpose. She would normally have leaped atop the container and balanced there with no problem, but she was so tired from the battles with the dog thief and Snatcher that it had taken several attempts before things worked out.

To make matters worse, Muffy had sat grooming herself while keeping up a running commentary. "The fluff ball leaps! Belly-flops on the lid! Skids off like a sea lion on a water slide! Lands on her head!"

When Roxxy had finally succeeded and was back in the yard, Muffy had made a show of scuttling up a nearby maple and leaping nimbly over the chain-link fence to land beside her.

"Show-off," grumbled Roxxy.

"Slug," purred the cat, giving her tail a flick of dismissal as she dashed away.

Roxxy yawned. Her claws clicked on the pine boards as she plodded up the steps of the deck. Tired though she was, she felt a sense of satisfaction in knowing Snatcher was no longer a threat. Too bad she didn't feel the same about the man who had attacked her and Leo. He could come back at any time. That pepper spray was no joke. The guy used it as if he'd had a lot of practice. In fact…

Her paw hung suspended above a stair tread.

Kindly old Mr. Jacobs…his missing dog…

AXEL

The signal light turned green, and Axel stepped on the gas pedal, hunching his shoulders in anticipation. *BANG! BANG!* The twin backfires exploded like a blast from a double-barreled shotgun. His cursing was interrupted when muffled yapping came from the sack on the passenger-side floorboard. The burlap twisted and heaved. He leaned over and slapped the material, wishing he could give it a real pounding but not wanting to damage the merchandise. The noise from the bag subsided into a snuffling whimper.

A horn blared. Axel jerked the steering wheel to pull the truck back into its lane and automatically raised a middle finger to silence the driver behind him. A left at the next intersection brought him to a quiet residential street. A flick of the stainless-steel lighter ignited a cigarette and obliterated the sweet aromas of tea olive and Autumn clematis shrubs wafting in through the open windows.

Axel whistled tunelessly and reflected on the snatch of the Jack Russell. The terrier had been in a fenced side yard gnawing happily on a bone-shaped chew toy. The house had no garage, and there were no cars in the driveway. Axel had knocked on the door to make sure no one was home. A biscuit had enticed the mutt close to the chain-link fence. After that, it was simple. A blast of juice and an easy vault over the fence. The unit was secured in the bag within minutes of spotting it. Just the way things were *supposed* to go. He fingered the Band-Aid folded over his ear. The Pom may have bitten him, but the real problem had been the interfering blond mutt. He still couldn't believe the dog had brought him down.

"*Yap! Yap! YAP!*"

Cords of muscle stood out on the sides of Axel's neck. He eyed the burlap bag flopping back and forth on the floorboard. Springs creaked as he stretched across the seat and raised a fist.

He could always find more merchandise.

CHAPTER 14

"Is that sappy or what?"

Roxxy paced the length of fence separating her yard from Toby's, trying to stay warm. That was the problem with fleecy curls. Cute, admittedly, but they didn't do much to keep out the chill. And why was it taking Toby so long to arrive for their usual morning chat? She needed advice, and he had a practical, level-headed way of looking at things that didn't, well, come naturally to her.

She reached the end of the fence at the rear of the property line and reversed course. The sudden rattle of chain links drew her attention to the eastern border of the yard. Her eyes widened in surprise as Leo squeezed through the small opening at the base of the fence. He wasn't usually out so early in the day. Other than the mangled mane, he didn't look the worse for wear from yesterday's ordeal. His gait was bouncy, and his tawny coat glowed in the strengthening sun.

"Hi, Roxx!"

"Hey, Leo."

She touched noses with him and went back to pacing. Her nerves were too jittery for her to sit still.

"Why so antsy?" asked the Pom, plopping down and watching her wear a path along the fence. He gnawed on an acorn the squirrels had missed. *Crack.* The nut's pebbled crown broke under his teeth. "Afraid Snatcher will come back?"

"No." Her tail bobbed in a shrug. "I'm sure he's gone for good."

"Darn right. He knows better than to mess with me again. Before you butted in, I had him right where I wanted him."

"Hungry and murderous?"

"Nah, I was lulling him into a false sense of confidence."

"Next time, more running, less lulling."

"I knew what I was—"

"Hang on a second." Roxxy's ears twitched as the back door of Toby's house creaked open.

Her eyes softened as the basset and his person, Kimberly, came onto the deck. Toby danced around the girl in a surprisingly graceful manner, considering his big paws and chunky frame. Kimberly was still in her pajamas, rubbing sleep out of her eyes with one hand and caressing Toby's floppy ears with the other. The girl bent further and scratched his back. A cascade of curly blond hair tumbled around her face.

Toby wriggled with pleasure as Kimberly crooned, "*Gooood* boy."

"Is that sappy or what?" grumbled Leo.

"Pipe down," huffed Roxxy, turning to give the Pom a piece of her mind, but she paused and giggled. "Your tail's wagging."

"Well, the *kid* is cute, even if she's wasting all that affection on a dog who smells like a wagonload of buffalo hides."

"You and Helen been watching old Westerns again?"

"Uh, some," Leo admitted.

Roxxy returned her attention to Toby and Kimberly.

The girl gave the basset a final pat and said through a yawn, "Go do your business, Toby-boy. I'll come get you when it's time to walk to school."

"Yip!" called out Roxxy.

Kimberly turned, putting a hand across her brow to shield her eyes from the the sun. "Hi, Roxxy! I didn't notice you over there. You're cute as ever! And Leo is there too. Hey, little buddy!"

"*Little buddy?*" growled the Pom. "I thought Toby was the dumb one in the family."

"I'll pretend," said Roxxy, eyeing the Pom beadily, "that I didn't hear that."

Toby leaned against the girl's knee and directed a woof toward the fence. "Good to see you, Roxx!" He snorted. "And you too, Leo."

"Wait for it," grumbled the Pom.

"*Little buddy!*" added the basset.

"See what the kid started?" Leo sighed. "Just shoot me."

Roxxy nodded. "Where?"

"Bye, pups!" Kimberly called out and went inside the house. The door banged shut behind her.

Toby's claws clattered against the steps as he lumbered from the deck. He reached the lawn and broke into an all-out dash toward the fence. Short legs created a rocking motion that caused his tail to spin like a propeller. Huge ears flapped up and down.

Leo snorted. "Looks like an elephant trying to gain altitude."

Roxxy ignored the remark and touched noses with Toby when he arrived. "How's it going?"

"Couldn't be better! Every day's a good one when I wake up next to Kimberly. I have my own blanket at the foot of the bed."

"How do you get up there?" asked Leo, surveying the basset's stubby legs. "Catapult?"

"Her dad made special steps for me, but thanks for asking, *little buddy*." Toby frowned. "What happened to your mane?"

"Snatcher. He grabbed me yesterday, but Roxxy and Muffy fought him off."

"*Snatcher?*" boomed Toby.

A squirrel on the opposite side of the yard scampered up a pine.

"Keep it down," Roxxy huffed. "I don't want my parents to know what happened. I wasn't supposed to be outside."

"Let's hear it," demanded Toby.

Roxxy outlined the encounter with the fox. Leo remained unusually quiet during the description.

"Wow, close call." Toby's ears flattened with concern as he turned to the Pom. "I'm glad you're okay. I…I wish I'd been there to pitch in."

"Me too. You're sturdy enough to make short work of Snatcher." Leo's bushy tail drooped. "I couldn't even defend myself."

"Listen," Toby ordered. "Don't talk like that. You survived the attack, and that's what counts. I'm…well, I'm *proud* of you."

"Really?"

"Of course, *really*," replied the basset. "You're plenty tough."

Roxxy said wryly, "It's lovely to see you two bonding."

The Pom frowned. "Who's bonding?"

"Yeah," Toby chimed in. "Leo's right. No bonding. We're just having a little chat."

"Thanks for the clarification." She rubbed a paw across her muzzle to cover a snort. "Anyway, I've been thinking about the dog thief who tried to capture Leo before Snatcher showed up."

"*DOG THIEF?*" Toby bellowed.

"*Shhhh!*" she shushed him.

"Let me get this straight. A human tried to snatch Leo *before* the fox attacked?"

She nodded. "Remember the guy who tried to pepper-spray me? You barked and ran him off?"

"Sure. Who could forget that creep?"

"He came back yesterday."

"You're kidding!"

"I wish." Roxxy paused and nosed an iridescent green beetle off her foreleg. The insect's rounded carapace shone like a glass bead.

Toby huffed. "Stop messing around with that bug and get on with the story!"

Roxxy described how the man had shoved Leo into a sack and nearly succeeded in carrying him off.

"Oh my!" Toby turned his chocolate eyes on the Pom. "I'm *really* sorry. Two close calls in one day!"

"Tell me about it. Pepper-spraying maniac followed by a killer fox. The neighborhood's going downhill."

"There's something I haven't told either of you," said Roxxy. She quickly outlined Mr. Jacobs's distress at the vet's office and his account of Wiggle going missing in the grocery store parking lot. She concluded, "Thinking about that kept me up most of the night. I'm sure Wiggle was taken by the same man who tried to capture Leo."

"I don't know, Roxx," said Toby. "That's kind of far-fetched."

All three dogs winced as a garbage truck on the next block hit its air brakes with a high-pitched squeal unpleasant to canine ears.

When the vehicle moved on, Toby continued. "Roxx, even if you're right, what can we do about it?"

"Put together a plan to stop the thief. Maybe even rescue the dogs he's stolen."

"W-Wait a minute!" Leo stammered. "Are you nuts?"

"We can do it."

"We? There's no *we*! I'm done with that maniac."

"I agree with Leo," said Toby. "The guy is too dangerous."

Roxxy growled, "But—"

"Do you smell that?" The Pom sniffed the air. "I think something was poking around the trash bins last night. Possum?"

"Raccoon," replied Roxxy. "And I know you're trying to change the subject."

"Is it working?"

She raked a hind paw through the curls along her flank. There was no point in trying to convince Toby and Leo until she knew how to track down the dog thief. Better to bide her time.

"Okay," she said. "We'll forget the plan for now."

"What plan?" asked Leo.

"Ha, ha."

"Oh, I meant to mention"—Toby's tail thumped the ground—"it's Kimberly's birthday! She's turning seven. Isn't that amazing?"

"Riveting!" The Pom's eyes opened wide in mock surprise. "First kid ever to turn seven! Let's arrange a parade!"

"Can it, twerp!" snapped the basset.

Roxxy sighed. "So much for the bonding."

"Leo," continued Toby. "We *should* have a parade! Kimberly is...is... *wonderful*!" His voice took on a dreamy note. "Take this morning for example. She looked so beautiful when she first woke up—crusty stuff in the corners of her eyes and a bit of drool on her snow-white cheek. Just adorable."

"Sounds like a zombie-fest," said Leo.

"Toby, ignore him," Roxxy intervened. "Is Kimberly having a party?"

"Two, actually. Her class at school is giving her one, and she'll have another in our back yard this afternoon with some friends." He glanced at Leo. "We're having a cookout."

The Pom sat up. "Weenies?"

"Yep. Kimberly's dad does the grilling. I saw the package." Toby scratched behind a big ear, sending it swinging like a pendulum. "The kind with the casings that snap when you bite them. Lovely."

Leo licked away drool from the corner of his mouth. "Weenies are my favorite!"

"I do recall you mentioning that."

"I'm not surprised. You've got a mind like a steel trap." Leo glanced at Roxxy for support. "How often have I said that?"

"Never."

"She's confused, Toby. I'm constantly remarking on the size of your brain."

Roxxy nodded. "I remember now. You said Toby's brain is the size of a walnut."

"Yeah," growled the basset. "That rings a bell."

"Pshaw!" said Leo. "Ancient history. The point is, I love me some weenies, and I'm sure Kimberly's dad grills them to perfection."

Toby nodded. "He *does* have a knack. Lightly charred exterior, juicy interior. Yummy."

Leo began to pant. "And does that delightful Kimberly sneak you a weenie or two?"

"Every time, and more than I can eat."

"Remarkable girl," gushed the Pom, tail wagging. "Cute. Generous. Crusty-eyed. She's got the whole package. She—"

"Not a chance."

"Come on, old buddy. Don't be that way! I know deep down that you really want to share."

"Well, I have to admit sharing doubles the pleasure of things."

"Whew! That's a relief. For a minute there, I thought—"

"With Roxxy," Toby interrupted. "Sharing with *Roxxy*."

"You droopy-eared freak. I ought to—"

"Leo," said Roxxy. "*If* you shut up, I'll share any weenies I get with you. I want to ask Toby a question."

"Fire away," replied the Pom. "You won't even know I'm here."

"If only," grumbled the basset.

"Toby," said Roxxy. "You mentioned the other day that you walk Kimberly and her friends to school." She rolled over and wriggled against the hearty fescue turf to scratch an itch along her spine, *ahhhh*. She flipped back to her stomach. "Is that right?"

"Every morning. Their moms pick them up in the afternoon."

Roxxy was certain the thick-bodied basset would be a good protector for the kids. He might have short legs and wasn't the nimblest dog in the world, but his massive jaws made him a formidable opponent for anyone who might want to harm the girls. His deep, baying bark could be heard for blocks. He'd no doubt defend Kimberly and her friends with his life. Still…there were dangers for *him* when traveling back home.

"Toby, aren't Kimberly's parents afraid you'll get hit by a car when you come back by yourself?"

"No. Marcy—Kimberly's mom—trained me special. She made sure I learned to sit and look both ways before crossing a street. I *always* do it."

"That's good."

"And the route I use to walk the girls to school has very little traffic. All the streets are residential except for one that's a dead end and blocked off. It has abandoned buildings that used to be businesses. The structures are surrounded by tall chain-link fencing. Marcy says they'll be demolished and replaced with houses. I use the street as a cut-through because there's a path at the end that links up to the road that Kimberly's school is on."

Leo yawned. "Wake me when one of you gets to the interesting part."

"Pipe down," ordered Roxxy. She turned back to Toby. "I thought you said the street with the old businesses is blocked off."

"Only to cars. There's an orange-and-white wooden barrier—kind of like a big sawhorse thingy—that keeps vehicles out. The girls and I can duck under it."

"Is it safe to take them down there?"

"Yeah, it's deserted. Marcy says the contractors won't start work for another couple of months."

Their conversation stopped when Kimberly appeared on the deck, blond hair glowing in the sunlight. Sparkly crimson clips held the tresses, which went well with the sky-blue dress adorned with pink polka dots. A breeze tugged at the lacy white hem. Pink knee socks depicted tiny blue basset hounds. White sneakers with a Velcro strap completed the ensemble.

Kimberly called out, "Come on, Toby-boy! Time for us to go!"

The basset gazed at the girl. "Kimberly's all dressed up for her party at school. Isn't she a vision, Roxxy?"

"Beautiful."

Leo said grumpily. "Looks aren't everything. Why doesn't Kimberly bring us a few weenies to sample? Kids today—no initiative."

Toby studied the Pom. "How about I initiate a paw upside your head?"

"Come on, Toby!" repeated Kimberly.

The basset flung a happy woof of farewell to Roxxy, followed by a growl of goodbye to Leo, and launched himself into an ungainly gallop. The thump of his huge paws echoed between the houses as he crossed the yard and ascended the steps of the deck like an army tank in top gear. Kimberly knelt and enveloped him in a fierce hug, giggling while he nuzzled her neck.

"I have to admit," said Leo grudgingly, "the pair are pretty cute together."

Roxxy snorted. "Going soft?"

"Momentary lapse." He rose and shook, but his mane didn't pop back into its usual perfect globe. Ragged patches showed where Snatcher's jaws had left their mark. "It's time for me to head home. Helen and I are going out."

"Groomer?"

"Yeah. My mane needs a trim so it'll grow back the right way."

"Just think," said Roxxy, eyes twinkling, "In a few weeks it'll be long enough for another bow."

CHAPTER 15

"We won't let that happen."

As soon as Leo left for home, Roxxy yawned and stretched out on a springy patch of clover. The smell of vanilla filled the air as her weight compressed the tiny heart-shaped leaves. She closed her eyes and felt the sun's warmth soak into her flank. A scarlet cardinal perched in a nearby holly. The bird's repeated trilling was like a lullaby. "Tweep…tweep…twee-twee-twee-twee."

The clover cradled the side of her face, and the delicate petals in front of her nose fluttered in rhythm with her snores. As sleep deepened, her legs began to twitch.

She felt the giant's presence before seeing him. Hobnailed boots shook the ground. The clover grew tendrils, encircling her limbs and trapping her in place. The man-thing stepped forward. A shadow swallowed her, and the metal-studded sole hovered above her head. She flinched as the stomp came again and again and—

BANG! BANG!

Roxxy woke and bounced upright.

There was no doubt about the origin of that noise—*the dog thief's truck!*

She went rigid. Could she follow the sound and trail the man to where he kept the stolen dogs? Her ears lifted, and she strained to hear, but another backfire didn't come.

Her tail drooped.

Ping…ping…ping…

Yes! She had forgotten about the distinctive sound produced every few seconds by the old engine. The noise was faint, but if she could get close enough, she would be able follow it. The problem would be keeping pace. She was fast but not *that* fast. Hopefully, there would be enough traffic lights to slow the truck's progress so that she wouldn't lose it.

She dashed to the wheelbarrow parked near the fence. A hop into the bed was followed by an explosive leap that sent her arcing upward. At the apex of the jump, she stared at the long row of neighbors' yards stretching before her.

So this is what it feels like to be tall!

Her legs buckled when she landed, but she scrambled upright and barreled into a dead run. She remembered her conversation with Toby and skidded to a stop before reaching the street. *Make sure no cars are coming!* All clear. She raced across the road. Accustomed to running on grass, the rough asphalt sandpapered the pads of her paws. She leaped the curb on the opposite side and sped between two houses to get to the next block over. By the time she reached the new street, the truck's motor was barely audible. She continued to follow, shortening her route at every opportunity by cutting through yards. At one point, she cleared a small picket fence and landed with a splash into a kiddie pool. The occupants, a toddler in a red swimsuit and her similarly clad mother, both shrieked—the kid with joy and the parent with surprise. Roxxy ignored them and pelted onward.

The yards and streets blurred together, although she did remember to halt and look both ways before crossing a road. Ragged panting tore at her lungs. Minutes had passed since she had last heard the truck. Was she still heading in the right direction? She was on the verge of giving up when she heard the familiar *ping...ping...ping*. The sound was close enough to give her a renewed burst of energy. The truck couldn't be more than a block or two away! She cut through a back yard and was glad there was a fence between her and the enraged Doberman on the adjoining property. Unfortunately, his barking drowned out the sound of the engine. She burst through a thick hedge and paused on the sidewalk to catch her breath, hoping the Dobie would shut up, now that she was out of sight.

Limbs trembling with fatigue, she dropped to the concrete and scanned the street in both directions. Small wood-framed houses lined the road, with well-kept yards and flower boxes hanging beneath many of the windows. Purple and yellow pansies crowded next to spiky crimson celosia and tight mounds of bronze mums.

The Dobie went quiet. Her ears lifted. *Yes!*

The labored sound of the pickup's engine was closer still. She was sure she could—

CRACK-CRACK-CRACK-CRACK! CRACK-CRACK-CRACK-CRACK! CRACK-CRACK-CRACK-CRACK!

Her ears clamped to the sides of her head. What is *that*? The pounding was deafening. There was no choice but to go in the direction where she'd last heard the truck. She scanned the street, then charged to the sidewalk on the other side. A quick dash took her between two houses separated by a darkened alley barely wide enough for the smelly garbage bins that lined it.

A whiskery gray rat strolled leisurely from behind one of the containers. Roxxy leaped over the startled creature and left it hissing in her wake.

CRACK-CRACK-CRACK-CRACK! CRACK-CRACK-CRACK-CRACK! CRACK-CRACK-CRACK-CRACK!

She burst from the alley and squinted against the light reflecting off the sidewalk. A glance to the right identified the source of all the racket. Halfway down the block, a man in a yellow hardhat was using a jackhammer to break up a section of cement next to a fire hydrant. His arms vibrated in sync with the blurred motion of the flat blade turning the surface to rubble. She grunted in frustration. The only thing to do was wait him out.

CRACK-CRACK-CRACK-CRACK! CRACK-CRACK-CRACK-CRACK! CRACK-CRACK-CRACK-CRACK! CRACK-CRACK-CRACK-CRACK! CRACK-CRACK-CRACK-CRACK! CRACK-CRACK-CRACK-CRA—

The sudden silence was jarring.

Roxxy gave a relieved huff. *Finally!*

The worker released the handles of the jackhammer. It landed with a thud. She noticed for the first time that the man was wearing earplugs. He picked up a silver thermos and unscrewed the red cap.

Her ears lifted, tilting forward and back and swiveling side to side. She groaned. *No sound of the pickup!*

She turned for home, tail curled between her legs. The chase had been useless. She might as well have taken another nap instead of—

"Aawwhhoooooo…"

Roxxy went still. *Couldn't be.*

"Aawwhhoooooo…"

An icy ribbon encircled her spine. The distant baying was filled with abject terror.

"Aawwhhoooooo…"

She was sure now. It had to be Toby. But why did he sound so desperate? Had the dog thief stopped the pickup and cornered her friend? She dismissed the idea. Wrestling the big-boned basset into a burlap sack was beyond even the thief's capabilities.

She gave herself an impatient shake. First things first. Find Toby, and *then* figure out what was going on.

"Aawwhhoooooo…"

Her ears pointed. *There!*

She sprang as if charging from a starting gate. Her paws barely touched the sidewalk as she raced into a park with walking trails and wooden benches. She glanced around without stopping. Empty. Still early in the day.

"Aawwhhoooooo…"

She grunted with satisfaction. The baying was closer. A headlong slide down a hillside created an avalanche of stones tumbling after her. Without slowing, she plowed into the wall-like boxwood hedge looming at the bottom of the incline. The thick, gnarly branches raked her face and flanks. She burst out the other side in a spray of tiny leaves that covered the sidewalk like green confetti.

"*AAWWHHooooo!*"

She turned onto a new street and trotted beneath a long orange-and-white-striped sawhorse spanning the thoroughfare. A corridor with sides composed of high chain-link fences stretched down each side of the pot-holed road, keeping trespassers away from abandoned buildings waiting to be demolished.

Her tail bobbed in a nod of understanding. *This is the shortcut to school Toby described.*

Some of the low buildings behind the fences still had rusty signs attached to metal siding or horizontal poles. A few swung in the wind, emitting a high-pitched creak that set her teeth on edge. One of the signs showed a car with a mechanic peering under the hood. Another portrayed a welding torch surrounded by a shower of faded yellow sparks. Farther down the block, a sign depicted a man in blue overalls pushing a hand truck loaded with a dented refrigerator. An unpaved lot next to this business held a jumble of old household appliances, such as washers and dryers, likely intended for recycling before the business closed.

"AAWWHHOOOOOO!"

She spotted Toby standing on the sidewalk in front of the lot with the worn-out appliances. His muzzle was shoved against the chain links barring access to the space, and his paws moved constantly in an agitated shuffle. He threw back his head.

"AAWWHHOOOOOO!"

The buildings lining the block trapped the noise and sent it echoing to and fro. She realized she'd only been able to detect it from several streets away because her hearing was so much more sensitive than a human's.

"AAWWHHOOachachach!"

Toby's cry broke off in a choking fit. *How long had he been calling for help?* As she watched, his restless movements slowed, and he sagged all over—his big ears drooped, and his thick tail hung limply. He gave no indication he was aware of her presence. Her nose twitched as the breeze brought a coppery tang. She chided herself for failing to notice a toe on one of his front paws was leaking red. And what was...

Her thoughts chittered to a halt. A thick white claw lay next to the fence. The chain links glistened with scarlet.

She broke into a dead run and didn't slow until she slid to a stop beside him. "Toby! What's *wrong?*"

He stared through the fence. His jaw trembled. Drool fell from the corners of his mouth and formed a glistening puddle on the sidewalk.

"Toby!" she barked, adding a shove with her chin.

"R-R-Roxxy?" he stammered, whirling to face her. "How did you get—"

"What's the matter?"

Toby shook. Big ears hit the sides of his face with a sound like towels flapping on a clothesline. He jerked his head toward the lot. "Kimberly's in there!"

Roxxy's eyes swept the area. No girl. Only a scattering of worn-out appliances left over from when the business closed. "I don't see her."

"That's the *point*!" barked Toby.

"*What's* the point?" A sudden thought occurred. "And where are the other girls who usually walk with her?"

"Couldn't come. Forget them! We've got to save Kimberly!"

"From *what*?" she blurted out, breathing hard. Her friend's panic was infectious. "I don't *see* her!"

"That's what I'm trying to tell you! Kimberly's in one of those freezers that opens from the top. She's trapped!"

Roxxy's eyes flicked over the appliances. Most were upright, but a few lay lengthwise on the ground. The doors and lids were either removed or wedged open with short, sturdy boards. Roxxy didn't see how it was possible for Kimberly to be trapped in something that couldn't be closed. "Toby, are you sure?"

"Of *course* I'm sure! *Look!*"

She followed his gaze. An old freezer lay flat on the ground. Bill and Carol had one like it—but newer—in the garage. The top could be raised by pressing a catch on the underside of the lip, causing the lid to swing upward.

"Do you see?" Toby stepped closer to the fence.

The chain links rattled as he shoved his bulbous nose into the diamond grid and pointed at the freezer.

"No, I *don't* see!" Roxxy growled, frustration growing as she looked where he indicated. "How could…"

A board rested on the ground next to the freezer.

And the lid was shut.

"Roxxy!" Toby barked. "It's right where—"

"I see it." A roach scuttled over the board and disappeared under the freezer. "How long has Kimberly been in there?"

"*Too* long! Why aren't people coming to help? I've been making enough noise to raise the dead."

"Your baying got muffled by all the buildings. Not to mention that stupid jackhammering going on."

"Let me try now!" Toby threw back his head. "*AAWwachachachachach!*"

Roxxy winced at the string of ragged coughs. "Your voice is shot, and I don't have the volume you do."

Toby whimpered. His tail drooped, and the white tip rested on a crack in the concrete.

"How did Kimberly get trapped in that thing?"

"It's all my fault! We were walking to school, and I heard a kitten mewling from somewhere inside the lot. I stopped and went over to the fence. Kimberly got curious and joined me. That's when she heard it too. She…she went inside to find it."

Roxxy glanced at the human-sized entry set in the fence. It was closed. There was no latch, just a knob.

She turned to Toby. "It wasn't locked?"

"I don't know! Kimberly kept yanking at it. Finally, a bunch of rust rained down, and the door creaked open just enough for her to squeeze through. She closed it before I could follow."

"Then what?"

"The mewling led her to the freezer. The lid was propped open with a board. She looked inside and got all excited, then leaned way over the edge and reached down." His tongue swept across his muzzle in a dry rasp. "She lost her balance and fell inside. Her heel caught the board. It went flying. The next thing I knew, the lid slammed down. *What are we going to do?!"*

"Take it easy. Everything will be okay."

"R-Roxxy, one time I heard Kimberly's mom say old freezers and refrigerators are death traps for kids. Something about the air inside getting used up."

"We won't let that happen."

"How are we going to stop it?"

"Let me think." Her eyes went to the knob on the entry. Humans and their stupid opposable thumbs! Always overcomplicating everything! *Okay...forget the gate.*

"Roxx," huffed Toby. "I heard the latch click when the freezer lid shut. Kimberly started banging from inside, but the sound got weaker. The noise stopped just before you got here."

"She's probably just resting."

"You don't believe that."

She looked away. *No...*

"Roxx?"

Her gaze swept the fence. The base rested on the sidewalk, making digging impossible. The inset gate was shut and a no-go. What did that leave? She craned her neck and looked up. The chain-link barrier was almost twice the height of the one at home and made more formidable by a coil of razor wire added at the top.

Her ears tilted back in submission.

"Roxx, it's hopeless, isn't it?" whimpered Toby.

"Stop being so dramatic!" she snapped, forcing her ears to lift perkily. "I'm fine-tuning the plan."

"S-Stop pretending."

Instead of responding, she backpedaled to get a broader view of the fence. After only a few paces, her rump hit something hard, producing a hollow metallic *bonnnggg*. She whirled. A rusty oil drum stood upright but rocked from the impact. The base settled on the grassy strip between the sidewalk and street. She wasn't tall enough to see the top—the thing was a good four feet high—but a metal lip curled around the upper rim, indicating a lid on top.

Her gaze swung from the drum to the fence and lingered on the razor wire topping it. The coils bristled with tight-packed pointy edges glinting in the sun. She sighed and glanced back at the old oil container.

"*Roxxxxy!*" yelped Toby. "I know what you're thinking, and I can't let you do it! You'll gut yourself on—"

Having no desire to hear the rest, she dashed to the opposite curb and leaned into a tight turn, claws scrabbling on asphalt. She charged back. Her leap landed her atop the oil drum with legs bunched and ready. Muscles uncoiled and her back paws pushed off the surface, sending the barrel clattering into the street behind her.

She shot upward. The wind stream flattened her curls. She soared up, up, *up*! Front paws cleared the razor wire as her trajectory leveled off. Joints popped in a desperate stretch to extend the leap. Razored edges tugged at the fur on her stomach, but her torso cleared without injury.

A triumphant yip burbled in her throat. *Made it! Made it! Made—*

Shock registered when the skin parted on the inside of her back leg. She convulsed and tumbled gracelessly through the air. The impact with packed dirt would have been jarring if black waves weren't already lapping at the edges of her consciousness.

"*Roxxy! GET UP!*"

Her eyes fluttered open. A mineral smell filled her nostrils, and she rolled in something sticky and wet as she got her paws beneath her. A determined push to stand resulted in a sideways topple and a fiery ribbon of pain tracing its way from leg to brain. She stared at the thin cut on the inside of her thigh.

Why is it bleeding so much?

"Roxx—" A shiver ran the length of Toby's flanks. "You can't walk. What are we going to do?"

"Who says I can't walk?" she grated, heaving herself upright in a three-legged stance.

She swayed in place, the injured limb dangling. An image came to mind of Snatcher limping away in defeat. She growled and raised her chin. She wasn't some moth-eaten fox.

"You hurt yourself for nothing," Toby said dully. "There's no way you can reach Kimberly, and—"

"Pipe down so I can concentrate," she snarled, wondering when the bleary edges at the corners of her vision would come back into focus.

No time to worry about that now. She shuffled toward the freezer, taking care to avoid a half-crushed forklift pallet with a row of jagged nails waiting to cause another injury. Her chin bumped into something hard. She blinked. How had she gotten here? She leaned against the freezer and tried to catch her breath. Why were her lungs working like a bellows? Better to focus on the appliance. Rust patches showed where the enamel had worn off. The latch to get inside was right where she expected—on the bottom of the lid. Too high for her to reach it with her chin, though. She'd have to…have to …

"*Roxxy!*"

She blinked, staggering sideways but remaining upright. "Stop yelling. My head hurts."

"You were about to pass out."

"Was not. I'm fibe…uh, *fine*…whatever."

"Doesn't matter now. Kimberly's been in there too long…" Toby's head hung so low the ends of his ears folded against the sidewalk.

Roxxy edged closer to the latch for a better look. *Squelch!* She flicked a front paw to dislodge the mud between her toes.

"Y-You're bleeding worse now," stuttered Toby.

She frowned. *What's he blathering about?* Let's see…the only way to open the lid would be to stand on her back legs—well, *leg*—and push the bottom of the latch with her front paws. Even then, she might not be able to stretch far enough.

Only one way to find out…

She pushed off the ground with her uninjured back leg and flattened her stomach against the cool surface of the freezer. Her tags beat out a jangle on the enamel. If she didn't know better, she'd think she was trembling. Focus! She stretched to her full length and *pushed*. The lightly ridged bottom of the latch dug into the pads of her front paws. The mechanism held. Without thinking, she put weight on her injured leg. An explosion of agony. Then darkness.

"Aachachachachachach! Aachachachachachach! Aachachachachachach!"

The hoarse yammering woke her. She rolled over. Why is Toby so upset? He's clawing at the chain links as if his life—

Kimberly!

Roxxy struggled to a sitting position and looked up. The world blurred. She blinked until the latch came into focus, then pushed off the ground with her good leg, once again leaning into the freezer and sliding her front paws upward. The pads slid smoothly over the enamel but slowed when they encountered a rust patch. A brick-red flake came loose and fluttered past her head. Her paws settled against the bottom of the latch. She *pushed*. Nothing. The stupid thing was never going to budge. Hadn't she done everything she could? Hadn't she tried?

A memory flitted through her mind.

Kimberly and Toby on the deck earlier that day. Small, delicate hands caressing the hound's big floppy ears. The bright tinkle of the girl's laughter.

Roxxy growled.

Stupid kids!

She planted the paw of her wounded back leg to the ground, snapped her body into an arrow-straight column, and *pushed* and *pushed* and *pushed!* Stars burst at the corners of her vision. The catch held firm. A strangled yelp got past her gritted teeth. One…last…*shove!*

Click!

The absence of resistance sent her tumbling sideways. She thought she heard a wet slap, and then all went black.

"KIMBERLY!"

The raw bellow woke Roxxy. She managed to lift her head and peer upward. The freezer lid was unlatched but hadn't yet been thrown back. Which meant that whatever was inside was…

"KIMBERLY! I know you can hear me! WAKE UP!"

Roxxy squinted. Did the freezer lid move a bit? She couldn't be sure. Her shivering made everything blurry. So…cold …

"KIMBERLY! KEEP PUSHING AND COME OUT *RIGHT NOW!*"

"All *right*, Toby-boy," wheezed a voice from inside the freezer.

The lid rose, pushed by a slim, pale arm. A blue-eyed girl with tangled blond hair appeared. She squinted against the brightness of the day.

"*Awwhhoooo-oooo-oooo.*" Toby's ragged baying sank to a hoarse but joyful rasp.

"Whew!" Kimberly steadied herself with a hand against the lip of the freezer. A thin line etched its way down each dust-smudged cheek. "It was so *dark* in there."

"*Awwhhoooo-oooo-oooo.*"

"I'm glad to see you too, Toby-boy!"

Roxxy snorted gently. The troublesome kid was a bit the worse for wear, but she glowed like a spring daffodil bathed in sunshine. In fact, the light reflecting off the girl's blond hair was almost *too* bright.

The side of Roxxy's head hit the ground with a soft *thock*.

"Roxx! You saved Kimberly! You—Roxx? ROXXY?!?!"

Her eyelids fluttered but she managed to keep them open long enough to see Kimberly swing a sneaker-clad foot over the side of the freezer. The girl had a squirming kitten tucked beneath her arm.

Roxxy grunted. *Figures. Cats are nothing but…*

The world turned black.

CHAPTER 16

"Cooperative as always."

The harsh medicinal smells were a dead giveaway. Vet's office for sure… but the surface beneath her flank wasn't the usual stainless steel. Instead, she was lying on surprisingly comfy padding. Warmth radiated through the terry-cloth cover, easing the ache in her joints.

Some kind of heating pad thingy?

Her nostrils quaked as she identified another scent. Healthy human sweat. She cracked an eyelid but quickly squeezed it shut. The overhead lighting was the brightest she'd ever seen. Ever so slowly, she tried again, allowing her vision to adjust to the glare. A boy—no, young teen by the faint hint of fuzz on his upper lip—stood next to the table, face pinched with worry. He lifted a trembling hand and pushed at strands of brown hair plastered to his forehead.

Did she know him? Her thoughts were as fuzzy as the film coating her tongue. The boy was wearing a splotchy brick-red t-shirt. His arms from the elbow down were coated with the same color.

Her nose quaked. The scent of copper hung heavy in the air.

Oh.

She lifted her head and studied the human, trying to place him.

"Whew!" The boy's expulsion of breath was like the release of air from a pressure valve. He smiled, but his bottom lip still trembled. "You're awake. Had me—us—worried for a minute."

The voice did it. *Jason!*

A slow thumping echoed in the room.

"Take it easy, girl. I'm not sure you should be wagging your tail. You could mess up your stitches or something."

Her tail went still. *Stitches?*

Jason scratched her behind the ears. "You were out cold when we got here. I knew where to bring you because of your tags. The vet—uh, Dr. Amy—will be back in a minute. She went to get something. Everything's going to be okay."

Hmph! *She* would be the judge of that. Fool boy looked worn out. She drew her legs beneath her to stand and give him a lick on the chin—and squealed like a puppy.

"Just lie still," Jason ordered, caressing her ears. "You're hurt."

She settled for craning her neck and giving his hand a lick.

His cheeks dimpled.

"You're a hero, pup. Heroine, I mean. When I found you and Kimberly, she was babbling, but I understood enough to know she got herself locked in the freezer. You were still passed out in your own, uh, on the ground. You must've opened the lid somehow." His weight shifted, and a grommet on the waistband of his blue jeans scraped against the table's side. "I wish I knew how you got past the fence."

Everything came back...*razor wire glinting in the sunlight.*

"You're shaking. What's wrong?" asked Jason, stroking the fur on the side of her face.

She leaned into the petting. Thoughts of impossibly high fences disappeared as she focused on the warmth of the boy's palm.

Her eyelids were closing when Jason mused, "Kimberly could have died trying to rescue that kitten. She's a lucky girl to have gotten out of the freezer."

Roxxy drowsily acknowledged the point. Kimberly *was* fortunate. The girl had a lot to learn. Putting herself in danger to help a feline? Who would be that dumb?

"The vet said this wasn't the first time you came to the rescue," said Jason. "She told me you took on a boxer to save your family's cat."

Roxxy sighed. Was she *ever* going to live that down?

The boy's fingers moved to her neck, and she shifted to give him a better angle to scratch under her chin. Jason knew his stuff. Her new position gave her a view of the glass-fronted cabinet on the opposite counter. The overhead lights shone on the surface, providing a reflection of her stretched-out form on the exam table. Her eyes widened as she studied a strip of shaved skin along the inside of her thigh. A short row of neat stitches was painted with a purple liquid.

She twisted to give the wound an experimental sniff but stopped when something pulled at her foreleg and sent a stinging pain through the limb. *What now?* Upon inspection, white tape covered the area. A thin tube snaked out and traveled upward to a clear plastic bag partially filled with scarlet liquid. The half-collapsed container hung suspended from a hook on a metal pole.

"Looks scary, huh?" said Jason sympathetically.

Before she could huff an affirmation, footsteps approached from the corridor outside. Jason was still focused on her and appeared not to have heard the sound in the hallway. *Poor human ears.* Nice enough to look at but useless for identifying anything less conspicuous than a brass band. Jason in particular had very nice ears. Fit his head neatly. Roxxy's mood changed to annoyance as Dr. Amy entered the room. The woman carried one of the dreaded cones meant to unjustly prevent a canine from licking something lickable.

The vet nodded at Jason. "Thanks for keeping an eye on her. Why don't you get washed up? There's a restroom down the hall. We'll trash that t-shirt and get you a smock to wear."

"That's okay. I'd better be going now."

"You should stay. Carol Anderson—Roxxy's owner—will be here any minute." Dr. Amy adjusted the drip on the bag. "She'll want to meet you."

"I know Mrs. Anderson through my Aunt Marcy—" The boy took a breath. "Sorry, this will sound confusing. Aunt Marcy isn't really my aunt, but I've known her all my life. She lives next door to Roxxy's owners."

"So you've met Carol and Bill?"

"Yes, ma'am. They're really nice." Jason took a step toward the door.

Roxxy heard that pesky whining again.

"Easy, girl," said Dr. Amy and Jason simultaneously.

The vet looked up from inspecting the stitches and smiled at the boy. "Roxxy likes you."

A shadow passed over Jason's eyes. "Uh, I like her too."

"Are you feeling all right?" asked Dr. Amy. "You ran all the way here."

"I'm good, but I'll go now. I don't want to be in the way." Jason's sneaker scraped the linoleum as he moved toward the door.

"You're not in the way at all. Carol will be thrilled to see you." The vet's tone became brisk as she bent and shone a light into each of Roxxy's eyes. "We took care of the urgent stuff, but I want a more thorough look at you, young lady. You had me worried when Jason brought you in. I thought we were going to lose you."

Roxxy yanked her chin from the woman's hand.

"Cooperative as always," said Dr. Amy. "Jason, can you hold her steady for me?"

"Sure."

Roxxy sighed as the boy gently placed his hands on either side of her head. His thumbs held her eyelids open while the vet shone the light in. His fingertips massaged the sensitive area below her ears.

"Jason, you've definitely got the touch."

"It's not me. Roxxy's good as gold."

"Wait until she's completely recovered from the anesthetic," replied Dr. Amy dryly. "You may change your opinion."

"No way."

"Hear that, Roxxy? You've fooled Jason into thinking you're an angel."

"She is!"

"If you say so." The vet pocketed the penlight and straightened. She put her hands on her hips. "Roxxy, no concussion, thank goodness."

Jason asked, "She's okay except for where the razor wire got her?"

"Surprisingly, yes." Dr. Amy ran her short fingernails down Roxxy's flank. "Missy, we've got to stop meeting like this. Who do you think you are? Lassie?"

Roxxy's bangs twitched in a frown. She'd watched old reruns of the show while curled up on the sofa next to Bill. All the people in the series were pleasant but surprisingly simpleminded, even for humans. They constantly fell down wells or got trapped in burning buildings. She could understand how somebody could be *pushed* into a well, but how do you *fall* into one? As for Lassie, Roxxy could never understand how the prissy long-haired collie remained perfectly groomed while fighting off mountain lions or dragging humans out of collapsed mine shafts. The dog acted *so* special. She—

Jason soothed the silky fur on Roxxy's forehead.

"I don't think she's a big fan of Lassie."

"What makes you say that?"

"Well, see the way Roxxy's eyes have gone kind of squinty behind her bangs? She looks…I don't know. Annoyed, maybe?"

"You've got a good instinct for dogs. Got one of your own?"

"Uh, no."

"You might want to think about changing that." The vet picked up the collar-cone from the counter. The sound of Velcro being separated echoed off the cabinets as a strip was adjusted. "Lots of dogs need loving homes."

Roxxy beadily eyed the cone and wriggled away.

"Stay still," Dr. Amy ordered. "I don't want you licking those stitches."

Jason said, "She doesn't like that cone."

"None of my patients do."

"Could we please try letting her get better without the cone?"

"Well…"

"Hey, you," said Jason, bending to look directly into Roxxy's chestnut eyes while cupping her face in his hands. "No licking, or Dr. Amy will put on the cone. Okay?"

Roxxy grunted an assent.

Jason turned to the vet. "See?"

"I'm not sure what I see, but I surrender. I'll give Carol the cone. She can put it on Roxxy if the little imp starts licking or scratching at the stitches."

"How come there are so few of them? With all that blood, I thought there would be more."

"The cut wasn't long, but it nicked the wall of an artery. You got her here just in time. If you hadn't, things would have turned out very differently."

The boy gulped. "It was pure luck that I found her. I was on the next block over and heard a dog barking in a raspy way that made me think something was wrong. Turned out to be Toby. I showed up as Kimberly was climbing out of the freezer. Then I saw Roxxy."

Jason's face paled.

"I tried to dial 911, but my hands were shaking so badly I dropped my phone, and it fell through a storm drain." Jason lowered his eyes. "I panicked. If I hadn't, I could've called somebody to get Roxxy here sooner. It's my fault she almost died."

Dr. Amy shook her head. Light danced off the tiny paw-shaped gold studs in her earlobes. "You carried a bleeding dog half a mile to this office. Give yourself some credit."

"Sure." Jason flicked a glance at the wall clock above the doorway. "I've got to go home and change. I'm really late for school."

"But—"

"If I don't stop by the principal's office by lunchtime, they'll mark me absent and phone my mom at work. She'll be worried."

"I'll give her a call now. I'm sure she'll understand why you didn't make it to school on time. In fact"—the vet smiled—"she'll be proud of you for saving Roxxy."

"No!"

Dr. Amy blinked. "Excuse me?"

"I...I'm sorry, but my mom's funny about dogs. She doesn't want me around them."

"But this was a special circumstance. She couldn't possibly be upset with you!"

Jason was silent.

The vet continued, "You *do* need to freshen up, though. Tell you what—we'll get you that smock. There's a restroom down the hall where you can change."

"But my mom—"

"Will be proud when she finds out what happened," Dr. Amy

insisted. "Any mother would be. I'm sure her feelings about dogs won't get in the way."

Roxxy grunted.

I've met the woman.

The door swung open, and a current of air sent Roxxy's curls aflutter.

"Oh, my!" Carol stopped dead in her tracks. She swayed and extended a hand to steady herself against the door frame.

"She's out of danger," Dr. Amy said quickly. "And she'll fully recover."

"But …" Carol whispered, gesturing at the stand holding the clear plastic bag, still partially filled with scarlet fluid.

"She lost a lot of blood, but she's bouncing back fine, and she came through the anesthesia like a trooper. All her vitals look good, and the stitches are holding nicely. She'll be able to put weight on the leg in a day or so. Give it a week, and she'll be good as new. They heal fast at her age."

Roxxy yipped a greeting to offer reassurance, but the sound came out weaker than she'd intended. Carol was instantly at her side, hands caressing and stroking while carefully avoiding the stitches and her taped foreleg.

"How's my *wittle girl*?" choked Carol.

Roxxy winced.

Baby talk? After the day I've had?

The vet patted Carol's shoulder.

"Like I told you when I called, Roxxy lost quite a lot of blood because of the nicked artery, but no muscle tissue was severed." A box of Kleenex appeared on the table. "Here."

"Thanks." Carol dabbed her eyes and drew in a steadying breath. "You didn't say anything on the phone about who brought her in."

Dr. Amy grinned.

"Somebody who says he knows you." She turned to where Jason had been standing a moment before. "Where'd he *go*?"

"Who?" Carol ran a hand through her red hair.

"The boy who carried Roxxy here. You walked right past him."

"I was too worried to notice anybody."

"I can't believe he snuck out."

Roxxy sighed. *Humans. Helpless as newborn puppies.* She was starting to understand how people kept falling into abandoned wells on the collie's TV show. They stumbled through life mostly unaware of their surroundings. Take Jason's exit, for instance. Carol and Dr. Amy had missed seeing him sneak out, but she'd spotted him as he edged through the open door. *Idiot boy.* He'd left so quickly she hadn't been able to give him a thorough nuzzling as a thank you. Her tail thumped the table. His parting wink had been adorable.

"Be careful!" Carol ordered.

"I've got her." Bill lifted Roxxy from the back seat of the car. He looked down at the bundle in his arms. "Haven't I, girl?"

By way of answer, Roxxy shoved her nose against the side of his neck and sucked in a whiff of minty aftershave.

"ACHOOO!"

"Gesundheit," he said with a grin. "Now be still while I carry you inside the house. If I drop you, my wife will murder me."

Carol nodded. "Glad you're clear on the concept."

A low hum drew Roxxy's attention to the freezer tucked against a side wall of the garage.

A growl rumbled in her chest. *Death trap.*

"What's the matter?" asked Bill. "Am I hurting you?"

Her scruff relaxed. She told herself to forget about homicidal appliances and enjoy being cuddled in Bill's arms. She licked his chin. A light stubble was present despite his morning shave, and she enjoyed the raspy sensation against her tongue.

He smiled. "Enjoying yourself?"

She delivered another lick as he carried her toward the door leading into the kitchen. Her leg was healing quickly, as Dr. Amy had promised. She was perfectly capable of walking on her own, but being carried was a pretty cushy deal. Still, she was restless after spending two nights at the vet's office. Her only real problem with the wound was that the stitches itched like crazy. She'd only stopped licking them when Dr. Amy waved the collar-cone at her and said, "What's it going to be?"

"Bill, watch your step." Carol held open the door. "And be gentle with her."

"I'm trying. I think she put on weight at the vet's office. She's heavy as a sack of potat—*Oomph!*"

She extracted the paw of her healthy back leg from his solar plexus.

"I think you kicked me on purpose," wheezed Bill accusingly while navigating the doorway into the kitchen.

"Let's see if she can walk on her own." Carol dropped the car keys on the counter. Metal jingled against granite. "Put her down next to the breakfast table but stay close in case she starts to hobble."

"Don't fret so much. Amy said she could get around fine, and—"

"Bill."

Roxxy and the man exchanged a glance. Both recognized the tone.

As soon as Roxxy's paws touched down, she trotted to Carol to show her the wounded leg was well on the mend. The woman's sigh of relief was audible, as was the popping of her knees when she knelt.

"Satisfied?" asked Bill.

Carol arched an eyebrow in his direction. "Immensely. Get over here and enjoy the fun."

Roxxy chest thrummed with a blissful grunt/groan/sigh as she soaked up the petting provided by four expert hands. An instant later, the floor vibrated with the growing thunder of paws pounding the hallway leading to the kitchen. Her parents and sibs barreled into the room in a scrambling melee that pushed Bill and Carol aside.

Canine noses sniffed and nuzzled Roxxy from one end to the other.

"I think we've been displaced." Carol smiled at Bill.

"Roxx," Max huffed. "Toby told us how you saved Kimberly, but I want to hear it from you. Start at the beginning."

"Yeah, Sis, *how* did you manage that?" asked Lulu.

"That's enough with the questions," Molly said. "Your sister needs her rest, but first I want to check out those stitches."

Roxxy rolled over. The wooden flooring was pleasantly cool on her back while her mother sniffed the injured leg.

"You're healing fast," acknowledged Molly. "But what were you thinking? You could have bled to death. I still can't figure out how you got out of the yard, much less ended up where you did. In any case…" Her furry tail, so similar to Roxxy's, lifted and curled over her back. "Your father and I are very proud of you for rescuing Kimberly."

"Darn right." Jake brushed his muzzle against Roxxy's. "Now go get some rest."

She rolled upright, staggering a bit. *I'm weaker than I thought.*

"Roxx?" asked Molly.

"I'm fine, Momma."

Roxxy plodded down the hall. She was about to enter the family room when Muffy appeared in the doorway and stopped, blocking the entrance. Roxxy noticed the feline's whiskers had fully grown back where that moron, Thor, had ripped them free.

The fine strands twitched and the small, darkish nose quaked.

Roxxy decided to head off the insult about her scent.

"I can't help it if I smell like the vet's office. It wasn't my idea to stay there overnight."

"What is it with you? Death wish?"

Roxxy groaned. The last thing she needed was another lecture on staying out of trouble. *Do they think I go around looking for opportunities to get hurt? I'm a napper!*

"I heard"—Muffy's emerald eyes shone with an indecipherable glow—"that you've been up to your usual antics. Drama, drama, drama."

"What's it to you?"

"Cat? Curiosity? How many times do we have to go over this?"

"Don't you have more important things to do? Those hair balls won't cough themselves up."

"So Kimberly tumbled into a freezer trying to save a kitten?"

"You know kids," Roxxy grated. "Lovable but dumb."

She glanced past Muffy into the family room. The nest of flannel sheets in the dog bed looked heavenly.

"A lot like you," purred the cat. "But without the lovable part."

"Fine. You done?"

"Not quite."

Roxxy steeled herself. She was too tired to avoid what would surely come next—flashing claws and a scratch on the nose. She scrunched her eyes shut. When she opened them, Muffy had already passed and was gliding down the hall. Roxxy stood dumbstruck, her cheek still tingling from the nuzzle of feline whiskers.

She remembered she had a reputation to uphold. "Don't *do* that! Creeps me out!"

Muffy looked back over her gray-cream-black shoulder. An amused purr echoed through the hallway. The sun streaming through the front door window at the far end made the space bright.

The cat snorted. "Why am I not convinced?"

Roxxy noticed the shadow waving back and forth on the wall. She sighed.

Stupid tail!

AXEL

"Everything's on schedule," Axel lied into the cell phone, watching the breeze push a yellow hamburger wrapper across the strip mall parking lot. He knew he was taking a chance by staking out a commercial lot so soon after the encounter with the security guard, but time was running out for assembling the shipment.

A gust of wind lifted the burger wrapper and plastered it to the pickup's side mirror. The smell of grease and ketchup filled the truck. Axel wadded the yellow paper into a ball and threw it on the asphalt. The thought of food sent a hot gas bubble rising in his throat. He belched and massaged his stomach while sliding down in the seat. His knee banged against the bottom of the dashboard. A knot of green and red wires dropped from underneath and dangled limply. He squinted and bit back a curse. Ethan nagging him, a hangover, *and* the truck falling apart? What's next? The day was starting off with a bang. He flipped down the sun visor, but he was slouched so low in the seat that the mid-afternoon rays still shone into his eyes. He adjusted his dark glasses and winced when one of the curved ends tugged at the Band-Aid folded over his ear. Who would've thought the Pom could wriggle out of the sack and nail him? Never would've happened if the blond mutt hadn't tripped him up. Miserable little—

"You're lying," said Ethan.

Axel sucked in a deep breath and let it out slowly.

He hadn't been able to concentrate since…well since that *mongrel* had yanked him off his feet. And sleep? Forget about it. Last night, he'd gone through a six-pack before finally nodding off, which explained why he hadn't woken up until noon. The inside of his mouth still felt like the floor of a chicken coop. He glanced at the glove compartment.

"What's the problem?" asked Ethan.

"I told you. There isn't one."

"You couldn't fool me when we shared a cell, and you can't now. What's going on?"

"Hang on a second," Axel grunted.

He put his phone on the seat and opened the glove compartment. A cascade of half-used matchbooks and empty cigarette packs tumbled out. He rummaged around until he found what he was looking for. The bottle had a pleasant heft, and the glass was cool against his palm. Keeping the container below window level, he carefully dribbled the bourbon into a half-filled soda can. His hand shook, and the bottle's neck rattled against the aluminum rim. Bringing the can to his lips, his tongue worked to suck down the harsh, smoky-sweet liquid.

He swallowed and blew out a breath, cheeks expanding like a puffer fish, and picked up the phone. "Like I said, the shipment's coming along. I'm making good progress."

"I'm not interested in progress. I want results. And don't *ever* leave me hanging on the phone again. Got me?"

Axel smiled lazily, letting the bourbon do its work. The pain in his ear eased, and thoughts of the meddlesome mutt faded. His mind dwelled on what he had planned for Ethan after the final delivery. A chuckle burbled at the back of his throat. *Got you?* He rubbed the back of his hand across his mouth to keep the chuckle from turning into a full-fledged laugh. *Yeah, Ethan, I got you right where I want you.*

"You losing it?" asked Ethan.

"Nah, I'm—" Axel sat upright.

He watched the dark blue minivan turn into the strip mall. The female driver had frizzy, bright-red hair that could've passed for a clown's wig. The vehicle also contained two middle-schoolers—a boy and a girl, also red-headed—positioned on opposite sides of the back seat. Both were crowded by a tan-and-white corgi. Each dog stood on a kid's lap and pushed a pointy muzzle through the gap in a half-open window. The triangular ears of the corgis stood erect, and the white tips of the short tails wagged happily.

Axel nodded as the van slid into an angled slot well back from the entrance to a grocery store. The parking space was next to an area designated for returning empty shopping carts. As the driver and kids piled out, the corgis gathered at a single window, whining as the people departed for the store.

A corner of Axel's mouth lifted as he studied the units pining for their humans.

I guess if you can't go with them, you'll have to come with me.

The woman stopped and frowned. The kids kept walking.

"Wait a minute," the woman ordered.

The red-headed youngsters turned.

"What is it, Mom?" asked the girl.

"Remember the posters we saw about the dogs going missing? You two better stay with Bonnie and Clyde."

"But *Mom*," pleaded the boy, "we want to—"

"Oh, stop whining. I won't be long."

The kids plodded back to the van.

Aluminum *crunched*, sending liquid burbling through the opening atop the can and over Axel's fingers. He hurled the mangled container out the window and wiped his sticky hand on his black t-shirt.

"You there?" asked Ethan.

"Sorry, I was watching a couple of units."

"Good prospects?"

"Thought so, but it didn't work out."

"You know what I think?"

"Can't wait to hear." Axel caught a partial glimpse of his face in the ketchup-smeared side mirror. He rubbed at the vein pulsing at his temple.

"I think you're a loser all around. You can't get your act together. You can't put together a shipment on time. You can't even train that pit bull you told me about—the one you bought off that guy a couple of months ago." Ethan laughed. "You still got that mutt? If I remember right, the only time you tried him in the pit, he set the record for jumping *out*."

Sour bile filled Axel's mouth. He wished he'd never overheard that guy in a bar talking about how much money could be made from illegal dogfighting. The man was a trainer who raised and sold pit bulls. Axel had jumped on the idea of making some easy cash. He'd gotten a loan from Ethan—his second mistake—and bought a dog. The mutt hadn't been tested in a match but looked like a winner. The animal had massive shoulders and a head as big as a toaster oven. The trainer said he was selling the dog cheap because he needed cash, but Axel soon discovered the real reason the guy wanted to unload it. The animal had no killer instinct. The first time Axel took it to an abandoned farm where local fights were held, the mutt had panicked and clawed its way out of the fighting pit. Axel had caught the dog and dragged it back. The animal promptly jumped out again and hunkered under the rickety, three-tiered spectator stands. It had cowered with its gray coat rippling in terror and its cropped tail trying futilely to curl between rear legs.

Axel rubbed his still-sticky palm on his jeans. Four months had passed, but he could still hear the taunts from the men in the stands. He'd wanted to wade into them and make them pay, but there were too many. The dog? That was a different story.

Ethan snorted. "I forget. What did you name that mutt? *Bashful*?"

"Basher," Axel replied in a voice that sounded like glass being ground by a boot heel.

"*Bashful* makes more sense. From what you said about him, he'd hide from his own shadow. Still got him?"

"Yeah. I've been waiting until I can recover some of my investment."

Ethan snorted. "Investment? Is that what you call it when some guy sells you a fighting dog that won't fight?"

"Knock yourself out."

"So what's the plan with the mutt?"

"I met a guy last week who's been to a few matches. Said he'd pay a good price for Basher."

"W-why?" Ethan stuttered through a guffaw. "Does the moron want a seventy-pound lap dog?"

"I told the guy Basher's a real terror in the pit. The mutt may be a wimp, but he *looks* tough. I'm driving him over to the buyer's house this afternoon."

"You're doing *what*?" snapped Ethan, all humor gone from his voice. "You should be out snatching units instead of wasting time getting rid of that useless piece of—"

"Won't take long," interrupted Axel. "The guy doesn't live that far from my place. Five-minute drive. I've got his address."

"Forget driving. Walk."

"What are you talking about?"

"The buyer will come looking for you when he finds out the dog won't fight."

"So? Let him find me."

"*Think* for once! If you take that junky pickup to deliver the mutt, the buyer will know what you drive. If he comes cruising around trying to find you, he could spot that rattletrap in your carport. The next thing you know, he's pounding on your door and making trouble. The neighbors could call the cops, and you end up back in the joint for breaking parole. Is that what you want?"

"You've made your point."

Axel watched the woman return to the minivan. She backed out of the parking space and drove toward the exit.

Follow it? He shook his head, remembering that the woman had mentioned the flyers to her kids. She was the careful type.

"Are you sure?" prodded Ethan. "With you, I sometimes have to repeat myself."

"I'll walk Basher to the guy's house. Satisfied?"

"Thrilled. Now, let's—"

"Gotta go," Axel interrupted. "Just spotted another unit."

He stabbed the disconnect button. There wasn't another prospect in sight, but he'd had a bellyful of Ethan.

A jangling rattle echoed from behind the pickup. Axel looked into the rearview mirror. A teenager was approaching, pushing a line of grocery carts that customers had left near the embankment at the rear of the parking lot. The boy's jaws worked on a wad of gum while his skinny frame leaned forward to add momentum to the slowly moving line of interlocked carts. The teen's course would pass within inches of the driver's-side door.

Axel did a quick scan of the lot. No looky-loos. The carts rumbled past, and then the boy's profile appeared in the open window. Axel delivered a stiff-armed blow with the heel of his hand to the boy's jaw. A pink glob of bubble gum and a scatter of white teeth with bloody roots sailed from the teen's mouth. The limp form collapsed like a steer in a slaughterhouse.

Axel stomped on the accelerator and swerved around the slowing line of carts. His spine pressed into the seat as the truck rocketed across the parking lot and produced its usual double backfire. Tires squealing, the vehicle careened into the street. The door to the glove compartment popped open. Axel reached over and slammed it, pleased he wasn't tempted to take a drink. In fact, he felt better than he had in days. His foot eased off the gas, and the pickup slowed to the speed limit. He shrugged. Ethan had a point about walking Basher over to the buyer's house. No need to let the guy lay eyes on the truck. Ethan was clever all right. Axel grinned. Just not clever enough.

CHAPTER 17

"He looks like a mean one."

"Settle down," huffed Max. "It won't be long."

Roxxy ignored him and paced the section of fence separating the back yard from the front. She was pleased her leg was pain free. The short line of stitches no longer itched, and the skin surrounding them was pink and healthy, already covered in blond stubble. Her leg wasn't the problem. Waiting was. Why hadn't Carol and Lulu come back yet?

She stared through the chain links, studying the sidewalk and the street beyond.

"You're just making yourself miserable," observed Max.

"No, that's your job," snapped Roxxy. "And you're a natural."

She stopped pacing and glared at him, going for a mixture of disdain and intimidation.

"Got something in your eye?"

"Forget it," she grumbled, deciding the subtleties of her piercing stares were wasted on him.

The big oaf sprawled contentedly beneath a nearby maple. Thick branches creaked in the breeze, and dappled sunlight played over his rangy frame. A large paw rested possessively on a red bone-shaped chewy composed of rubbery material that she knew from personal experience was indestructible and lacking in flavor. She had no interest in the thing. However, Max's claim on it made her want to snatch it away. Was she quick enough? Certainly. Was it worth the effort? Probably not. Without opposable thumbs, there was no way to beat him over the head with it.

What was taking Carol and Lulu so long?

A revving engine echoed from the street. Roxxy peered through the chain-link fence as a big delivery truck barreled into view. The driver-side door was open, and the airstream sent the man's shoulder-length scraggly blond hair fluttering behind him. He had one hand resting casually on the steering wheel. His eyes were fixed on a cell phone cupped in his other hand. Roxxy sucked in a breath as the vehicle swerved and nearly took out a mailbox. Her ears flattened. *The idiot could have run over someone!* An explosion of barks erupted from her throat. The driver gave her a wide-eyed glance as he corrected the truck's path and zoomed out of sight.

She released another tirade.

Moron!

"What are you yammering at?" asked Max.

She whirled. "Didn't you see that truck?"

"The one that just went by? So what?"

"The driver wasn't paying attention! He could've jumped the curb and run down Carol and Lulu."

"You're just mad because you're the last one in the rotation when Carol is leash training us. She saves you for the end." Max snorted. "And who could blame her?"

"What's that supposed to mean?"

"You forget there's a person holding the end of the leash. After your rabbit-chasing incident, Carol spent a whole afternoon picking leaves and twigs out of her hair."

"That was the rabbit's fault! I didn't tell him to dart under the box hedge." Roxxy went back to pacing. She silently acknowledged that Max made a couple of good points, but she wouldn't admit it out loud if her life depended on it.

She was a bit, well, *enthusiastic* on the walks, and she definitely didn't like being the last one to go. Carol always walked the dogs one at a time because it was the best way to leash train them. Max had already had his turn today, and Lulu was currently enjoying hers. Roxxy flicked her tail impatiently. *Life was so unfair!* Why did she have to go last when she was by far the most energetic walker? The new smells were amazing! Yesterday, she'd picked up the musky scent of a raccoon near a plastic trash bin one of the neighbors had left on the curb. But every walk offered new aromas—possums, groundhogs, rabbits, and, of course, other canines. She enjoyed discovering a spot some strange dog had marked. She'd then squat and claim the area as her own—except when some *male* canine had lifted a leg to mark a spot on a tree or a telephone pole too high for her to reach. *The nerve.*

She stopped mid-stride and growled at Max.

He blinked. "What did *I* do?"

"Exist," she replied, and went back to prowling the fence line.

If she was being honest—a trait, in her opinion, that was right up there with obedience in being overrated—she wasn't as well behaved on walks as Max and Lulu. When Carol had first started the leash training a few weeks previously, Lulu had been perfect as usual. Roxxy had envied the way her beautiful sister exuded a refined dignity as she held her head high and maintained a steady pace. Even Max, whom Roxxy considered as quick-witted as a fire hydrant, had easily learned to walk placidly next to Carol's knee.

Roxxy's own aptitude for leash training was...well, *modest* was the most charitable description. And was it her fault? Of course not! She simply became so engrossed in various scents that she forgot Carol was even *there*. Roxxy sighed. She spent half the walks rooted in place, nose buried in an interesting patch of grass while resisting all Carol's efforts to move along. And the rest of the time? She lunged forward like a runaway sled dog, dragging the human with her in pursuit of a fascinating smell somewhere ahead.

Her tail drooped when she recalled the 'rabbit-chasing incident.' She hadn't intended to pull Carol *through* the hedge. Still, you had to give the woman her due—the grip on the leash had never faltered. Roxxy sighed. Shame about the torn cashmere sweater.

Stupid rabbit!

Roxxy blamed her nose for her leash-training problems. Like her tail, her nose had a will of its own and drew her irresistibly in whatever direction was most fascinating in the moment. Carol, usually doting, had looked at her after yesterday's outing and muttered, "Walking you is like trying to leash train an alligator."

Roxxy ducked when a bluebird dove out of nowhere. The bird's sharp beak opened to snatch a grasshopper in mid-hop, only inches above Roxxy's head. The azure bird soared into an oak's canopy, where its outstretched wings killed its momentum and it dropped neatly onto a branch. Roxxy admired the creature's perfect control. She vowed to do better on the walks. Starting today!

Max looked up from the chewy he was trying to maul. An amused glint shone in his cinnamon eyes. "Poor Carol. She's probably taking her time with Lulu because she wants to put off walking you as long as possible."

Roxxy measured the distance between them. One leap should do it.

"Now, Sis—" Max stiffened and pushed away the chew toy. "I was just having a little fun."

Hmmm...right ear or left?

"I know that look!"

Left, she decided. Strands of tan fur intertwined to form an inviting tuft at the triangular tip. Her legs bunched, but before she could pounce, dog tags jingled from the sidewalk.

Finally!

Roxxy turned from Max—making a mental note that she owed him a hard nip when she got back from the walk. She gave a chuff of impatience as she watched Carol and Lulu. They were taking their sweet time as they approached, leaving foot and paw prints respectively in the front lawn. The pair finally arrived and stopped just outside the gate. Lulu sat primly while Carol unsnapped the leash.

"*Good* dog!" the woman cooed while scratching Lulu under the chin. "You're a perfect walker! Such a little lady!"

Roxxy frowned. *What's next? An awards ceremony?*

"And you," Carol said, pointing a well-manicured index finger at Roxxy, "would do well to imitate your sister."

Roxxy felt a pang of guilt. Carol was right. She promised herself she would remain calm and walk demurely once they set out. But what was taking so long? Why was Carol adjusting Lulu's collar instead of opening the gate? *Let's get going!*

"Take it easy!" Carol laughed.

The air tugging at Roxxy's curls was the first hint. The second was the realization that her eyes were on the same level as Carol's. How had she gotten airborne? She glanced down. The flattened grass below indicated it wasn't her first leap. She landed and sat quivering with anticipation as Carol attached the leash to her collar. The snap of the catch was too much. A jolt of adrenaline shot through her, and she twirled in circles. The motion sent the leash wrapping around her legs. She toppled over and hit the ground with a *whump*.

"Impressive," observed Max. "If you're the main attraction at a calf-roping event."

"Don't be mean," said Lulu, fighting the giggles and losing as she gave a half snort, half hiccup. "Roxxy's doing the best she can."

"That"—Max nodded—"is the sad part."

Roxxy growled. "Enjoying yourselves?"

"All of you, quiet down." Carol knelt and began untangling the leash but stopped and studied Roxxy. "Hmm… Maybe I should quit while I'm ahead and pull you around the neighborhood in a little red wagon."

Roxxy's nose skimmed the sidewalk and her hindquarters swung in a victorious sashay as she kept pace with Carol's easy stride. The walk might have started out…uh, a bit rough, but things had gone well since. Who said leash training was hard? She put a bit more swagger in her step.

"Proud of yourself?" asked Carol, chuckling softly.

Roxxy gave an absentminded tail wag in response, but her head stayed bent as she sifted through the smells rising from the cement. A raccoon had come this way the night before, and she was trying to pinpoint where it had stepped off the pavement.

"Good girl," murmured Carol. "You're doing great."

Roxxy huffed in modest acknowledgment. The outing was turning out *very* well, and she was pleased to be fulfilling her resolution to be a more cooperative walker. So far she'd paused only sparingly to investigate the most interesting scents, and since she wasn't stopping constantly, Carol was giving her plenty of time to sniff.

A flutter of movement drew her attention. A male cardinal landed in a nearby holly, its feathers bright against the shrub's green leaves and berries. The bird scolded her with a slow distinctive call—*cheer...cheer...cheer*—that ended in a series of rapid-fire trills—*perty-perty-perty*. All of it amounted to *move on*!

She stopped and yipped to tell the cardinal to get over himself. She had better things to do than worry about his territory. A slight tug on the leash got her moving.

"*Very* good girl," cooed Carol.

Roxxy didn't slow again until she heard the excited cries of a group of kindergarteners swarming over playground equipment in a fenced schoolyard. Most of the kids were playing on an elaborate framework of multicolored climbing bars and sliding boards, all connected by tubes through which the children scurried like hamsters navigating a maze. Two of the little boys were off by themselves playing on a teeter-totter. The narrow board pivoted up and down, center hinges squeaking as a child rose high on one end while the youngster on the opposite side sank almost to the ground. She loved seeing the repeated soaring and plunging.

"Time to go." Carol tugged on the leash.

Roxxy planted her paws. The kids were such fun to watch! Another tug and she remembered her pledge to be cooperative. She allowed herself to be pulled along, but not before producing a loud, martyred sigh. Was there an answering chuckle from Carol? Roxxy ignored it and focused on matching the woman's pace.

"I'm *so* impressed. You're finally getting the hang of this. How about a long power walk as a reward?"

The *power walk* reference was a mystery, but Roxxy knew an approving tone when she heard one. Air stirred behind her.

Carol nodded. "There's my answer."

Roxxy shifted into a faster trot as the woman's stride lengthened. Block after block slipped past. Gradually, she realized the houses lining the streets were smaller than the ones she was used to. Another few blocks and the homes looked decidedly rundown. Paint peeled from the exteriors, and a few had cars in the front yards—wheels missing and bare rims resting precariously on cinder blocks.

"We'd better head back." Carol glanced around. "It's getting late, and I don't usually walk in this part of town after dark. We'll go to the corner and turn around."

Roxxy was only half listening. She'd picked up the sound of a dog's panting that was too far away for Carol to hear. A moment later, a pit bull rounded the corner ahead, pulling enthusiastically on a taut leash held by a big man with a shaved head. The pair were on the opposite side of the street from her and Carol but quickly approaching.

Roxxy frowned. The dog's ribs stood out starkly beneath a dull gray coat that she suspected would have a silvery sheen if he was properly nourished. His flat nose, small eyes, and short-cropped ears were the same washed-out gray. The middle of his broad chest was marked by a white diamond-shaped patch. However, all of that was secondary to his most dominant feature.

The pit bull's jaws were so massive that his head was oval shaped.

Roxxy gulped. He looked bred to wreak havoc. She wondered if he was as aggressive as those jaws made him appear.

Her nose quaked, but she was upwind and unable to detect his scent.

A glint of metal drew Roxxy's eye to his throat. Was that…a *prong collar*? She'd heard about them but hadn't believed a person would be cruel enough to make a dog wear one. She shivered. The tips of angled chrome prongs pressed against the pit bull's broad neck as he tugged at the leash. She was certain the metal tines must be painful, but the discomfort didn't seem to bother him. His nose eagerly swept the sidewalk while vacuuming up smells. He was clearly fascinated by the variety of scents wafting off the cement.

She snorted softly. *Me and you both, buddy!* The thought was instantly followed by a command to herself to stay vigilant. Those jaws were no joke. Some dogs were peaceable when distracted but could be ill-tempered when exposed to other canines. He would notice her soon and might be aggressive.

A muttered curse drew her attention to the dog's human companion as the pair approached an untended crepe myrtle extending a sturdy horizontal branch across the sidewalk. The limb was as thick as an ax handle and hung heavy with knots of fading pink blossoms. The pit bull slid beneath the obstacle. Roxxy expected the man to duck under. Instead, his free hand curled around the limb and snapped it cleanly. He hurled the branch into the depths of the shrub.

Roxxy grunted in response to the casual display of strength, but her pace next to Carol didn't falter. The rapid clicking of Carol's nails on her cell phone indicated the woman was oblivious to the man and dog on the opposite side of the road.

Roxxy studied the guy and was surprised to feel her hackles rising. Her default response to people was positive—treats, petting, what wasn't to like? But there was something about the man that was off. His sleeveless black t-shirt revealed muscled arms with crude tattoos packed from wrist to shoulder. She couldn't make out the words, but the image of a snake slithering out of the eye socket of a skull made her flinch.

The man's broad shoulders tapered to a slender waist. His jeans rode low on his hips, and the denim was stiff with motor grease. The pant legs were stuffed into high-laced, scuffed leather boots. The footwear was adorned with chains that ran down the outer calf, across the toe, and up the inside ankle. Short, spiky studs interspersed the links.

Roxxy shivered, imagining the damage that a kick from one of the boots would produce.

A delighted woof drew her attention.

"Hi there, I'm Basher! What's your name?"

The pit bull's ears folded back, and his frame wiggled in an all-over-body wag, signaling both pleasure at their meeting and total submission.

Roxxy's tail wagged. *So much for aggression!*

She yipped cheerily, "Hi Basher. I'm Roxxy. Great to meet you!"

The wind changed direction, and a discarded Styrofoam cup tumbled across the street toward her. The scents of the pit bull and the human followed. Her nose quaked as she took in the pungent smell of Basher's oily, unwashed coat. A pang of pity touched her heart. She was no fan of baths, but she knew that they were a way for people to show they cared about you. How many times had Bill and/or Carol plopped her down in a tub of soapy water, given her a good scrubbing, and rubbed her dry with a fleecy towel? All the while cooing that she was an adorable fluff ball. *Hokey, but sweet.*

Poor Basher smelled as if he'd *never* been bathed.

She turned her attention to the man and sifted the scents wafting off him. Her nose wrinkled. He was also a stranger to soap. A sour funk rose from the crescents of crusty dried sweat below the armholes in the sleeveless shirt. The heavy reek of cigarette smoke clung to him like creosote lining an untended chimney.

"Roxxy, I'll come say hello!" Basher strained against the leash, apparently forgetting the human attached to the other end. The tines of the prong collar dug into his neck, but he appeared to take no notice.

"Don't!" snapped the man, leaning back to counter the dog's pull.

Roxxy watched the reddening of the man's heavy features. The sawtooth outline of a vein pulsed beneath the skin of his temple.

Roxxy stopped dead.

"Why put on the brakes?" asked Carol, looking up from the phone. "You were doing so—"

Roxxy felt the woman stiffen at the sight of the pit bull and his owner.

Carol whispered, "That dog looks half starved."

The comment barely registered with Roxxy. Her focus was on the man's profile.

Could it be…was it possible…despite the different clothes and footwear…

During her encounters with the dog thief, her nose had been numbed by the effects of pepper spray. She hadn't been able to imprint his scent. He'd spoken rarely, and most of the comments were muttered curses, and the uniform-like shirt he'd worn had covered his arms. The billed cap had cast his features into shadow and prevented her from determining how much hair—if any—he had. Sunglasses had obscured his eyes.

Was a pulsing vein enough to go by?

"I'll be right there!" bellowed Basher in a series of cheerful barks. His claws scrabbled against the sidewalk as he lunged to reach the street.

Carol gasped and shoved the cell phone into her pocket. Roxxy understood the woman's reaction. The heavy-jawed, excited dog would be intimidating to a human who didn't have the benefit of knowing his scent communicated friendly enthusiasm rather than aggression.

"I'm coming, Roxxy!" Basher reared on his hind legs, throwing himself against the restraining leash. "I can't wait to meet you, and—"

"*SHUT IT!*" The man's bellow coincided with a yank on the leash that sent the dog into a backflip. A squealing yelp cut through the air as Basher thudded to the pavement next to the human's heavy boots. The metal spines of the collar dimpled the dog's neck, but no blood appeared.

Roxxy's heart went out to him as he hunkered low, his eyes rolling in terror. A shudder rippled down his flanks.

The man drew back a foot.

"*RARF-RARF-RARF-RARF-RARF!*" barked Roxxy at the same instant Carol yelled, "*DON'T!*"

The man's boot froze in mid-kick, and his head swiveled toward the sounds of protest. He squinted, trying to see through the sun's glare as it was setting behind Roxxy and Carol. Shaking his head, he pulled a baseball-type cap from his back pocket and put it on. The brim had a sharp crease, and the design above pictured two metal-framed towers, wide at the base and narrow at the top, with cables strung between them.

Roxxy gulped. *It's him!*

The thought had barely formed when the man's gaze settled on Carol. His lips drew back in a wet grin.

Roxxy was reminded of Snatcher's expression when the fox had held Leo trapped in his jaws. A tremor from the leash informed her that Carol was squirming under the man's scrutiny.

"I'm Axel," the pit bull's owner called. "What's your name? Live around here?"

"I s-saw what you were about to do."

"Do?" He shrugged. "I wasn't about to do anything."

"You were going to kick your dog."

"Nah, I wasn't planning to go through with it. I just wanted to throw a scare into him so he'd stop pulling on the leash. Besides," the man's voice hardened, "it's my dog, and I can do what I want with it."

Carol's trembling hand pushed a strand of her straight red hair behind an ear. "There's *no* justification for being cruel to a dog!"

"Don't get all agitated, lady. It's not good for your health."

"There are online videos on how to leash train—"

"Can it. I've had enough of your mouth."

"How d-dare you—"

"You ought to see somebody about that s-stutter," Axel mocked with a laugh.

A sharp scent caused Roxxy to glance at Carol. Fear sweat popped out across the woman's upper lip.

"Sir," said Carol in an unsteady voice. "I can't stop you from being rude, but I *can* contact the ASPCA if you hurt that dog."

"Told you"—the man pointed an index finger like the barrel of a gun—"name's Axel. Not *sir*. Just another example of how you don't listen."

He stepped off the curb and began crossing the street. The chains on his boots clinked with each step. Basher followed in a cringing crawl.

Axel's grin returned as he came within a stride of Carol. "Guess you're the one who needs a lesson."

Roxxy's leash vibrated with the thudding of Carol's heart.

Enough is enough!

"*RARF-RARF-RARF-RARF-RARF!*"

Barks erupted from Roxxy like a string of exploding firecrackers. Axel stumbled backward. She bunched her legs to spring, intending to grab a pant cuff and yank him off his feet, but a hard tug on the leash stopped her.

"Easy, girl, *easy!*" Carol ordered. "And stop that growling."

Roxxy hadn't realized the sound—reminiscent of a stump grinder chewing through hardwood—was coming from her.

"*RARF-RARF-RARF-RARF-RARF!*" She lunged again, but there was no play in the leash.

She leaped like a fish breaking the surface of a lake. Her body twisted to snap the restraint.

Axel stood frozen on the yellow line dividing the street. His eyes widened.

"*RARF-RARF-RARF-RARF-RARF!*"

Yeah, moron, it's me!

"Sit!" Carol ordered.

Roxxy ignored the command. Who *sits* when confronted with a dog-stealing scumbag? She threw herself forward, hoping to pull the leash from Carol's hand.

"*SIT!*"

Roxxy bunched her legs for another leap, but Carol kneeled next to her. Strong fingers slid through her fur as the woman gripped the nylon collar and gave it a determined shake.

"*SIT!*"

Roxxy reluctantly plopped her hindquarters on the sidewalk's rough surface. Her eyes remained fixed on Axel. She made no effort to control her growling, even when Carol enveloped her in a hug. The woman's heartbeat registered against her flank—slower now.

"Lady, if you can't control that mutt, I will."

The skin across the man's cheekbones drew so tight his face resembled the skull tattooed on his bicep.

"How? By *kicking* her?" Carol tightened her arms around Roxxy. "That's what you were going to do to your dog, right?"

Axel took a step forward, dragging the cowering Basher with him. "Lady, I'm going to—"

"*RARF-RARF-RARF-RARF-RARF!*" Roxxy's barking bounced off the houses lining the street.

Axel stopped dead in his tracks. His eyes narrowed as he weighed his options.

"*RARF-RARF-RARF-RARF-RARF!*"

"What's going on out here?"

Roxxy went silent and glanced past Axel, searching for the source of the new voice. She spotted a heavyset older lady with pink curlers in her hair, silhouetted in the open door frame of the house across the street. A cell phone was half raised to the woman's ear.

"Mind your own business!" yelled Axel, half turning and glaring.

"I'll mind what I want! I'm calling the police!"

"Okay, okay!" said Axel. "No need to get the cops involved. Just a misunderstanding."

The woman frowned and looked at Carol. "You okay, hon?"

"She's fine!" snarled Axel before Carol could respond. "I'm leaving. Got things to do."

He gave the prong collar a vicious yank and strode away. Basher yelped and followed.

"Thank you!" Carol called out to the woman.

"I'd stay away from that guy. He looks like a mean one."

Roxxy half listened as Carol again thanked the lady. She was watching Basher, who moved in an odd, jerky shuffle as he accompanied Axel. His belly skimmed the ground as his wide, terrified eyes remained riveted on the human's boots.

She felt herself lifted from the ground. Warm breath fluttered the curls on the side of her face.

"Roxxy, there's no law against those horrible collars, and the guy didn't actually kick the dog. I don't think there's anything I can do. I don't even know where he lives."

Roxxy licked Carol's cheek.

"Nice try, but it'll take a while to get that creep out of my head. Okay, let's go home. It's past your suppertime."

As they retraced their path, Roxxy couldn't shake the image of the cringing pit bull or put aside other troubling thoughts. If Axel was that cruel to his own dog, how was he treating the pets he'd stolen? And what did he have in store for them? Poor Mr. Jacobs. He must be worried to death about Wiggle. He's probably wondering if she's scared and hungry.

The tip of Roxxy's tail dragged the sidewalk as she plodded along next to Carol. She made a halfhearted attempt to raise it. What was the point of thinking about the stolen pets? She remembered her conversation with Leo and Toby. They'd been right to discourage her from trying to stop Axel. Even if she found out where he lived, the dogs he'd taken were certainly being kept someplace else. The situation was hopeless.

Shadows spanned the sidewalk as the day slowly died. She and Carol reached the top of a hill and halted at an intersection. A city bus rumbled by, leaving them in a cloud of diesel fumes. Carol stepped back from the curb, and Roxxy followed in response to a tug on the leash. Idly, Roxxy's gaze went to the distant mountains rising behind the buildings on the opposite side of the street. Forested hills traced a path across the darkening horizon. The sun disappeared below a purple crest, leaving only a fading golden radiance to outline the rounded summit. The sky deepened from blue to indigo, and a scatter of glittering pinpricks appeared. One twinkled far brighter than the rest. Unbeknownst to Roxxy, a matching light kindled deep within her chestnut eyes.

I wish I could help the stolen dogs! I wish I—

A dazzling starburst pinned her like a butterfly to a cork board. Tiny craters revealed themselves in the cement beneath her paws. The grass strip between sidewalk and street glowed so brightly the emerald spine of each blade was visible. Overhead, a chimney swift froze mid-flight. Every quill stood out on the underside of the fanned bronze-gray wings.

"What's up?" Carol asked. "Why did you stop?"

Roxxy blinked. The burst of light disappeared as quickly as it had come. The chimney swift glided toward its evening roost. The grass faded to dull green.

"Come on, sweetie," added Carol, her voice weary but otherwise normal.

Roxxy resisted the insistent pull on the leash and stared disbelievingly at the woman. Was it possible that Carol hadn't seen the dazzling display? A memory niggled at the corner of Roxxy's mind. *In the back yard at home, I was the only one who noticed the starburst. My parents had been droning on about—*

"Young lady." The toe of Carol's sneaker tapped an impatient beat on the sidewalk. "Come *on*."

Roxxy planted her hindquarters on the cement. She wasn't moving until she figured out what was going on. Was she really the only one who could see the starbursts?

"Hey!" woofed a black Newfoundland from behind a chain-link fence enclosing a nearby yard. "Why are you just sitting there? Your person wants you to get a move on."

Roxxy glared at the Clydesdale-sized dog. Newfies were well-known suck-ups, eager to please any human in sight. This one clearly felt entitled to give unsolicited advice.

"Keep your opinions to yourself!" she replied in a series of angry yips. A thought brought her up short. "Did you see that blast of light?"

"Roxxy," said Carol. "Stop yapping at that dog, and let's go! I'm exhausted!"

"Well?" Roxxy continued to focus on the Newfie.

"What light?" A tongue the size of a dish towel swept away drool. He glanced at his home. "I'm going inside before I miss dinner."

Roxxy went rigid as she remembered the previous time she'd seen such a flash of light—in her back yard, right before suppertime, when the stars were coming out. Her parents had been giving a lesson on how to be a good family dog. Which of the qualities had they been talking about? Let's see... *being a good protector!*

"*Roxxxxy!*" said Carol in exasperation. "Home!"

"Bye!" Roxxy called out to the Newfie, allowing herself to be pulled into motion by Carol.

She used her chin to bump the woman affectionately on the ankle and threw in a cheerful yip for good measure.

Carol's green eyes narrowed. "What's put you in such a good mood? Up to something?"

Roxxy felt the air stir from behind.

CHAPTER 18

"You're good for something."

Basher swallowed a whimper and kept pace with his master's long strides as they entered the back yard just after nightfall. *Finally, home!*

A *ping* sounded.

Basher stopped alongside his master as the man removed a cell phone from his back pocket and studied the screen. The device's eerie blue light shone upon features hardening like cement.

Basher averted his eyes, but the action provided little relief. He stared at the thin chains adorning the boots only inches away and resisted the urge to lick the line of pebbly skin stretching across his right shoulder. Instead, he kept as still as possible and slowly swiveled his head to inspect the yard.

The rear of the man's one-level dwelling was dark except where the moon reflected off two small windows flanking the back door. The house, like others in the neighborhood, was small, with warped boards beneath its blistering once-white paint. Basher's nose quaked as the wind stirred. A sweet scent wafted from the tiny, white blossoms of a sprawling Autumn clematis. The shrub was as high as a stepladder and as wide as a garden shed. The plant bordered the outside edge of the worn pathway from the back door to the rear of the carport. The smell mixed unpleasantly with the odor of moldy siding drifting from the house.

Other than the clematis, the only other sizeable shrub in the back yard was a holly taking up a far corner. Small, tight clumps of ribbed-leaf stinging nettles grew here and there in low mounds. Most of the yard was littered with scattered junk—balding tires, an upended sofa with tangled springs sprouting from the moldy base, and other barely recognizable deteriorated objects. Prickly weeds and crabgrass poked through the areas not covered with discarded items.

The breeze quickened and brought the aroma of burgers being grilled at an unseen neighbor's house. Saliva flooded Basher's mouth. He choked but swallowed quickly enough to avoid making a sound. His eyes flicked to the boots again, then away.

The crescent moon cast a weak light on an old metal shed anchoring the corner opposite the holly. A narrow section of corrugated roof had blown off in a storm and was canted against the rear of Basher's chain-link pen. He looked longingly at the enclosure, wishing he was safely inside instead of standing so close to his master.

Basher knew the dimensions of his rectangular space by heart. The narrow sections at the front and back required two strides to cover. The sides took four strides. The ground inside the enclosure was devoid of greenery and would've blunted a pickax. Nevertheless, a well-worn path was etched into the interior perimeter. Basher spent each day pacing within the man-high chain-link pen. He began when the first rays of sunlight appeared over the rooftops and continued until only a sliver of sun was visible above the distant hills in the west. Still, the pen was better than where he'd spent his puppyhood. *That* space had been so small he and his sibs had practically lived on top of their mother. The memory drew a keening whimper from his chest.

"Shut it!" snapped Axel without taking his eyes off the phone.

Basher chastised himself. *Why* couldn't he stay quiet? He stared at his sanctuary inside the pen—a battered wooden crate positioned near the middle of the enclosure. A faded label on one of the slats indicated the container had once been used to ship oranges. Bands of moonlight slanted through the gaps where some of the boards were missing. Basher couldn't wait to curl into a tight ball so that he could fit inside it.

"I hope that text is enough to get Ethan off my back," said Axel.

Basher's ears perked up. His master liked to talk aloud, even when only the two of them were present. The man seemed to enjoy an audience.

"Let's get you back in your pen. Would you like that, boy?"

Basher's stubby tail wagged madly. Maybe he hadn't disappointed his master. Maybe—

"But first," continued Axel, "let's talk about how you made me look like a fool today. The deal fell through because the buyer saw you were scared of your own shadow. Still," Axel paused and grinned, "you're good for something. I could use a little exercise."

Basher gulped. *Oh no, oh no, oh no…*

Chains clinked softly as the boot drew back. Moonlight glittered on the edges of the links.

Bzzzzz, bzzzzz, bzzzzz.

"Great timing," snarled Axel, pausing in mid-kick. He pulled the vibrating cell phone from his pocket and put it to his ear. "What now, Ethan? I just texted you… Yeah, just getting back home… No, I didn't sell him… The buyer changed his mind… You writing a book? Forget Basher. He's history. Why'd you call?"

Basher gulped. History? What did that mean? One more mystery in a day full of them. He'd been shocked when his master had taken him for a walk. *That* was a first. The last time he'd been out of the pen was months ago. His master had driven him late one night to an open field behind a barn. A ring of pickup trucks—mostly old but some new with shiny wheels and oversize tires—sat with headlights on, illuminating three tiers of wooden bench seating. The arrangement surrounded a shallow pit dug into clay soil. Raucous men were crammed shoulder to shoulder on all three tiers, jostling each other and shouting to be heard as they placed bets. Occasionally, a head tilted back to expose an unshaven throat as one of the men took a long pull from a bottle.

Basher recalled how he had taken in the scene while waiting in the cage in the back of the pickup. His master had spoken to one of the men in charge. Before Basher knew what was happening, his master had hustled him to the pit and shoved him in. A coppery smell rose from the red clay floor, and his paw pads grew sticky as he paced, too agitated to stand still. The air was thick with raucous laughter and bloodlust oozing from human pores. Basher was so distracted he didn't notice the other dog being thrown into the pit until its heavy paws thudded softly against the clay.

Basher stood paralyzed as he faced the slavering canine across from him. One look told him something terrible had been inflicted on the poor dog to turn him into such a mindless killer. Basher leaped from the pit before he could be attacked and tried to take refuge beneath the bottom row of seats. The spectators' taunts and laughter rained down. His master had thrown him back into the pit, but he'd sprung out once more and run to the pickup and the open cage. He'd tried to make himself small and wedge into a far corner. His master was too smart for that. His thick fingers had curled around Basher's collar and dragged him around to the side of the truck where no one could see, and…

Basher grunted. The rest of the memory was a blur, which was just as well. Still, why could he never please his master? Today was a perfect example. He'd seen Roxxy and gotten so excited at the prospect of making a friend that he'd pulled his master into the street without thinking. He still couldn't understand why Roxxy and the nice lady had gotten so upset when he was about to be kicked. Didn't they know what happened to bad dogs? He'd expected to be taken home after his master had gotten into the argument with Roxxy's owner, but the walk continued until they'd reached a neighborhood much like his own. The streets were narrow, and paint peeled from the clapboard houses. Yards were filled with scattered beer bottles and junked cars.

His master had stopped in front of one of the most rundown dwellings and half led, half dragged him up the steps of a rickety front porch. Axel had banged so hard on the front door that the windows had rattled in the frames. Startled by the noise, Basher had wet himself and crouched in shame just as the home's occupant threw open the door. The man had looked angry at first, but then his close-set eyes had settled on the spreading yellow pool on the warped boards of the porch. The stranger had burst out laughing and asked Axel if he wanted to borrow a mop. The words had caused his master's face to flatten into the featureless stare. The stranger had turned white and slammed the door so fast flecks of fading paint fluttered down from the frame overhead.

"Hang on a second, Ethan. I can't hear a thing. This stupid dog's teeth are chattering."

Basher could hardly believe his luck when Axel unsnapped the leash from the prong collar. The gate creaked as it swung open. Basher was halfway through the opening when the kick landed in the soft flesh just behind his rib cage. He bounced off the gatepost and staggered forward, managing to avoid most of the piles his master didn't bother to pick up anymore. He heard a familiar wet sound—*ahemmmacCCHHHH!*—and a fat glob of spit splattered on his skull and dribbled down the sides of his head. The next kick landed between his back legs and sent him rolling past the crate to the rear of the pen.

"Useless."

Basher waited until the padlock snapped shut before crawling to the old metal coffee can just inside the gate. The rusting container served as a bowl for those times when his master remembered to feed him. Basher stuck his head inside and sniffed the curved bottom. Not even a morsel. His gaze shifted to the red plastic bucket resting on its side. He nosed it upright and licked the interior. The rasp of his tongue was loud within the confines of the surrounding plastic.

His master used to fill the bucket regularly, but the man had begun skipping days recently.

Basher moved in a scuttling crawl to his crate. The boards lining the bottom were rubbed smooth from where he'd lain before. He curled into the tightest ball his aching ribs would allow. Sleep beckoned, but his master had resumed his phone conversation.

"Just a couple more days, Ethan… Uh huh… Uh huh… Everything's on schedule. I just need to tie up some loose ends."

Something in the man's tone made Basher lift his head and peek from the crate. He accidentally met his master's eyes. As dizziness rocked him, he ripped his gaze away.

"Yeah, he's one of them. It's time to cut my losses. I'll take him up to the Outpost day after tomorrow… Yeah, it's nice and private, even though it's not a long drive to get there. Plus, those foothills deaden sound. Nobody will hear anything."

Basher flattened his cropped ears, but the phrase echoed. *Nobody will hear anything…*

CHAPTER 19

"Remember me?"

Roxxy lay still. The deep, regular breathing of her sibs and parents washed over the family room. The weak light of a crescent moon slanted downward through the picture window at an angle, indicating it was high in the sky and near the middle of its nighttime passage.

Being careful not to disturb Max and Lulu—whose warm bodies nestled on either side of her—she stood. Her claw caught in the flannel blanket of the dog bed. Roxxy froze as Lulu grunted and rolled over. When Lulu's breathing became regular, Roxxy freed the snag with her teeth and stepped out of the bed. A moment later, she was creeping along the hallway, hugging the wall and avoiding the annoying board in the center that creaked when the slightest weight settled on it. A turn into the kitchen and a passage under the breakfast table brought her to the back door. She lowered her head and pushed through the flap near the bottom.

The thick plastic slid along her back. Her tail caught the covering and lowered it into place before it could clatter against the frame.

She paused on the deck, feeling the tightness ease in her muscles. So far, so good. She drew in a breath and tasted the air, checking for the possibility of rain. Good. The night would stay dry. Her nose twitched. Possum. A tilt of her head picked up the soft rustling of leaves behind the fence at the yard's rear. If this was a normal nighttime jaunt, she'd have investigated and barked to warn the critter to keep moving, but tonight she had other priorities.

She trotted down the deck steps and crossed the yard. Dew-covered grass turned the fur on her paws into a soggy tangle. The wheelbarrow was right where she had hoped it would be. The muscles bunched in her legs. A dash/hop/leap sent her sailing over the chain-link fence. She landed gracefully—well, as graceful as a belly flop can be—and scrambled upright.

The blocks zoomed past as she charged down the sidewalk, stopping only to look both ways before crossing any streets. The spot where she'd met Basher was easy to find. She zigzagged across the area, her nose skimming over the cement as she soaked up his scent. A final sniff brought a tail flick of satisfaction.

I could track him anywhere.

Her bangs twitched in a sudden frown. There was a trace of dried poo where his paws had made contact with the cement. Very strange. Canines were usually fastidious about where they stepped. Time to move on. She set off, following Basher's scent and resisting the urge to stop and squat whenever she passed a spot some other presumptuous dog had claimed.

The trail split so suddenly that her head swam. How could it lead in two different directions? She stood indecisively for a moment, then chose the path with the strongest scent, hoping it would take her to Basher's home. After a few blocks, she came to a two-story house with plywood nailed over the windows on the ground floor. Upstairs, moonlight shone on the sharp edges of broken panes in the frames. Loud snoring rumbled past one of the openings. Maybe Axel, maybe not. She didn't need to go up the warped wooden steps leading to the sagging front porch. Even from the yard, she could smell the spot where Basher had wet himself near the front door.

She made a quick circuit of the house. Basher's scent was confined to the steps and the front porch. Had he and Axel come to visit someone? That would explain why the trail she'd followed had the stronger smell. The pair had taken it and then doubled back. A glance at the moon brought a double ear flick of concern. The crescent had dropped more than she'd expected. The night was slipping away! She set off and returned to the spot where the scent divided. A quick sweep over the ground pointed her in the direction she'd passed on before.

Her claws clickety-clicked on the sidewalk, and her breathing deepened as her dead run ate up block after block. She was finally rewarded when Basher's scent led her off the pavement and into the back yard of a corner lot. She slipped beneath a huge holly. Stiff, pointy leaves tugged at her fur as she settled herself. She had a view of the back yard as well as the rear of a small home that squatted on a cinder-block foundation. The windows on either side of the back door were dark, but a bare light bulb burned weakly above the entry, casting a yellow glow that reached only a few feet into the shadowy yard. A sprawling Autumn clematis stood in isolation near a worn path leading from the back door to a covered carport at the side of the house. Axel's pickup was parked with the rusted tailgate facing her.

She blinked. The yard wasn't fenced! That could only mean Basher was in the house with Axel. What to do now? She was torn—pleased that the pit bull wasn't relegated to an existence as a yard dog but disappointed she wouldn't have the opportunity to ask about any of Axel's activities.

What now? A little rest wouldn't hurt before heading home. She yawned and idly compared Axel's messy back yard to Bill and Carol's well-kept garden. The area before her was strewn with items like old tires and discarded furniture. Beyond, a dilapidated aluminum storage shed sat in a corner of the yard. A narrow section of the shed's sheet metal roof had come off and was leaning against the rear of a rectangular chain-link enclosure. Roxxy frowned.

What was that used for?

She nosed aside a holly branch and scooted forward to get a clearer view. A stem caught her collar. A yank freed the snag but caused a clump of berries to rattle alarmingly. She went still and cut her eyes to the house. The windows remained dark.

Definitely time to go!

Being more careful, she wriggled from beneath the holly and trotted to the sidewalk. She couldn't wait to get home and snuggle up with—

Clink…clink…

She stopped in mid-step, swiveling her ears to pinpoint the location of the sound.

Clink…clink…

She crept back to the shrub and slid under the low-hanging branches. Her gaze fixed on the fenced enclosure, which contained a couple of buckets and a wooden crate with several slates missing.

A formless shadow shifted within the crate.

Clink…clink…

Her breath caught as moonlight glinted on the prongs of the collar surrounding Basher's thick neck. He twitched again in his sleep.

Clink…clink…

She tried to process the situation, but her mind refused to accept what she was seeing. Basher couldn't be confined to such a small area. Didn't make sense. How was he supposed to *live*—to patrol the yard, to discover interesting scents, to run and play?

Roxxy squeezed her eyes shut and reopened them. Nothing had changed.

She understood now why Basher had been so excited on the walk. The new smells and sights must have been wondrous. The pen wasn't a home. It was a prison! And what were those small piles scattered around the interior of the enclosure. Was Basher a digger? She was still trying to figure it out when the breeze shifted, and the smell hit her full in the face. She vomited and half-digested kibble splattered the ground between her front paws. Another retch followed. When her stomach was empty, she crept from beneath the holly and cleaned her muzzle by rubbing both sides on a patch of crabgrass. Somewhat dazed, she trotted to the pen. Basher lay half outside the crate, still sleeping fitfully.

Roxxy hesitated. *I need to wake him gently, or he'll sound an alarm.* She huffed a quiet greeting and tensed as Basher stirred. He half rose on trembling legs and stared at her. Terror shone in his gray eyes, constricting his irises into tiny dots surrounded by widened rounds of white. He crept from the crate in a crouching shuffle, dipping a shoulder to avoid a jagged nail sticking from a broken slat. The tips of his cropped ears drooped in submission.

Realization hit her. Basher was so abused by Axel that he'd lost the basic canine instinct to challenge a trespasser on his own territory. Her heart constricted. What kind of torment must he have suffered? She forced the thought away and focused on the mission at hand—get information about Axel's dog-stealing operation.

"Hi, Basher," she huffed quietly. "Remember me? I'm Roxxy."

CHAPTER 20

"Be ready."

Roxxy waited as Basher's eyes widened in recognition. The corners of his mouth tugged back in a goofy smile of welcome, exposing mottled pink-and-black gums. An all-over-body wag sent his narrow hips swinging from side to side.

"Listen," she began, "I've come to—"

"How did you find me?" interrupted Basher in an excited babble.

Chain links rattled as he jammed his face against the mesh to touch noses. "I'm so glad you came!"

"Hush!" she ordered, throwing a glance at Axel's house.

She waited—heart pounding—but the windows remained dark. When she looked back, Basher was trembling like a chastised puppy wondering what he'd done wrong.

Roxxy continued in a huff that was little more than a whisper, "Sorry if I sounded mean, but you need to be quiet as a mouse. I don't want Axel to know I'm here."

She gently pressed her nose against the chain-link fence, and Basher did so as well. She noted that the metal was cool, but his rubbery pink nose was hot and dry. A glance inside the pen revealed the reason—overturned buckets.

She pulled back and suppressed a growl. *How long had it been since Basher ate or had a drink?*

"I-I'm sorry I barked," said the pit bull. "I'm always messing up."

"Take it easy. You were excited. No big deal."

"You're just being nice." His front paws kneaded the dirt. A thin string of silvery drool fell from the corner of his mouth and slid down his gray foreleg. "I can't do *anything* right!"

She groaned. If he didn't calm down, she'd never get any sense out of him. Inspiration struck.

"Basher," she said. "You're a *good* dog."

His ears lifted. "You really think so?"

"No doubt about it." She wondered yet again why the term had such a magical effect on canines. She suppressed a snort. Well... *most* canines.

"Roxxy, do you mean it? I'm really a good dog?"

She tilted her head to the side and studied him. "I guess you don't hear that very often."

"Never!" Basher flicked his eyes to Axel's house. "I'm a big disappointment to my master."

"Your what?"

"My master—Axel—you met him when he was walking me."

Roxxy frowned. What was this *master* stuff? She was fond of people in general, and she adored Bill and Carol when they weren't blathering on about some rule or other, but she never thought of humans as her *masters*. In fact, Bill and Carol would be lost if she and the other dogs weren't around to look after them.

Basher continued. "Speaking of my master, I'm sorry he was mean to that nice lady who was walking you."

"Not your fault. I—*Aaachooooo!*" She rubbed a paw across her muzzle, trying to forestall another sneeze.

The eye-watering stench rising from the scattered piles was almost more than she could take.

"Sorry," said Basher.

His head bowed in shame, and his legs trembled so violently that he sagged against the side of the enclosure. The chain links pressed a diagonal pattern into his short coat.

"I'm used to the smell, but I know it must be terrible for you. I don't remember the last time my master cleaned up the poop. Don't get me wrong," he added quickly. "It's not his fault. If I wasn't such a disappointment to him, he'd take better care of me."

Roxxy hesitated, wondering if it would do any good to tell Basher *no* animal deserved to spend its life in such a small pen, much less surrounded by its own waste. She gave a mental shrug. There wasn't enough time for her to try and convince him, and he probably wouldn't believe her anyway.

"Whoo-whoo-whoooooo…"

A great horned owl glided into view, skimming past the roofline of Axel's house. The tufted tips of the raptor's ears ruffled in the glide path, but the gray-and-black form was perfectly silent. Its wide wings sliced through the air like scythes, and the luminescent yellow eyes scanned the ground. Roxxy was suddenly glad Leo wasn't with her. Owls and Pomeranians didn't mix well—at least for the Poms.

"Some birds are pretty," said Basher, studying the owl as it passed overhead. "But I don't like those things."

"Me either," replied Roxxy. "But let's get back to you. How long have you been cooped up in this pen?"

"A couple of months. Ever since my master bought me."

"Why did he bother getting you"—she gestured at the enclosure with her chin—"just to leave you out here? Dogs are meant to live *with* people, not in solitary confinement."

"My master got me to be a fighter." Basher shuddered. "I was terrible at it."

"Wait a minute," said Roxxy, thoroughly mystified. "Fight *who*?"

She glanced at Axel's house to be sure the dwelling was still dark. So far, so good.

"Don't you know? Some humans make dogs fight in pits. People bet money on who's going to win." He frowned. "*Why* are you staring at me?"

"I-I didn't know something like that even existed." She swallowed. "You poor thing."

Basher replied gruffly, "I wasn't trying to make you feel sorry for me."

"I know you weren't. I…" She picked up the sound of a car engine.

Roxxy glanced past Axel's house to the street. An old vehicle with a cracked windshield drove slowly past. The female driver yawned and absently picked at one of the curlers in her gray hair. On the passenger side, a girl only slightly older than Kimberly was in the process of throwing folded newspapers out the window. Each landed with a soft *smack* as it hit precisely in the middle of a driveway. The car passed by Axel's house without making a delivery.

Roxxy glanced to the east. The night sky had lightened to cobalt.

"Do you need to go?" asked Basher.

She nodded. "Yeah, but first I have to ask you something."

"Okay."

"Do you know that Axel steals dogs?"

"*What?*"

"Quiet!" she ordered. "He steals pets. I saw him almost snatch my next-door neighbor—a little guy named Leo. Axel zapped him with pepper spray and shoved him into a burlap bag, but Leo got lucky and escaped."

Basher gulped. "I knew my master didn't like *me* because I'm a disappointment, but I never thought he was capable of stealing pets. What does he do with them?"

"That's what I was hoping you could tell me. He has to keep them somewhere. Does he have a big storage building?"

"Not that I know of. I mostly just get a glimpse of him when he comes and goes. He usually leaves before mid-morning and sometimes makes a stop back in the afternoon, but he often doesn't."

"Does he go out much at night?"

"He leaves late *every* evening and stays away for a couple of hours, but he usually gets back around midnight."

"Weird that he goes out so late," said Roxxy.

"Very." The tight skin across Basher's forehead wrinkled in a thin line. "The only thing I know about where he goes is what I overheard him say on the phone today."

"What's that?"

"My master was putting me back in here"—Basher indicated the pen with a sweep of his jaw—"when a guy phoned, and they talked about a place that my master goes to sometimes. It's in the foothills and called the Outpost."

"Outpost?"

"Could be a cabin, I guess."

"Did you hear anything about stolen dogs?"

"Sorry, not a word."

"Okay." Roxxy fought to keep her tail from drooping.

All her hopes had rested on Basher knowing where Axel was keeping the stolen pets. There were undoubtedly too many to be stored in a cabin. The realization that she was at a dead end left a bad taste in her mouth, like the time she'd snatched up a lemon wedge that had fallen to the kitchen floor. Her tongue curled at the memory.

"Now that I think about it," continued Basher, "my master didn't *say* the Outpost is a cabin. I assumed it was because of the foothills remark. I guess the Outpost could be a storage building of some kind. I was kind of distracted."

Basher paused and gulped.

"What?" asked Roxxy.

"When my master was talking on the phone, he said he was planning to take me up there and cut his losses. He was staring right at me when he said it. I…I think maybe…he's going to do something bad to me."

"So, the Outpost could be a storage building?" Her heart pounded so hard a tiny web of veins registered at the corners of her eyes.

"I think you're missing the point," said Basher, edging closer to the chain-link fence. "Whatever the place is used for, something terrible is going to happen to me there."

"Uh huh." *Can I find the building before Axel moves the stolen dogs?*

"Roxxy, are you listening? When my master said he planned to cut his losses, he was talking about getting rid of *me*!"

"Obviously," she muttered. *What was the best way to find the Outpost?* Her mind raced. Follow Axel? Impossible. That left only…

"Basher, I'll be back in a second." She dashed away.

"What? *Wait!*"

He shifted impatiently from paw to paw as the blond figure disappeared around the corner of Axel's home. He heard her nails click against the carport's cement floor. She returned at an even faster clip.

"What were you doing?" he demanded.

"Had to check something out." She sighed. It was the only way to locate the Outpost, but Toby and Leo were going to have a fit.

"Well, don't let me *distract* you!" said Basher. "I tell you my master's going to kill me, and you go haring off in the middle of the conversation."

"Oh, that." She flicked an ear dismissively.

The tip of his stubby tail pointed at the ground. "Can't you at show some sympathy?"

"What good would that do?"

Basher sputtered. "How can you be so *heartless*?"

"Wait a minute." Roxxy looked at him, dumbfounded. "Don't you understand?"

"Understand *what*?"

"I'm getting you out of here."

Basher's jaw dropped.

"Stop looking so shocked," she grumbled. "What did you think I was going to do? Let that maniac have his way?"

"Roxxy, there *isn't* a way out. Besides, my master—"

"Enough with the *master* stuff. Just say creep, and I'll know who you're talking about."

"That's not the point. Regardless of what we call him, he's going to get rid of me soon."

"How soon?"

"Very." Basher glanced to the east.

Roxxy followed his gaze. Cobalt had given way to light blue.

"From what Axel mentioned to that guy on the phone," continued Basher, "he'll be c-cutting his losses tomorrow."

"Well, that means I need to come back tonight and get you out."

"No!"

Her ears perked forward at the sudden firmness in his tone. She waited.

"I can't let you risk that, Roxxy."

"Why?"

"Well, a few weeks ago, a raccoon made a racket trying to get into the garbage. Axel charged outside with a baseball bat and cornered the animal against the side of the house." Basher stared at the bare dirt between his front paws. "There was hardly anything left of the raccoon afterward. I c-can't let the same thing happen to you."

A desperate squeal drew her attention to the yard next door. The owl was on the ground, its talons sunk into a rabbit's neck. The bunny's back legs kicked, sending tufts of grass flying, but the predator's curved beak struck. Bone crunched, and the rabbit went still. The owl launched itself from the ground and hung suspended as its wings beat once, twice, three times before catching air. Drops of blood—black in the moonlight—fell from the rabbit's limp form.

"Bad sign," croaked Basher.

Roxxy suppressed a shiver. *No kidding.*

He continued. "Even if you found a way to help me escape, Axel would track me down."

"He's planning on getting rid of you. Why would he care if you ran off?"

Basher looked at her pityingly. "Roxxy, you're so…so *innocent!*"

"That's not the general consensus," she said wryly.

"You don't understand," insisted Basher. "My master doesn't want me, but he doesn't want anybody *else* to have me. I'll never be safe from him."

"I'll find you a forever home," she said confidently, wondering when she'd lost her mind. Hard to pinpoint that kind of thing. She gave herself a brisk shake. "Axel will never find you."

"But—"

"Hush and let me think." She gnawed absently at a paw pad to dislodge a pebble caught in the soft webbing between her toes.

The little stone rolled away and plinked against one of the pen's support poles. Hmmm…how to get Basher out? The chain-link fence was too high for any dog to jump, and there were no gaps to squeeze through. And the ground at the base was too hard packed for digging.

Feeling less confident by the minute, her gaze swept the perimeter of the enclosure.

And stopped abruptly.

"Basher," she said slowly. "Here's what we're going to do when I come back tonight."

The outline of the plan went quickly.

"So that's it," she finished. "All good?"

"All good?" Basher asked. "How about, all *bad*? I appreciate the risk you're willing to take, but there's no way your idea will work."

He backed away and wiggled his hindquarters into the opening of his crate, flinching as the rusty nail grazed his flank. "Roxxy, I can't let you put yourself in danger, especially by trying something so crazy. There's no point in *you* getting killed trying to save *me*! Stop and think about everything that could go wrong."

Her gaze drifted to the eastern sky. Cobalt had lightened to violet, and a thin line of robin's-egg blue outlined the distant hills. Above, a familiar star burned brightly, refusing to yield to the coming dawn. She waited for a burst of encouraging light, but it didn't come.

Thanks a lot.

"Roxxy, what are you frowning at?"

"Nothing. Just be ready when I come back tonight."

"But—"

"Be ready," she repeated.

In the east, a sliver of sun edged above the curve of the earth. The star winked out.

AXEL

Axel's nostrils dilated as hickory smoke drifted into the cab of the truck. Saliva filled his mouth. The makeshift barbecue stand near the parking lot entrance was doing a brisk business selling ribs and chicken to customers visiting the strip mall. He turned and spat out the window. The barbecue guys were having better luck than he was. He'd been parked in an inconspicuous corner for nearly—

Beep-beep-beep.

Axel cursed and killed the timer on the cell phone. He was using the feature to help him avoid staying too long in one spot, but he resented having to find a new location every half hour. Had to be done, though. Even more flyers had gone up around town. Worse still, they pictured that stupid dachshund he'd snatched from the old man's car and warned that a dog thief was in the area.

He started the engine and guided the pickup past the barbecue stand. The smell of roasting pork filled the cab. His stomach rumbled as he turned onto the street and carefully accelerated. Maybe the key to avoiding the double backfire was—

BANG! BANG!

The sounds exploded from the muffler, and an instant later a curse ripped from Axel's throat. The heat of a lava-like flush spread from neck to chest. He canted his upper body toward the side window and let the airstream wash over his face. A few more days and things would be different. He'd deliver a full shipment and collect the money. A truck dealership would be next on the list—after taking care of Ethan, of course. The thought brought a grin of anticipation.

The cell phone vibrated in his pocket.

Speak of the devil...

"Ethan, how are you doing this fine afternoon?"

"Why so jolly?"

"Just my sunny disposition."

"Keep it to yourself. You going to meet the deadline?"

"Absolutely. A few more units, and I'm good to go," replied Axel.

"You sure?"

"Relax. I'll make delivery on time."

"By the way," Ethan said casually. "You never gave me the details on what went wrong with selling Bashful. Did the buyer wise up?"

"You're fading," grated Axel.

"Reception seems fine to me," replied Ethan. "What happened to your sunny disposition?"

Axel thumbed the button to end the call. The traffic light ahead turned red, and he stomped on the brake. The pickup's tires screeched. A muscle twitched in his jaw as yesterday's events came flooding back. One disaster after another. First, he'd somehow crossed paths with the blond mutt who'd been nothing but trouble since day one. To make matters worse, its owner had the nerve to give *him* advice on how to control

Basher. He was about to put her in her place when the mutt had gone crazy and tried to snap its leash.

A creak from the steering wheel alerted Axel to loosen his grip. No use cracking the rounded plastic. He hadn't been *afraid* of the dog. No way. The mutt couldn't have weighed over thirty, thirty-five pounds. So, why hadn't he waded in and given it a taste of the boot? Was it that ear-splitting bark? Or something about the eyes? Almost like they were burning with...

Axel shook his head. *Stop imagining things!*

The day had gone downhill after the encounter with the woman and the mutt. When he'd finally arrived at the buyer's house, the jerk backed out of the deal to buy Basher. One thing after another.

The traffic light changed, and Axel stepped on the accelerator.

BANG! BANG!

The backfire was still reverberating as a vintage black Corvette sped past in the adjoining lane. The low-slung obsidian car gleamed with the luster of a black pearl, and the dual chrome exhausts under the back bumper burbled with controlled power.

Axel's eyes tracked the Vette. It was well ahead when a taillight blinked bright red, signaling the intention to enter Axel's lane. He cursed and floored the gas pedal.

BANG! BANG!

The pickup caught the Vette and cut it off. The two vehicles came within an inch of trading paint, but the nimble sports car swerved back into its lane. Axel pulled alongside and got a good look at the driver—a balding, burly guy wearing a short-sleeved shirt that revealed a skull-and-crossbones tattoo on a muscled bicep.

The Vette accelerated.

Axel stomped the gas—*BANG! BANG!*—and kept the truck wheel to wheel with the glistening car.

The driver's face darkened to a mottled purple, and his hand shot up with a raised middle finger. He pumped his arm to emphasize the gesture.

Axel caught the man's eye and slackened his features into a dead-eyed stare.

Blood drained from the Vette driver's face. He gave a hard wrench of the steering wheel. The car rocketed into a side street, veering side to side while the man tried to regain control.

Axel followed but kept well back.

The Vette jumped the curb. The *screech* of metal on metal sounded as the front quarter panel slid into a yellow fire hydrant. Momentum carried the car forward. The side-cap on the hydrant gouged out a horizontal strip from bumper to bumper. A ribbon of glistening black metal lay in the street like a snake with a broken back.

Axel grinned as he left the slowing Vette behind.

He eased back in his seat and rethought the situation with Basher. What difference did it make that the scheme to sell the mutt hadn't worked? *The dog will be history by tomorrow.* And a few days after that? Ethan will follow.

Axel's grin widened as he thought about the fat stacks of cash he'd be raking in. He made a pistol of his right hand by extending the forefinger and cocking the thumb. He pointed through the windshield and stomped on the gas while dropping his thumb twice in quick succession.

BANG! BANG!

As the double backfire faded, Axel pantomimed blowing a curl of smoke from the barrel of the imaginary gun.

CHAPTER 21

"You don't want bacon? Are you dying?"

Roxxy's puppy-length legs were so short that clearing the bottom lip of the dog door was a challenge. She stumbled as she passed through. A glance at her paws revealed her blond fur was now ghostly white under the light of the full moon. Her nose quaked as she sifted the scents of mulched rose beds, a savory burger wrapper in a nearby trash bin, and a hint of field mouse beneath the nearby garden shed. The aromas were familiar from her trips outside with her parents and sibs during the daytime, but the smells were somehow heavier at night.

She knew she shouldn't be outside so late. Her parents had warned her it wasn't safe for puppies, but what could be the harm? She'd almost asked Max and Lulu to join her on the adventure, but they were such goodie-goodies when it came to following the rules. Totally brainwashed by the lessons in how to be a good dog. Ugh! She could think for herself, thank you very much, which was why she was here. She'd picked up the musky scent of a raccoon earlier in the afternoon. The critter had passed along the back fence sometime the previous evening. They were only active at night, which meant she had to sneak out to get a glimpse of one. Her tail twitched with excitement as she imagined telling Max and Lulu that she'd laid eyes on a big fat raccoon! Of course, she'd make sure her parents weren't in earshot. She could just imagine her Momma's and Poppa's reactions if they found out.

Good dogs don't sneak out, blah blah blah!

Her legs were so short that her body rocked side to side as she navigated the steps down to the yard. The height of the treads was tough on a puppy's short limbs. She couldn't wait to be as big as her parents—or at least her mother, who Bill and Carol said she was the spitting image of. *Spitting* was a human thing. One of their few traits that she envied.

The dew-covered lawn seemed to drag at her paws. Had she made the right decision in sneaking out? She put the thought aside and trudged toward the rear of the property. Halfway to the back fence, an icy ribbon etched its way down her spine. She paused and looked over her shoulder. The moonlight illuminated each of her footsteps. The paw prints were dark against the glistening lawn, exposing a track that led right to her. She shivered. Maybe trying to find the raccoon wasn't so smart.

"Bad doggy."

She faced forward so quickly that pain blossomed behind her eyes. A human giant loomed in front of her, raising a baseball bat as thick as a tree trunk. Air whistled as he swung the club toward her skull! She tried to dodge, but the wet grass had grown over her paws and held her tight.

"Wake up, Sis!" demanded Lulu, shoving a cold nose against Roxxy's ear. "You're whimpering."

"Am not," she huffed shakily, squinting against the morning sun streaming through the family-room window.

She groaned. A half hour of sleep, tops. She had crawled back into bed just as her housemates began to stir from *their* good night's rest. She'd hoped they'd let her doze away the morning, but her sister clearly had other ideas.

"Come *on*, Roxx!" Lulu woofed. "Bill's cooking bacon. If you do your baby-seal thing, he'll cave. Make those bangs tremble!"

"Not hungry. Go 'way."

"You don't want bacon? Are you *dying*?"

"Okay, okay, I'm coming," she grumbled, not wanting to rouse suspicions. "Can you tone down the youthful enthusiasm?"

"Don't be so grumpy. Besides, I'm *older* than you. Hurry up!"

Roxxy watched the black tip of Lulu's tail disappear around the doorway, followed by the merry clatter of claws on hardwood. *It's not the age,* she thought grouchily, *it's the mileage.*

Roxxy licked the inside of the bowl, enjoying the last morsel of savory bacon-y goodness. She stared at her reflection in the bottom of the stainless-steel dish, and chestnut eyes narrowed accusingly. *Idiot!* Why had she told Basher she'd help him escape? Even worse, why had she been dumb enough to promise to place him in a forever home?

Her reflection—if not her mood—brightened as she polished the interior of the bowl with a final desultory lick. She left the laundry room and plodded across the kitchen to reach the dog door.

The sun was pleasantly warm on her shoulders as she patrolled the perimeter of the fence. A dry rustling drew her attention to a pile of leaves neatly raked into a gold-and-crimson mound at the base of an oak. A young squirrel exploded out of the mound and soared straight up. He landed and rolled playfully in the multicolored pile, sending leaves flying. Coming upright, he launched himself in an arcing leap and settled amid a wide patch of acorns near the oak's trunk. His cheeks rapidly filled to bulging. Roxxy gave a halfhearted woof to put the rodent on notice that she was the boss of him. He paused in his nut gathering, studied her briefly with shining black eyes, and went back to stuffing himself.

She suppressed a fleeting temptation to bark more assertively. Who was she kidding? The pesky squirrel was the least of her worries. She continued along the fence, no closer to solving the dilemma of how to get Basher into a loving home. All this fretting was cutting into her naptime. At this rate, she might as well be human. *They* never seemed to relax.

She trotted past the well-kept garden shed. Forest-green walls supported a pitched red-shingled roof. A small front porch contained two rocking chairs. Cobwebs stretched from the tips of the curved bases to the plank flooring. She snorted. Makes my point about humans. Bill and Carol rarely used the cozy porch. They were diligent about *working* in the yard, but she wished they would savor *relaxing* in it. She decided the next time she found them weeding or engaging in some other compulsory activity she'd sidle alongside and ramp up the cuteness until they couldn't resist taking a break to pet her.

She sighed. *A giver, that's what I am.*

She reached her destination—a stretch of low-growing mint on the shed's south side. She plopped. A refreshing scent rose from the crushed petals, and the springy stems created a soft pallet against her flank. She ordered herself not to go to sleep. She still had to come up with a plan to find Basher a forever home. Maybe she could—

"*Ouch!*" she yelped, more startled than hurt by the bite on the tip of her tail.

Max's snort echoed off the side of the shed. "Got you!"

She whirled and leapt in one motion, enjoying the way his eyes widened at her quickness. He spun and took a single bounding stride, but she landed on his back and rode him to the ground. Her teeth clamped on a triangular ear. She applied pressure. He went still.

"Gib?" she asked.

"Let go, Roxx. I was just teaching you to be more alert."

Her jaws tightened. "Gib?"

"Okay." Max grunted. "I *gib*. Happy now?"

"Reasonably so," she said brightly, wriggling off his broad back. "Using you as a chewy always lightens my mood."

"Glad to be of service." He lifted his hind paw and scratched the damp ear. "How did you get airborne so fast? That was quick, even for you."

"Really? I thought I was a bit slow."

"I bet you do."

"Maxey, you did a good job of sneaking up on me." She settled back on the bed of mint. "Now run along. I've got some planning to do."

"I'll keep you company." He sprawled next to her. "And try to talk you out of it."

"Why?"

"The plans you come up with usually involve the destruction of property or some kind of mayhem."

She'd be able to concentrate better if he left, but…well, the good-natured oaf was comforting to have around.

She leaned over and licked the ear she'd gnawed. "Sorry, big brother. I hope I didn't hurt you. I'm just tired and irritable."

"As opposed to your usual state of being—*rested* and irritable?"

"Very quick-witted, Maxey." She yawned. "For you."

"Roxx?" He cocked his head and studied her. "You *do* look tired. Exhausted, even. What's up?"

"Yeah," added Lulu, trotting over to join them. Her dark eyes were soft as she studied Roxxy. "At breakfast, you didn't try to coerce Bill into giving us a second helping of bacon. You live for second helpings."

Roxxy hesitated. She considered telling her sibs about Basher and her intention to pull off a rescue, but she knew Max and Lulu would insist on helping. She couldn't risk that.

"Come on, Roxx," said Max. "Give."

Lulu added, "Please, Sis. Whatever's going on, you don't have to deal with it alone."

Roxxy's mouth went dry as she imagined her sibs facing Axel.

She shot upright and snarled. "Can't you leave me alone? For *once*?"

Max and Lulu stared wide-eyed, huddling together for comfort.

She dashed away before the urge to apologize became overwhelming. *It's for their own good!*

Her legs churned as she charged up the deck steps. They didn't slow until she reached the dog door. She pushed through and was midway across the kitchen before she noticed Carol sitting at the breakfast table. The woman wore comfortable flannel pajamas and a pink terry-cloth robe. Steam rose from an ignored coffee cup by her elbow.

"Vicky, I'm *so* sorry. I know how hard this must be for you," said Carol, pressing a cell phone to her ear.

Roxxy stared worriedly. The woman's slender form slumped in the chair.

Carol dabbed her eyes with a tissue before she continued hoarsely. "We both knew it was coming, but still…"

Roxxy instantly went into comforting mode, positioning herself next to the chair and whining with concern as she tried to make eye contact. Carol seemed oblivious, though, completely absorbed in the phone conversation. Roxxy decided to stay put in case she was needed to provide an adoring look or an encouraging tail wag. Her eyes swept the floor in case a bit of bacon might've fallen from the table during breakfast. No harm in multitasking. Unfortunately, the hardwood was spotless. She leaned against Carol's pajama-clad ankle. The flannel and the woman's body heat were a soothing combo. Roxxy's eyelids fluttered and closed even as she ordered herself not to go to sleep…

She woke with a start and sat up straight.

Stupid flannel.

"Vicky, I'm looking forward to seeing you tomorrow morning… Uh huh. Give me a call if you want to talk before then. No, you won't be bothering me, I promise… Yes… Yes… Take care, and don't forget to call if you need anything at all… Bye now." Carol pressed a button on the phone and said softly in the tone that humans use for talking to themselves, "So sad."

Roxxy frowned. *Enough was enough!* Carol needed to be comforted, and she had a willing canine right next to her. Roxxy didn't embrace all the traits involved in being a good dog—*obedience* was a total scam—but providing comfort was her specialty. She rose on her back legs and placed her front paws on Carol's thigh.

"Oh, hi, Roxxy." A weak smile brightened the woman's features. "Didn't notice you were here."

Roxxy deepened her breathing to the vibrating thrum she could initiate on demand. The skill was her only useful inheritance—as far as she could tell—from the unknown pug ancestor. The sonorous sound was her version of a purr and could soothe humans as effectively as tucking a warm blanket around them on a cold night. She gazed at Carol with a wide-eyed expression of dewy adoration while wondering if she was laying it on a bit thick. Probably not. Subtlety was usually wasted on humans.

"You're a cutie," said Carol. "But even you can't make me feel better right now."

Roxxy lifted one ear and dropped the other. *Seriously?*

She rested her chin on Carol's thigh and gazed upward while batting her lashes to send fleecy bangs aflutter. Her paws curled while gently kneading the flannel-clad leg.

Carol's dimples appeared. "You win."

Roxxy suppressed a snort. It almost wasn't fair.

Job finished, she started to push away but found herself encircled in the woman's arms and hoisted into a warm lap.

"And you're *definitely* not a puppy anymore." Carol grunted. "You're heavier than Molly."

Roxxy forgave the comment about her weight and licked away the salty remnants of a tear on Carol's cheek.

"You"—the woman's voice caught—"are a fluff ball of love. You know that?"

Fluff ball?

The next lick caught Carol full on the lips.

"Ewww!" The exclamation was a half squeal, half giggle. "You did that on purpose!"

Roxxy tried to squirm free so she could go and think about finding Basher a forever home, but Carol's arms held her fast.

"Poor Vicky. She had to have Ferris put down yesterday. He was *such* a sweetie, and they were so close. The worst part? He could always comfort her when she was sad, but now she's sad because he's gone." Carol placed her chin on top of Roxxy's head. "Ironic, huh?"

Roxxy yawned. She didn't get *ironic*—humans and their overly complicated concepts! She supposed it had something to do with their brains trying to keep up with those active thumbs. *Or was it the other way around?* Even *that* idea made her head hurt. In any case, human ingenuity should've stopped with the can opener. Every invention after that seemed to distract people from the real pleasures in life—snuggling, napping, checking for new smells in the yard, and snacking. Never forget snacking.

Irony aside, Roxxy understood why Vicky was devastated over Ferris's passing. The pair had come to visit often since she was a puppy. Carol and Vicky would have coffee at the mahogany table in the dining room.

Ferris would lie at Vicky's feet, his gray chin resting on the carpet. Roxxy enjoyed ambling in and huffing a respectful hello to the old Lab. His filmy eyes would brighten when they settled on her, and his thick tail beat the floor as he woofed his usual greeting. "There's my favorite troublemaker! What kind of mischief have you been up to?"

She sighed.

Once you get a rep, it's hard to live it down.

She snuggled deeper into Carol's arms and inhaled the almond-scented hand lotion along with the clean, musky aroma of sleep that still clung to the woman's skin. News of Ferris's passing wasn't a surprise but was nevertheless heart-wrenching. Roxxy had noticed during the last few visits that the old dog had grown more and more frail. His skin hung on his bones, and he could barely rise without yelping in pain. When she had last seen him, he'd told her in a raspy huff that Vicky had no family other than him. He couldn't stop fretting about how she'd cope after he was gone.

"Vicky's coming over for coffee tomorrow," continued Carol, as if musing aloud was helping to organize her thoughts. "She's heartbroken and all alone now. I wish she'd get another dog, but she's determined to wait a while. I guess that makes sense, although I think Ferris would want her to have a new—*hey*! What's gotten into you?"

Roxxy wiggled out of Carol's arms and leaped to the floor. Her claws scrabbled on the hardwood as she tried to get traction. Her shoulder thumped a table leg, and the coffee cup rattled in its saucer. She launched herself for the dog door leading to the back yard.

"Stop!" snapped Carol.

Roxxy groaned but obeyed by stiffening her legs and leaning back to come to a sliding halt. Some of that stupid good-dog stuff had apparently sunk in without her realizing it.

Inconvenient.

"What"—Carol's manicured nails drummed the tabletop—"are you up to?"

Roxxy tried to appear guileless. Her tongue lolled from the corner of her mouth while her ears tilted at half-mast in an expression of simple-minded confusion. She sent Max a silent thank you for modeling the look.

Carol rolled her eyes. "Nice try, but it doesn't suit you."

Roxxy dropped the act and grunted impatiently. *I have things to do!*

"That's more like it, but I'll tell you this—I'd better not find anything chewed to pieces. And don't think I haven't noticed my birthday scarf is missing."

The comment found its mark. Roxxy's tail drooped. *Stupid cashmere!*

Carol sighed. "Scoot, but *please* stay out of trouble."

Roxxy whirled and pushed through the plastic flap. She paused on the deck and spotted Max and Lulu in a far back corner of the yard. The pair circled a gopher hole, sniffing enthusiastically. Good. They were too distracted to notice her. She descended the steps, being careful to make as little noise as possible, and trotted around the corner of the house. The muscles in her shoulders relaxed once she was out of Max and Lulu's line of sight. She peered through the chain-link fence separating the back yard from the front. On the other side of the fence, the entry to the crawl space was just as she remembered it—a square wooden door about her height set in a narrow wooden frame, surrounded by the house's brick wall.

Her gaze shifted when a black lizard sporting iridescent blue stripes along its tail climbed up the brick wall and stopped at eye level with her. The creature crooked its head with a jerky motion and settled a shining ebony eye on her.

A growl burbled in her throat, but she stopped short of unleashing a bark to send the lizard on its way. Her will was tested when the reptile's tiny legs pumped in a series of push-ups to claim its territory.

Her growl deepened.

As if!

She dismissed the impudent creature and stared through the chain-link fence at the latch on the crawl space entry.

Why did humans make everything so complicated?

CHAPTER 22

"Run!"

Just as she had the previous night, Roxxy waited until everyone in the household was asleep before sneaking out the dog door. The deck's pine boards were cold against her paw pads. She sucked in a startled breath of frigid air. *First frost!* She exhaled, sending a billowy cone streaming before her as she trotted down the steps. Stiff blades of grass found their way between her toes. Trying to warm up, she did a quick circuit around the yard's perimeter before using the trusty wheelbarrow as a jumping-off point to clear the fence.

The journey to Basher's house went much faster than the night before. She arrived after a quarter hour or so of steady cantering. Her throat was raw from sucking in icy air. She slithered beneath the holly she'd used previously as a vantage point and stayed low to avoid the pointy ends of the leaves. Everything in the yard was as she remembered it, including

Basher's pen at the back of the lot, but tonight, he wasn't curled up in the dilapidated crate that served as a makeshift doghouse. Instead, he sat bolt upright just inside the gate. His only noticeable features were his eyes—two white orbs, wide with fear.

Her throat made a dry click as she swallowed.

We're dead if he panics at the wrong moment.

Her gaze shifted to the object that had caught her attention the night before—the two-foot by eight-foot length of sheet metal propped against the rear of Basher's pen. One narrow end canted over the top of the chain-link wall. The other rested on the ground outside. The metal surface shone silver under the sickle moon's light. The nearby shed had a gap in the roof that was the same size.

Roxxy gave a soft huff of satisfaction. Thank goodness Axel hadn't moved the panel during the day. Speaking of... She glanced at his house. The good news was the weak light that had burned over the back door last night was now off. The bad news was that the glow of a television set came through the grimy windows at the rear of the dwelling. Worse still, Axel's braying guffaws mingled with the show's canned laughter.

A shiver ran through her that had nothing to do with the cold. She'd hoped Axel would be asleep when she arrived. Freeing Basher from the pen was going to create a tremendous racket. The noise would certainly cause the man to come out and investigate. Dealing with a bleary-eyed, sleep-addled Axel was one thing, but confronting a wide-awake, weapon-wielding maniac was another. Oh well. She still had the element of surprise working for her. But then again, Axel had the bat.

Her eyes narrowed as a wisp of fog curled across the flickering light coming through the window. She'd been so preoccupied with her concerns about Axel that she hadn't noticed the misty tendrils starting to rise from the ground. She sucked in a breath, tasting a mix of frosty air and heavy dew. A satisfied growl tickled the back of her throat. *Come on, fog!*

She slid from beneath the holly and trotted to Basher's pen, navigating around the junk scattered in the yard.

"R-R-Roxxy?" The metal links in Basher's prong collar clattered against a support post when he thrust his pink nose against the chain links.

"Stop making that racket," she ordered.

"S-Sorry."

She leaned forward and touched noses in greeting—and pulled back quickly. His panting was rank with terror.

"Are we s-still going to—"

"Yes," she interrupted. "Just like we talked about. Take a couple of deep breaths and calm down." *His stuttering was making her nervous.* "Once we start, we've got to keep moving. No stopping for anything until we're off the property."

"I-I'll try." Basher glanced at Axel's house. "I freeze up sometimes when I'm near him. He scares me so much that I can't even think. I might do the opposite of what you want me to do."

Roxxy swallowed the angry reply that came to mind. *Couldn't you have mentioned that before?* Shame filled her, and she reminded herself what Basher had been through.

"I get it," she said. "Axel's a scary guy, but you know what he has planned for you. Think he'll have a change of heart? Think he *has* a heart?"

Basher's mottled tongue swept across his muzzle. "Well, when you put it like that."

"Right. Get ready." She ran to the rear of the pen but didn't stop until she was several strides past. A quick whirl and she was facing the aluminum panel propped against the back of the enclosure.

Yeah, reminds me of the teeter-totter that I saw at the playground when I was watching the kids. When one end goes down, the other goes up.

"Whooo, whoo-whoo-whoooooo…"

The owl was easy to spot, high in a maple whose fallen leaves were scattered among the junk in the yard. The bird's squat body perched on a thick branch, anchored by tapered talons. A soft breeze stirred the wispy tufts atop the predator's head. Roxxy tensed as the owl's eyes settled on her and dilated into flat black disks surrounded by gold bands. She knew she was too big for the bird to be a threat, but why hadn't her jangling nerves gotten the message?

"R-Roxxy?" called out Basher in a ragged huff.

She focused back on the pen. Basher was standing on trembling legs and facing her. His wide chest heaved as he sucked in great gulps of air.

Her eyes darted to the house, then back to the enclosure. She ran through the plan one more time. Charge up the improvised teeter-totter, and her weight would push it down to land inside the pen. Basher would hop on, and the two of them would run up the ramp to the other end. Their weight would drive the teeter-totter to the ground outside the pen.

What could be easier?

She sprang forward. Her ears flattened in the wind stream of her dash. The base of the ramp was a stride away when a front paw clipped an old radiator hose hidden by a clump of weeds. She turned her charge into a clumsy leap. Her stomach crashed into the ramp at the point where it rested against the pen.

CLANG!

The sound was like a gong being hit with a sledgehammer, and it passed through her in a jarring, teeth-rattling shudder. Her claws raked metal as she crawled to the top end. As she'd hoped, the ramp tipped toward the inside of the pen. *The plan was working!* She was still congratulating herself when the downward momentum halted. Uh, oh! She wasn't heavy enough to drive the end all the way to the ground! Her stomach lurched as the ramp reversed course and swung upward. She flattened herself to keep from falling off and being trapped *with* Basher. Why hadn't she thought things through?

She blinked when big paws appeared an inch from her nose and curled around the end of the panel. Basher levered himself over the edge and sprawled across her. Their combined weight sent the teeter-totter rocketing to the ground.

CRASH!

"Oomph!" exclaimed Roxxy.

"Sorry!" said Basher, crawling off her but staying on the ramp. "Didn't mean to smush you!"

"You were terrific!" Roxxy shook. "You caught the end just in time."

"I didn't want to get left behind."

"You won't be."

"Promise?"

"Promise," she assured him.

"What now?"

"We're right on schedule." Her gaze traveled up the ramp. The ascending slope shone invitingly in the glow of the moon. "Let's get to the top, and our weight will—"

Her voice died as yellow light blossomed from the fixture above Axel's back door. The thickening fog transformed the illumination into a fuzzy glow. She drew in a calming breath. The enclosure would be difficult to see from the house. With luck, she and Basher would be well away by the time Axel figured out what was going on.

"He heard us!" yelped Basher. "What do we *do*?"

"Get up the ramp!"

Bang-bang-bang-bang!

She winced at the noise made by his big paws, but speed was more important than stealth. She pelted after him, adding to the racket. The strip of sheet metal began to tilt even before they reached the end. Their combined weight slammed it into the ground.

CLANG!

Roxxy tumbled off and hit her head on a dented toaster with no electrical cord. Stars burst at the corners of her vision. She felt teeth slide through the fur at the back of her neck, and a tug on the collar as Basher pulled her upright.

"You did it, Roxxy!" he barked. "I'm free! I—oh, I *forgot* it!"

"Forgot what?" she mumbled, still dazed. Her paws felt clumsy as she followed Basher to the pen.

"See there?" He pointed his chin toward a well-gnawed square of thick ribbed rubber beside his crate. "I wish I'd remembered to grab my chewy. Axel threw it in the pen when I first got here to strengthen my jaws. It was the only thing I had to keep me company."

A hard lump formed in Roxxy's throat. Basher's chewy was a hacked-off piece of old tire tread.

"*What's going on out here?*"

Roxxy turned as the bellow rolled across the yard. The voice seemed oddly disembodied in the fog. Axel's bulk filled the doorway to the house. She squinted. Something about his silhouetted form was off. One arm was unusually long. No...it just looked that way because of the baseball bat.

"Run!" she ordered Basher.

"But—"

"*Now!*" she barked, already in full flight. Once past the holly, they could cross the street and lose themselves among the neighborhood's houses.

"Stupid mutt must be trying to get out."

Roxxy snorted at the muttered words. *Too late, creep!* Axel would never catch her and Basher now. She put on an extra burst of speed, and her ears lifted with each bounding stride.

A low whimper registered from somewhere behind her.

The distraction caused her to plow into the holly. Waxy leaves tore at her coat, and branches whipped across her face and chest. Berries flew from the shrub and rolled into the street beyond.

The whimpering was louder now. She backed out of the holly and turned.

This can't be happening!

She gulped. Basher's head was wedged beneath the pen, and his muzzle rested an inch from the tire-tread chewy. The bottom of the chain-link fence had bowed inward to accommodate his chunky skull. The wire mesh rested on the nape of his neck and was snagged in one of the prongs in his collar, preventing him from backing out.

Roxxy looked over her shoulder. A streetlight showed the red berries strewn across the road. A quick dash and she'd be past them, on her way home. She'd done her part, right? The teeter-totter idea had worked. Well, sort of. But the point was, she'd gotten Basher *out* of the pen. Was it her fault he'd hung around trying to reach that stupid chewy and gotten himself stuck?

She threw a final look at the enclosure to confirm the hopelessness of the situation. Basher's narrow rump stuck up, and he flung himself backward again and again, putting all his weight into the effort to pull free. The chain-link fence rattled as if it was being beaten with a mallet, but the collar remained snagged.

"Stop that!" snapped Axel, appearing through the fog like a mystical giant and looming over Basher.

The pit bull instantly went still. Axel lifted the baseball bat and smacked the fat end against a palm.

"Dumbest mutt ever. You somehow get *out* of the pen, but don't even have the brains to run away. You're useless." He chuckled. "Even to yourself."

"*UNHN, UNHN, UNHN, UNHN, UNHN!*"

Roxxy winced as Basher's string of staccato, high-pitched yelps pierced the night. The cries signaled surrender and a plea for mercy. She glanced at the hard planes of Axel's face.

No mercy there…

The man cleared his throat with a sound like marbles shaken in a tin can. His mouth worked, and he spat. Brown-streaked mucus splattered between Basher's shoulder blades.

A shiver ran down the pit bull's gaunt flanks.

"Too foggy for anybody to see what's going on," said Axel, surveying the neighboring houses. He looked down at Basher and tapped the dog's spine with the bat. "You cost me money today. I'm going to take it out of your hide."

Axel took a wide stance and centered his weight on the balls of his feet. Biceps bulged as he raised the bat high overhead and let the fat end drop to the small of his back. His knees bent for maximum power.

"*Unhn, unhn, unhn, unhn, unhn.*"

Roxxy flattened her ears to the side of her head. Basher's voice was quieter now—the helpless keening of the doomed.

Axel's upper body snapped forward. The head of the bat leaped in an ascending arc, gaining speed.

"*WHA—UGH!?!*"

Roxxy's jaws closed on the smooth, rounded wood, catching it on the upswing as it came level with Axel's rippling shoulders. The timing of the leap had been the tricky part. Too soon and Axel would've noticed her coming. Too late and…well, better not to think of that. Her momentum ripped the weapon from his hands as she sailed past. His startled grunt and the thud of his body hitting the ground were nice bonuses. The weight of the bat brought her down faster than expected. The jarring force of the landing ran up all four limbs. She gasped, and the bat tumbled away. She was glad to get rid of the awful gamey taste embedded in the wood. Basher's story about the pulverized raccoon flashed through her mind.

She promised to throw up as soon as she had a moment to spare. A *thunk* sounded when the bat rolled into one of the pen's support posts.

She rose on shaky legs and took stock. Axel was sprawled on the ground near the front of the enclosure. She was at the rear. Basher was between them. His big head was still stuck under the fence, trapped by the snagged collar.

"Great, *another* mutt," said Axel, levering himself to his elbows and squinting at her. "Where did *you* come from?"

"Your worst dreams!" she snarled. Thank goodness the fog was making it hard for him to get a good look at her. The last thing she wanted was for him to recognize her and come to the house looking for trouble. The thought caused her hackles to rise. She barked. "*Moron!*"

"Shut that yapping!" Axel waved a hand in front of his face to clear the mist, but the effort only stirred the tendrils into an impenetrable swirl. He rolled onto his side and massaged the base of his spine. "Landed funny."

Roxxy stiffened. *Now's my chance!* Three quick steps brought her to Basher. He was so terrified, some kind of paralysis had set in. She jabbed him hard in the ribs with her chin. "I'll bite down on your collar, and we'll pull together!"

"No use," he croaked. "Get out of here while you can."

She thundered, "*SHUT UP AND PULL WHEN I TELL YOU!*"

Basher stared at her from the corners of bulging eyes. "Whatever you say!"

Roxxy clamped her jaws on the collar, being careful to avoid biting down on a prong. She took a good grip and grunted, "Now!"

Basher gave an ear flick and flung himself backward. She matched his effort. The bottom of the chain-link fence bowed out each time they tugged, but the collar remained snagged.

A sound registered.

Was that the scuff of a boot?

She pulled harder. Her saliva and the collar combined to leave a metallic taste on her tongue. Another scuff sounded from behind. No doubt about it this time. As if on cue, the air overhead split with a *whhooossshhh*! She gave a mighty yank and desperately twisted her torso.

Ting!

A link in the collar snapped so suddenly that Roxxy and Basher were flung from the pen as if launched from a catapult.

WHUMP!

Roxxy jack-knifed out of the rolling tumble that had carried her halfway across the yard. She stared back at the pen. A tennis-ball-sized divot gouged the dirt where her head had been a moment before. The bat lay on the ground.

Axel cursed and shook out his hands.

"I'm *free!*"

Basher appeared beside her and raked a hind paw across his collarless neck. "Ahhh!"

"Let's go," said Roxxy, unable to shake the queasy feeling brought on by the sight of the depression in the hard ground.

Too close! She dashed away, with Basher close behind. A leap took her over an upturned yard rake with the spiky tines pointing skyward.

"You did it!" woofed Basher. "Thank you! Thank you! Thank you!"

She continued at a dead run past the holly, pausing only to throw a quick glance both ways before charging into the street. The berries she'd dislodged from the shrub earlier squished under her paws, and the pulp found the gaps between her toes. Her ears swiveled backward at the sound of a grunt.

"Duck!" she yelped.

"What?" huffed Basher.

Roxxy stopped and crouched as the pit bull kept running. The spinning baseball bat parted the curls on top of her head and flew past. She gave silent thanks the throw hadn't been aimed at Basher, who'd failed to duck. The weapon had been hurled with enough force to split a skull. She came out of her crouch and quickly caught up with him. The bat rolled down the middle of the road. She leaped it, but Basher—whom Roxxy was beginning to think wasn't cut out for high adventure—stepped on the rounded handle and face-planted. She nudged him upright, feeling bony ribs against her muzzle, and directed him to a yard at the end of the block. A pedestrian alley beckoned between two houses. Roxxy could see a dimly lit streetlight in the distance where the passage opened out to another road.

"I'LL FIND YOU!" roared Axel.

She glanced back for a final look. He stood next to the holly with arms raised and fists pounding the air.

"BOTH OF YOU ARE *DEAD!*"

"R-Roxxy," whimpered Basher. "It's not over, is it?"

"No," she admitted, leading him between the houses. "We—*YELP!*"

Sharp yellow teeth snapped at her foreleg. She leaped off the rat's tail and dashed to the end of the alley. The rodent—bigger than any she'd ever seen—didn't follow.

She gasped. "If I get through this night without heart failure, it'll be a miracle."

"That was close!" remarked Basher.

"Yeah, you could put a saddle on that rat."

"I mean escaping Axel."

"*Too* close," she confirmed. "And he's not giving up. You were right. He'll try to find you."

"W-What are we going to do?"

"Don't worry. I've got a plan."

A stride later, she cocked an ear in Basher's direction. "Was that a groan?"

CHAPTER 23

"Shouldn't we be hiding someplace?"

The sickle moon had fallen so low that Roxxy could see only the yellow, triangular tip jutting above the roofline of the house across the street. She had taken refuge in the foundation plantings of the home opposite. The cloying scent of a late-blooming tea olive lay upon her like an unwelcome blanket.

She cocked an ear at the weary cadence of claws clacking on the sidewalk. A moment later Basher appeared beneath a streetlight half a block back. She rose to meet him when he arrived.

"Almost there," she said encouragingly, but she received only a grunt in reply.

She veered off the sidewalk, taking a diagonal path across a well-tended front yard. Her trot slowed to a fast walk, allowing the cool lawn to soothe her stinging paw pads. She led Basher around a group of red-hatted garden gnomes lounging within a bed of sunburst dahlias.

As far as she was concerned, the jury was still out on the garden gnome issue. Creepy or cute? Too close to call.

"You said we were almost there," groaned Basher.

"We are. How are you holding up?"

The only reply was ragged breathing that reminded her of the time Bill sandpapered a wooden post. Guilt filled her. She'd pushed the half-starved pit bull to the point of breaking, but there was no other choice. Hiding him was the priority. Axel's threat still rang in her ears. *I'LL FIND YOU!*

Basher huffed weakly, "I can't go any…"

"We're here," she said.

Instead of stopping at her house, she led him into Leo's back yard and halted in front of a birdbath positioned on short wrought-iron legs in the middle of a flowerbed. The water was level with Basher's chest.

"Drink up," Roxxy ordered. "Every drop."

"Aren't you thirsty?" His flanks still heaved from the journey.

"Yes," she said. "But I'll have some water later."

"But—"

"Drink!"

Basher complied. When the birdbath was empty and his tongue finished rasping over the cement bottom, he asked, "What now?"

"Come on." She turned and trotted through Leo's side yard—scanning the base of the shrubbery for signs of Snatcher, even though logic told her he wouldn't take her on again—and stopped at her house.

The white-painted entry to the crawl space shone a weak but ghostly silver from the streetlight out front.

"What now?" repeated Basher. He shifted from paw to paw. "Axel might already be trying to find us. If he drives by, he could see us from the road."

"Hang on." She sniffed at the crawl space door.

The smell of the paint had an oily undertone, distinctly different from the chalky odor of the stuff used on the walls inside the house. The panel was held closed by a sideways oak peg shoved between two side-by-side metal rings—one attached to the door and the other to the narrow wooden frame. Roxxy sighed. Canine brains weren't meant for dilemmas like this. If you wanted something licked, sniffed, or scratched, call a dog. But opening doors? Where was a human when you needed one? There was probably some trick to removing the peg, and no doubt the process would be easy for humans born with jointed fingers and an acrobatic thumb. Not so simple if you had four furry toes and a dewclaw.

"Why are we just standing here?" asked Basher. "Shouldn't we be hiding someplace?"

A metallic clamor came from somewhere down the street. Both dogs froze.

"What—" began Basher.

"Shhhh!" Roxxy cocked her head one way, then the other, narrowing down the source of the sound. The rattling slowly died out. "Garbage can," she said. "A possum or raccoon probably got inside and tipped it over."

"Are you positive?"

"Well, I'm positive it wasn't a pickup truck."

"But—"

"Pipe down. I'll have you hidden in second."

"Where?"

"Behind there." She gestured at the door with her chin. "Let me concentrate."

Basher frowned. "I'm—"

"*Not* piping down." She studied the panel.

A growl tickled the back of her throat. She didn't know how a smarty-pants human would get the door open, but there was nothing to prevent her from simply ripping the peg and rings free. She rose on her hind legs and propped one front paw against the wooden door and the other against the brick wall. Her mouth settled around the peg. Hmm…oak. Too bad. Her teeth would've sunk deeper into pine. Jaws worked as she bit down and yanked for all she was worth.

After a long moment of futile effort, she gave up and dropped to the ground. The peg was almost flush against the panel. She couldn't get her back teeth into play for a really strong grip.

Movement caught her eye. Basher trotted to the front of the house and leaned forward, swiveling his head from side to side. Her tail bobbed in a shrug. He probably expected Axel's truck to cruise down the street at any second. Truth be told, she was worried about that as well, not to mention the concern that one of her family members—probably her mother or father since they slept more lightly than the sibs—would hear her fumbling with the door and come outside to investigate.

She imagined explaining the pit bull's presence. *Well, Momma and Poppa, I decided to save my new friend, Basher, by taking on a bat-wielding maniac, and…*

Yeah. That would go well.

She again braced herself against the door and bit down on the peg. Her front legs stiffened as she *pulled*.

Nothing.

She was about to unclamp her jaws when her back paws slid out from under her. A mad scramble resulted in a sideways fall. Her flank hit the ground with a decisive thump.

This just gets better and—

The dry taste of oak lay on her tongue. She opened her mouth and the peg rolled free. How had *that* happened? She was still pondering the deviousness of human engineering when a nose pressed against her ear. She jumped as if doused with a bucket of ice water.

"Don't *do* that," she growled at Basher. "Between dealing with Axel and stepping on a giant rat, my nerves are shot."

"You're amazing, Roxxy! How did you get the door open?"

She resisted the urge to say *No clue*. Basher needed all the confidence in her he could get. Tomorrow was going to be…challenging.

"Well?" he prompted.

"All part of the master plan," she replied with a nonchalant ear flick.

"Unbelievable!"

She blinked. *You have no idea.*

"Can we hide now?" asked Basher.

She turned to the partially open door and nosed it to widen the gap. The hinges creaked, and she slowed her effort until the noise was minimal.

When the space was big enough for Basher to pass through, she said, "Slip inside, but don't hit your head on the top of the frame. Get a good night's sleep and be *really* quiet so no one in the house hears you. We don't want Bill coming out with a flashlight to see if some critter has gotten into the crawl space. If he discovers you, he'll bring Carol out for a look. She'll recognize you from the walk, and we'll be sunk. She didn't like Axel, but she'd feel obligated to put up flyers so he could come get you."

"Why? She seemed nice."

"She *is* nice, but she doesn't know how awful he really is. She'd think he'd be worried about you."

"But he'll k-kill me if I go back."

"We're going to make sure that doesn't happen."

"If you say so." The tip of his stubby tail pointed at the ground.

"Cheer up, you big goof," she said brightly. "You'll be in a loving home by tomorrow night."

I hope!

"How? You haven't told me yet."

She lay down and explained what she had in mind, stopping

occasionally to gnaw at the residue of squished holly berries between her toes. The pulp was mealy and bitter. She knew from experience that it would make her sick if she swallowed the stuff, so she wiped her tongue on the grass to keep the goo from accumulating in her mouth.

When she finished describing the plan, she asked, "What do you think?"

Basher snorted. "It sounds as crazy as the scheme you came up with to get me out of the pen, but you made it work. I'm pretty sure you could pull off anything you put your mind to."

"Well, uh, thanks," she replied uncomfortably, wondering if his opinion would be different if she told him pure luck had allowed her to open the crawl space door. *No need to find out.* She tilted her head at the entry. "Okay, let's get you settled. I'll go first."

She stepped off the opening's bottom lip and dropped the length of a foreleg to the hard-packed dirt floor. The crawl space was more inviting than she'd anticipated. Her paws rested on dry ground, and the overhead floor joists were set high enough to provide plenty of room to stand comfortably. The spaces between the joists were filled with fluffy pink lengths of insulation.

She sniffed and was pleased that there was no mold. The perimeter of the foundation held louvered vents that allowed air to circulate and illumination to filter in from the streetlights out front. Cinder-block pillars squatted in rows and supported the house. Only a few items were scattered about—a fertilizer spreader with a wheel missing, a cracked garden hose, and some bent tomato cages.

Her nose twitched from a slight funk coming from the far end of the space where two cast-iron pipes joined together. The only other drawback was all the cobwebs draped about the pillars. She frowned. The space wasn't cozy, but it was acceptable for one night.

"I'm not staying in there, Roxx." Basher pushed his blocky head inside the crawl space but came no further. "The place is all spidery."

"I thought pit bulls were tough."

"Would *you* like to stay here?"

"No. It's all spidery."

"See?"

"I'm kidding. It's fine. You won't be in here very long. Just—" A sudden yawn overtook her. "Sorry. Just keep thinking about how snuggly you'll be in your forever home."

"You promise I won't have to stay here for more than one night?"

"Absolutely."

If everything goes right. And when was the last time that *happened?*

"Okay, Roxxy." Basher stepped down to the floor. He sniffed his way over to the cinder-block pillar with the fewest cobwebs and curled up next to it. "G'night."

"Sleep well." She closed the door from the outside by shouldering a plastic milk crate against it. Bill kept the container around to carry garden shears and trowels when he tended the flower beds.

A leap landed her atop the wheeled garbage bin. The subsequent jump over the fence and into the back yard was a snap. A few minutes later, she padded into the family room and wedged herself into her usual spot between Max and Lulu. The warmth of their bodies and the soft murmur of communal breathing enfolded her like a gentle cocoon. As she drifted off, she reminded herself to avoid oversleeping. Getting a late start would be bad...*very* bad.

AXEL

Axel blinked awake and turned his head away from the band of sunlight slashing across his face. Pain exploded at the base of his skull. There was no pillow under his head, which accounted for the crick in his neck akin to a spike embedded in a railroad tie. He tried to shift on the coverless, grimy mattress, but the sweat-soaked surface glued him in place. The open window blinds hung at a crooked angle. He fumbled for his cell phone on the improvised night table—an upended wooden spool that had once held electrical cable—and squinted at the screen. *7:32 a.m.*

He sat up with an effort of will and belched. The bubble of gas coated his tongue with the sour taste of last night's whiskey and cigarettes. Opening the second bottle of bourbon had been a bad idea, but it was the only way he could temporarily blot out the image of Basher and the other mutt disappearing into the night.

A wave of nausea hit, and he dropped his head between his knees. The urge to vomit passed, and he lit a cigarette and stared unseeingly through the wafting gray swirls of smoke. He remembered the smooth handle of the wood against his palms as he raised the bat high. He'd had Basher right where he wanted when the other dog charged out of nowhere. Something about the mongrel seemed familiar, but he hadn't gotten a good look because of the fog.

He took a final drag and dropped the glowing butt on the oak planks. It would burn itself out among the other blackened scars. The landlord would have to refinish the hardwood before renting the house to someone else, but so what?

Axel shuffled into the bathroom and propped his hands on the sides of the sink. He leaned forward and looked into the cracked mirror. The whites of his eyes were sickly yellow and webbed with red veins, but his black irises were flat with determination. He rotated his neck. The sound of popping cartilage was loud in the small green-tiled room. A turn of the faucet released a stream of cold water. A roach skittered out of the drain and up the side of the stained sink. Axel splashed water on the insect to send it back down the pipe. Making a bowl with his hands, he flung icy water into his face—again and again and again. His skin tingled as the rivulets dripped from his chin to his chest. Head now clear, he planned out the steps for locating Basher. If the other mutt was with him, so much the better. The dog would make a good unit for the shipment.

Axel stared at his grinning reflection in the mirror. Time to go to work.

CHAPTER 24

"Are you crazy?"

Roxxy's limbs twitched in fitful sleep.
She put on a burst of speed, but the giant was gaining on her. The ground shook each time his boots struck the earth. Clods of dirt ricocheted off the trunks of barren trees. How close was he? She heard a grunt and the snap of a pants cuff. She juked left to avoid the kick. A rusty tine on an upturned yard rake pierced a paw pad. Her legs tangled, and she tumbled end over—

She rolled from the dog bed, and her claw caught the wicker frame and flipped it into the air. Padding and blankets rained on top of her. The bed followed. Her eyelids fluttered open. Speckled sunlight—filtered by the wicker—filled her little cave. *Hmmm…nice and cozy.* She wiggled into a tight C and tucked her tail around her paws. The fleecy tip settled over her eyes. Sleep had almost returned when the soft clatter of a cup and saucer came from the dining room. *Hmmm…sounded like the good* china. Were Bill and Carol having company? Groggy but curious, she swiveled her ears toward the hall.

"Vicky," said Carol's gentle contralto, "I think you're coping really well."

"I agree," added Marcy's lighter soprano. "Especially under the circumstances."

Roxxy wished her brain wasn't so sleep-addled. What were Vicky and Marcy doing here?

"Thanks," replied Vicky. "I'm trying."

Roxxy frowned. Why did Vicky's voice sound so thick? Did she have a cold?

"I'd be a basket case," said Marcy. "You're holding up better than anyone could expect."

Roxxy yawned. There was something she was supposed to do. She was certain of it. But what?

"I'm lucky to have such good friends," said Vicky. "And Carol, I'm glad I got my dog fix before Bill took your crew to the park."

"I can't believe it's almost noon and Roxxy's *still* conked out in the family room. She wouldn't even get up when Bill called her."

"Sleeping the sleep of the innocent?" Marcy chuckled.

"I wish," replied Carol wryly. "Roxxy gets into more trouble than the rest of the dogs combined."

The tip of Roxxy's tail flicked in annoyance. *Everybody's a critic.*

"And I'm glad to see Toby," said Vicky. "Thanks for bringing him over, Marcy. The big lug has been lying next to my feet all morning."

"My pleasure. He's a sweetie."

Carol asked, "Vicky, do you want me to go wake Roxxy?"

"No, let her sleep. I peeked at her when I got here. She was snoring like a freight train. And cute? She's so angelic with those blond curls."

"*Angelic?*" gasped Carol. "Please, not when I'm taking a sip of coffee.

Have you noticed that three-legged chair in the corner? Does that say *angelic* to you?"

Vicky gasped. "Oh, my! She must be part beaver."

"That's no way to talk about the dog who rescued my little girl," said Marcy. "Roxxy's perfect!"

"A perfect *mess*!" declared Carol.

"Not true!" admonished Vicky. "Roxxy's the mellowest dog in the world, or she wouldn't be sleeping like a rock at this very minute."

Carol sighed. "She's probably trying to recover after getting into some kind of mischief."

"And what might that be?"

"Better not to know!"

Roxxy's indignant huff was lost under the humans' laughter echoing from the dining room.

Always judged, never understood.

"Well, time for me to go," said Marcy. "Carol, do you mind if Toby hangs out here for a little while?"

"Happy to have him. What's up?"

"Susan's coming by. She's not really comfortable around Toby, even after all these years."

"*Why?*" blurted Vicky. "He's as threatening as a throw rug."

"Long story. Goes back to when she and I were kids."

"Toby's always welcome here," said Carol. "Roxxy will be glad to see him when she wakes up."

"Thanks," replied Marcy. "I'll go out through the kitchen and leave him in the back yard. Susan should be here any minute. She and her husband are heading out of town for a few days, and Jason's staying at our place."

Roxxy flicked an ear in approval. The boy was a natural at petting, and his pesky mom wouldn't be around to spoil things.

"I'll see you two later," continued Marcy. "Vicky, call me if you want to talk."

Roxxy was drowsily aware of Toby's clicking claws and Marcy's soft footfalls as the pair proceeded from the dining room at the front of the house to the kitchen at the rear. The back door closed behind them.

Good. Should be quieter now, and I can get back to sleep. Her breathing deepened.

"Vicky, are you sure you'll to be okay on your own? Bill and I have a guest room. You're more than welcome to stay for as long as you want." Carol paused. "Your house may seem empty without Ferris to keep you company."

"I've been thinking about that, but I'll be fine. I'm planning to stay busy. In fact, I should get going. I need to swing by home and pick up an unopened bag of dog food. I want to take it to the shelter."

"Speaking of the shelter…" Carol's voice trailed off.

"No," Vicky said. "I'm not ready for a new dog."

Roxxy sprang up as if the carpet was on fire. The wicker frame went flying and landed silently on the sofa.

BASHER!

How could she have forgotten? She must've been completely befuddled by exhaustion. He would be worried out of his mind.

More cups and saucers rattled from the dining room.

"Carol, let me help you tidy up," said Vicky.

"It's just coffee stuff. I'll take care of it."

"Sure?"

"Positive," replied Carol. "Come on. I'll walk you to your car."

Vicky chucked. "If you do, we'll spend another fifteen minutes chatting in the driveway."

"That's the plan."

The front door opened, and a breeze drifted its way into the family room. Roxxy's nose twitched at the almond scent given off by the purple clematis that climbed the posts supporting the porch roof. The instant the latch clicked shut, she streaked from the family room and made the turn into the kitchen without breaking stride. Paw pads skidded over hardwood as she fought to stay upright. Her lowered head hit the dog door flap so hard stars burst at the corners of her vision. Rather than taking the steps, she leaped off the side of the deck. Her tail clipped a thin branch on a bordering wax-leafed tea olive, releasing a burst of sweet perfume. She landed neatly and barreled for the wheelbarrow's usual spot. All she had to do was leap the fence, fetch Basher from the crawl space, and—

She threw her weight back and stiffened her legs. Paws carved furrows in the lawn as she slid to a stop.

Where was the wheelbarrow?

A glance around the yard revealed it sitting uselessly—for her purposes—in the center of the yard next to a rose bed. Her nose twitched at the aroma of freshly spread mulch. Bill's handiwork, no doubt. He must've started early so he could take the dogs to the park. What now? A glance at the fence confirmed there was no way for her to clear it without using the wheelbarrow as a platform.

A faint whimper came from the crawl space.

She swallowed. *I got him into this …*

The whimpering grew more desperate.

Sunlight sparkled on the twists of chain links lining the top of the fence. Her tail bobbed in a shrug. She wouldn't get high enough to impale herself. More likely, she'd break her neck when she crashed into the barrier a foot below the top. She crouched to get a running start.

"*Roxxy!*"

She whirled and stared dumbstruck. Toby stood behind her, jowls wobbling from the woof to get her attention. How had she forgotten that Marcy had left him here?

Toby's eyes narrowed. "Were you planning to try and jump the fence? Are you crazy?"

"I have to!" she blurted. "There's a dog named Basher in the crawl space under the house."

"*What?*"

"I helped Basher escape from his owner last night. The man was planning to do something terrible to him. *No questions!*" she ordered when Toby's chest expanded in preparation for a query. "I'll explain later, but right now I have to jump over the fence. I don't have a second to waste!"

"Tell me what you need."

"We have to get the wheelbarrow closer to the fence." She saw his wrinkly forehead buckle in confusion, but continued before he could ask a question. "I use it as a platform to clear the fence."

"I'll be your wheelbarrow."

She stomped her paw. "This is no time to be joking around."

"Who says I'm joking? Get a running start and leap from my back. What could be easier?"

"Forget it. You're uh…sturdy, but not *that* sturdy. I don't want to injure you."

"You won't. Well, at least not much." He snorted. "Besides, I can't wait to tell Leo I helped while *he* was somewhere getting his mane teased."

"You're sure?" she asked.

"Where do you want me?"

She led him to the right spot, then looked on approvingly as he anchored himself by digging thick, sharp claws into the earth.

She trotted to the middle of the yard. "Ready?"

"Hurry up!"

Tufts of grass flew from her paws as she rocketed forward. An arcing hop brought her down on his broad shoulders, and then she exploded upward. His yelp of pain sent a chill through her as she soared over the fence and landed next to the crawl space door. She flung a look over her shoulder. Toby lay sprawled on his stomach, all four legs splayed flat on the lawn. A wince twisted his features.

"T-Toby." Her voice caught in her throat. "Are you okay?"

"I'll live." He grunted. "I think. Get a move on!"

She did, shouldering away the empty crate holding the door closed. The panel crashed open and smacked her soundly on the nose. She tumbled backward, smelling the rush of musty air released from the crawl space.

Basher burst out and stood quivering, head whipsawing from side to side before he spotted her on the ground. "S-Sorry! I thought you'd forgotten about me."

She rose and swept her tongue across her smarting nose.

"I, uh, overslept," she admitted.

"*Overslept?*" yelped Basher, goggle-eyed. "When Axel could be looking for us? I didn't sleep at all."

"Quiet!" she snapped, and immediately felt guilty when his ears folded back in submission. She leaned forward and brushed her muzzle along his. "I've got this under control. Just follow the directions I gave you last night and everything will be fine."

"Whatever you say, Roxx." Basher paused and nodded toward Toby. "Who's that?"

She couldn't resist. "My assistant."

"*Assistant?*" Toby's jowls quivered. "I—"

"Okay, okay," she interrupted, a smile lightening her eyes. "How about, *my partner in crime.* Happy now?"

"Not until you've finished doing whatever crazy thing you're up to and get back inside the fence."

"Right." She turned to Basher. "Take a couple of deep breaths and try to relax. Everything's on schedule." *Liar.* "Remember the plan?"

"Sure. Only…I was hoping you might have thought of a better one."

Toby snorted.

She glared at the basset, but before she could say anything, she heard a chirp signaling a car being unlocked. Human voices drifted around the front corner of the house. Roxxy cocked an ear and listened.

"Carol," said Vicky. "Thanks for walking out with me. I've taken up your whole morning."

"I'm glad we could talk. Call me later and let me know how you're doing."

Roxxy bolted, flinging an order without stopping. "Basher! Get ready!

CHAPTER 25

"Grab her!"

Roxxy rounded the corner of the house and skidded to a stop, watching Carol and Vicky release each other from a hug. *Oh no!* Vicky was already gripping the handle of the car door! Roxxy took a deep breath and forced herself to approach the two women at a leisurely trot. She'd just started when her attention was drawn to the light jingle of chains and the heavier sound of boot heels smacking the sidewalk.

Axel!?

An electrical charge shot through her, reminiscent of the time she'd licked a three-prong opening on an electrical plate. The man was two houses away and coming right for her. Thankfully, the tingling left her limbs when he turned off the sidewalk and strode to the entrance of Mrs. Brown's home. She was a nice elderly lady who sometimes stopped by on Sunday afternoons to swap heirloom tomato seeds with Bill.

Roxxy's mind raced as Axel banged on the woman's door. What if he happened to glance toward Vicky's car at the wrong moment? What if he—?

Stop what-if-ing and get on with it!

Roxxy woofed a quiet but friendly greeting at Vicky.

"Oh, my!" said the woman, eyes widening. "Roxxy, what in the world are you doing here?"

"And how," added Carol, "did you manage to get out of the back yard?"

Roxxy charged Vicky and leaped.

"*Eeek!*" Vicky plucked Roxxy neatly from the air and embraced her in a warm hug. "You scamp! You nearly scared me to death!"

"I'm still wondering," Carol interjected, crossing her arms, "how the scamp navigated the fence."

Roxxy snuggled, enjoying the warmth of Vicky's embrace and the fragrance of floral body lotion with a peach undertone.

"Isn't she *adorable*?"

Carol rolled her eyes. "Captivating."

"Roxxy, I'm *so* glad I saw you before I left!" Vicky paused and winked at Carol. "Do you think you'll figure out how she got out of the back yard?"

"Probably not." Carol's features softened. "Roxxy, *what* am I going to do with you?"

"You'll figure something out." Vicky chuckled. "In any case, it's time for me to go."

Roxxy managed another lick to the woman's cheek before finding herself deposited on the driveway. She flung a glance at the corner of the house. Basher's head stuck out. He panted so hard a line of spittle ran to the ground. She was certain he'd seen Axel. Her only hope was that the dog would stay put instead of dashing away in panic.

"Carol, I'll call you later." Vicky opened the car door.

The muscles bunched in Roxxy's legs. *Here comes the tricky part!* The door swung open. She leaped past Vicky to land behind the steering wheel.

"Wow!" said Vicky. "She's quick!"

"Uh huh," agreed Carol from her position on the opposite side of the car. "Especially when it comes to doing something she shouldn't be doing."

"Munchkin," Vicky addressed Roxxy. "Time to get out of the car. You're cute as a button, but I have errands to run."

Roxxy leaped into the back seat.

So far, so good!

Carol cocked an eyebrow at Vicky. "See what I mean?"

"She does seem to have a mind of her own."

"That's one way of putting it." Carol's dimples appeared, and she opened the sedan's back door. She made a grab for Roxxy's pink collar. "Out, you!"

Roxxy ducked and launched herself under Carol's outstretched arm. Butter-soft flannel slid along her back. She landed well past the driveway and hit the ground running.

Vicky exclaimed, "Forget *quick*. She moves like lightning!"

"Get her before she reaches the street!"

Roxxy raced away, leading the pair toward the road. She was nearly at the sidewalk when she stopped and spun. Carol and Vicky were almost on top of her, their backs to the car and house. She looked past them and settled her gaze on Basher. He was partially hidden by the corner of the house.

"*NOW!*" she barked.

The pit bull raced to the Toyota and leaped through the back door Carol had left open.

Twin shadows fell on Roxxy.

"Grab her!" gasped Carol.

"Don't worry! I've got the little—" Vicky's wheezing voice cut off as Roxxy zipped between the woman's legs and darted back toward the vehicle.

From behind, a thud sounded as the two humans collided. Roxxy felt a pang of guilt but didn't slow. *All for a good cause!* She leaped when she neared the car, leaning back so all four legs extended in front of her.

Bang!

Her paw pads crashed into the door. A teeth-rattling shockwave ripped into her shoulders and hips. She dropped like a stone and landed hard on her rump.

"Finally!" said Carol.

Roxxy went limp as she was enfolded in a fierce hug and lifted from the ground. She could feel Carol's heart thudding through the flannel.

"*Bad* dog! With all that dashing around, you could've gotten into the street and been run over."

Roxxy ignored the comment. Her concern at the moment was Axel and whether the creep had noticed the commotion caused by Carol and Vicky's efforts to catch her. Worse, had he seen Basher leap into the car? She shivered.

"What's wrong, sweetie?" asked Carol. "I didn't mean to scold you. You're not *really* a bad dog."

Roxxy huffed impatiently. Bad dog, good dog, who cared? Her main concern was remaining an *alive* dog, which meant keeping Axel unaware that Basher was close by. A glance at Vicky's car revealed sunlight sparkling on the windows. The effect was mirror-like and reflected the yellow leaves falling from a nearby maple and twirling gently to the driveway. The interior of the vehicle was obscured. Nevertheless, Roxxy hoped Basher was following her instructions and flattening himself on the floorboard behind the front seat. He probably was, being the obedient type. She snorted. *Good* dog!

She wriggled to peek over Carol's shoulder. Axel was still talking to Mrs. Brown. He had one hand extended palm down to indicate Basher's height. The old lady shook her head. Axel took a step closer and loomed over the bent figure. The screen door rattled in the frame as Mrs. Brown reached behind herself and fumbled for the handle.

"Carol," said Vicky tentatively. "Have you and Bill thought about keeping—"

"You know we can't," interrupted Carol. "Not with the changes in Bill's job."

"I'm sorry. I know you don't have any other choice."

"I didn't mean to snap at you. It's just that…"

"I get it."

Roxxy was only vaguely aware of the byplay. Axel had finished interrogating Mrs. Brown and was striding along the petunia-lined flagstone path leading to the sidewalk. Boot heels scraped on the cement as he turned toward Toby's house.

Roxxy gulped.

When he's finished there…

She flung herself into a squirming fit to force Carol to end the conversation with Vicky.

"Hold still, Roxxy! And mind your manners."

RAP-RAP-RAP!

Her ears swiveled toward Toby's front porch.

RAP-RAP-RAP!

"Anybody in there?" Axel demanded, continuing to pound on the door frame.

RAP-RAP-RAP!

A hanging basket of orange chrysanthemums, suspended from the roof of Toby's porch, swayed as a gray-and-white nuthatch shot from a concealed nest and took flight.

"Just a second," came a response from inside the home.

Roxxy knew the voice. *Jason!* She had a sudden urge to put herself between Axel and Toby's front door. She placed a paw against Carol's rib cage and shoved.

"Oomph! What's gotten into you?"

Roxxy went still when Carol's arms tightened. The woman knew how to hold a dog. Frustrated, Roxxy watched Jason step onto the porch. He tilted his head back and gazed up at the man looming over him.

"Yes, sir?" asked the boy in a squeaky voice.

"I'm looking for a pit bull." Axel waved to shoo away a yellow-and-black bumblebee. "Have you seen a dog running loose? Maybe with a smaller mutt in tow?"

"I'm just visiting," replied Jason, taking a half step back. The heel of his tennis shoe brushed a yard-long metal watering wand propped next to the door. The implement toppled over and clattered against the concrete floor. The boy jumped as if he'd backed into a hot stove. His head brushed the hanging basket of mums, sending the container swaying like a pendulum.

Axel shot out a hand and steadied the pot without looking at it. His mouth twisted in a sneer. "You're a jumpy little pu—uh, kid."

Red patches appeared on Jason's cheeks. "I haven't noticed any loose dogs running around."

"Anybody inside who might've spotted them?"

"Just my Aunt Marcy. And my mom. We don't live here." Jason licked his lips. "I mean, my mom and me."

"I don't need your life story. Go inside and ask if anyone saw the mutts."

"You said one's a pit bull?"

Axel nodded and leaned away from the determined bumblebee.

"What does the other one look like?"

"Can't be specific." Axel paused and his forehead wrinkled. "It was about the size of a cocker spaniel. Light colored. Never seen it before, but it was in the yard when my dog got out of the pen."

"I'll be back in a second." Jason turned and slipped through the door.

Roxxy silently told the boy not to hurry. Carol and Vicky were taking *forever* to wrap things up. Her breath caught as Axel's hand moved in a blur to swat away the bumblebee. The insect's wings tore free from the force of the blow, and it tumbled toward her yard. Axel's gaze followed the bee's path. His eyes swept past her, then jerked back and narrowed.

Carol said, "Good girl. You've finally settled down...in fact, you're stiff as a board! What's wrong?"

Roxxy gave a halfhearted tail wag to keep Carol from worrying, but most of her attention was on Axel. He was turning to survey the block from end to end. He'd apparently been so consumed by the search for Basher he hadn't realized he was on a street where he'd previously tried to steal dogs.

Hinges creaked on the screen door as Jason stepped onto the porch.

"Well?" demanded Axel.

Jason shook his head, causing a comma of auburn hair to fall across his eyes.

"Sorry, sir. I checked, but no luck." A hand swept the lock back into place. He brightened. "But your dog may wander by later. I bet I could get him to come to me. Do you have a photo?"

Axel snorted. "Why would I take a picture? It's just a dog."

"But—"

"I put some notices up with my cell number," Axel said. "There's one on a telephone pole at the end of the block. If you see the mutt, there's a couple of bucks in it for you."

He cleared his throat with a ratcheting sound like a wire auger reaming out a drainpipe and sent a stream of phlegm arcing into the container of mums.

The orange petals fluttered under the brown splatter. Axel dragged a forearm across his mouth. "That animal's going to pay for the trouble it caused. Know what I mean?"

Jason's face blanched.

"Call if you see the mutt," Axel added. He turned without another word. The chains adorning his boots jangled with each step.

When he reached the sidewalk and pivoted toward Roxxy's house, a cloud edged in front of the sun to darken the day. She took it as an omen and glanced at Vicky's car. Sure enough, with the sun obscured, no light reflected off the windows to conceal the interior.

Basher's docked ears and bulging eyes were visible as he peeked from the back seat and gazed at Axel.

"*Get down!*" Roxxy barked.

The pit bull stayed frozen in place.

"Hey, you!" admonished Carol, giving Roxxy a little shake. "What are you yapping about?" And as an afterthought. "You weigh a *ton*."

"I think she's getting restless," Vicky said. "I'd better get going so you can take her inside."

"Don't feel like you have to rush."

Vicky smiled. "I think we've passed the rush stage and shifted into lingering." Her eyes glistened. "And thank you for taking the time. It means a lot to me."

"I'm glad I could help."

Roxxy watched with growing dread as Axel approached the end of her driveway.

I've got to get loose and create a diversion before he sees Basher!

She braced her back paws against Carol's stomach, determined to jackknife out of the woman's arms, but hesitated. What if her claws ripped through the flannel shirt and scratched Carol?

"Hey, mister!" called Jason, eyes wide as he glanced from the car at Roxxy's house to the big man.

Roxxy gulped, certain that Jason had spotted Basher.

"Mister!" Jason repeated.

"What?" snapped Axel, turning and glaring.

"You said there's a reward if I help you find the dog?"

"I said a couple of bucks, but I'll make it worth your while."

"I did see a pit bull."

Roxxy's tail drooped. She couldn't believe Jason would—

"I saw him running loose over there."

The boy pointed in the opposite direction from Vicky's car.

Roxxy chided herself. *I should've known better!*

"What did it look like?" demanded Axel.

"Huh?"

"Describe the dog you saw."

"Well," said Jason uncertainly, "he was tan or gray. Maybe even black. Hard to remember."

A sheen of sweat appeared on his upper lip.

"That's it? Notice anything unusual about the markings?"

"Err…you mean like brindle-colored or something like that?" Jason wiped his mouth on the shoulder of his t-shirt.

Axel glared. "The dog I'm looking for is gray with a white star on its chest. Can't miss it."

"A star? Right, a star. I forgot to mention that."

"Save it, kid. You just want the finder's fee, and you're wasting my time." Axel turned away.

Roxxy's limbs tingled with growing panic. Axel had almost reached her yard, and Basher was still peeking above the bottom edge of the window. The man could spot him at any second.

She barked, *"Basher! Get down!"*

"What's gotten into you?" Carol admonished. "Stop that racket!"

"Wait, mister!" Jason's eyes again flicked to the car and away.

Roxxy followed the boy's glance. Basher trembled so violently his ears quivered like tuning forks.

Jason continued, "Mister, I saw the dog from the side. That's why I wasn't sure about the star on his chest."

"Punk, I think you're messing with me. I just don't know why."

"N-No, sir. I w-wouldn't do that."

Roxxy was grateful to Jason for stalling Axel's approach, but the kid was playing with fire. She had to get Basher out of sight.

A series of barks exploded from her chest, *"GET DOWN ON THE FLOORBOARD!"*

"That's *enough*!" snapped Carol.

Roxxy growled with satisfaction as Basher's head dropped from view. *Now to move Vicky along!*

"And what are you growling—*ooof*!"

Carol grunted as Roxxy exploded into a flurry of movement, lashing out with her back legs.

"R-Roxxy! You *kicked* me!"

"I'd better get going," Vicky said hurriedly. "I've got lots of errands to run, and Roxxy's getting uh…restless."

"It's like trying to keep a grip on a kangaroo," acknowledged Carol with a gasp. "Call later and let me know how you're doing."

Roxxy stopped struggling as the two women engaged in an awkward hug with her in the middle.

A moment later, the car pulled out of the driveway.

She went limp with relief.

"Typical," stated Carol. "You settle down *after* Vicky leaves. Did you wear yourself out? I—what's *he* doing here?"

Roxxy had been wondering when Carol would notice Axel. The man was still on the sidewalk, glowering at Jason.

"One more chance, kid," said Axel softly. "Did you see the dog or not?"

Jason didn't respond. He was watching Vicky's car as it turned the corner at the end of the block.

"Well?"

"Uh, sorry, mister. Now that I think about it, the dog might have been a boxer."

"Punk." Axel's voice rasped. "You been yanking my chain? You need a lesson in manners?"

"What seems to be the problem?" Carol called out.

Axel whirled. "Lady, this is none of your business."

"Maybe, maybe not, but there is no need call someone a punk." Carol turned and raised her voice to reach Jason. "You'd better go inside while I talk to this…gentleman. Marcy's probably wondering where you are."

"No, ma'am. I'll stay."

"Jason, go inside, please. Everything's fine."

The boy shook his head. Roxxy saw the glint of the metal watering wand clutched in his fist. Her tail thumped. She doubted the makeshift weapon would have any effect on Axel, but the sentiment was appreciated.

"Stubborn dogs and stubborn kids," Carol muttered.

"What?" asked Axel, biting off the word.

"Nothing. How can I help you?"

Axel spat on the sidewalk. "Mighty polite, aren't you?"

"I'm trying to be," replied Carol. "For all the good it's doing."

The man's features slackened into a dead-eyed stare.

Roxxy felt Carol's breath upon her ear as the woman pulled her close and whispered, "I wish Bill was home."

"What?" snapped Axel, approaching.

"Nothing," said Carol.

A growl tickled the back of Roxxy's throat as Axel neared. She squirmed to be let down where she could maneuver, but the effort had the opposite effect. Carol's slender arms tightened around her. To make matters worse, Axel showed no signs of stopping. Roxxy wondered if he'd plow into them, but he halted inches away. His loomed over her and Carol, casting them in shadow. Roxxy's nose twitched at the acrid scent oozing from Axel's pores, reminding her of the alcohol disinfectant used at the vet's office. Strong as the smell was, it didn't blot out the stench of his unbrushed teeth or sour armpits. She heard Carol swallow and knew the woman was trying not to throw up.

"Problem?" asked Axel. The corners of his lips curled to expose yellow teeth.

"W-What do you want?" Carol stepped back.

The man followed, staying so close Roxxy could see a tiny flake of tobacco stuck between his crooked bottom teeth.

"I'm looking for my dog. Pit bull. He got out of his pen last night. Have you seen one around?"

"S-Sorry, no."

"Are you sure? He—"

"I have things to do inside."

Carol's about-face was so sudden that Roxxy's head swam from the swinging motion.

"Don't turn your back on *me*!"

Roxxy stiffened as heavy footsteps thudded from behind.

Carol must've also heard because she turned and gasped. "Oh no!"

Axel's nostrils dilated like those of a charging bull as he closed in on them.

Roxxy bounced as Carol backpedaled frantically. Flower stalks snapped under the woman's sneakers.

Axel stopped and laughed.

Roxxy frowned. What's he up to?

Thunk!

Her teeth rattled as the retreat came to a jarring halt.

A mockingbird atop the porch's peaked roof took flight while mimicking the outraged call of a blue jay. *"Aun-aun-aun!"*

Roxxy realized what had happened. Poor Carol! The *thunk* had been the back of her head slamming into one of the support posts.

"Sting a bit?" Axel smirked.

He extended a hand toward Carol's shoulder-length red hair, still swinging from the impact.

"RARF-RARF-RARF-RARF-RARF!"

Axel jerked his fingers away so quickly he tripped and went down on the seat of his jeans.

Slaver flew from Roxxy's jaws in a glistening arc.

She twisted, trying to break free of the reflexive clench of Carol's arms. *"RARF-RARF-RARF-RARF-RARF! RARF-RARF-RARF-RARF-RARF! RARF-RARF-RARF-RARF-RARF!"*

"Easy, girl. Settle down," said Carol.

Roxxy ignored the command. The relief in the woman's voice belied the words. Roxxy kept her eyes fixed on Axel. Her lips skinned back from her teeth in a snarl that would've done credit to a she-wolf.

She whipsawed back and forth, trying to break free of Carol's clenching embrace.

"RARF-RARF-RARF-RARF-RARF! RARF-RARF-RARF-RARF-RARF! RARF-RARF-RARF-RARF-RARF!"

"That animal's out of control!" Axel scrambled to his feet.

"Not yet," replied Carol. "But you never know what might happen."

"Listen, you—" He paused, recognition dawning in his eyes. "We met the other day, right?"

He nodded in answer to his own question.

"Yeah, you're the busybody who was giving me advice on how to walk my dog." He jabbed a finger within inches of Carol's face. "I ought to—"

Roxxy's jaws snapped. Axel lurched away. She spat out a sliver of nicotine-stained fingernail.

"Bad dog." Carol rubbed her cheek against the side of Roxxy's face.

"That mutt could've taken off my hand! If you don't make it behave, I will!"

"If you're implying you intend to hurt my dog, I'll call the police. There are laws against cruelty to animals."

"I'm justified in protecting myself."

"Interesting point. When the officers get here, I'll ask their opinion."

Axel's eyes shifted as if taking stock of his surroundings. "Hey, cool it, lady. Sorry if I got a little testy. I'm just…uh, upset about my dog."

"The one you were walking when we met?"

"Yeah. He ran off, but he's probably still somewhere in the area. Have you seen him?"

"I already told you I haven't." Carol's tone softened as she continued. "It must feel terrible to lose a pet. Have you put up flyers with your contact information?"

"Yeah. I want that dog back. He's my property."

"I…see."

Carol's undertone of disgust was evident to Roxxy. Axel must've recognized it as well. A red flush crept up his thick neck. She tensed, waiting for him to charge, but he turned abruptly and clomped away.

Carol stood frowning at the man's back.

A whispery sigh of relief drew Roxxy's attention to Toby's yard. She'd been so focused on Axel she hadn't noticed Jason leave the porch and come close enough to help if things got out of control. The silvery length of the watering wand was still clutched in his hand.

Roxxy acknowledged the boy with a *thank you* tail wag. His dimples appeared, and he trotted back to Toby's home with the wand lowered. The nozzle parted the grass and left a thin dark band paralleling his footprints. Hinges creaked on the screen door as he disappeared inside the house.

She wondered when she'd see him again.

"What are you whining about?" asked Carol.

Roxxy huffed in annoyance. *Who's whining?*

A moment later, Carol deposited Roxxy on the cool hardwood floor of the front hallway. The dead bolt on the door clicked into place. Carol knelt, and Roxxy felt the pleasant tingle of fingernails sliding down her back.

"You were great. *So* protective. But I can't stop thinking about that awful man." Carol shook her head. "Some people shouldn't be allowed to have pets."

Roxxy's tail swished in agreement. Fortunately, the creep *didn't* have Basher anymore. Her new friend was on his way to a loving home.

Carol said regretfully, "I wish… Well, I guess it doesn't matter what I wish. If I run into someone who's found the dog, I'll have to say who the rightful owner is. He said his phone number is on the flyers."

Roxxy's tail stopped in mid-wag. *Oh no!* Carol would make the connection the minute Vicky phoned and reported a pit bull had found its way into the back seat of her car.

Carol would feel obligated to…

"What's the matter, sweetie? You're shaking like a leaf."

CHAPTER 26

"What about me?"

Roxxy paced from room to room, too preoccupied to investigate the corn chip aroma wafting from beneath Bill's recliner in the den. The man enjoyed watching football on the big-screen TV above the fireplace. When the game was close, his excitable gyrations sent chips flying around the room like candy exploding from a piñata. Roxxy and the other dogs would encircle him, snapping the salty treats out of the air. One or two occasionally slipped through and would be discovered later. Always a delightful surprise. Too bad she was too distracted today to do more than pay passing notice.

Was Vicky ever going to call?

As she continued pacing, her claws rat-a-tat-tatted crisply against the laundry room's tile, clicked dully on the hardwood in the hallway and kitchen, and sank into the carpet upon her reentry into the family room.

She paused in front of the large picture window, studying the sunlight slanting through. How could only an hour have passed since Vicky left with Basher? It felt like days. Why no call? Discovering a stowaway pit bull in the car's back seat was a big deal. Vicky would certainly want to phone Carol and share the news.

From the corner of her eye, Roxxy spotted Carol passing by the doorway with a laundry basket of bedsheets. She raced after her, slowing only when her muzzle was an inch away from the heels of the woman's pink tennis shoes. A spicy hint of lemon thyme tickled her nose. Carol must've gone to the herb garden earlier that morning.

"Darn. Forgot the pillowcases," muttered Carol, and she did an abrupt about-face.

Roxxy tried to dodge, but the toe of the canvas footwear bopped her on the chin. The laundry basket catapulted from Carol's hands. Linen tumbled out and buried Roxxy. She sat in darkness and fumed.

What's next? Locusts?

She squirmed until her head popped free.

"*Bad* dog," said Carol, failing to stifle a giggle. "Just be glad I haven't washed those yet. Otherwise, you'd be in *big* trouble."

Roxxy yawned. The sheets were soft and smelled comfortingly like Carol and Bill. She wiggled to create a nest for herself. The only thing that would make the situation better was a nice belly rub. She rolled onto her back and waggled her paws in the air.

"Forget it." Carol tucked a stand of silky red hair behind her ear. "I'm already behind in my Saturday chores."

Eyelids batted to send blond bangs atremble.

"You're not as adorable as you think you are."

Roxxy allowed a whimper of disappointment to escape, wondering if she was laying it on too thick.

"I give," said Carol, chuckling ruefully.

Roxxy arched her back and grunted, enjoying the sensation of smooth palms gliding across her belly. She shifted to guide Carol's hand to an itchy spot below her breastbone. The movement put her face in a sunbeam slicing through the front door's frosted glass. Her eyes closed, and the underside of her lids glowed pink. She was drifting off when the buzzing of a cell phone jolted her awake.

"Hi, Vicky," said Carol. "I didn't expect to hear from you this soon. Is everything okay?"

Roxxy lay still as a shadow came and went when Carol stepped past her. The rubber-soled shoes were silent on the hardwood as the slender form disappeared into the kitchen.

Roxxy followed and found Carol pulling out a chair at the breakfast table. "Vicky, I don't think I heard you right."

Roxxy leaned against Carol's denim-clad ankle and wished the woman would turn on the cell phone's speaker function. Normally Roxxy could make out both sides of a conversation, even when a phone was clamped to someone's ear, but her heart was hammering so loudly she could only hear Carol's words.

"Vicky, let me get this straight. There was a *dog* on the floorboard of your car's back seat when you got home… Uh huh… What kind of …" Carol sat forward. "A pit bull? What does he… Oh… White diamond on his chest, thin as a rail, and half starved?… I see. He's next to you on the couch right now… That's sweet… Uh huh… You want to know if anyone around here has reported a missing dog? I, uh…" Carol slumped in the chair. "Yeah, I think I know what's going on. The dog—"

"*RARF-RARF-RARF-RARF-RARF!*"

Carol jerked the phone from her ear and stared at Roxxy.

"*RARF-RARF-RARF-RARF-RARF!*"

"What's gotten into you? Quiet down so I can talk to Vicky."

"*RARF-RARF-RARF-RARF-RARF!*"

"I'm not giving you a treat. Knock it off!"

"*RARF-RARF-RARF-RARF-RARF!*"

"*Quiet!*" Carol turned sideways in the chair, so her back was to Roxxy. "Sorry Vicky, I'm dealing with a pest… Of *course* it's her. How did you guess? Now, about that dog you found in your car, the truth is—"

"*RARF-RARF-RARF-RARF-RARF!*"

Roxxy dashed around the chair and leaped to paw the phone out of Carol's hand. An elbow fended her off. She landed but sat poised, ready to try again.

"Hang on, Vicky." Carol laid the phone on the table. Her smooth brow creased with horizontal lines. "Roxxy, what's wrong?"

Roxxy lifted her front paws and settled them on Carol's thigh. She gazed into the woman's eyes, not bothering with "baby seal" or any of her other tricks. Seconds passed. The spell was broken by a faint voice coming through the forgotten phone.

Carol blinked.

Her features were troubled as she put the phone to her ear and said, "Vicky, I can identify the dog from the description you gave."

"*RARF-RARF-RA—*"

A hand gently enfolded Roxxy's muzzle.

"Vicky, just after you left, a neighbor stopped by and told me about a dog that fits the description of the one you found… Uh huh, a pit bull. Has to be the same one… Right… The dog's name is Basher." Carol took a deep breath. "The dog's owner is totally out of the picture. He moved away and abandoned the poor thing."

Carol released Roxxy's muzzle.

Metal tags clattered against hardwood as Roxxy's limp form collapsed to the floor, but her eyes tilted upward, unable to leave Carol's face.

"In fact, Vicky—" Carol's dimples appeared but her voice remained serious. "Basher's technically a stray now. I guess you'll have to take him to the shelter. You may not want him, but somebody will."

Roxxy's heart had slowed enough to hear Vicky's outraged reply.

"Carol, are you suggesting I abandon Basher? After everything he's been through?"

"You're not abandoning him by taking him to the shelter. I'm sure they'll find him a good home. Besides, what's the alternative? You know our situation. We can't take him."

"What about me?"

"You?" asked Carol. "I thought you wanted to wait before finding a dog to adopt."

"This is different! Basher found *me*!"

"So what?"

"Don't you see?" replied Vicky indignantly. "Basher and I were meant to be together, and—"

Carol burst out laughing.

"Carol Anderson, how can you... Oh." Vicky chuckled. "You think you're *so* clever."

"I know what a softie you are."

Roxxy could hardly believe it. The plan had worked! Basher was in his forever home. She closed her eyes and pictured her sweet-natured friend curled up next to Vicky.

Maybe a little nap was in order.

"Vicky," said Carol. "That's a good question. How *did* Basher get into your car?"

Roxxy's eyes snapped open. *Time to go*. She leaped to her paws but managed only a step before Carol's fingers curled through her collar and tugged her to a halt.

"Vicky, I'm not sure either, but do you remember when Roxxy was running around out front... Yeah, and leaping up to slam the rear door shut… Do you believe she, well …" Carol listened for a moment and then laughed. "You're right. I don't know what I was thinking. Thanks for the reality check."

The call ended. Roxxy didn't resist as she was hoisted into Carol's lap. She even seized the opportunity to lick an earlobe, searching for the tiny hole that sometimes held an earring.

"Tickles," giggled Carol. She shifted Roxxy to a position that put them face to face. "Can you believe I thought for a second you planned all this? Is that crazy or what?"

Roxxy yawned. *Humans. You had to love 'em.*

AXEL

Axel sat slumped, staring at the scarred top of the yellow Formica table. The early morning sun sliced across a corner, creating a bright wedge in contrast to the surface still in shadow. He winced at the glare.

He knew he was too old to stay up all night drinking, but yesterday had been such a bust...

The rounded head of a cockroach appeared above the table edge opposite him. Sensitive antennae waved, probing the air. Apparently satisfied, the insect climbed onto the surface, exposing the full length of the shield-shaped carapace that glowed bronze beneath the sun's rays.

Axel blinked, lids sliding over eyes grainy with fatigue. The roach was the length of his thumb. The creature shot diagonally across the table. A sibilant sound traced the path as tiny claws scuttled toward a greasy crust of pizza with a sliver of pepperoni clinging to congealed cheese.

A dull pain throbbed at the base of Axel's skull, pulsing in rhythm with the faucet dripping in the kitchen sink. He drained the last of his whiskey from the pint bottle and slammed it down. A crunch sounded as the roach's carapace shattered, and a filament of goo squirted from beneath the bottle to land in the open sugar bowl. Glistening white granules swelled and darkened to brownish orange.

Axel cursed. Could things get any worse? He'd wasted hours yesterday, going door to door trying to find Basher. And what had he gotten for his trouble? Zip. He wished he'd slapped the woman holding the yappy mutt. She'd looked at him like he was something scraped off the bottom of her shoe. And he still couldn't believe how the dog had tried to jump from her arms and go after him. He should have taken the dog by the neck and—

His cell phone buzzed to announce an incoming call. *Yeah, things can get worse.*

He picked up the device and snarled. "I'm not in the mood, Ethan."

"Your mood doesn't interest me."

"Listen—"

"*You* listen. Time's up."

Axel ran a swollen tongue over cracked lips, tasting the bourbon residue. Searching for Basher yesterday and then hitting the bottle had been a mistake. He'd missed the opportunity to snatch the last couple of units to fill the shipment on time. "Look, Ethan. I know I messed up, but—"

"Forget it. You're either coming today or not. What's it going to be?"

Axel picked up the empty whiskey bottle. A spiky roach leg hung from the bottom. He upended the pint with a shaking hand and sucked until a drop slid across his tongue.

"You going to answer me?"

Axel winced and pressed a thumb against the side of the phone to reduce the volume.

"Take it easy, okay? Give me an extra day or two, and I'll be ready."

"Bring what you have," said Ethan flatly. "Now. *Right* now."

"I told you. I don't have the full shipment."

"Fine, I'm cutting the price by twenty percent."

Axel rubbed a hand across a three-day growth of beard. The rasp was like a metal file on a rusty nail. He tried to concentrate, but the bourbon muddled his thoughts. He needed full payment at delivery. There would be start-up expenses after he took over the operation.

"I'm tired of being jerked around," warned Ethan. "Take it or leave it."

"Leave it," Axel snapped, his mind clearing. Ethan wouldn't be calling if the buyer wasn't applying pressure. "I want full payment. I'll gas the units before I let you rob me."

"Gas them? Are you crazy? Those mutts are worth—"

"*Units.*" A grin lifted the corner of Axel's mouth. "Remember?"

He waited, listening to Ethan's harsh breathing.

"Fine. You've got two more days, but there'd better be thirty in the shipment."

"You're the boss, Ethan." Axel's grin widened. "I want you to get everything coming to you."

CHAPTER 27

"Never a good sign."

Roxxy woke but lay still, drowsily listening to the breathing of her parents and sibs. The picture window glowed with soft ambient light from the sun rising in the east. She sighed and snuggled deeper into the blankets. Basher was probably sleeping at the foot of Vicky's bed this very minute. She was glad he was now in a loving home instead of with that horrible creep. Thoughts of Basher triggered a memory. What had he said when she first visited him at that awful pen? Something about...*yes*! He'd mentioned Axel was planning to take him to a remote area where the man had a storage building. She gave an ear flick of satisfaction. The place had to be where Axel was keeping the stolen pets. With any luck—well, a *lot* of luck—she could find it and free the captives before the monster moved them.

She was too excited to go back to sleep. A yard patrol was in order, and she wanted to do it alone so she could come up with a plan. She carefully rose and made her way into the kitchen, pausing automatically beneath the breakfast table. Bill and Carol usually ate in the cozy kitchen rather than in the dining room. Roxxy had a firm policy of giving the floor beneath the table a good sniff, even though there was rarely anything to scavenge. What was it with Carol? Compulsive cleaner? Roxxy flicked her tail in a shrug. No one was perfect. She eased through the dog door and stood on the deck. The treetops stirred in a morning breeze that rippled pleasantly through her curls. She stretched while congratulating herself on having made a stealthy exit.

"AWHOOOOO!"

She flinched. *So much for stealth.* Toby stood just on the other side of the fence that separated their yards, glaring at her through the chain links. Behind him, a line of robins marched across the lawn, heads bobbing as spiky yellow beaks probed the grass with each step.

"AWHO—"

"Hush!" she said in a low woof. "Don't wake the whole neighborhood. I'll be right there."

"Hurry up!"

Her paws pitter-pattered as she descended the pine steps. A quick dash brought her to the fence.

She greeted him with a nose touch and asked, "What are you doing up so early?"

"Dying of curiosity. We haven't talked since you used me as a platform to jump the fence! How did everything turn out?"

"It went—"

Her answer was interrupted by a high-pitched yip from behind her.

"Hi, guys!"

Leo squeezed through the little gap in the chain-link fence that he customarily used for entry to her yard. He shook out his mane—still a bit worse for wear from the encounter with Snatcher—and dashed toward her. Behind his bounding form, tiny dark patches showed on the dew-covered grass where his paws had touched down. She noticed with amusement that he wasn't bothering with the prancing, show-dog gait he normally adopted to irritate Toby.

She and Leo touched noses when he arrived. The Pom moved to the fence to offer a similar greeting to Toby. The basset leaned forward to accept, but the pair suddenly pulled back as they realized they were about to exchange a friendly hello. Leo swept a paw across his muzzle to hide a look of embarrassment while Toby suddenly seemed interested in a black-and-yellow caterpillar inching its way up a metal fence post.

Roxxy broke the silence. "Good morning, Leo." She tracked a ladybug as it landed on the Pom's right ear and folded crimson wings. She made a small wager with herself. Two naps this afternoon if she won, none if she lost.

"Hi, Roxx," said Leo. He shifted his attention to the basset, wrinkling his nose as he did so. "Toby, there's something I don't understand."

"Not surprising. There's so much you're unclear on. Where to begin?"

"What I don't *understand* is why you smell like you slept in a dumpster. How would you climb inside? You've got the vertical leap of an inchworm."

Roxxy noted the ladybug was still perched on Leo's ear. *Two naps.* Easy bet. The bickering had started before the insect could take flight. She huffed, "Would it kill you two to admit you like each other?"

"Preposterous," said Toby.

"Ridiculous," added the Pom.

"Now," added Toby, a twinkle appearing in his chocolate eyes, "back to my leaping ability. Leo, I'll concede that I'm not a great leaper, but my legs are plenty strong. In fact, they supported me when Roxxy used my back as a platform to jump the fence."

"*What? When?*"

The Pom's animation caused the ladybug to rise with a blur of tiny wings.

"Yesterday," responded Toby. "You were probably getting a bubble bath and a comb-out, but *I* helped Roxxy rescue a dog hidden under her house."

"B-But," Leo stammered. "What are...who was...where did—"

"Stop babbling," interrupted Roxxy, "and I'll explain."

"Start at the beginning. Where did the dog come from?"

"Yeah," Toby added. "I'm interested in that part, too."

Roxxy outlined the whole story, starting with how she'd met Basher while Axel was walking him. When she got to the part where she'd first visited the pit bull and saw his living conditions, Toby's eyes took on a hard glint, and Leo issued a surprisingly deep growl. However, their strongest reactions came when she mentioned how close she'd come to getting her head bashed in with the baseball bat. Her friends' horrified expressions told her she should've kept that information to herself.

"What possessed you to take that kind of chance?" demanded Toby. "Axel could've killed you!"

"Yeah, Roxx," added Leo. "What were you thinking? I know you felt sorry for Basher, but that's no excuse for putting yourself in danger."

"What was I *supposed* to do? Just leave him in that terrible situation?"

"You should've—" Leo blinked and turned to Toby. "I got nothin'. You want to take a shot?"

"Not really, but I'll try," said the basset. "Roxxy, I can—"

All three dogs jumped when a squirrel thudded to the ground behind Toby. Overhead, the broken end of a low limb bobbed from the release of the critter's weight. Dried seedpods rattled with the bough's movement. The squirrel bounced upright and ascended the trunk with a clatter of claws.

Toby resumed as if the interruption hadn't occurred, "Roxxy, I can certainly understand why you wanted to get Basher away from that awful man."

Her eyes narrowed. "Something tells me there's a 'but' coming."

"There is." The basset lifted an ear and let it drop in a nod. "You were *really* fortunate it all worked out. You've got to stop pushing your luck."

Leo huffed. "Toby's right, Roxx."

"I'm glad you two finally agree on *something*," she said.

"Don't joke around," snapped Toby. "This is way too serious."

"Roxx," added Leo, his usual bantering tone absent. "I want you to promise never to go near Axel again."

"No." She extended a paw, dragged one of the long papery seedpods toward her, and tore it open with her teeth. The flattish oblong seeds were brown. A single lick left a bitter tingle on the back of her tongue.

"Don't eat those things," warned Leo. "They won't kill you, but they can make you sick."

"Squirrels eat them."

"Forget squirrels!" barked Toby. "And Roxxy, don't you 'no' us! You've got to stay away from Axel."

"Yeah!" added Leo. "We won't let you put yourself in that kind of danger."

"I've got to stop him." She flicked away the seedpod. "That's all there is to it."

Toby and Leo exchanged helpless glances.

Roxxy continued. "Basher said Axel has a place in the mountains just outside of town. The guy calls it the Outpost. I think that's where he's keeping the pets he's been stealing. If I can find it, I might be able to set them free."

The Pom's ears went limp with relief. "So, you don't actually know where this building is?"

"Well, uh…I don't," she admitted.

"Good."

She glared.

"Be mad if you want," said Leo. "I'm just glad you're at a dead end, which might keep you from becoming actually, you know, *really* dead."

Roxxy twitched an ear to dislodge the partial crown of an acorn that had been dropped by a squirrel in a nearby oak. The ribbed segment had bounced off a root before lodging itself in her fur. A quiet crunching came from the squirrel as the rodent chewed the remaining nut meat. She envied the contented critter.

"Roxx," said Toby. "Leo's making a good point. Axel's hideout could be anywhere. There's no way to find it, so you might as well give up."

"I guess," she admitted. "I only wish... Wait a minute!"

"What?"

She sat bolt upright. "Repeat what you just said."

"I said, 'what.'"

"Before that! You said something about the Outpost."

Toby frowned. "Why are you asking?"

"It made me think."

"Never a good sign," said Leo, holding the acorn crown between his front paws.

Roxxy eyed the Pom, and he hastily began gnawing on the ribbed cap.

"Toby," said Roxxy. "What did you say about the place where Axel is keeping the stolen pets?"

"Can't remember. In fact, it's time we all went inside for breakfast. I'm starving." He cocked an eyebrow at Leo. "How about you?"

"Famished," agreed the Pom. "Helen bought a new kibble that's extra crunchy, and—"

"Hideout." Roxxy stared into the distance.

Leo barked. "Lose that train of thought! Let your mind go blank. Pretend you're Toby!"

"Yeah, Roxx. Let—" The basset glared at the Pom. "What did you say?"

"Don't take it personally. I'm trying to distract her from whatever crazy idea she's about to come up with."

"Too late," she huffed with satisfaction.

Toby plopped down on the lawn and rested his jowly chin on a wide paw. He sighed heavily, and blades of grass fluttered in front of his bulbous nose. "Let's hear it."

"The first night I went to visit Basher, I took a close look in the carport and noticed an old tarp covering the bed of Axel's pickup."

"Please," Leo muttered with a groan. "Tell me you're not thinking what I think you're thinking."

Toby flicked a floppy ear to cover his eyes. "Why didn't I sleep in?"

"This is *great*," gushed Roxxy. "All I have to do is hide under the tarp, and Axel will take me to where he's keeping the captives. Get it?"

"Yeah, we get it," growled Leo. "And no, don't do it."

"Right, bad idea," agreed Toby. "In fact, bad, *baaaad* dog for even thinking of it!"

She snorted, "Doesn't work on me."

"It was worth a try."

"Back to the plan," she said. "Basher said Axel usually makes a trip to the storage building late in the evening."

"Why then?" asked Leo.

"I don't know. Maybe to feed the captives. Axel wouldn't go to the trouble of stealing them if he didn't intend to keep them healthy until he"—she shuddered—"goes through with whatever he has planned."

A cold light shone within Toby's normally warm eyes. "And what would that be?"

"I don't know that either, but I'm going to free them before it gets that far."

"Let's say you're right," acknowledged Leo. "You hide under the tarp, and Axel drives to this outhouse—"

"Out*post*," she corrected.

"Whatever. You get to where he's keeping the captives. Then what? You jump out and wrestle the creep to the ground? Knock him out? Take the keys to his truck?" The Pom snorted. "Your paws won't reach the gas pedal."

"Well…after I get to the Outpost, I'll sneak from under the tarp and hide nearby. Then…uh… Then, when Axel leaves, I'll set the dogs free and lead them back to town." She gave a double ear flick of satisfaction. "Easy as pie."

Her stomach rumbled. She liked pie—especially chicken. She didn't understand humans' attraction to fruit.

"Easy…as…pie?" Toby echoed hoarsely. "I don't even know where to start."

"*I* do," growled Leo, stepping so close to Roxxy she could see her reflection in his shining black eyes. "What makes you think Axel won't discover you once you're hidden? All he has to do is check under the tarp for a tool or something. He'll grab you or zap you with that pepper spray, and you'll end up like all those other poor dogs."

"I have to try."

Toby and Leo looked at each other. The ends of their tails flicked in unspoken agreement.

Roxxy's eyes narrowed. "What…?"

"We're in," Toby said.

"Yeah," Leo added resignedly. "Roxx, tell us what to do."

"Forget it. This is my idea. You two stay out of it."

"You're not the only one who can be stubborn," said Toby. "Leo and I are going with you."

"No offense, but neither of you could leap into the bed of a pickup."

"We'll find some way to be useful, Roxx," insisted Leo.

"Provide a distraction, something like that," agreed Toby.

"Roxx, get used to the idea," said Leo. "If you're taking on Axel, Toby and I are coming with you."

Why, she asked the universe, *can't I filter?*

"Well?" demanded Leo.

"Doesn't sound like I have a choice."

"You don't." The basset rose and shook.

A floppy ear smashed a dandelion ball. Dozens of wispy white seeds caught the breeze and sailed through the chain links.

"Right, Toby." Leo wriggled to the side to avoid having the tiny filaments lodge in his mane. "We'll team up to protect Roxxy from herself."

"Don't mind me," she huffed. "Just carry on as if I'm not here."

"When do we go to Axel's?" asked Toby.

"My parents and sibs usually take a nap after dinner. I'll sneak out tomorrow night. I want to be at Axel's before he drives to the storage building."

Leo resumed chewing on the acorn crown. He asked idly, "Not tonight?"

She yawned. "I'm still worn out from dealing with Basher. I want to be fresh when I make the trip to help the captives."

"Sounds good." Toby's morose tone suggested otherwise. He craned his neck to see past Roxxy. "Glad the wheelbarrow is back where it usually is. Do you think Bill will leave it there?"

"I hope so, or I won't be going anywhere."

"*We* won't be going anywhere," corrected Leo.

"That's what I meant." Her glance took in both of her friends. "Guys, thank you for helping me. It means a lot."

"We'll be there," confirmed Toby.

"And be on time. I won't wait for you."

"Don't worry," said Leo. "We don't want to get left behind."

"Good. I'll catch up on my rest, and we'll meet tomorrow night."

She was grateful when Toby and Leo said goodbye and departed. Her rumbling stomach reminded her breakfast was in order. She trotted up the deck steps. The anticipation of a good meal followed by a nap was somewhat diminished by the guilt of lying to her friends.

Still, if a fib was necessary to keep them safe, so be it. Toby and Leo would be snug in their beds tonight.

She'd be in the back of Axel's pickup, on her way to the Outpost.

CHAPTER 28

"What have I done?"

Roxxy waited until everyone in the household gathered in the family room in various stages of a post-dinner food coma, and then she eased through the dog door and padded to the edge of the deck. The crescent moon had already turned the dew-covered lawn into a silvery lake. She pointed her muzzle toward Toby's property and quaked her nose. There was the usual aroma of hound—his oily coat's scent lingered after he went inside—but it wasn't strong enough to indicate he'd been in the yard in the last hour or so. *Good.* She turned to Leo's property and took a deep breath, checking for the flowery bubble bath Helen loved and he tolerated.

Roxxy's bangs twitched in a frown. Spicy aromas of sage, lemon thyme, rosemary, and cilantro from Helen's herb garden blotted out everything else. Her eyes roamed over Leo's yard. No sign of the Pom. She wasn't surprised. He rarely went out at night. *Owls.*

The wheelbarrow was right where she'd hoped, and the leap over the fence was becoming routine. Her fast trot to Axel's home through the intervening neighborhoods was effortless. The quiet cadence of her nails on the sidewalk kept her company. Confidence built with each step. She'd gone head to head with him before and held her own. Why should this time be different?

"EERK!"

The high-pitched yip—*not* a terrified squeak, she told herself—flew from her mouth when a hump-backed possum shot from behind a garbage can onto the sidewalk in front of her. She was airborne in a leap that would've carried her over a pony. A glance down did nothing to soothe her nerves. The possum's beady eyes stared back, shining with a feral glint as they followed her trajectory. The creature's pale lips lifted to expose spiky teeth. Its knobby, hairless tail lay flat behind it on the cement. She landed well past and flung an indignant woof over her shoulder, letting the animal know that if she wasn't on a mission she'd show it who was boss. In reply, its narrow jaws opened in a scathing hiss. She bolted.

Stupid possums!

A few minutes later, she slid beneath the big holly at the edge of Axel's property, rustling fallen pointy leaves under her paws as she settled. A quick scan of the yard and she'd wiggle under the tarp in the bed of the pickup. The light over the back door burned dimly. No fog tonight, but no problem. The windows at the rear of the home were dark. Was Axel in the front part of the house? That would be a bonus. Her gaze moved on, tracing the shortest path through the scattered junk to the carport, and…

A dry click accompanied her swallow. Where was the truck? She'd been so preoccupied with her overview, she hadn't noticed the pickup was gone, which was definitely *not* part of the plan. Wasn't it too early for him to have already left for his nightly trip to the storage building? Her chest fluttered with a thousand butterfly wings. Should she go home? Stay?

The whine of the pickup's engine echoed from the street in front of the house. *Yes!* She shot from her hiding place and dashed for the covered parking pad. The route sent her slaloming around a rusted, upended water heater and the rim of an auto tire with the lug nuts still attached.

She skidded to a stop at the back corner of the carport farthest from the house. A loose grouping of metal trash cans near a support post provided a hiding place. She wormed her way to the middle and hunkered down. In front of her, narrow spaces between the cans provided a view that extended through the carport, down the length of the driveway, and to the road in front of the house. A streetlight shone down on the home's dented aluminum mailbox.

Behind her hiding place, a well-worn dirt path stretched from the rear of the carport to the back door.

Tires hissed as the truck turned into the driveway. Headlights carved an arc across the front yard. She blinked as a thin vertical band of illumination passed between two cans and swept briefly across her face. The truck eased to a stop in the carport, and the engine died with a rattling cough. Her nose wrinkled from the acrid scent of hot motor oil. Boot heels thumped on concrete, growing louder with each step.

She peeked through one of the gaps, catching sight of Axel from the knees down, coming right for her.

RUN! RUN! RUN!

Her legs bunched in response to the command from her jangling nerves. She caught herself in time and stayed put. If she dashed away now, Axel would see her, and the plan would be finished before it even got started! Mr. Jacobs's dog and the other stolen pets would be lost forever. The image of the old man flitted through her mind—back bent with age, hands knobby and gnarled, yet his eyes were bright and his crooked fingers gentle. She clamped her jaw to keep her teeth from chattering and waited.

Bang-bang-bang-bang-bang-bang-bang-bang-bang-bang-bang-bang-bang-bang-bang-bang-bang-bang-bang!

A heart-stopping second elapsed before she identified the sound—aluminum cans cascading into the metal bin in front of her. The racket concluded with a *clang* when a lid slammed into place.

Axel's voice came out thick and half slurred. "Can't have empties with me. Might get stopped by the boys in buu, *hic*, blue."

His voice was followed by the faint buzz of a vibrating cell phone.

"S'up, Ethan old buddy?... Yeah, stopped for happy hour... Don't be so sherious, *serious*. It's all good... Yeah, I just came home for a pit stop and a quick cup of coffee, then I got to make a run to the Outpost to feez—*hic*—feed the units. Doody—" Axel laughed wetly and belched with a sound like carpet ripping. "*Duty* calls."

She stiffened.

Outpost? I'm just in time!

"Wha?" asked Axel in a tone that indicated his good humor had vanished. "Don't tell me how to do my jog, *hic*, job! Gubbye!"

She put an eye to a gap as Axel stepped from the rear of the carport and took the path to the back of the house. The light above the back door left a weak shadow in his wake, weaving in sync with his unsteady gait. She waited until the door closed behind him, then did a quick circuit of the truck. The side windows in the cab were rolled down. She cocked an ear, fearing she might hear the whimper of a captured dog trapped in one of those horrible bags, but the only sound was the steady *tick-tick-tick* of the cooling motor.

A leap carried her over the pickup's closed tailgate. She landed awkwardly atop a thick canvas tarp. Dust flew up, and she responded with three quick sneezes that left her dizzy. *Would Axel come charging out to investigate?* Her heart hammered as she waited. When enough time had passed for her to feel certain she hadn't been heard, she turned her attention to the oversize tarp beneath her paws. The rough material covered the bed of the pickup, concealing a jumble of who knew what, and was rolled at the edges to fit the space. She clawed back a corner and burrowed underneath. The opening she'd created allowed a little ambient light to filter in behind her. She crawled to the middle of the space, inching past engine parts smelling heavily of motor oil. Scattered tools added to the obstacle course. A claw caught on the ridged edge of a socket wrench. She jerked it free. By good fortune, the movement tugged at the canvas. The corner where she'd entered flopped back into place. Total darkness enveloped her. She grunted in satisfaction. If Axel happened to glance in the back of the pickup, the lump she made under the tarp would blend in with the bulges made by the other stuff. She frowned. *Or would it?* There was no guarantee that Axel wouldn't notice her outline and pull back the canvas to investigate—pepper spray in hand! Her mouth went dry. Worse, he might simply fling aside the tarp to look for something among all the junk. Panic growing by the second, she bit the underside of the covering and rolled over again and again to create a cocoon. She realized instantly she'd made a mistake. The wrapping was so tight that her limbs were pressed against her body. Now she was *really* trapped! She wriggled this way and that, but her efforts only tightened the material.

Her mind raced as she tried to figure out how to get free. An idea began to form but evaporated when a muffled sound reached her—the back door of the house just slammed shut! Axel's footsteps followed, steadily growing closer. What was that accompanying noise? It registered as a slow, repetitive rhythm—*jingle, slap, jingle, slap, jingle, slap.* Where had she heard that before? Memory stirred. Bill had the same habit of tossing his keys and catching them while walking to the car. The thought barely finished when the series of *jingle-slaps* ceased.

Roxxy held her breath. Would Axel notice the disturbed tarp, or would he climb into the cab?

Creeeaaakkk...

The protest of rusty hinges sent a wave of relief rolling through Roxxy. *YEESSSS!* Axel was opening the door to the cab and not bothering to check the cargo bed. She'd soon be at the Outpost and could figure out how to free the captives from—

The creak of hinges stopped.

"Tarp's all twisted," muttered Axel.

Roxxy went as cold and still as an ice sculpture.

The bed of the truck dipped slightly. She envisioned Axel levering himself against the side to get a better look. Her beliefs were confirmed when the rank odor of beer and cigarettes seeped through the tarp. His face must be only inches from the other side of the canvas.

"Better see what's going on."

Roxxy felt a tug on the covering. In another second, Axel would unroll the canvas like a rug, and she'd lay exposed. One huge hand would seize her by the neck while the other shoved the can of pepper spray in her face and zapped her at point-blank range. Toby and Leo had been right. She'd been stupid to think she could stow away, and—

"*Yip-yip-yip-yip!—Roxx, it's me!*"

The tarp went slack.

Axel snorted. "Is this my lucky day or what?"

"*Yip-yip-yip-yip!—Get out of there while I distract the guy!*"

Numbly, she ordered her limbs to move, but shock paralyzed her. There was nothing wrong with her hearing, though. She'd recognize that bark anywhere! *Leo! But how?*

"Quick bugger," wheezed Axel.

Leo's mad yipping filled the air. Roxxy could follow the sound, circling the truck. Axel's heavy footsteps followed.

"*Roxx, he'll never catch me. I'll-GAK!*"

"Got you! Can't outrun the juice!"

Roxxy flinched at the triumph in Axel's voice.

She whispered in a ragged huff, "What have I done?"

Leo's choked whimpering was replaced by the snap of burlap unfurling and a soft *whish* from the drawstring being pulled tight. The vehicle's door closed with a metallic clang. The motor whined, coughed, but didn't start.

"Flooded the engine," said Axel disgustedly. "I'll give it a minute."

Roxxy woke from her state of stunned surprise. She had to free Leo! If she could get out of the tarp, she could circle to the passenger side and…and…yes! Leap through the open window, take the sack between her jaws, and jump out before Axel knew what was going on! But could she act before he drove away?

First things first. Get free of the tarp!

The pickup's engine whined once again but didn't catch.

"Don't force it," grumbled Axel.

Roxxy stifled a yip of exultation. *Great advice!* She was trying to fight her way free, but she needed to *ease* her way out, like…like…like the striped garter snake she'd seen gliding through the grass in her back yard! She would *slither* from the tarp.

Forcing herself to go slowly, she wove her body from side to side, gently pushing against the canvas to create more space to operate. *Keep it up!* A few more wriggles and her head slid free. She squinted, temporarily blinded by the streetlight's reflection off the oval window on the back of the pickup's cab. A blink cleared her vision, and a final slithery movement freed her limbs and landed her crouched on the cargo bed.

Ooonh, oonh, ROARRRR-BANG-ROARRRR-BANG-ROARRRR!

The truck's motor surged to life, sending a vibration that traveled up Roxxy's legs and rattled her teeth. *Oh no!* She had to get to Leo! Staying low so Axel wouldn't see her in the rearview mirror, she threw herself over the closed tailgate. A back paw caught the lip, and she tumbled end over end before slamming onto the cement. The revving motor drowned out the impact. She lay dazed next to the rear tire on the passenger side. At the opposite end of the carport, the truck's headlights came on and flooded the back yard.

She had to get to the passenger door and jump through the window!

She staggered upright and leaned against the back bumper, waiting for a wave of dizziness to pass. Axel didn't seem in a hurry to leave. He was gunning the engine, probably in an effort to make sure it didn't stall again. Confidence surged through her. As soon as her head cleared, she'd snatch Leo right from under Axel's nose!

A plume of oily smoke belched from the muffler and hit her in the face. She choked as the vehicle surged backward. The license plate crashed into her flank, and she went down hard. All went dark when the pickup's chassis passed overhead. The rolling tires bracketed her sprawled form without making contact.

She was counting her good fortune at not being squashed when the oil pan caught her on the left side of the head. Her ears rang, and she could barely hear the truck as it continued down the driveway. She lay exposed in the beams of the headlights, expecting a screech of brakes and Axel running toward her with a burlap bag at the ready, but the vehicle didn't slow. She squinted past the glare. Axel was turned sideways on the seat and looking through the back window as he guided the truck into the street. The headlights swung away from her. The pickup paused while gears ground noisily, then it accelerated toward the end of the block.

BANG! BANG!

The double backfire crashed through the night and cleared her thoughts. She gulped. *Leo!*

She rose on wobbly legs. Maybe a loud bark would bring the truck to a stop. She opened her mouth and let fly—or tried to—but her throat was swollen shut from the exhaust. Her bark was a wheezing huff. The vehicle was already halfway down the block, leaving a trail of white vapor.

Move!

She managed a shaky trot, cutting diagonally across the front yard to the street. The truck slowed as it reached the corner. She found another gear and raced down the middle of the road. A manhole cover lay in her path. Her stride lengthened and she sailed over it. *Don't catch a claw in the rim!* Her nose wrinkled at the streams of funky air rising from the small round openings in the steel plate. Ahead, the truck rolled through the intersection without coming to a complete stop. She leaned forward into a full-out charge. The gap began to close, but with the truck in motion, there was no way for her to run alongside *and* leap into a window. Her only option was to jump into the cargo area and figure out a way to free Leo once they reached the Outpost.

Still at a dead run, she focused on the space just above the tailgate. She took a deep breath and sprang, extending to her full length and carving a graceful arc through the air. The cargo bed appeared beneath her. She saw a spot where the bunched tarp would cushion her landing. Hope surged through her. *Don't worry, Leo, I'll stay close!* The airstream tugged at her curls as she descended toward the pickup's bed.

BANG! BANG!

The vehicle shot forward, surging well beyond the span of her leap, and leaving her suspended over the street. The asphalt surface shone with the glow of dwindling red taillights.

The road rushed up to meet her.

AXEL

Gravel crunched under tires as the pickup crested the top of the hill. Axel parked in front of the Outpost and switched off the ignition. Moonlight shone through the windshield and cast his weary features in sharp planes and hard edges. The beer had worn off, and a dull ache pulsed behind his eyes. He massaged his temples until the discomfort eased. Why had he gotten drunk when he was almost at the finish line?

He vowed silently to stay off the booze until he delivered the shipment and settled up with Ethan. The thought lifted his spirits. He leaned across the seat and lifted the burlap sack from the floor. The unit inside began thrashing wildly. A bash against the dashboard put an end to *that*. A whimper filtered through the heavy material.

Axel grinned. *They all learn.*

His cell phone vibrated. He glanced at the screen, and the headache returned. *Another call?*

He pressed the button to accept. "What's up, Ethan? You keeping vampire hours?"

"You were wasted when we talked earlier. I'm just calling to make sure you got to the Outpost okay."

"Aww, I'm touched. You're worried about me."

"I'm worried about the shipment. And watch your mouth. I'm calling the shots."

Axel's laughter shattered the surrounding stillness.

A roosting mourning dove burst from a nearby tree, unleashing a panicked *Coo, coo, coo!*

Axel grunted as he curled forward and reached under the seat. A ping sounded when the flick of a horny thumbnail contacted metal.

"What's so funny?" demanded Ethan.

"Nothing." Axel pinched his nose to kill the laughter.

"How many more units do you need before the shipment is ready?"

"Only one. I'll snatch it in the morning."

"Good. I'll have your cash ready when you get here tomorrow night," said Ethan.

"No. I'll be there day after tomorrow. Early."

"Why wait a day?"

"I got things to do after I snatch the last unit."

"Like what?"

"Like pack all my stuff at the house. I'm clearing out. Even selling the pickup. I'll put a down payment on a new ride after we settle up."

"I don't need your life story. Just get here day after tomorrow. First thing, like you said."

"No problem. I'll—" Axel realized he was talking to dead air.

He pulled the revolver from under the seat. The ball of his thumb settled against the hammer's ridged edge. *Yeah, we'll see who's calling the shots…*

CHAPTER 29

"It's all my fault."

The day was dying in a final blaze of light. Rays from the setting sun pierced the lone window in the laundry room, casting a blood-red square on the cream wall opposite. The tiled floor below remained dark by comparison. Roxxy's tags clanked against the stainless-steel bowl as she listlessly quenched her thirst. Finished, she hesitated, unsure of what to do next. Drops of lukewarm water dripped from the blond fur below her chin and plinked into the half-full bowl.

"Everything okay, Sis?" Max asked.

She turned. Her sibs stood side by side in the doorway, examining her worriedly while blocking the way out. Each stood in a determined, stiff-legged posture that announced they weren't going anywhere until they received some answers.

"Roxx," said Max. "You've been acting weird all day. Like you're sleepwalking or something."

"And you've hardly gone outside at all," added Lulu. "What's wrong?"

"Wrong?" Roxxy gave a halfhearted shake. The water remaining on her chin splattered against the washing machine's white enamel surface. "There's nothing wrong with staying inside and taking it easy."

"True," acknowledged Max. "But there's a difference between taking it easy and moping around in a daze."

"I'm not moping." She took a breath and tried for a playful tone. "Besides, if anyone knows about dazed, it's you."

"Nice try," replied Max. "Now stop messing around. What's up?"

"Nothing."

"Roxx," interjected Lulu. "You didn't finish the scraps of pot roast Bill gave us at dinner. What's going on?"

"I wasn't hungry."

"Since when?" asked Max. "You'd eat an armadillo if you could get one to stand still."

"I'm sick," she replied flatly.

"Oh!" he exclaimed. "Why didn't you say—"

"Of you. And getting more so by the minute."

Max's triangular ears fell.

"Roxx, don't say such things!" Lulu admonished. "Max adores you. We all do."

"Then get out of the way. I mean it."

Lulu stood her ground. "Does this have anything to do with Leo going missing?" Roxxy flinched.

She'd gotten home from Axel's just as everyone was doing their bedtime routine. No one had noticed she'd been gone. The rest of the night had dragged on forever. She'd lain wedged between Lulu and Max, taking no comfort from their presence, and staring unseeingly into the dark. A thrush's trill announced the coming dawn, but the songbird was soon drowned out by the repeated ringing of the front doorbell. Bill was already in the shower, but Carol answered, with Roxxy and the other dogs close on the heels of the woman's fuzzy bunny slippers. Helen—normally as meticulously coiffed as Leo—was in a misbuttoned quilted dressing gown. Her graying hair stood in unbrushed peaks. In a trembling voice, she reported she'd gone to bed early, and when she'd awoken, Leo was nowhere to be found. Helen went on to say she'd already driven through the neighborhood, but there was no sign of him. Carol's face paled as she listened. Within minutes, the two women left the house together to continue the search.

"Roxxy!" Lulu insisted. "*Please* tell us what's bothering you. Max and I can—"

"*LEAVE ME ALONE!*" Her bark was followed by a nip to Lulu's velvety ear.

"*Ouch!*"

Roxxy spat out a few strands of black fur. "I told you to stop bothering me."

"R–R–" Max's cinnamon eyes were wide with shock.

"R–R–" She mimicked cruelly. "Both of you stay away from me!"

She plowed through her stunned sibs before they could react and dashed down the hall. A leaning turn brought her into the kitchen. She crossed the space in a clatter of claws on hardwood and lowered her head to smash through the plastic flap of the dog door. The impact left her dizzy. She paused on the deck. Her nose twitched at the vanilla scent wafting from a stand of yellow cone flowers growing in the perennial section of the garden. A tiny wren atop a nearby birdhouse released a piercing trill reminiscent of steam escaping from a teakettle. The sound cleared her head, and she remembered why she hadn't wanted to come outside. She whirled toward the flap still swinging from her exit.

"*WOOF-WOOF-WOOF-WOOF-WOOF!*"

The series of deep, commanding barks froze her in place.

"ABOUT TIME!" The bellowing continued. "GET OVER HERE!"

Roxxy's tail curled between her legs.

"NOW!"

She reluctantly glanced across the yard. Toby stood on the other side of the fence that separated their properties. His stubby limbs were rigid, and his normally warm chocolate eyes were hard and accusing. She plodded down the steps and shuffled toward him. A squirrel chittered as it dashed across her path, but she didn't track the rodent.

She arrived at the fence. After a second's hesitation, she leaned forward to touch noses with the basset through the chain links.

He ignored the gesture. "Let's hear it."

"What?" She pulled back and lay down, chin on paws.

A beetle with an iridescent, greenish-blue carapace ambled along the fence's base. She focused hard on each movement of its angular spiky legs.

"Cut it out," growled the basset. "Helen came by this afternoon and told Marcy that Leo's gone. Where is he?"

"I don't know," she replied, still watching the insect.

"*Who* has him?"

She lifted her eyes to Toby's but said nothing.

His back legs folded, and his hindquarters hit the lawn with a thud. He gave a single, ragged huff. "Axel."

Roxxy swallowed. "How did you know?"

"You're not as clever as you think you are. Leo and I didn't fall for that stuff about you needing another day's rest before going to Axel's to hide in the pickup."

"But—"

"We worked up a plan to take turns keeping watch so one of us could follow you when you set out. We knew there was a good chance you'd get yourself into a mess and need help. When I came outside for my watch, Leo was gone." His voice deepened into a growl. "What happened?"

She looked away. *So that's how Leo came to be there.*

"Well?" demanded Toby.

"I…I went to Axel's last night. When I got there, I hid under a tarp in the back of his pickup, but I panicked and managed to wrap the thing around me."

"Then?"

"Axel noticed the tarp didn't look right. He was about to discover me when Leo charged in." Roxxy numbly watched a black-striped chipmunk unearth an acorn at the base of the big oak.

"Stop making me drag it out of you," snarled Toby.

She blurted out, "Axel-pepper-sprayed-Leo-and-shoved-him-in-a-sack."

The basset closed his and his big head tilted forward. The tips of his drooping ears brushed the grass.

"I…I know," said Roxxy. "It was horrible. I wanted to help, but I was tangled in the tarp. By the time I got free, the truck was already driving away. I almost caught it…"

"But you didn't."

"No." Roxxy sat up and squared her shoulders. "It's all my fault."

"You got that right!" barked Toby.

The chipmunk threw an alarmed glance at the basset and darted up the oak. Its tiny claws skittered on the trunk, dislodging a filmy patch of gray-green lichen.

"I'm *so* sorry," whimpered Roxxy.

"That doesn't change anything. Leo's stuck in a cage someplace, and he knows Axel has something horrible planned for him."

She winced and rose on unsteady legs. "Well, I…I guess I'd better get back inside."

Toby continued as if she hadn't spoken. "And what about Helen? She's heartbroken."

Roxxy staggered.

"If you'd accepted our offer to help, Leo and I could've tag-teamed Axel. We would've run circles around the creep and distracted him while you got free of that stupid tarp. Axel would never have gotten close enough to score with his pepper spray. But no," continued Toby in an acid tone. "You had to try and sneak away on your own. And you managed to get Leo caught."

"I'm n-not arguing," she choked. "I'll n-never forgive myself."

"Good." Toby stomped a big paw. "Maybe you've finally learned something."

She shrank into herself as if absorbing a blow.

"Stop looking so miserable," huffed the basset. "Tonight, then?"

"Huh?" The change of subject caught her off guard. "What about tonight?"

"Leo. The annoying Pom. Remember?"

"I already admitted I'm to blame for getting him captured," she said wearily. "What else do you want?"

"To get him *un*-captured. Stop feeling sorry for yourself and come up with a plan to rescue the little pest."

Roxxy's eyes widened.

"And stop looking so surprised," ordered Toby. "What did you think we were going to do? Leave the little pest to fend for himself?"

"You believe I can figure out a way to save Leo? Even after everything that's gone wrong?"

"Of course, I do," said Toby gruffly. "You saved Kimberly when she was stuck in the freezer. You didn't give up on her. I'm not giving up on you."

"I, uh, well... *Thank* you."

"Less thanking. More thinking. We need a plan."

She lay down and gnawed on a dewclaw, trying to ignore Toby's heavy pacing on the other side of the fence. Her foreleg was soaked with saliva by the time she gave a confident ear flick.

"Toby, I think this will work." She outlined a revised plan and concluded by warning, "Axel's faster than he looks, and he's deadly with that pepper spray. *Don't* let him corner you!"

"No problem. I'll scamper out of range before he can do any damage."

"Scamper?" A hint of a smile crept into her voice. "You?"

"I can scamper with the best of them. Bassets are known for their agility."

"Compared to what?" she asked innocently. "Anvils?"

"Okay, I'll *lumber* away if Axel gets close."

"Fine," she conceded. "But be careful."

"Look who's talking. When should we set out? After everyone's asleep?"

"No."

"But—"

"We can't wait that long." An unseasonably cold wind prickled the skin beneath her curls. "We're running out of time."

CHAPTER 30

"Does a plan ever go smoothly?"

"I'm...slowing..."

Roxxy's ears swiveled to the rear, but her fast trot continued without breaking stride.

"You...down," wheezed Toby.

She sighed and stopped. *No kidding.* And immediately felt guilty when she turned.

Toby's lumbering form was half a block back, illuminated by an overhead streetlight that buzzed like an angry wasp. His big paws slapped the sidewalk as he rumbled forward in a weary rocking gait. She reminded herself that bassets were built for rooting through densely packed thickets, not for moving quickly over distance. She stepped off the sidewalk. Cool blades cushioned her aching paw pads as she waited on the lawn of an aging two-story house. Her gaze traveled up the dwelling's clapboard siding. A low chimney squatted dead in the center of a sagging roofline. Atop rested a sliver of moon whose tip was as sharp as a scythe. It was poised perfectly, as if balanced by an unseen hand. Hmm...not as late as she'd feared. Even with her friend's slow pace, they'd arrive at Axel's before he left for his nightly trip to the Outpost. If everything went well, she'd be stowed away under the tarp in the back of the pickup, and *this* time she'd avoid making a mess of it.

She tried not to shuffle impatiently as she waited for Toby to catch up. His thick claws clacked against the sidewalk like a horse's hooves. She'd stuck with the plan for them to sneak away from home just after their respective dinners. *Risky, though.* She was counting on her parents and sibs failing to notice she was gone until bedtime. When they did, they'd start whining until Bill and Carol caught on. Her ears drooped at the prospect of worrying everyone. Bill in particular was a softie. He'd be frantic. Carol was likely to keep a cool head and organize the search. By then, Roxxy hoped to be on her way to the Outpost.

Toby had mentioned that his absence from home might go completely unnoticed. Kimberly and her father were on a dads-and-daughters camping trip sponsored by her Brownie troop. Marcy would be home but deep into a book, and Jason—who was staying over while his parents were out of town—had upcoming finals and would be studying. Toby hoped the pair would assume he was asleep at the end of Kimberly's bed as usual.

"Oomph!" Roxxy staggered as Toby stumbled into her.

"Sorry," he apologized. "Lost my balance."

"No problem," she replied, eyeing her friend with concern.

His stubby legs trembled with fatigue, and his panting reminded her of a laboring vacuum cleaner when the bag needed changing.

She huffed. "Maybe you should turn around and—"

"Lead the way," growled Toby.

She set off at a somewhat slower trot, expecting him to lag again, but he somehow kept up. When they arrived at Axel's corner lot, she led Toby to the holly that offered a good view of the back yard and the rear of the house. They slipped beneath the shrub so Toby could catch his breath and scope out the property.

As soon as they were settled, he blurted out, "Did Basher live in that thing?"

She followed his gaze. Axel hadn't bothered to clean the cramped pen. "Yeah."

"I never imagined"—Toby's throat rippled in a dry heave—"anything like *that*."

"He's in a good home now," she remarked absently. "Stop thinking about the pen. We've got bigger problems. Take a look at the carport."

Toby did so.

"Uh, Roxx, I thought you said Axel had a pickup…with a tarp in the back…that you could hide under."

"Yep, I did say that." Then, almost to herself, "Does a plan *ever* go smoothly?"

No pickup was in sight, but it was hard to miss the large white panel truck with an extended cargo section. The vehicle was so long that only the back half fit in the carport. Orange lettering stood out boldly on its side. A closed and latched cargo door faced the back yard.

"What now?" asked Toby.

"Let's take a closer look at the truck."

"How is that going to help?"

"It couldn't hurt. Come on, and don't trip on all the junk in the yard."

She eased from beneath the holly with Toby close behind. They padded across the weedy ground, navigating around a bald tire and a rusting shovel with the metal tip broken off.

They were almost at their destination when the light above the back door blazed on. They froze, illuminated like lawn statuary. Roxxy was the first to recover. She bit down on Toby's nylon collar and pulled him under a sprawling Autumn clematis beside the footpath curving from the back door to the carport.

"Quiet!" she huffed as they huddled beneath the low branches. The blossoms' sweet fragrance was oppressive in the confined space.

Hinges creaked on the back door, followed by heavy footsteps approaching along the path.

An acrid odor penetrated the floral scent. Roxxy wrinkled her nose.

"I hate that cigarette smell," whispered Toby.

"Me too," she replied with barely a breath. "Now pipe down before Axel notices us."

As if on cue, the footsteps stopped. Roxxy shifted to peer through a tiny gap in the foliage. Axel stood so close to the clematis that he could have reached out and crushed a handful of the tiny white blossoms. Fortunately, he was peering around the shrub and studying the corners of the back yard. His head swiveled smoothly from side to side in that creepy mechanical way she'd noticed the very first time she'd spotted him on Leo's property. Only days had passed, but it seemed somehow long ago.

Focus, she ordered herself, watching as Axel's hands curled into fists the size of cantaloupes.

"For a second there, I thought Basher might have come back. Wouldn't that be a treat?"

She heard Toby swallow drily.

Axel finished scanning the yard, shrugged, and continued toward the carport.

"He is one scary human," whispered Toby. "If he is human."

Roxxy was too absorbed in watching Axel to reply. As he walked, he idly flipped a set of keys into the air. The porch light glinted on the silvery objects as they rose and fell, accompanied by a rhythmic *jingle*, *slap, jingle, slap, jingle, slap,* hitting his palm before being tossed again. The pattern continued in rhythm with his strides.

Roxxy frowned.

Where have I...? Her tail flicked in recognition. She'd heard the same sounds when hiding under the tarp. *Must be a habit of his.*

She inched forward and parted the branches with her chin. Axel was at the rear of the vehicle with his back to her. Muscles rippled under his black t-shirt as he lifted the roll-up door. The hinged panel rumbled in the tracks. The only items in the open cargo area were collapsed cardboard boxes and rolls of packing tape. He pulled a cell phone from his pocket and began tapping on the screen.

Toby huffed quietly. "I guess he's changed his routine for tonight. We can come back tomorrow evening. Hopefully the pickup will be here, and you can hide under the tarp."

"No."

The basset's head whipped toward her. A floppy ear slapped her across the muzzle.

He croaked, "No?"

"Toby, look at all that packing stuff. I think Axel's planning to box up his belongings and leave for good. This is our last chance."

She hesitated, listening to moths pinging off the porch light.

Toby is going to hate this...and I'm not crazy about it either.

She said, "Even if Axel's moving on, he has to stop by the Outpost to pick up Leo and the other dogs. He's not going to just leave them there after he's gone to so much trouble to steal them."

"I think you're right, but what can you do?" Toby pointed his muzzle at the carport. "No pickup. No tarp. No place for you to hide and go with him."

"Same plan, different vehicle," she said, trying to sound more confident than she felt. "When he's almost done loading the panel truck with what he's taking from the house, I'll leap into the back and hide myself behind some boxes. Should be a snap."

"Snap?" said Toby faintly. "It'll be a snap all right. Probably your neck."

"Don't be so...graphic."

"Let's say by some miracle that your idea works, and you conceal yourself for the ride to the Outpost. What then? You've never gone into detail about how you're going to free the dogs."

She snorted softly. "I'm sensing a lack of confidence."

"Roxxy."

"I'll figure it out as I go along. The first step is getting there."

"But—"

A loud metallic rumbling came from the rear of the truck. Axel pulled a steel ramp from a slot beneath the cargo area. He walked backward into the yard and dropped the end of the narrow ribbed panel. The ramp crashed against the hard-packed earth with a *CLANG*.

A window slid open in the house next door. The thick torso of a man in a sleeveless t-shirt was backlit by a flickering television. His hairy muscled arms supported him as he leaned on the sill. The tattoo of a fanged snake coiled around his neck. He snarled, "Keep it down out there!"

Axel's features slacked, and he turned.

"Uh," the man said hoarsely. "I didn't mean... I don't..."

"Want to come out and talk it over?"

"S-Sorry," said the man. "I mean, for the interruption!" The window slammed shut, and the bottom pane toppled free. The house's interior went dark even before the glass struck the ground and shattered. Yellow shards shone in the moonlight.

"Roxx," rasped Toby. "There's got to be another—"

"There isn't," she interrupted, watching Axel saunter up the ramp.

He filled his arms with packing materials and reversed course. Roxxy and Toby held their breaths as he passed the clematis and returned to the house. He hooked a heel in the door and pulled it shut behind him. Once inside, he opened one of the small windows at the back of the dwelling. Roxxy's nose wrinkled at the odor of unwashed dishes and old take-out containers.

"What a slob," remarked Toby, whose sense of smell was more powerful than Roxxy's, despite her pug ancestor. "Should we move to another spot while Axel's packing or stay put?"

"Here's fine. We've got good cover, and the truck is only a quick dash away." She tilted her head toward the house. "Let's be quiet though. I don't want him to hear us through the open window."

"Sure, Roxx." Toby swept his wide tongue across his muzzle. "I'm thirsty."

"Join the club. Quiet now, okay?"

Toby rolled onto his side. "I'll just rest my eyes."

Roxxy placed her chin on her paws and settled down to wait. The noise coming through the window indicated Axel wasn't wasting any time. The high-pitched screech of packing tape pulled from a roll was followed by the thud of objects thrown into boxes. Time dragged on. She gave a soft snort when she noticed Toby had fallen dead asleep. His nostrils dilated and contracted in rhythm with his deep, regular breathing, pushing away the fallen petals in front of his nose and leaving a wedge-shaped space of bare dirt.

She shifted to ease the pressure of a twig digging into her belly, careful not to wake her friend. He needed the rest, and she needed to think. Something niggled at the back of her mind. What was it? Try as she might, she couldn't pin it down. She was so preoccupied it took a moment before she realized the packing sounds had stopped.

"Toby—" She nudged him hard with a shoulder. "Wake up."

"Washn't...*wasn't* asleep," whispered Toby indignantly. "Resting my eyes is all."

"I was about to check for a pulse."

"I'm awake now. What's up?"

"I think Axel's ready to load the truck."

"What makes you…"

Toby's voice trailed off as the house's back door opened.

Axel sidestepped through with a cardboard box tucked under each arm. Roxxy and Toby spent the next half hour watching from beneath the clematis as the man methodically loaded the truck. She was surprised by how neatly Axel stacked the boxes, wall to wall and almost to the ceiling, filling the front third of the cargo area. Roxxy dug her claws into the drying leaves scattered on the ground. *Probably leaving room to pack the captives.*

"The way he's arranging those boxes," whispered Toby, "there's nowhere for you to hide."

"Don't be so negative," insisted Roxxy. "He's not finished."

"Almost finished," muttered Axel as he trudged past the clematis on the way to the truck.

"You were saying?" Toby quirked an eyebrow.

Roxxy grunted in reply.

Axel clomped up the ramp and lifted a box to fill one of the two empty slots in the top row of a wall of cardboard containers several layers deep.

Her eyes narrowed as she studied the space between the boxes on top and the interior roof.

Axel jumped from the cargo area without bothering to use the ramp.

Roxxy and Toby were silent as the man passed in front of the clematis. The light above the back door sent his shadow rippling across the shrub. Roxxy waited until he disappeared inside the house before turning to Toby.

"Thanks for coming with me tonight." She brushed her muzzle against his, feeling the coarseness of his whiskers. "Be careful going home."

The folds in the basset's wrinkly forehead deepened. "What are you—? *Roxxy!*"

The shrub's branches raked her back as she shot from beneath the clematis. Three bounding strides and she was at the base of the ramp. A sudden thought—*claws clang against metal*—sent her swerving at the last instant. A flailing jump lifted her over the back bumper. She landed on the smooth wood of the cargo area. Unchecked momentum sent her sliding across the boards. The wall of boxes loomed ahead. She bunched her legs and sprang. The arc of her leap carried her over the top row of containers, but her back paw caught a cardboard edge and sent her into a wild tumble over the surfaces. She smacked into the front wall of the cargo area. A smell rose from the box digging into her ribs. Hmm…Axel's unwashed socks or a dead rat? Hard to tell.

She stiffened as the back door to the house slammed shut and a lock snapped into place. The scuff of Axel's footsteps grew louder. Her eyes darted wildly. *Toby had been right!* The carefully stacked containers offered no place for her to hide. Axel was tall enough to spot her the minute he entered the cargo area, and—*what's that?*

A blackened rectangle of shadow was notched between the front wall and an adjacent box. She hurried over. The gap would be a tight fit, but it was deep enough to conceal her. However, once she was in, getting out would take some scrambling.

Bang-bang-bang-bang-bang!

Axel's boots rang on the metal ramp. Roxxy gulped and dropped into the narrow space. One flank slid over the smooth wall panel while the other brushed cardboard. Her paws settled on the box below. She felt like a piece of bread in a toaster, but she was completely hidden.

Thump!

The box against her shoulder vibrated. Axel must've added one to the last slot in the outermost stack.

"Done," said the man.

The sudden cell phone buzzing nearly startled a yelp out of Roxxy.

"What's up, Ethan… Yeah, going fine… Just finished putting my stuff in the truck… Will you stop worrying? There's plenty of room for the cages… That's right, I'm leaving for the Outpost in a few minutes… I'm not sure, I've got a few things to do there… Lay off, Ethan, I'll be on the road to your place by dawn… Yeah, should be there around noon. See you then."

Roxxy gulped.

Going to the Outpost was what she wanted. Right?

"Why is this uneven? Hmm…a box in the back must be caught on something."

Roxxy gasped as the container beside her pressed against her flank. The sound was lost under Axel's grunts as he put all his weight against the outer box that corresponded to her hiding place. Air whooshed from her lungs, and her rib cage creaked as if compressed in a vise. A spiderweb of red veins pulsed across her field of vision. Consciousness was slipping away when the pressure along her flank eased as suddenly as it had started. She sagged within the narrow space and greedily sucked in air.

"I don't get it," mused Axel. "Better crawl on top for a better look."

Roxxy shivered. *Uh oh.*

"Awhoooooooo! Awhoooooooo! *AwhooooOOOOOOO!*"

"What the…?" Axel's voice trailed off.

"*AwhooooOOOO! AWHOOOOOOOO! AWHOOOOOOOO!*"

Bang! Bang! Bang! Bang! BANG! BANG! BANG! BANG! *BANG! BANG! BANG! BANG!*

Roxxy listened as sixty pounds of basset charged up the loading ramp.

"*AWHOOOOOOOO! AWHOOOOOOOO! AWHOOOOOOOO!*" bellowed Toby. "Roxx, I saw what Axel was about to do! I'll distract him!"

"You squatty mutt!" Axel shouted. "Get out of here!"

"*AWWHHOOOOOumph!*"

Roxxy winced as the baying was cut off by a boot thudding into flesh.

"*Oomph!*" grunted Toby. "Those chains *hurt*!"

"How's that feel?" crowed Axel. "Ready for another one?"

CRACK!

A sliver of wood appeared above her head. The object ricocheted off the ceiling and the pointy end embedded itself in the top of the box beside her.

"*ARRGH!*" bellowed Axel.

"Roxx!" barked Toby. "I dodged his last kick! He smashed his foot into one of the boards supporting the wall. Little pieces went everywhere!"

THUD!

"He missed again and fell! I'd better get out of here while I can. Good luck!"

BANG! BANG! BANG! BANG! BANG! BANG! BANG! BANG! Bang! Bang! Bang! Bang!

Roxxy listened as her friend descended the ramp. She suppressed a snort. *Toby* can *scamper with the best of them.* A new thought sobered her. *What would Axel do now? Go back to examining the boxes, or—?*

The roll-up door hissed in its tracks and banged shut. Total darkness enveloped her. A faint rumble sounded as the loading ramp settled into the slot below the floor. An instant later, the engine roared to life, sending a shiver through the cargo area. The truck lurched into motion. Wearily, she crawled from the cramped hiding spot and collapsed atop a box, instantly asleep.

CHAPTER 31

"Get back here!"

Toby's thick claws scraped the sidewalk as he shuffled forward. Only two more blocks to go. His tail wagged wearily as he envisioned his special blanket at the foot of Kimberly's bed. Without thinking, he drew in a deep breath and grimaced. The pain in his side was a reminder of Axel's kick. Roxxy had warned him that the man was fast, but Toby still couldn't believe a human so big could move that quickly. Where was Roxxy now? Still on her way to the Outpost? Or—he swallowed drily—had Axel discovered her? She could be stuffed in a sack right this minute.

Or a cage…

He paused beneath a streetlight and gave himself a head-to-tail/tail-to-head shake that slapped his ears against the sides of his head. Feeling better, he cut across a corner yard with a wide, well-kept lawn.

His street was only a block away. He passed a two-story house and saw the bottom edge of the crescent moon hanging well above the chimney. Nearly midnight. The walk home from Axel's had taken longer than expected. Fatigue and sore ribs had forced him to take several rest breaks.

A rosebush at the corner marked the entrance to his street. The fat yellow blooms seemed to float against the foliage that blended with the night. The sweet scent reminded him of Kimberly's shampoo. She and her dad would be back tomorrow from their overnight Brownie outing. In the meantime, he was grateful to be nearing home. Soon, he'd be easing through the dog door and sneaking up the stairs to Kimberly's room. Once there, the custom steps would allow him to reach his usual sleeping place at the foot of her canopied bed.

He brushed past the roses, being careful to avoid the thorny stems. The silky-smooth petals slid caressingly down his flank. He turned the corner and stepped onto the street leading to his house.

And stopped dead.

All the houses were dark except for two—his and Roxxy's. They sat side by side and shone like beacons, the porch lights spilling out onto front lawns. The tip of Toby's tail brushed the sidewalk before curling between his legs. Even half a block away, he could tell what was happening. The search was on for him and Roxxy. Thank goodness Kimberly was away. Otherwise, the little angel would be worried to death about him. And Marcy? He could almost hear her already. *I've been so concerned for you! Bad dog! It's not like you to run off!*

He snorted. Then she would cave and give him a treat.

Toby's heart stuttered as a piercing trill split the air—*chuck-will's-widow, chuck-will's-widow, chuck-will's-widow*. The volume suggested an animal the size of an ostrich. Toby glanced at a low branch of the nearest maple. A bird no bigger than his paw stared back beadily and fluffed its mottled brown-and-black feathers. The tiny chest puffed and another high-pitched *chuck-will's-widow, chuck-will's-widow, chuck-will's-widow,* ripped through the night.

Toby ordered himself to get moving and take Marcy's scolding, but he was still dawdling when his front door opened. Marcy hurried down the porch steps. Jason followed at a slower clip.

The boy yawned and rubbed his hand over his eyes. Pajama bottoms peeked below the legs of his jeans, and his white sneakers were untied. "Aunt Marcy, you haven't told me what's going on."

"Roxxy and Toby are missing," the woman replied without stopping.

Jason's eyes widened. "*What?!*"

Marcy stopped at the rear of her car, parked in the circular driveway. A chirp sounded as the trunk opened. "Where did I leave that flashlight?"

"What do you mean missing?" asked Jason.

"As in *gone*," said Marcy testily. She bent forward, and her upper body disappeared inside the compartment. "I know it's here somewhere."

"Start at the beginning," Jason pleaded.

"A few minutes ago, I discovered Toby wasn't here. That's why I woke you up."

"I'm confused." The boy pushed away a lock of auburn hair from his forehead. "What makes you think Roxxy went with him?"

"I didn't say she was *with* Toby," replied Marcy, still rummaging. "I said she and Toby were missing."

"How did you find out about Roxxy?" pressed Jason.

"Before I woke you, I called Carol to see if Toby might be over there. No luck." Marcy sneezed.

"Bless you."

"Thanks. I need to vacuum out this trunk."

Jason prompted, "And Roxxy?"

"Carol said she noticed Roxxy was gone hours ago." Marcy straightened and massaged her lower back. "She and Bill took separate cars to cover more area. I asked why she didn't call me to help, but she said they thought they'd find Roxxy pretty quickly."

"But Mrs. Anderson's back." Jason excitedly pointed at the Honda SUV parked in the driveway of Roxxy's house. "Maybe—"

"No," Marcy interrupted, again leaning forward to search the trunk. "Carol said she's come home for a quick break and to check on the other dogs. She's going back out in a few minutes."

"And you and I are taking your car to look for Toby?" asked Jason. "And hopefully Roxxy?"

"Uh huh. We'll—*finally*!" Marcy lifted a flashlight from the trunk. "I knew I'd left it here."

She flicked a switch, and a weak cone of light appeared.

"I'd change the batteries, but I don't want to waste time." She studied Jason in the ambient light cast by the beam. "Honey, you're flushed. Are you coming down with something? Let me feel your forehead."

The boy dodged her hand. "I'm fine, Aunt Marcy. Just worried. Let's hurry, okay?"

"I'm concerned too, but I'm sure we'll find them. Besides, Toby's not the kind of dog to get into trouble."

"What about Roxxy?" asked Jason.

"Well, that's a different story. She's a handful."

"*Woof!*" bellowed Toby in affirmation, then quickly clamped his mouth shut.

He hadn't meant to draw attention to himself. The flashlight's yellow beam rippled over the lawn.

"Toby?" called Marcy. "Is that you, boy?"

"Near that bush!" said Jason.

Toby squinted as the cone of light found him. The chuck-will's-widow released another raucous call.

"Get over here, mister!" commanded Marcy, voice trembling with relief.

Ears drooping, he obeyed. Marcy was a sweetie. Causing her to worry was the last thing he wanted. He felt even guiltier when she knelt and enveloped him in a tight hug. He inhaled the aromas of fresh soap and warm skin, so much like Kimberly's.

"*Bad* dog!" Marcy scolded unconvincingly. "I can't believe you ran off."

Jason squatted to bring himself eye-level with Toby. "Where's Roxxy? Where's our girl?"

"I wish I knew," replied Marcy as if the question had been addressed to her.

"We have to find her." Jason scratched Toby behind the ears.

"*Woof!*"

The bark's force blew the lock of hair away from Jason's forehead.

Marcy chuckled. "I think Toby agrees with you."

"Dogs are smart." Jason sighed. "I just wish my mom…"

"She might feel differently one day."

"You really think so?"

"Well…"

"Yeah," Jason said despondently. "Me neither."

The scuff of a sneaker drew Toby's attention to Roxxy's home. Carol stepped onto the porch and eased the screen door closed behind her. The strap of her tan purse was thrown over her shoulder, and car keys glinted in her hand. She waved half-heartedly at Marcy and Jason, then strode down the steps. She was wearing a green baseball cap, and her long red hair was pulled through the little gap in the back. Her makeshift ponytail swung from side to side as she walked, causing Toby to feel slightly queasy as he recalled an experience with a pony at Kimberly's last birthday party. The kids had spent all their time fawning over the creature while ignoring him, despite his role as loyal canine protector. To add injury to insult, the sneaky horse had delivered a solid kick to his shoulder when no one was watching.

Toby put aside the memory of the diabolical pony and focused on Carol as she approached. The corners of her mouth and eyes were lined with worry, and the knuckles of the hand clutching the car keys were bloodless. He wagged his tail in greeting. She stopped in mid-stride, obviously just noticing him. Relief smoothed her features. Blue eyes scanned the area around him, and then her anxious frown returned.

Toby felt his tail go still.

Carol looked at Marcy. "Roxxy?"

"No sign. I'm *so* sorry."

"That means…she's out there all by herself." Carol dabbed her eyes with a crumpled tissue from her purse.

"I'm sure she's fine," said Marcy, blinking away tears of her own.

"Cut it out," Jason snapped. "*Both* of you. Boohooing isn't going to help Roxxy."

Marcy placed her hands on her hips. "You know better than to speak—"

"He's right." Carol gave Jason an appraising look. "Thank you."

"Uh, yes, ma'am."

"Carol," said Marcy, absently reaching out a hand to ruffle Jason's hair. "Have you heard from Bill?"

"He just called. No sign so far. He's going to continue searching the east side of town, and I'll take the west. We started close in, but now we'll head farther out." She straightened her shoulders. "I'm glad Toby's home, but I'd better get back out there and look for Roxxy."

"You mean *we*," corrected Marcy. "Jason and I will come with."

"I might be driving around all night," said Carol. "You two should go to bed."

"Forget it," said Marcy and Jason in unison.

The pair looked at each other. Marcy arched an eyebrow. The boy's face reddened, but he held her gaze.

Marcy grinned and turned to Carol. "You heard the kid. All for one and one for all."

A ghost of an answering smile flickered across Carol's face. "Good. The company would be nice, and three pairs of eyes are better than one. We'll take my SUV."

"Right," replied Marcy.

Toby huffed in agreement as a knot of tension uncoiled in his chest. The thought of Roxxy taking on Axel by herself had been worrying him. He wanted to be there when—

"I'll take Toby inside and lock the dog door," Marcy said. "He'll be fine until we get back. I don't want him disappearing again while we're gone." She paused and grabbed his collar. "Come on, buster."

Toby tried to pull away, but Marcy was dragging him to the front door before he could stiffen his legs to resist. In desperation, he went limp and tried to belly-flop.

"Up!" Marcy snapped.

Toby felt himself hoisted upright by the collar—his thick neck ensured the brief maneuver wouldn't injure him—and propelled forward. He tried digging in with his back paws.

"That doesn't work when it's your bath time," said Marcy with a grunt of effort. "And it won't work now."

Toby glanced over his shoulder. He had a direct view of the driver's side of Carol's white SUV. She was already behind the steering wheel. Jason was sitting in the back seat on the same side. The boy gripped the handle of the rear door but hadn't yet pulled it closed.

"Come on!" wheezed Marcy, skirting a coiled hose near the front porch. "In the house!"

Toby stopped resisting and plodded along beside her.

"That's better," Marcy said approvingly. "We're almost there."

The grip loosened on his collar.

"I'll pour you a bowl of kibble," began Marcy, "and then—"

He flung his weight backward and pulled free.

"*Toby!*"

He evaded a grab and raced toward the SUV. Jason still hadn't pulled the door closed.

"*Woof!*"

Toby wondered if his bellow would do the trick. Some humans were a little slow. He didn't think Jason fell into that category, but you never knew. Fortunately, recognition dawned on the boy's face, and he withdrew his hand from the car door.

"Get back here!"

Toby ignored Marcy's command and charged past Kimberly's abandoned pink bicycle, resting on the lawn. He crossed into Roxxy's yard and barreled toward the SUV. Jason waited in the back seat, dimples showing. Toby heard Marcy's footfalls in pursuit. He put on a burst of speed. Chrome trim outlined the frame of the open door, beckoning him. He leaped, intending to clear Jason and land on the seat beyond.

"Oomph!"

Sorry, thought Toby, rising from the boy's lap.

"Wow," said Carol, who had turned to watch. "That was like a walrus wallowing onto an ice shelf."

Toby threw her an offended look before scrambling off Jason and wedging himself into the far corner.

"*Bad* dog!" Marcy exclaimed breathlessly as she arrived and peered past Jason. "Toby, out of there. Now!"

He sank into a deadweight sprawl.

"No you don't!" Marcy leaned across the boy and made an awkward grab for Toby's collar.

"Oomph!" Jason grunted, rubbing his stomach.

"Sorry about the elbow." Marcy took a step back but remained bent at the waist and glared at Toby. "Get over here before I come around to the other side and drag you out."

He sank deeper into the seat.

"Toby!"

"We need to get going," said Carol. "Why is he acting so weird?"

"Your guess is as good as mine." Marcy paused before adding in a tone heavy with meaning, "Dogs."

"Tell me about it."

"Aunt Marcy," said Jason. "Let Toby go with us. He's as worried about Roxxy as we are."

"What are you? A dog whisperer?"

"I don't have to be," replied Jason reasonably, "to figure out he's pretty determined."

Carol shrugged. "The kid's got a point."

"I give," said Marcy, throwing her hands in the air. "Toby, move closer to Jason so he can grab you if we brake suddenly."

Toby obeyed.

Marcy raised an eyebrow. "*Now* you're cooperating?"

"He wasn't misbehaving," said Jason. "He didn't want to be left out."

Toby gave the boy's ear an enthusiastic lick. Saltier than Kimberly's, but not bad.

"Yuck!" Jason lifted his shoulder to wipe the side of his face.

"Serves you right," observed Marcy. "Co-conspirators."

Toby watched with satisfaction as Marcy closed Jason's door and walked around the car to slide into the front passenger side.

"Seat belt," Carol reminded Jason as she looked over her shoulder while backing the vehicle down the driveway.

Marcy tilted down the sun visor and opened the flap on the underside to expose a lighted mirror.

She frowned while examining her frizz of blond curls. "I wish I'd never gotten this perm."

"You look great," replied Carol.

"I look like a dandelion." Marcy flipped the visor back in place. "What's the plan?"

"We'll take it slow to be sure we don't miss Roxxy, but we'll go as far out as we have to. You know that little scamp. She"—Carol's voice faltered before recovering—"could be up to anything. She might be miles away."

"I'm *sure* she's fine," said Marcy. "Probably chasing a rabbit right now. She'll wear herself out and come home."

"Maybe." Carol glanced into the rearview mirror and made eye contact with Jason. "You watch on the left while Marcy keeps a lookout on the right. I'll try to scan both directions, but I have to pay attention to the road."

"Got it," said Jason, peering out the side window as the car neared the end of the block.

Toby brushed his muzzle against the soft hair at the nape of Jason's neck, hoping the boy would turn and give him a scratch behind the ears. Instead, Jason stayed focused on what lay behind the glass. Toby licked the slightly salty skin above the collarless t-shirt.

Jason scrunched up his shoulders. Without turning, he muttered, "Tickles."

Toby studied the pinched features reflected in the window. Jason's jaw was set in a hard, determined line. The hazel eyes flicked back and forth, scanning each passing property.

A prickle rippled down Toby's spine as Jason's mouth moved and a bloom of condensation appeared on the glass.

"I'll find you, Roxxy. I promise."

CHAPTER 32

"I'm on my own."

The truck braked hard. Roxxy's body—curled atop a box—maintained its forward momentum and smacked into the cargo area's front panel. She bounced off the metal surface and, by sheer happenstance, dropped paws-down into the narrow slot where she'd previously hidden. The tightness of the space kept her from toppling over as the vehicle turned sharply before coming to an abrupt stop. The engine quieted to an idle. Hinges creaked on the driver's-side door.

Her ears swiveled, tracking Axel's footsteps by the crunch of gravel. He paused in front of the truck. *Click!* The sharp sound was followed by the rattle of a chain. The footsteps returned, and the vehicle crept a short distance forward before halting again.

The sequence of sounds reversed, beginning with Axel moving behind the truck and concluding with the same, *Click!*

Roxxy shifted uneasily.

Great. Axel has the road to the Outpost chained off.

A soft huff escaped without her realizing it. "I'm on my own."

Gears ground together, and the truck climbed at a slow, steady pace. Stones pinged off the undercarriage. Unpaved road? A sudden jostling bounce from a pothole sent the boxes atop the outermost columns crashing to the floor. The truck climbed in a series of sharp back-and-forth turns. The contents of Roxxy's stomach swayed in rhythm with the rocking motion. Drool dampened the corners of her mouth. *Don't puke!* After what seemed an eternity, the course straightened, and the pitch angled upward as the truck crested a final rise. A short stretch of welcome flat terrain followed before the ride paused. Gears ground, and a curving reverse sent another wave of nausea through Roxxy. The truck braked a final time, and the engine died.

Roxxy's stomach settled and her hackles rose. *The Outpost!*

Footsteps moved from the cab and approached the rear of the truck. Roxxy's bangs twitched. What was that other noise? The regular light clinking? She was sure she'd heard it somewhere before… Oh yeah. The noise's origin popped into her brain, and with it an idea. She blinked in the darkness. Could the solution be *that* simple?

Casters rattled as the roll-up door slid open on curved rails. The purple-tinged illumination of an outdoor light flooded the cargo area. She ducked in her hiding spot, nose wrinkling as pine-scented air rushed in, sharp with tannin-rich sap. Her nose quaked. *Not many hardwoods.* She recognized several familiar animal scents, among them squirrel, fox, and raccoon. Some of the smells were new. One odor was so rank and powerful it sent her tail between her legs. Some ancestral trait identified the source…*bear.* She shifted restlessly. How far away from home *was* she?

A blast of cursing came from the open cargo door, trailing off with, "I should've run a strap across the load. I'll check on the units and then get this junk straightened out."

Footsteps retreated.

Roxxy blew out a relieved breath. Her chance to get out of the truck was coming sooner than expected. She peeked above the lip of her hiding spot. A gravel parking pad spanned the short distance from the rear of the vehicle to a barn-like metal structure. Axel's broad back was visible as he approached the building. Roxxy's first impression was that the structure looked abandoned. Uneven rust bands flowed down corrugated walls leaning on the foundation. A pedestrian door was directly across from Roxxy's position. The upper half of the panel probably once contained a window but was now covered by a ragged square of metal siding. Above the door, moths pinged noisily off a blazing lightbulb before circling back in swooping arcs for another bash.

Axel stopped in front of the entry and slipped a key in the lock. The knob turned. He pushed, but the panel didn't budge. He took a wide stance and placed a palm in the center of the door. Muscles bunched across his shoulders as he shoved. No movement. Another try met with the same lack of success.

"Always sticks..." he grumbled before turning slightly and slamming a shoulder against the door.

It crashed open and bounced off an inner wall. As if on cue, an explosion of yowling erupted.

"Shut it!" commanded Axel, reaching inside to flip on a light switch.

The torrent of anguished barking continued, rolling past Axel and crashing into the truck's cargo area like a tsunami. Roxxy flattened her ears to little effect. The cries came in waves of hopelessness. She raked a paw across the side of her face, trying to rip away the sound. *The captives have already given up! There's nothing I can do to—*

A single, defiant voice rose above the defeated chorus.

"*YAP! YAP! YAP! YAP! YAP! YAP! YAP!*"

Roxxy ears lifted.

Leo!

"Shut it!" shouted Axel.

"*YAP! YAP! YAP! YAP! YAP! YAP! YAP! YAP! YAP! YA—*"

"*SHUT IT!*"

The barking stopped. She supposed even Leo knew not to push Axel past a certain point. The thought barely finished before the man disappeared inside the building and slammed the door behind him. The panel wedged in the frame rather than settling neatly. She wasted no time. A squirming hop freed her from the narrow slot. She trotted to the edge of the stack and eyed an area on the floor where none of the boxes had fallen. A leap down and a dash carried her to the lip of the cargo area.

Roxxy landed on the parking pad in a spray of gravel. A soft *yip* escaped when a sharp rock wedged between her toes. *No time to stop!* She rounded the back bumper and ran along the side of the truck until she reached the front wheel well. It was a tight fit, but a determined wiggle allowed her to slide between the tire and the curved metal frame.

Concealed, she mulled over the plan for preventing Axel from leaving with the captives while she went for help. She was confident she'd figured out a way to pull it off. The problem was execution. Precise timing *and* help from the captives would be needed at the critical moment.

Roxxy shifted to get more comfortable, and flakes of smelly road grime rained down on her back. The desire to shake was almost overwhelming, but there wasn't enough room. She settled for peeking around the edge of the frame to get another look at the Outpost. A pair of garage doors were positioned next to the pedestrian entry, but the large panels had been welded shut with a hardened lumpy bead of gray material. No windows were in sight. She was willing to bet the other sides of the building contained none either. Axel wouldn't want anyone seeing inside. The pedestrian door was probably the only way in or out.

The wheel well was too cramped for her to stretch out, so she belly-crawled to the middle of the undercarriage. She carefully avoided the black oil dripping from some type of inverted bowl thingy beneath the engine. Getting comfortable on the gravel wasn't easy, but she found a suitable spot—she was acknowledged in the family as an accomplished lounger—and settled down to wait. She had a clear view down the length of the vehicle and could see the bottom third of the door to the Outpost. She'd be ready the moment Axel appeared.

She spent the time inspecting the bottom of the paw where she had registered a twinge of pain after jumping from the truck. A bit of gnawing revealed a pointy sliver of gravel wedged into the base of a nail. She shivered. *Could have pierced the pad and been much worse!* Her teeth worked the sliver free, and she ran her tongue across her muzzle to get rid of the grit that had clung to the stone.

Her thoughts returned to Axel. She was now clear on how to prevent him from driving away with the captives. Unfortunately, she needed *them* to provide a distraction at the critical instant. But how to tell them without Axel spotting her? Hmm... Her best bet was to sneak into the Outpost while he restacked the fallen boxes.

Scccreech!

The Outpost's warped door was wrenched open with a sound like a saw ripping through sheet metal. Roxxy's heart hammered as Axel approached the rear of the truck. *Yes!* The instant she heard him moving around in the cargo area, she would dart into the Outpost. Her muscles tensed, but he unexpectedly veered around the back bumper. She tracked his footsteps to the driver's door. The hinges creaked, but he didn't climb in. Instead, his boots were planted less than a yard from where she lay beneath the undercarriage. The black rounded toes were dusty, and the chains' sharp edges glittered like diamonds.

CHAPTER 33

"Hair trigger."

Roxxy cocked an ear at the noise coming from above. It was so close that Axel must be fumbling for something under the driver's seat.

"Must have slid back...got it!" A pause. "Needs a good cleaning to get rid of the rust."

The truck door slammed with enough force to dislodge several fat drops of oil from the engine. Roxxy made herself small and avoided being spattered. Her eyes stayed on Axel's boots as he retraced the path to the Outpost and clanged the door shut behind him.

Her eyes narrowed. At the front corner of the building, a cone of light—unnoticed by her until now—streamed through a jagged, tennis-ball-sized gap at ground level. She wriggled from beneath the truck and darted to the spot. The hollow carcass of a long-dead beetle lay speared on a spiky prong of twisted metal at the opening. She sniffed the air flowing through the gap. The eye-watering reek reminded her of Basher's pen—only worse because the smell was concentrated from being confined in a building. There was nothing to see through the gap other than the rounded side of a metal trash can, but there was plenty to hear. Axel whistled off-key. The captives whimpered at a volume plain to her but inaudible to human ears. What was that other noise? *Rasp-rasp-rasp.* It reminded her of when Bill sharpened the blades of the garden shears with a whetstone.

Snap!

Roxxy jumped.

"Hair trigger." Axel paused before continuing with a snicker. "Units, I've got a nice surprise for your Uncle Ethan."

She suppressed a growl. *Bullies like an audience…but what's a hair trigger, and why is he so pleased about it?*

"Ready for a ride?" asked the man. "Let's get your cages stacked by the door to make the loading easier. And no yammering while I work. I'm sick of you mutts."

Roxxy listened to the rattle of pens being roughly handled. An explosion of barking followed. She jerked away from the opening, and her chin brushed the dead beetle. The husk disintegrated into powder. She sneezed before she could help it, but the sound was lost under the yowls and protests caused by the cages being moved about.

"*QUIET!*"

The command silenced the captives.

"I said no yammering, and I meant it. Hmm, looks like I need to show you what happens when you disobey me." He chuckled. "Ever seen any bowling?"

Roxxy frowned. Bill and Carol sometimes tried lawn bowling in the back yard with a ball the size of a grapefruit and some flat-bottomed wooden pins. "Tried" was the operative word that crossed Roxxy's mind because the humans rarely finished a game before she snatched one of the pins and started a far more interesting game of keep-away. But what was Axel talking about? Seemed unlikely he'd have a bowling layout inside the building.

A cage rattled, and the high-pitched squeal of a dachshund pierced the air.

"I've seen your photo on flyers all over town," said Axel. "Bet your old owner would have a fit if he knew what was about to happen."

Leo yammered, "*YAP! YAP! YAP! YAP! YAP! YAP! YAP! Stay away from Wiggle, you gutless creep! Look at the way she's cringing!*"

Roxxy stiffened. Wiggle? Where had she heard that name before? And more importantly, *why* couldn't Leo keep his mouth shut?

"*YAP! YAP! YAP! YAP! YAP! YAP! YAP! If I could get free, I'd sink my teeth—*"

"Guess I'll forget the poster dog," said Axel with a snort. "I've got a volunteer."

"*Yiiipppppp…*"

Leo's terrified wail died under the banging rattle of metal bouncing across concrete. The noise ended with an explosive *clang*!

"You mutts see that?" Axel wheezed with laughter. "The little yapper's cage knocked over those old oil cans at the back of the building. Strike!"

"I've got…"

Roxxy was relieved to hear her friend's voice, but it was so weak she could barely understand what he was saying. She tossed her head and flicked back an earflap, exposing the pink canal beneath. Carefully, she placed the side of her face against the opening.

"To…hang on…until…"

She pressed harder, wincing as a razor-thin sliver penetrated her tender flesh.

"Roxxy gets here."

She sat back and numbly watched a single scarlet bead drip from a twist of rusty metal.

"Let that be a lesson to the rest of you," said Axel.

Roxxy felt a breeze stir her curls. The bead dropped and splattered.

How did Leo know I'd come?

"Cages stacked," said Axel with a satisfied grunt.

She blinked, realizing she'd barely heard the clatter of pens being gathered.

"I'll get the boxes in the truck sorted out, and then I'll start loading you mutts. Don't go anywhere." He laughed. "Get it?"

Roxxy eased from the front of the building and backpedaled along the side wall. Seconds later, the door was pulled open and crashed against an interior wall. Axel's heavy footfalls moved to the truck.

Roxxy padded softly forward and peeked around the corner. Axel was at the vehicle, gripping the loading ramp stored beneath the cargo hold. He walked backward. The ramp rumbled in its track as it slid free.

She glanced at the entry to the Outpost. Her breath caught. The door stood open! She reached the threshold without scattering gravel and paused to allow her eyes to adjust to the harsh light spilling out. Details were a blur, but there was no hiding the glint of metal cages or the dull coats and bent backs of the cringing captives. Her nose quaked at the reek of neglected pens and canine hopelessness.

She charged straight in.

CHAPTER 34

"Nice of you to drop by."

As soon as she was through the entry, Roxxy pivoted hard left and stumbled over a sharp-edged metal toolbox resting on the floor. She stayed upright, but her shoulder brushed against the front of an old refrigerator. Brick-red flakes flew from the rust-pitted enamel. She skidded to a stop and scanned her surroundings, giving only a passing glance to the cages stacked near the door. Her first priority was to locate a hiding spot in case Axel returned before she could brief the captives and get out.

The Outpost's interior was about the size of a storage barn she'd explored when the family had visited Carol's parents in the country, but the farm building had been divided into neat, well-maintained sections that held tractors and harvested crops. The Outpost was one big space and so dank and dilapidated it looked like it might collapse at any second. The rough concrete beneath her paws extended from wall to wall and was etched by brown stains that worked their way in crooked paths to a slotted drain in the middle of the floor. Above, the metal roof was dotted with holes where rivets had sprung free. Wooden rafters supported the span and were liberally dusted with white mold.

Roxxy flinched when a wind gust beat against the exterior of the building. The structure swayed on the foundation, and shadows swirled as boxy light fixtures—suspended on chains from the rafters—swung this way and that. Air whistled through the holes left by the popped rivets. A *snap* sounded, and a splinter the length of her foreleg separated from a beam and plummeted toward her head. She sidestepped. The makeshift spear hit the floor and cracked in two. A fat gray termite waddled out.

The wind died, and the light fixtures ceased swinging. The shadows settled and revealed that the front half of the building was better lit than the back. The fluorescent tubes were missing in the rear. She cocked her head and peered into the depths of the building. Too dark for humans to make out much, but she could see well enough to identify the items near the back wall—scattered oil drums, rusting metal shelves, lumpy bags of sand, and dusty footlockers. Plenty of places for her to hide if Axel unexpectedly returned.

A squarish object rested near the oil drums, but her eyes skittered away from it.

Not yet…

She turned her attention to the well-lit area around her. Fresh white scratches traversed the cement, starting at the side walls and ending at the cages stacked haphazardly near the door. The captives had been silent since she'd entered the building, which wasn't surprising. She'd counted on her appearance being so unexpected they'd be in shock…but that wouldn't last long.

She did a quick scan of the cages' occupants. About half the captives were purebreds and the rest mixes of this and that. Among the dogs with pedigrees, a cocker spaniel hunkered in a cage atop a stack three high. His white-and-chocolate coat was lumpy with knots of matted fur, and his flanks moved like bellows as he panted. In the adjacent stack, a miniature Doberman pinscher paced nervously, claws chittering against the hard plastic panel that served as a base for the pen. And below that, a flat-faced, brown Pekingese stood trembling. Specks of half-chewed kibble clung to the corners of his mouth.

The mixed breeds included a Chihuahua-schnauzer mix with gray torso and legs, short black beard, and white-tipped ears. The next pen housed a tan dog whose wiry body and large triangular ears signified a universal mix of breeds. She sat shivering and oblivious to her surroundings. A strand of silver drool dangled from her mouth.

In a cage atop one of the other stacks, a black-and-white beagle mix stood on short sturdy legs. The expression on her thin face was bleak, and her big paws constantly kneaded the pen's base. The enclosure below held a small dachshund. The little dog had curled itself into an impossibly tight ball—the posture of a canine withdrawing deep inside to block out the pain of existence.

Roxxy took a deep breath and met the gazes of the dogs who seemed aware of her presence. The captives' eyes were every shade imaginable—tan, amber, honey-gold, chestnut, chocolate, black, startling blue, and even striking green—all glazed with despair.

Roxxy swallowed. *So many dogs…*

Realization dawned. No wonder Axel had limited his belongings to a quarter of the space in the long panel truck. There were enough cages to fill the rest of the cargo area.

"H-Hi," stuttered the Pek with the crumbs stuck in his short muzzle. "My name is—"

"Quiet," interrupted Roxxy, not yet ready to tell the prisoners what she needed of them.

She instantly regretted cutting off the Pek's greeting. His bushy tail curled between his legs, and he started to shiver.

Roxxy added hurriedly, "Sorry, I'll explain everything, but I need to check something first."

I can't put it off any longer.

She trotted to the back of the building. The dented cage rested in the murky area where the overhead lightbulbs had burned out. As she approached, a tiny form struggled upright within the confines, swaying on wobbly pipe-cleaner limbs. The figure stumbled sideways but righted himself and stood. Roxxy noted the dullness of the matted orange-brown coat. Leo's normally flawless mane had collapsed into warped folds like a deflated basketball…but his amber eyes were bright and hard despite the gloom. She leaned forward and touched noses. His was worrisomely warm. A deep scratch along his shoulder oozed crimson.

"Hi," she said.

"Nice of you to drop by," growled Leo.

"I was in the neighborhood."

He snorted.

"I'm going to get you out of here," said Roxxy.

"Hang on a sec." He looked past her and huffed quietly to the captives. "I *told* you guys Roxxy would show up."

The remark snapped the prisoners out of their communal sense of despair. An explosion of yaps, barks, and howls filled the building.

All amounted to variations of "*HELP!*"

The sound wave shook the building. A metal rivet dropped from the ceiling and bounced off Leo's battered pen with a *ping*!

"Roxx!" barked Leo in a voice loud enough to carry over the roar. "I didn't mean to set them off."

"My fault," she replied. "I shouldn't have expected them to stay quiet for—"

"*The man's coming!*" yipped the miniature pinscher, pressed against the back of his cage and staring through the doorway.

"Hide, Roxx!" snapped Leo.

She dashed to an old footlocker in a rear corner of the building. A slot gaped where the rotting chest didn't quite meet the back wall. Scattered rat droppings littered the narrow space. *Gross!* She sighed and wriggled fanny first into the opening, knowing a fast exit might be needed. The moldy smell of the old leather was nearly as bad as the rodent poop. Her rump hit the corrugated wall, and she crouched down, completely hidden. The corner was dark enough that Axel could be almost on top of her and not know it unless he pointed a flashlight into the space. Of course, that meant she couldn't see him either. She edged forward and peeked around the edge of the footlocker. Her line of sight ran the length of the building.

"*SHUT UP!*" roared Axel, striding over the threshold.

The chorus of barking died as if the captives' vocal cords had been slashed.

"That's more like it!" Axel put a thumb over a nostril and blew a wad of yellow snot into a pen. The glop splattered against the curly white ear of a cringing bichon.

"Bullseye. As for the rest of you, if I have to come back in here before I finish getting those boxes restacked…"

Roxxy listened for the remainder of the threat. It remained unspoken, which was somehow scarier than if he'd finished. She hoped he would go back to the truck. The last thing she needed was for him to wonder what had caused the captives' outburst.

He turned to the doorway.

Her gut unclenched.

Axel suddenly stopped. He pivoted and stared at the cages, scratching his chin. Fingernails rasped against the stubble. "Why *did* you mutts start barking? Something set you off?"

Roxxy groaned. *Is the creep a mind reader?*

"Better take a look around."

She knew she should slip back to be completely hidden, but the desire to keep an eye on Axel won out. She stayed very still as he approached the rear of the building. His path carved a line down the center of the floor space, and his head swiveled in the creepy side-to-side motion she'd noticed on their first meeting. The overhead lighting and his heavy brow left his face devoid of features except for hard planes and knife-edge shadows. A boot heel clanged against the drain in the middle of the floor.

His form became less distinct as he moved into the half of the building where the overhead fluorescent tubes were missing. A kick sent a hubcap spinning out of his way. Sparks shot from under the disk as it bounced across the floor before clanging into an oil drum. The container rang hollowly. Axel passed Leo's cage without stopping. Another stride and he'd be close enough to spot her if she didn't slink back into her hiding spot. Ever so slowly, she withdrew until completely concealed.

Maybe he'll give up…maybe he'll return to the truck to finish securing the boxes…maybe…

The wishful thinking died when his footsteps stopped next to the footlocker. She risked a quick peek. And froze. Axel stood within a yard of her. By sheer luck, his face was turned away, or he would've instantly spotted her. Roxxy's nose twitched at the sour smell of old sweat. He was wearing greasy jeans and a sleeveless t-shirt. Short, wiry strands of hair curled from the edges of his armpits.

Her legs tensed. She was seized by an overwhelming urge to bolt—zipping past him was doable, as long as his attention was elsewhere—but she forced her muscles to unknot. The critical moment hadn't yet come in her plan to save the captives. When it did, everything would depend on surprise.

She had to stay put.

Her stomach settled on the mouse droppings as she sank into her cozy hiding place. *Cozy* sounded better than what it felt like—*deathtrap*. Now, if the creep would just go back outside and—

Thunk, thunk.

The footlocker vibrated and released a shower of dust. A fine layer settled on her nose. She tried to lick it away, but her tongue was so dry she made it worse by smearing it.

Thunk, thunk.

If she hadn't been lying on her tail, the tip would have twitched in understanding. Axel was toeing the footlocker to see if something would run out from behind. Where were those stupid creatures who'd left the poop?

There's never a rat around when you need one.

"Forgot this old thing was here. Better check that gap in back."

A hand appeared overhead, descending slowly as if unsure of what it would find. She eyed the pale crescent of flesh between thumb and index finger. A hard bite wouldn't allow her to escape—Axel had her hemmed in—but she could go out fighting. Her lips skinned back in readiness as she waited for the hand to come closer.

"*YIP! YIP! YIP! YIP! YIP! YIP! YIP!*"

She jerked as the high-pitched, rapid-fire barking ripped from a single throat and battered the walls.

"*YIP! YIP! YIP! YIP! YIP! YIP! YIP!*"

Roxxy was so startled by Leo's maddened yammering it took her a moment to realize the hand was no longer in sight.

"You?" exclaimed Axel. "*Again?*"

Roxxy's ears lifted to funnel in sound. The man's voice was further away now. In fact...*oh no!*

"I bet you got the other mutts stirred up while I was outside. Maybe it's time to forget bowling and try a different sport." The man snickered. "How about football? I've always wanted to kick a field goal."

"Yip! Yip! Yip! Don't worry, Roxx! The jerk's focused on me now. Yip! Yip! Yip! Yi—"

CLANG-CLANG-CLANG-CLANG-CLANG-CLANG-CLANG!

Roxxy looked around the edge of the footlocker and saw Leo's cage tumbling end over end toward the front of the building. His tiny body bounced around the interior like a rag doll in a clothes dryer.

CLANG-CLANG-CLANG-CLANG-CLANG-CLANG-*CLANG*!

The rolling frame smashed into the trash that had blocked her view while crouching at the corner outside. The mangled pen bounced off and settled in a heap of broken wire spokes. Leo lay crumpled at the bottom of the wreckage. The fluorescent lights shone through the ruined cage and left a tangle of shadows covering his still form.

"Serves you right," snarled Axel, striding through the door without bothering to look at his handiwork.

Roxxy waited until the man's boot heels rang on the truck's loading ramp, then dashed to Leo's pen—or what was left of it. She chose a gap and shoved her nose through, but the limp form was too far away to reach. Her nostrils quaked, and she sighed with relief. Leo didn't have the dead smell that set in when life left the body. *But why wasn't he moving?*

"Leo," she whispered, "Wake up."

Nothing.

"Leo!" Her huff was louder and more desperate. "You're scaring me! Please—"

The Pom's flanks expanded in a breath, but he remained otherwise limp. She didn't allow herself to dwell on the possibility he might never regain consciousness. A quick trot took her to the stacked pens. She surveyed the occupants, who were clearly stunned after seeing Axel kick Leo's cage the length of the building. They stood stiff-legged and trembling…

well, except for one dog. The small dachshund was still curled in a tight ball of deadened withdrawal.

A flicker of motion drew Roxxy's gaze to the doorway. Just outside, a brown, pebbly toad landed, and a piece of gravel rolled from beneath its splayed foot, cracking against the metal jamb. The creature's pink tongue shot out, stretching like a piece of well-chewed bubblegum. The globular end smacked into a low-flying fat moth and reeled in the struggling insect. Madly fluttering wings disappeared into the toad's pink maw.

Roxxy grunted. What would it take to get a good omen for a change? She turned to the captives.

"Who's ready to go home?" she asked.

CHAPTER 35

"We thought you'd be bigger."

"G-g-go home?" stammered the Pek with the crumbs around his mouth. "You really mean it?"

Roxxy flicked an ear in assent, wondering how the loaf-shaped bundle of fur was able to breathe out of that squashed-up nose. Her muzzle—she wrinkled it daintily—was a bit shortish because of the distant pug ancestor, but it was practically *pointed* compared to the Pek's. Poor little guy.

He asked, "What are you staring at?"

"Nothing," she replied guiltily. "Let's talk about getting you home."

"We'll do anything you want!"

"Great. What's your name?"

"Bam-Bam."

"Nice to meet you. I'm Roxxy. I want to—"

"S'cuse me," interrupted a male bichon. He raked a paw across the ear that Axel had spat upon, but the sticky substance was embedded in his curls. "Leo promised a dog named Roxxy would come and rescue us. Is that you?"

Her tail flagged at the mention of her friend's name. She forced it back up. "Yeah, that's me."

"Does Leo know more than one Roxxy?"

She felt the fur bunch at the scruff of her neck. "What's the problem?"

The bichon exchanged a look with Bam-Bam.

"Roxxy," blurted the Pek. "We thought you'd be bigger."

"Than what?"

"Just…you know, *bigger*. Leo said you'd find a way to deal with Axel. We thought you'd be huge like a Great Dane."

"Or fierce like a rottweiler," added the bichon.

"No offense, Roxxy," continued Bam-Bam, "but you're a blond fluff ball with an underbite. You look like a cuddler, not a fighter."

Roxxy sighed. *I do like a good cuddle.* She recalled the times she'd hopped onto the couch and wedged herself between Bill and Carol or lounged in a tangle with her parents and sibs. She shivered. *Will I ever see them again? And what about that boy, Jason? He's good at petting. Too bad his mother doesn't like—*

"Roxxy," prompted Bam-Bam.

"Sorry." She cocked an ear to make sure Axel was still shuffling boxes in the back of the truck. Satisfied, she returned her attention to the Pek. "I'm tougher than I look, and I *have* taken on Axel before."

"You've come out on top?"

"Absolutely."

If by "on top" you mean "escaped with my life."

"Roxxy," whuffed a brown-and-white Welsh corgi in the top row of cages. "Hasn't anyone ever told you to stay out of trouble?"

"Constantly," she acknowledged.

"Clearly with no effect," said a shih tzu, leaning forward and pressing a furry face against the wire mesh. Square imprints appeared on the gray-and-black cheeks. "Tell us about your plan."

"How did you know I'd have one?"

"Leo said you've always got a plan."

Bam-Bam added, "And he said to go along with it, no matter how crazy it sounds."

And a lot of good it did him, came the unbidden thought.

She forced her eyes to remain on the Pek instead of wandering to the crumpled cage that held her friend's body.

"We need to keep Axel from driving off with you guys"—she absently placed her paw on a crushed cigarette butt and flicked the smelly thing behind her—"so I can go get help."

"How do we keep him here?" asked Bam-Bam.

She quickly went over the plan.

When she finished giving instructions, she asked, "Questions?"

There was no reply. Instead, the captives' ears drooped, tails fell, and postures sagged.

Why, she wondered, *am I the only one who likes my plans?*

"Roxxy," said Bam-Bam dubiously. "I know Leo said to go along with whatever you—"

"I'm for the plan," came a weak huff.

The miniature dachshund uncurled from the tight ball she'd previously made of herself. She tried to initiate a head-to-tail/tail-to-head shake, but the movement sent her staggering. The pen rattled as her thin body bounced off the side. She righted herself and stood on trembling legs. A brown patch shaped like a bow tie sat dead center in her narrow chest.

She turned to Bam-Bam, whose cage was next to hers, and gave a soft snort. "Let's go with the fluff ball's crazy idea."

"Thanks," said Roxxy. "Feeling better?"

"Some." The dachshund began panting, revealing white gums. A long pink tongue made a pass across her pointy muzzle. "Thirsty is all."

"I'm sorry," replied Roxxy. "Hopefully you'll be home soon, and Mr. Jacobs can fill your water bowl."

"I'd love a drink of—*you know my Rodney?*" Her eyes changed from dull brown to a glowing honey-gold.

"Nice elderly man? Beautiful hands?"

The dachshund's curled tail went into overdrive. "Yes!"

"And you're Wiggle?"

"Right again! Is Rodney okay? I've been *so* worried about him."

"He misses you."

"I miss *him*! Rodney's legs cramp up horribly sometimes. He cries when it's really bad. The only thing that makes him feel better is if I put my head under his palm. He'll rub my ears and smile no matter how bad he's hurting."

"Your Rodney's waiting for you, Wiggle. You'll be back with him in no time."

"Promise?"

Roxxy started to reply with an automatic yes but paused when a sudden wind gust pressed down on the metal roof. The wooden support rafters groaned. The weight of the structure—and the fate of the captives—seemed to settle on her spine.

"Wiggle, I'll do my best."

"Fair enough. We'll be ready when you give the signal." Wiggle glared at Bam-Bam. "*Won't* we?"

The Pek wagged his tightly curled tail. "You got it."

The other captives added huffs of agreement.

Roxxy stiffened as footsteps approached from the truck. She hesitated only long enough to sweep the dogs with narrowed eyes—*be ready*—then darted to the front wall and crouched on the far side of the old refrigerator.

The spot would keep her out of Axel's line of sight when he reentered the building. She wedged in tight beside the fridge, feeling its condenser hum against her side.

A boot heel rang on concrete. She peeked around the edge of the fridge. Axel was facing away from her. His muscles rippled across his shoulders as he hefted a pair of pens. She'd noted the occupants earlier—a cocker spaniel and a beagle mix. The dogs yelped at the careless handling of the cages. Axel cursed and gave the containers a violent shake. The spaniel toppled over and lay panting. The beagle mix stayed balanced on splayed paws and slid across the plastic bottom. She crashed into the side of the pen but somehow remained upright on sturdy legs.

Axel turned to the doorway. The spaniel was still sprawled on his side, flanks heaving and gasping for air, but the beagle mix had assumed a ready crouch and was watching Axel from the corners of her brown eyes. The dog's lips fluttered in a silent snarl. Her gaze shifted and met Roxxy's.

The beagle mix blinked twice to show she'd be ready when the time came.

Roxxy grunted with satisfaction. *I can count on that one.* She waited until Axel's boot heels rang on the loading ramp, then darted from behind the fridge.

Before reaching the doorway, she flung a quiet huff to the captives. "Remember the signal!"

No replies came. She frowned as she crossed the threshold. Were they being careful to avoid drawing Axel's attention? Or was their resolve waning? She rounded the corner of the building. A few strides and she was out of Axel's line of sight. She planted herself and leaned against the cool metal siding.

Might as well relax.

Soon her front teeth gnawed worriedly at a dewclaw. She made herself stop and sniffed the breeze funneling along the side of the building. The acrid smell of pine resin was overwhelming. She swallowed to clear the bitter taste pooling at the back of her throat. Giving up on the dewclaw, she turned all her attention to fretting. How long would it take for Axel to load the truck? Would the captives follow their orders? Would—

Yikes!

A bat zipped from behind her, and a clawed wingtip yanked a whisker from her muzzle as it passed. The animal took the corner ahead by flipping sideways and disappearing around the edge of the building. She barely had time to blink before a reverse maneuver bought it zooming back with a fat moth wriggling in its mouth. She sat frozen as the flight path settled on a course that would intersect with a spot between her eyes. A last-second twitch of a wing sent the bat skimming by.

She gulped. *The great outdoors is highly overrated.*

"Almost done."

Roxxy's ears perked up when she heard Axel's muttered comment drifting from the cargo area. She had momentarily forgotten about him. A feeling of nervy excitement swept through her. She crept forward and slid half of her face around the corner, just in time to see Axel place a pair of pens atop stacks in the nearly full cargo area. One contained Wiggle, whose eyes still shone with the possibility of being reunited with her Rodney. The other cage contained Bam-Bam, whose throat was working as if he was trying to avoid throwing up. Roxxy couldn't blame him. Her stomach was flitting about like a butterfly in a gale.

Axel's cell phone rang. He cursed before putting it to his ear.

"What now, Ethan?"

Roxxy was pleased to see Axel's face flush with anger as he listened to the caller. Maybe he would be thinking about this Ethan guy when she made her move.

"Take it easy," Axel said. "I'll be headed your way in a minute…

Yeah… Yeah… I got all thirty. Had an extra, but he didn't make it. Little yapper got what he deserved."

Roxxy's nose twitched at the smell of freshly turned earth. She tugged a front paw from the ground and shook a ribbon of soil from her claws.

"Lay off!" Axel snapped. "I said it was an extra. Sometimes you need to make an example to keep the other units in line… Yeah, whatever… Just have the cash ready when I get there… Leaving now. Well, after I lock up. Don't want any hikers wandering inside the Outpost and finding the dead unit… Uh huh, see you later."

Dead unit?

Roxxy's stomach dropped. Had Leo died while she was waiting for Axel to finish loading the truck? Numbly, she shoved the thought away.

Focus!

The next few minutes would determine whether Axel drove off with the captives or whether he'd be stranded here. If she could keep him from leaving, she'd have time to backtrack the route the truck had taken—*hopefully*—and bring help. The dog on the TV show did stuff like that all the time. How hard could it be?

She backpedaled to put more space between her and the corner so she could be at a dead run when she cleared the side of the building. A sharp pain caused her to glance down. Her front paw rested on a lime-green pinecone covered in densely packed short spines. She flicked it into the underbrush.

She leaned forward, straining to hear. Sure, there was the crunch of gravel as Axel approached the door to the Outpost, but so what? Where was the sound that everything depended on? Her ears vibrated in tiny rhythmic movements like twin tuning forks…nothing but crushed rock shifting under Axel's boots. Well, there was also her nervous panting, but that didn't count.

Could she have been so wrong? Had she chanced too much on—?

Jingle, slap, jingle, slap, jingle, slap, jingle, slap, jingle, slap...

Roxxy streaked around the corner of the Outpost. Her paws left the ground as she rose with limbs extended, arrowing toward the target. She unleashed a deafening bark that split the night to signal the captives.

"RAHR-RAHR-RAHR-RAHR-RAHR- RAHR!"

CHAPTER 36

"You're starting to worry me."

"AWWOOOOO!" bellowed Toby.

The sound echoed around the SUV's interior like an avalanche of boulders bouncing down a canyon. The vehicle swerved and sent him toppling into Jason's lap.

"Sorry!" gasped Carol, jerking the steering wheel to bring the big Toyota back on track. "I've never heard him bay like that."

"*AWWOOOOO!*" reiterated Toby.

He'd begun to think they'd *never* find Roxxy.

"Toby, quiet!" Marcy swiveled to stare into the back seat. "What's gotten into you?"

"*AWWOOOOO!*" Toby leaned across Jason and pressed his nose against the cool surface of the window.

He squinted at the thorny hillside sliding past. Why wasn't Carol slowing down? His ears lifted, and he frowned in concentration, listening for more of Roxxy's frantic barking.

"*AWWOOOOO!*"

"Aunt Marcy," said Jason excitedly, "I heard something!"

"Me too. A crazy basset hound."

"*Before* that! I think I heard Roxxy."

"*AWWOOOOO!*"

Jason said, "Toby heard her too."

"*AWWOOOOO!*" He gave the boy a sloppy lick on the chin.

"Toby!" snapped Marcy. "I'm not going to tell you again. Be quiet! And what"—she glared at Jason—"are you talking about?"

"*AWWOOOOO!*"

"*Toby!*"

"Aunt Marcy," replied the boy, wiping his chin on his shoulder. "I *know* it was Roxxy. I heard her barking in the distance when we passed that side road a few seconds ago. The one leading up the hillside. I'm sure Toby did as well."

"I didn't hear anything until you two started up." Marcy's cheeks puffed as she blew out her breath. She resumed in a softer tone, "Jason, it's nearly four in the morning, and we're all getting loopy. Let's agree you and Toby were imagining things and leave it at that." She glanced at Carol. "Right?"

"I...I'm not sure. I didn't hear anything, but I'm so tired I might have missed it." Carol began slowing the car. "Maybe Jason and Toby are onto something."

Tires crunched on loose stones and twigs as the vehicle edged to a stop on the side of the deserted road. The engine idled quietly.

Marcy lifted a hand to cover a yawn. "Carol, I know you're frantic about Roxxy, but she couldn't have gotten this far from town. We shouldn't even be looking out here. Let's go home and get a couple of hours of sleep. We can start searching again when we're fresh."

"But what if they're right?" Carol tilted her head toward the back seat. "What if Jason and Toby *did* hear Roxxy? They seem pretty certain."

"*They*," said Marcy wryly, "are a basset hound who barks at the TV during dog food commercials and a kid who adores Roxxy so much that wishful thinking's getting the best of him."

"I just like dogs," said the boy.

"Sure," replied Marcy.

"Wait a minute," said Carol. "Does Jason adore Roxxy? News to me."

Marcy snorted.

"He was like a zombie when I woke him tonight, but the minute he found out Roxxy was missing, he went to DEFCON Four." She rubbed her temples. "Or is it, DEFCON One? I can never remember which is the scariest."

"You *are* getting loopy." Carol glanced in the rearview mirror and met Jason's eyes. "Roxxy is pretty adorable, but Marcy's right. We should head back."

"Hang on," insisted Jason. "Let's turn around and check. The side road's only about a quarter mile back."

"I saw it, but the entry was blocked by a chain stretched between concrete posts."

Marcy nodded. "And there were steep banks on either side. No way for us to get around."

"What's wrong with you two?" Jason slapped the seat with an open palm. "This is Roxxy we're talking about."

Toby stared wide-eyed. *Go Jason!*

"You're starting to worry me," said Marcy, reaching over the seat to press a palm against the boy's forehead.

Jason shook her off. "Look, the chain blocking the road might not be padlocked. If we can get past it, we could drive up the hill. Roxxy might be hurt or something."

Marcy shook her head. "We can't trespass on private property in the middle of the night."

The boy's lip trembled. "Sure, we can. We just—"

"Jason," interrupted Carol, "Your heart's in the right place, but you're not using your head. Listen to your Aunt Marcy. We'll go home and get some rest and then start again in a few hours."

Jason nodded and slumped in the seat.

Carol put the SUV in gear. The vehicle rocked as it eased onto the road.

Toby planted his paws wide apart on the vinyl to keep his balance. Acceleration pushed him back and he plopped down on his haunches. He noticed Jason staring out the side window. Toby frowned. Why had the boy given up instead of insisting Carol turn around?

"Jason," said Marcy through another yawn. "I'm sure Roxxy will turn up, and—"

Toby blinked in astonishment as the door beside Jason opened wide and the boy dove from the speeding SUV. A white sneaker was bright against the darkness before he was swallowed by the night.

"*What the*—" Carol slammed on the brakes.

Toby dug his claws into the seat to avoid being thrown to the floorboard. The vehicle slid to a stop. He rose and twisted to peer out the rear windshield. Twenty feet back, the taillights illuminated Jason in a red glow. The boy was on his hands and knees in the sparse grass bordering the pavement. Toby gave a huff of encouragement as Jason staggered into the road and pelted away. In the distance, moonlight glinted on the chain barring the entrance to the side road.

"We'll go back," Carol said shakily as she wrestled the steering wheel.

Tires screeched as the vehicle careened across the road in a tight turn. The unlatched door flew open and bounced against the hinges.

"Wait!" Marcy turned in the seat and made an unsuccessful grab for the rear door's handle. "I need to shut this before—"

Toby sprang for the opening but was jerked upright when Marcy's hand tightened around his collar.

"Stop right there, buster! You are *not* following Jason!"

Toby went still. Marcy had a firm grip on his collar. Her knuckles pressed into the scruff of his neck. Could he break the hold? *Should* he break it? The requirements of being a *good dog* demanded he obey her. Marcy wasn't only Kimberly's mom but a lovely person in her own right. The woman deserved absolute respect. All this flashed through his mind in an instant.

"That's better," said Marcy. "Now settle down and—"

Sixty pounds of basset hound lunged for the open door.

"*Toby!*"

"*Marcy!*" Carol ducked away from her friend's knee as Marcy began climbing into the back seat.

"Toby seems determined to go after Jason," groaned Marcy. "Which is the *last* thing we need."

Carol put the car in park and set the emergency brake. "I'll hop out and close the back door."

"Thanks! He's about to pull my arm out of the socket!"

Toby felt a pang of guilt but redoubled his efforts. In the corner of his vision, the SUV's headlights splashed over Carol as she hurried around the front. He torqued and twisted like a marlin trying to break a fisherman's line.

Crack!

The pressure on his neck disappeared as pieces of the plastic collar hasp ricocheted off the padded ceiling.

"Oh no!" wailed Marcy.

Toby launched himself toward the open door even as Carol pushed from the outside to close it. He realized he'd been a half step slow and flinched in anticipation of his tail being smashed, but Carol—*bless her*—caught the handle just in time.

He threw her a grateful "woof!" and hit the ground running.

"RAHR-RAHR- RAHR- RAHR- RAHR- RAHR!" Roxxy gave the signal as she tore around the corner and charged straight for Axel.

His jaw dropped. She leaped, and time slowed. *Why aren't the captives barking?* Her yapping had been the cue for them to unleash an answering roar that would've split Axel's attention. She had no chance of success without their help. Grimly, she focused on the key ring spinning well above the man's open palm. Aluminum and copper glittered in the light cast by the bare bulb hanging over the Outpost's entry. And Axel—always faster on his feet than seemed possible for such a big man—shifted his weight to meet her with a kick. She could do a midair flip and change trajectory to avoid the blow…but that would eliminate any chance of snatching the keys…not to mention reneging on her pledge to Wiggle to do her best.

Roxxy sighed and stayed on course.

Stupid promises!

Time accelerated. The keys fell toward Axel's waiting palm. Denim snapped as his foot lashed out. Her eyes remained on the keys even as she flinched in anticipation of the blow.

"BARK-BARK-BARK-BARK-BARK-BARK-BARK-BARK-BARK-BARK-BARK-BARK-BARK-BARK!"

Axel froze mid-kick, and his head whipped toward the explosion of noise. The keys were an inch from his palm when Roxxy nipped them out of the air. They jingled merrily in her clenched teeth as she sailed past.

The plan's working!

All she had to do now was land and find her way back to town. The creep would be stuck at the storage building until she returned with help. She extended her front paws to hit the ground running.

"YEERRPPPP!"

Her surprised cry was distorted by the key ring clamped between her jaws. Axel's hand tightened like a steel clamp on one of her rear legs.

"BARK-BARK-BARK-BA—"

The captives' voices died as one when Axel plucked her from the air. He pivoted, swinging her in a flat circle.

Pain lanced through the ball socket in her hip…but by then, little mattered. The world spun out of control.

THE SHARP SCENTS OF sumac and sage triggered a massive sneeze as Toby galloped past the tangle of low shrubs bordering the road. Behind him, tires squealed as the SUV was wrenched into a turn to pursue. Toby kept his eyes firmly ahead. Jason was bent double at the entrance to the side road. The boy's pale fingers splayed across his knees and his narrow chest heaved.

"Woof!"

A weak grin appeared on Jason's sweat-soaked face.

"I guess I'm not the only one who's crazy."

Toby slid to a stop, scattering stones beneath the heavy chain that blocked the road leading up the steep hill. He gave Jason's denim-clad knee a playful shoulder bump and felt guilty when the boy staggered and grabbed the chain for support. The thick metal links clinked dully.

Toby frowned. The chain completely spanned the road, and each end was padlocked to a sturdy metal ring set in a cement post. Steep slopes rose on both sides of the blocked entry and prevented a vehicle from driving around. A zigzag pattern of gravel switchbacks etched their way to the top of the hill and disappeared over the crest.

As if echoing Toby's thoughts, Jason said, "It's going to take longer to reach the top than I thought."

Toby shook briskly.

Time to get going.

The tip of his tail brushed the chain as he ducked under, but he managed only a step before a hand closed on his scruff.

"Sorry," said Jason. "But we need to stay together until we know what's going on."

Toby raked a paw through gravel as he tried to pull away.

"I'm anxious too. Give me a second to catch my breath, and—"

"*BARK-BARK-BARK-BARK-BARK-BARK-BARK-BARK!*"

Toby and Jason jerked at the avalanche of sound shearing down the hillside.

"*BARK-BARK-BARK-BARK-BARK-BARK-BARK-BARK!*"

"How…how many dogs are *up* there?" Jason released his grip on Toby and stepped over the chain, nearly tripping when the toe of a tennis shoe caught the heavy links. "And why are they barking like that?"

Toby charged up the hill, sending loose stones pinging off the cement posts. *Only one way to find out!*

"*YEERRPPPP!*" gurgled Roxxy.

Her surroundings blurred as Axel swung her in a circle. The crushing grip combined with the centrifugal force to bring her leg to the breaking point. She readied herself for the sickening *snap*, but the pressure disappeared.

She whirled away like a thrown Frisbee.

Whack!

Her tail lashed the door frame as she spun through the Outpost entry. The speed of her flight slowed. The floor rushed up. Her head bounced across the surface repeatedly as she tumbled out of control. Her mouth opened reflexively, sending the keys clattering away. By sheer chance, momentum carried her after them. A final roll, and she came to rest almost dead center in the middle of the building. Her tongue lolled on the concrete. The chalky dryness was like a wick leaching away the last moisture in her mouth. The key ring lay only inches away, glinting enticingly, but she was too stunned to move.

"Wait for me!"

Toby ignored the command. They hadn't even reached the first bend in the road, and Jason was already struggling to keep up. The kid's rubber-soled sneakers kept slipping on the gravel.

Toby increased his trot to a run, but a sharp pain brought him to a halt. He lowered his head and gnawed at a stone wedged under a toe. Getting up the hillside was going to be tougher than he'd imagined. The switchbacks would be the killer. Would it make sense to ignore them and charge up the incline in a straight line? Probably not, he decided. Dense forest and thorny undergrowth blanketed everything except for where the road was carved out.

A shadow blocked out the moonlight. Toby glanced up at Jason, who was panting like a runner after crossing the finish line of a marathon. The boy smelled of fresh sweat and a lingering scent of minty toothpaste. Toby huffed a greeting and received a pat in reply. Screeching brakes drew their attention to the main road, fifty yards below. Carol and Marcy piled out of the SUV.

"Great," muttered Jason.

"You two get down here!" Marcy yelled. "*Now!*"

Toby ran for the switchback. His ears lifted as Jason's sliding, uneven tread followed. Carol and Marcy's footfalls joined in from below.

SNAP!

"AAAAARRRHHHHHHHHH!"

Toby whirled so quickly his big paws tangled and he face-planted. A scramble brought him upright. He spat out a pebble and peered around a frozen Jason.

Marcy lay on her back just inside the chained barrier. She hugged her knee to her chest. The ankle below was bent at an angle that sent a wave of nausea through Toby. Her lips pulled back in a rictus of pain, and her teeth gleamed ghostly in the moonlight.

"AAAAARRRHHHHHHHH!"

The scream was followed by the rasp of ragged breathing echoing up the hillside.

Marcy needs me! Toby sprang downhill but slid to a stop after only a few steps. He twisted to view the summit. *Roxxy's life might be in danger!* He looked back and forth wildly, ears slapping the sides of his face.

"Easy, boy." Jason's gentle hand caressed the back of Toby's neck. "I think Carol's got it under control."

Toby shook off the hand but followed Jason's gaze. Carol knelt beside Marcy's hunched figure.

"See?" asked Jason.

"Marcy, hold still," said Carol. "I need to see if it's broken or just sprained."

Toby squinted as a cone of light shone from a cell phone.

"Marcy," continued Carol shakily. "It's broken for sure. I'd better call—"

The light winked out. Toby sucked in a startled breath, getting a bracing lungful of sage. The moon's glow was enough for him to see Carol frantically jabbing at the phone.

Her slim shoulders sagged. "Marcy, it's dead. I should've charged it before we left. Let me use yours."

"I…forgot…to bring it," replied Marcy through gasps.

Toby stood frozen as Carol sat back on her heels and pulled the brim lower on her baseball cap. Her red ponytail swung as she scanned the hillside.

"Jason," she yelled. "I need your phone."

"I forgot mine, too," the boy called out. "Will Aunt Marcy be okay?"

"She'll be fine, but we need to get help right away. Come down here."

"C-Can't. I've got to find Roxxy!" Jason turned and pounded up the hillside.

Carol sighed. "I used to like that kid."

"Go…after…him," said Marcy.

"No. You're the priority right now."

"But—"

"No buts! The footing's too bad for me to get you safely to the car. We'd both fall and be worse off. I hate to say it, but the best thing is to leave you here while I drive to that all-night convenience store. Remember the one we passed? I'll use their phone to call an ambulance. I can be back here in twenty minutes, and the paramedics should arrive soon after."

"Sounds…good."

"Okay." Carol reached down and brushed away the hair sticking to Marcy's sweaty forehead. "Try and keep still while I'm gone."

"I…won't…run off." Marcy's low chuckle morphed into a groan.

"I'll hurry," promised Carol, knees popping as she stood.

Toby threw one last glance at Marcy before dashing after Jason.

"This must be my lucky day."

Roxxy blinked awake. How long had she been out? She shifted on the cold concrete and tried to stand, but her body was having none of it. The face of the man standing over her came into focus, and the fluorescent lighting cast a yellow sheen on his broad, oily features.

"Got to admit, you caught me off guard." Axel hooked a thumb over his dandruff-coated shoulder, indicating the parking pad outside.

She tried to growl but choked.

"Me and you got a history," continued Axel. "Crazy how you keep turning up."

His eyes flattened to the color of old tar. He pointed at the keys near her head.

"I'll take those, and then I'll take care of you." He bent and extended his hand toward the glinting metal but paused and tilted his head toward the crushed pen in the corner. "Just like I did that yappy little Pom."

CHAPTER 37

"Gotcha."

A cramp in Toby's flank slowed him from a wobbly lope to a walk, but he was close now. The final switchback lay just ahead. He sucked in a deep breath. The pine-scented air at the hilltop was refreshing after the dusty stuff that hung over the sage and underbrush below.

I need all the invigoration I can get.

Every muscle ached, and the pads of his paws felt as if they'd encountered a belt sander. Still, he was better off than Jason, who was last seen moving on all fours like a spent but determined land crab.

Toby stopped as a low-pitched buzzing penetrated the noise of his own raspy panting. He edged around a rock outcropping and made the angled turn past the switchback. His tail brushed gravel in a weary wag. Ahead, the road curled over the crest of the hill. *Finally!* The bluish-white glow of an outdoor light formed a weak halo over the summit, revealing the source of the buzzing. Higher in the sky, the star-strewn canopy held a hint of purple. He blinked. How had it gotten so late? Or early?

Toby felt eyes on him and glanced into the underbrush bordering the road. A fox's pointed muzzle parted the broad variegated leaves of a dome-shaped hosta. The animal came no closer, but the slit black pupils narrowed in the yellow irises as the predator weighed the situation. Toby's lips skinned back from his teeth in a snarl, and he sent a silent message. *Yeah, I'm weak, but not* that *weak.*

The fox disappeared in a whisper of rustling leaves.

Toby loped toward the hillcrest—aching ribs and sore paws forgotten in the adrenaline rush produced by the appearance of an animal that reminded him of Snatcher. More importantly, Roxxy was nearby. He could feel it.

The "yappy little Pom" remark sent blood surging into Roxxy's weakened limbs. She came off the floor in a wild lunge before Axel's fingers could curl around the keys.

CLACK!

Her jaws closed on air as Axel jerked his hand away and stumbled back. She snatched up the keys. A metallic taste filled her mouth as she clamped down for a good grip that wouldn't crack a tooth.

The plan could still work!

She sprang for the open door, but once again, Axel was faster than she'd anticipated. He jumped in front of her and sent a kick whistling at her head. She juked. The boot's edge grazed her shoulder and sent her rolling across the concrete. She was up in an instant, having somehow maintained her hold on the keys.

Axel stood poised between her and the door—knees bent, stance wide, and weight balanced on the balls of his feet. She sighed around the keys.

Good luck getting past that.

"Here, pooch," coaxed Axel.

Her eyes narrowed as he pulled a packet of beef jerky from his pocket and tore the cellophane open with his teeth. A forefinger and thumb worked a piece free. He extended it toward her. His lips turned up in a smile that never reached his eyes. "Take the nice treat. Yummy, yummy."

She growled.

Right.

The smell of the jerky reached her. Drool slipped past the keys and dripped on the concrete. She backed up. Axel followed. She sidled one way and then the other, trying to find an angle that'd give her a chance to dash past him to the open door, but he moved with her, nimbly side-stepping to cut her off. The soles of the heavy boots tapped a light cadence on the floor.

"Catch!" said Axel suddenly, tossing a piece of jerky.

She let the strip hit the floor in front of her. Did he really think she was stupid enough to drop the keys and snatch the jerky out of the air? How dumb did he think she was? Still, the morsel *was* appealing! Her nostrils quaked at the beefy scent. If she ever got out of this mess, she was definitely going to find herself a nice, yummy—

Click.

Her mouth opened in shock, leaving the key ring dangling from a bottom tooth. Axel thumbed the red safety tab on a narrow canister almost hidden in his massive hand. A black, recessed nozzle was leveled at a spot between her eyes.

Pepper spray! Maybe I am *as dumb as he thinks!*

Bright orange fluid shot toward her in a hissing stream. She bit down on the key ring and juked right. Acrid fumes flooded her nose as the spray sizzled past. The cone tracked her. She backpedaled in a zigzag pattern, somehow avoiding the liquid and the splash zone. As the distance between her and Axel widened, the trajectory of the spray rose to capture her beneath the falling torrent. Her only hope was to get farther away. She turned and bolted.

Well done, you! As long as she had the keys, there was still a chance to get past Axel and leave him stranded while—

Clunk!

She whirled. The canister lay at Axel's feet. Her tail flicked in satisfaction. *Empty!*

A roach lay on its back in the area she'd fled from. Its angular limbs wriggled, trying to right itself. A sheen of orange pepper spray lightened the black form. Its angular legs slowed and went still.

Roxxy shivered, thinking that it could've been her.

A gravelly chuckle drew her attention to the entry.

Axel grinned and placed a palm against the open door. His weight shifted and he shoved.

BANG!

The building reverberated as the warped panel was forced into the frame. A shower of dry rot rained from the rafters. Roxxy stood in dumb shock as flakes worked their way through her curls and settled on the skin beneath. A desire to shake and remove the itchy material registered somewhere in the depths of her mind, but she was unable to crack the icy despair that froze her in place.

Axel smirked. "Gotcha."

Toby cleared the crest of the hill in a loping bound.

BANG!

Panicked, he skidded to a stop and stared at a corrugated structure, still vibrating from some type of impact. *The Outpost!* Parked in front was the panel truck where he'd almost had his ribs crushed. The orange-and-white vehicle was backed up to the building. He wished he could see into the cargo area, but he didn't have the right vantage. To complicate matters, he was upwind and couldn't detect the scent of what was loaded inside.

With a start, he realized he was standing in the open and would be seen the instant Axel appeared. He fled into the bordering trees, careful to avoid the fat drops of resin oozing from the trunks. He sank into a quivering crouch, wondering what to do.

Moonlight flickered. He glanced up and spotted an owl traversing the glowing crescent. The predator was a danger to tiny dogs like Leo. Speaking of… Where was the Pom? And where was Roxxy?

The breeze shifted, placing Toby downwind of the truck. His pulse quickened, and his thick tail brushed across pine needles. Scents poured over him. His nose quaked, stopped, then quaked again. *Impossible!* There couldn't be *that* many captives in the vehicle. A growl rumbled deep in his throat. The cages must be stacked and jammed together like containers of merchandise.

And none of the scents were Roxxy's or Leo's.

His ears tilted forward. Odd that the dogs were quiet now after unleashing such a ruckus before. Had they seen something that terrified them into silence?

Well, if Roxxy and Leo weren't in the truck, they must be inside the Outpost…with Axel. Toby's flank still throbbed from his last encounter with the man. The thought of drawing the human's attention brought a whimper of fear. Still, he had to let Roxxy and Leo know he had arrived to help.

He threw back his head to unleash a bellow that would penetrate the Outpost's walls, but before he could make a sound, fingers closed around his muzzle.

"Don't," whispered Jason.

Toby yanked free, hackles rising.

"Take it easy. Let's figure out what's going on before you start barking. Gives us more options."

Brown and white fur smoothed. *Point taken.*

"Come on. Let's start by going around to the back of this dump. There may be a window where we can see inside. After that, we'll check out the truck." Jason licked his lips. "I've got a bad feeling about this place."

AXEL STOOD WITH HIS back to the closed door. A smile revealed a jagged crack in a yellow incisor. His irises expanded to create black bottomless pits as lifeless as a skull's empty eye sockets.

Roxxy gulped but was determined to show she wasn't afraid. She lifted her chin defiantly, settled into a springy crouch to emphasize her readiness to evade a charge, and tilted her ears forward to signal a haughty indifference to threat. She even managed a somewhat realistic growl… before feeling the tip of her tail brush the concrete.

What is it with that thing?

She groaned and accepted the reality of her situation. The plan was dead. It was only a matter of time before Axel cornered her and took the keys. He'd haul away Wiggle, Bam-Bam, and all the rest to some horrible place, and they'd never be reunited with their loved ones.

Roxxy's heart twisted. She had made things worse by giving the captives hope. Why couldn't she just mind her own business and…

Could hope ever be bad?

Her tail rose of its own accord and assumed its usual jaunty upward curl. She slipped her tongue through the loop of the key ring and pulled it deeper into her mouth to settle it more firmly. She sucked in a deep breath, noting the keys' metallic taste. If Axel wanted them, he'd have to take them.

As if reading her mind, the man strutted forward. Boot heels rang against concrete. She backpedaled. How long could she hold out? The sun would be coming up soon. Maybe an early-morning hiker would come along and see the captives in the back of the truck. The police might even be called. If she could evade Axel long enough to—

Her rump smacked into the rear wall.

Uh oh.

She looked left. Old tires rose in tightly clustered stacks. Their white underlining showed beneath dried cracked rubber. She glanced right. Rows of ribbed oil drums extended from the wall, piled high and forming a makeshift barrier. The wall behind meant she was hemmed in on three sides. The footfalls stopped. Her gaze snapped straight ahead. *Make that four.* In front of her, Axel's broad shoulders spanned the distance between the tires and the oil drums.

"Nowhere to go?" asked Axel.

The keys rattled in sync with her trembling jaw. Axel would need only a couple of long strides to be on her. She abruptly rolled to her back and exposed her throat and belly to signal complete surrender. Seeing Axel from an upside-down position sent a queasy feeling rippling through her gut. Her jaws opened and the keys tinkled when they slid to the concrete. She whimpered piteously.

"Asking for mercy?" Axel snorted. "You got the wrong guy."

There's one thing you can count on with this creep, she thought, *he likes to run his mouth.* She arched her back, creating an inch of space between her and the floor.

"Lesson time." Axel stepped forward and shifted his weight to deliver a kick.

She slammed her spine into the concrete and twisted in one fluid motion to bring herself upright. A juke to the right avoided Axel's boot, but the attached chain ripped a tangle of fur from her shoulder. She snatched the keys and shot beneath the man's raised leg.

"You *miserable...*"

She tuned out the cursing that followed and didn't stop until she reached the center of the building. The spot offered the best place to dash in any direction when Axel made his next try for her. He'd eventually wear her down, but she was determined to buy as much time for the captives as possible.

The cursing stopped, which was somehow more ominous than when he was ranting. A wince tightened the corners of her eyes as muscles cramped in her flanks and legs. How much longer could she go without a drink? A shake of her head dispelled the thought. She had bigger problems. No, *one* big problem, and he was getting closer by the second. A few more strides and he'd be close enough to try another kick. The lighting here was better than in the building's rear, and she could see a greasy sheen of sweat coating Axel's heavy brow. He was probably worried about getting a late start and keeping that Ethan guy waiting. Good. The more impatient Axel got, the more likely he was to rush her. She was confident she could outmaneuver him, as long as she stayed away from the walls or... or until he tired her out.

Roxxy tossed her head to settle the key ring more firmly between her teeth. Her jaws ached from clutching the stupid things, and the unnatural taste caused drool to soak her chin and chest. She stayed put and watched Axel's approach. He moved carefully, with his knees bent and his weight balanced on the balls of his feet. His wide chest rose and fell in deep even breaths, pushing forth the smell of his unbrushed teeth.

Her tail bobbed in a nod. *Time to get moving.*

She managed only a half step back before coming to a jarring halt. A glance down revealed the reason. The claw of a front paw wedged beneath the rounded rim of a metal grate. She'd forgotten about the drain in the floor. A panicky shiver rippled through her and sent the keys jangling like castanets. She leaned back and put all her weight into a yank to free the claw. *Ouch!* Pain flared in the toe joint, but the claw remained stuck.

"You got this coming," said Axel.

Air whistled as his foot swept toward Roxxy's face.

She gave a final, desperate pull. A ribbon of agony raced up her foreleg as she ducked away. The bloody root of a claw remained fixed in the grate.

The sole of the boot passed harmlessly through the fur atop her head. Axel's foot rose in an arc driven by momentum. His arms windmilled as he fought to keep his balance.

She dashed past, leaving a line of neat red paw prints on the cement, but stopped so abruptly a smear marked the spot where she slid to a halt.

A grate?

She stood transfixed. Her concentration was so intense she didn't notice Axel's next kick until it arced toward her rib cage.

CHAPTER 38

"Did you hear that?"

Roxxy dropped to let the boot sail past, but Axel—*why* did she always underestimate his quickness—corrected the kick's trajectory at the last second. The adjustment slowed the blow and prevented it from breaking her ribs, but the impact was powerful enough to send her breath *whooshing* from her body. She was counting herself lucky when the side of her head smacked into an old radiator and the room went black.

Roxxy stirred at the sound of ringing. She shook her head. The pain put a fast stop to that. *No* more head shaking, thank you very much. The ringing changed to a hum like a swarm of bees inside her skull. To make matters worse, she couldn't figure out why her teeth were clamped on something metal. She almost unclenched her jaw, but a vague recollection stopped her.

"It's time to finish this. I got things to do."

The wall next to her moved. She was no longer in shadow. Her eyes squinted against the sudden brightness. Wait a minute. How can a wall move? The silhouette shifted. *Not* a wall. Human? Too big, surely. Something with a familiar curve was centered over her head, rising higher and higher. Had she chewed on something similar in the past? Maybe, but she didn't remember any crusted mud in the wedged area where the sole sloped up to meet the heel.

"*YIP! YIP! YIP! YIP! YIP! YIP! YIP! YIP! YIP! YIP! YIP!*"

The high-pitched warning ricocheted off the metal walls and turned the building into the inside of a snare drum. Awareness flooded through Roxxy in time to see Axel jerk. His stomp veered off course and crashed into the floor next to her head.

"*OOWWWWWW!*" The man lifted his injured foot and hopped in place on the other.

Flaky dried mud rained down on her.

"*YIP! YIP! YIP! YIP! YIP! YIP! YIP! YIP! YIP! YIP! YIP! GET UP, ROXX!*"

A jolt of adrenaline brought her upright. She threw a tail flick of thanks at the figure in the upended cage.

Leo shouted, "*MOVE!*"

She backed away from the still hopping Axel but stopped when the grate's cool surface registered beneath her paw.

"Don't just *stand* there!" ordered Leo. "Get as far away from the guy as you can!"

"I'm going to—*agghh!*" Axel's voice rose in a shout as he slipped on an iron rivet.

His rump hit the floor hard enough for Roxxy to feel the impact through the paw resting on the grate.

"Roxx! Get further away while you can," ordered Leo.

"Ah ab an adee." A toss of her head shifted the keys to the other side of her mouth. "I have an idea," she repeated.

"I'll just bet you do. Run while you—*duck!*"

The rivet whizzed past her head. An inch lower and it would've cracked her skull. Her ears swiveled, tracking the knob of bouncing metal to the back of the building. Her eyes stayed on Axel as he struggled to an awkward standing position. A grimace contorted his features when he rubbed the small of his back. Her eyes narrowed. He was no more than four of his long strides away, but he clearly wasn't going anywhere at the moment. Her front paws shuffled until each found an outside edge of the metal grate.

"*Roxxy!*" yapped Leo. "*Get moving while you can!*"

She lowered her head and studied the narrow slotted openings. Beneath the top plate, a pipe extended straight down and curved out of sight.

"What are you up to, mutt?" asked Axel.

His throat worked. A gob of phlegm arced toward her but fell short, splattering on the cement in a spray of green streaks. He dragged the back of his hand across his mouth.

"You troublemaking little—"

She tuned out the rest. If things went as expected, she was about to make a *lot* more trouble for the creep.

"*MOVE, ROXX!*" pleaded Leo. "*GO!*"

Eyes still on Axel, she opened her jaws, allowing the key ring to drop from her mouth. She didn't bother to look down. The clatter of metal on metal told her the keys hit the target. They would now be passing through the slotted grate and plummeting along the pipe to eventually come to rest in a place where Axel couldn't reach them. Half the day would pass before he could have another set sent from town. Maybe the person who brought them out would see the captives barking and be curious enough to alert the authorities.

As for her? Well, Axel was right about one thing. She was finished. Her legs quivered with fatigue, her head pounded, her flank ached with each breath, and her tongue was thick and foreign. He'd soon corner her, and…well, she'd done the best she could. She'd fulfilled her promise.

She blinked.

So what was he waiting for?

He had both feet on the floor and seemed recovered from the missed stomp. The overhead lights gleamed on his bald head, and the corners of his mouth formed a lazy grin. Why did he look so smug when she'd made it impossible for him to drive away? Unless…

She looked down. The key ring rested atop the grate, balanced across two slots. She swallowed. *Am I* ever *going to catch a break?*

"ROXX!" shouted Leo. "*RUN!*"

"No windows," said Jason as his gaze swept the rear of the building.

As he stepped back, his tennis shoe landed on a brown dried pinecone whose scales were open to expose the central stem. The brittle cone disintegrated with an alarming *crunch* that bounced off the side of the structure.

Toby growled.

"Sorry," whispered Jason.

Toby could understand why the boy had wanted to find out if there was a window to see inside. Made sense, but no luck. Why were they still wasting time? They needed to get inside the building *pronto*, which meant using the front door.

Toby rammed the bony ridge of his skull into Jason's jean-clad ankle.

"Ow! What was that for?"

Another growl sufficed for a reply. *Stop dawdling!*

Jason pushed a lock of auburn hair off his forehead.

"I wish we knew what we were getting ourselves into, but when all else fails"—he squared his shoulders, and the comma of hair fell again—"let's use the direct approach and try the front door."

Toby grunted. *Why didn't I think of that?*

Roxxy's ears flattened as waves of laughter washed over her.

"For a second there," said Axel, wiping his eyes, "I actually thought you were *trying* to drop the keys in the grate. I must be losing my—*HEY!*"

She concentrated, tuning out the approaching footsteps and putting all her weight on her paw, which was pressed against the key ring.

"*ROXX! HE'S NEARLY ON YOU!*"

She wished Leo would shut up so she could concentrate. Her head dipped, and she nosed the ring back and forth along the grate. Eyes watered from the fumes of an astringent chemical rising from the drain. A delicate nudge lined up the loop with the slot. The keys vanished.

"*ROXX, YOU'VE GOT TO—*"

Axel's boot smashed into her side. A *crack* sounded as she rose into the air. The blow was too shocking to be painful—at first. The agony came when the floor rushed up to slam into the flank that received the kick. She tumbled halfway to the front of the building. The world was still a gray haze when a vise—or something that felt like one—closed on her scruff. A human grunt sounded, and she was airborne again. A calendar taped to the front wall absorbed some of the impact when she hit. The Outpost rang like a gong struck with a mallet.

TUNNN…uuuunnnnnnnnn…unnnnnn…unnn…

She bounced off the metal siding, rolled halfway back to the drain, and convulsed. The contents in her stomach emptied, pooling and soaking into her limp fur.

"*YIP! YIP! YIP! YIP! YIP! YIP! YIP! YIP! YIP! YIP! YIP! STAY AWAY FROM HER, YOU CREEP!*"

She dragged her stiff tongue across her muzzle and grimaced at the sour taste. Had she vomited? Was something wrong with her? A welcome distraction came when the thud of approaching footsteps registered through her flank pressed against the concrete. Maybe someone was bringing her a nice bowl of water.

TOBY DIDN'T BLAME JASON for shaking his head as if he didn't believe what he was seeing. They had just arrived at the front of the Outpost and gotten a glimpse of the cargo area facing the building. The cages were stacked like merchandise waiting in a storeroom. The captives hunkered in terrified silence. Toby couldn't imagine what they'd seen to have left them so stunned.

"Well," said Jason weakly. "I don't see Roxxy in any of the pens."

Toby huffed impatiently.

"Right. Let's see who's inside the building."

The boy lifted a hand to knock on the door.

Toby stood just behind Jason, brisling with anticipation. The minute the entry was opened, he'd dash past, and—

TUNNN...uuuunnnnnnnnnn...unnnnnn...unnn...

Jason's knuckles stopped an inch from warped metal. "W-What was *that*? Sounded like somebody hit the wall inside with a sledgehammer!"

The fur bristled along Toby's spine. *We've got to get in there and—*

"*YIP! YIP! YIP! YIP! YIP! YIP! YIP! YIP! YIP! YIP! YIP! STAY AWAY FROM HER, YOU CREEP!*"

"Did you hear that?" Jason pressed his ear to the door. "Toby, I think that's the little dog who was with you and Roxxy in her back yard—the one who went missing."

A cold lump settled in Toby's stomach as Leo's words sank in. *Stay away from her...*

"YIP! YIP! YIP! YIP! YIP! YIP! YIP! YIP! YIP! YIP! YIP! STAY AWAY FROM HER, YOU CREEP!"

"Pom, you're never going to learn."

Roxxy frowned as the footsteps changed course and receded. No water? She tried to lift her head to see what was going on, but something sticky glued her cheek to the floor. Was Max playing a practical joke on her?

Determined now, she pulled to free herself. A *squelch* sounded as wet fur came away from concrete. She gathered her paws beneath her and pushed. An explosion of agony detonated in her chest. She collapsed, whimpering, but her eyes tracked a big man striding toward a dented cage. The enclosure sat upended next to a garbage can in the corner. A grid of shadows—cast by the unrelenting fluorescent lights—penetrated the mesh and covered the occupant. Fuzzily, she tried to identify the little dog. She was sure she knew him, but the name didn't come. Lenny? He retreated to the pen's rear corner as the human approached.

"YIP! YIP! YIP! YIP! YIP! YIP! YIP! YIP! YIP! YIP! YIP! THAT'S RIGHT! FOCUS ON ME!"

Roxxy's mind snapped into focus as Axel stopped in front of Leo's cage and raised a foot. Her eyes widened in horror.

CLANG! CLANG! CLANG!

The sound of the stomping slowly faded.

"*That* should shut you up for good!" Axel wrenched his boot from the tangled wreckage. A link of chain caught on a wire spoke. He ripped the snag free.

Twaannngggg!

Roxxy swallowed. Leo's fawn-colored body lay crumpled at the bottom of the mangled pen. A spiky length of crushed frame penetrated his mane like a harpoon. There was no way to tell whether the spear pierced flesh.

"That's done," said Axel, squatting to retie his boots.

He stood and stomped one foot on the concrete, then the other.

"Snug."

His flat gaze fell on Roxxy.

"Now it's your turn."

She swallowed a whimper.

So this is what it feels like to be a mouse dropped into a tank with a boa constrictor.

"Just so you know," said Axel in the taunting tone he'd used with the captives. "Once I'm done with you, I'll call the truck rental place and have someone bring out another set of keys. You've been a pest, but nothing more than that."

A growl vibrated deep in Roxxy's chest as he approached. She rolled to her stomach and gathered her legs beneath her. Her paw pads were from the vomit pooled on the floor. She inched to a drier spot and waited.

One good bite. Her gaze settled on the crease in the pant leg that revealed where the boot stopped. Axel's ankle was protected only by denim. Her jaws tingled. *One good bite...for me...for Leo...for the captives...*

As the man neared, the boots' chains produced a disconcertingly merry jingle. She squinted against the light dancing on the links. He was a single stride away. *Now!* She heaved herself upright. A grating sensation registered as the ends of her broken rib found each other, followed by something far beyond her concept of pain. She didn't remember collapsing, but how else could she have the now familiar taste of concrete on her lolling tongue.

A shadow fell on her.

"Hate to do it," said Axel sincerely. "But I'm going to put you out of your misery."

"Should I forget about knocking and just go in?"

Toby rammed the top of his head into the boy's ankle.

"Ouch! *Again?*"

Toby responded by growling and pointing his muzzle at the entry.

"Okay, okay, I get it." Jason turned the doorknob and pushed.

The creases deepened across Toby's forehead when the panel didn't budge.

"Let's try this." Jason flattened a palm against the door. His face grew red as he shoved.

The panel stayed closed.

Jason's feet slipped, and he fell. His knees left indentations in the loose rock.

Toby's growl deepened.

"*Stop* that! I'm doing the best I can! The thing's either stuck or bolted from the inside."

Toby tossed his head impatiently.

"You and me both," snapped Jason, correctly interpreting the gesture. "I'll try something else."

Toby wondered what *something else* might be. A battering ram? Dynamite? He wasn't encouraged when Jason strode well away from the building.

You're going in the wrong direction!

Toby was on the verge of following the boy to deliver another head-butt, but Jason suddenly turned and charged the door.

Toby scrambled out of the way as Jason swept past and lowered his shoulder like a football player rushing a tackling dummy.

Axel set himself and drew back a foot.

"Too bad I can't take my time."

A whimper worked its way up Roxxy's throat, but she swallowed it.

I won't give him the satisfaction.

The fur on her cheek flattened as a sweeping kick whistled in, driving a pocket of air before the blow.

SCREECH!

The warped door flew open with an ear-piercing protest. Jason bounced backward and landed flat on his spine. Toby didn't wait. He hurtled past the boy, but once over the threshold, his legs stiffened, and he slid to quivering halt, staring in goggle-eyed horror.

CHAPTER 39

"Do you ever listen?"

*S*CREECH!

Roxxy flinched at the sound resembling a buzz saw chewing through a nail in a two-by-four. The door swung open in the bent frame with a force that sent a shudder through the building. Brick-red flakes showered down from the rusty ceiling, parted by the blocky tan-and-white form shooting through the open door. The newcomer's progress died when his short, stubby legs backpedaled to a stop. Big ears swung back and forth in response to the sudden halt in momentum. His chocolate eyes, glazed with shock, riveted on her.

She sucked in a breath.

Toby!?

Before she could bark a greeting, a skinny boy in jeans and t-shirt leaped over the stunned basset. Jason slowed and waved a hand in front of his face to clear the falling dust. His eyes widened while taking in the scene, but instead of freezing like Toby, he warily approached. His trembling fingers brushed a lock of auburn hair from his forehead.

Jason flicked a glance from Roxxy to Axel's foot—frozen mid-kick.

She ground her teeth. Just when she thought things couldn't get worse. How could she protect Jason when she couldn't even protect herself? What was the idiot boy doing here? Didn't he realize he was in danger? He probably had some kind of half-baked idea that he could help.

A soft thump echoed off the floor behind her.

Stupid tail.

"Wasn't expecting visitors," said Axel mildly.

Jason stopped out of Axel's reach and stammered, "I've c-come to g-get Roxxy."

Axel frowned and lowered his foot. "I know you, right? You're the kid who lives next door to the mutt."

The man pointed down at Roxxy.

"J-Just let me take her, and I'll go."

"How did you get here?"

Roxxy had been wondering about that as well, but Jason didn't respond to the question. Instead, he began a slow sidestepping motion, circling around Axel while maintaining a deliberate distance between them. Jason's tennis shoes left footprints in the rust flakes that had settled on the floor.

"Stay put, kid!" snapped Axel.

Jason continued to circle.

Roxxy realized with horror he was moving deeper into the building. *What* was the boy up to? He kicked aside a socket wrench lying in his path. The tool skidded across the concrete and banged off a side wall.

"Punk, I'll give you one more chance. Stand still and tell me how you got here."

"Mister, I don't want any trouble. I'm just here to take Roxxy home." Jason licked away sweat from his upper lip but didn't stop moving. "Please."

Axel pivoted to follow the boy's progress.

Roxxy flicked her tail away to keep Axel from stepping on it. His back was now to her.

What was that bulge covered by his t-shirt at the rear waistband of his jeans?

She peered between Axel's spread feet and focused on Jason as he halted after making a half circle from the door. The three of them were lined up. She was closest to the entry. Axel was between her and Jason, and the boy was farthest away. A low growl registered deep in her chest. The boy had cut off his own escape route! Was he *insane*?

She was still fuming when Jason locked eyes with her. A slight lift of his chin indicated the clear path she had out of the building. A hard lump formed in her throat.

Oh...

"Please?" repeated Axel with a sneer. "Kid, you're mighty polite. Especially for somebody who's trespassing. This is private property. *My* private property."

A broad sweep of Axel's hand indicated the surroundings as if it were a palace. Roxxy watched a roach the size of a belt buckle crawl unnoticed across the toe of his boot.

"I'm just here to get Roxxy." A thin muscle twitched in Jason's jaw. "Let me have her, and I'll go."

Axel gave an impatient headshake. "Anybody waiting for you outside?"

"No," answered Jason automatically. "Uh, I mean—" His Adam's apple bobbed in his throat. "But I called the police. They should be here any minute."

"Good for you. Let me take a look at your phone just to be sure you're telling the truth."

Jason's mouth opened…and closed. His shoulders slumped.

Axel nodded. "That's what I thought."

Roxxy eyed the back of Axel's ankle. She tried to push upright, but her legs folded.

"Punk, I'll get to you in a minute, but I got something to finish." Axel turned to Roxxy. "Where was I?"

She cringed as a kick swept toward her head but before it could land, air exploded from Axel in a gasping *"OOMPH!"*

He staggered past her with Jason's shoulder buried in his back. The boy's legs churned, driving Axel toward the open front door. Roxxy stared in disbelief. The kid was probably trying to push the man over the threshold, slam the door, and wedge something against it. *Brave, but crazy.* The thought was barely finished when Axel set his feet and turned, stiff-arming Jason in the chest. The boy reeled past her and didn't regain his balance until he was near the grate in the middle of the floor.

The ring of boot heels on concrete alerted her. She rolled out of the way as Axel stomped where her head had been an instant before. He skidded on the drying vomit but didn't fall.

"Leave Roxxy alone!" yelled Jason.

Axel turned from her and stalked toward the boy. "You telling me what to do?"

Roxxy's mind raced. *I have to keep the creep away from Jason! But how?*

She clenched her teeth against the pain sure to come and struggled upright. Her vision blurred as the ends of cracked bone grated together in her flank.

"Roxxy!" yelled Jason while backpedaling from Axel. "Run!"

"You run!" she snarled, wishing the lovable idiot would get his priorities straight.

The sole of Jason's sneaker rolled across a yellow-handled screwdriver, and his rear end hit the concrete.

Axel let out a shout of laughter and charged.

The boy scuttled away like a land crab, moving on palms and heels. His gaze settled on Roxxy. "Go!"

The tip of her tail flicked in annoyance. Did he expect her to leave him? He didn't *look* stupid.

She threw back her head and unleashed a raging bark that echoed off the ceiling. "*RARR! RARR! RARR! RARR! RARR! RARR! RARR!*"

Axel whirled and stared at her in disbelief. "Never thought I'd see you upright again."

"*RARR! RARR! RARR! RARR! RARR! RARR! RARR! THAT'S RIGHT, CREEP. KEEP YOUR EYES ON ME!*"

"Mister!" yelled Jason. "You can still let us go!"

Axel didn't bother to look back at the boy. "Keep your mouth shut while I finish this mutt off."

She gulped as Axel approached. *That worked better than I thought.* Her legs wobbled as she held her ground. Now, if Jason would just have the sense to dash out of the building while Axel was distracted, whatever happened to her would be worth it.

"Hey!" shouted the boy, scrambling to his feet. "Mister! Answer my question!"

"*RARR! RARR! RARR! RARR! RARR! RARR! RARR! JASON, RUN!*"

"Quiet down, Roxxy!" yelled Jason.

"*RARR! RARR! RARR! RARR! RARR! RARR! RARR! YOU QUIET DOWN! AND GET OUT!*"

"Mister! You're just a bully!"

Axel's stride faltered for only a second before continuing toward Roxxy. She directed a string of barks at Jason. "*RARR! RARR! RARR! RARR! RARR! RARR! RARR! DO I HAVE TO DRAW YOU A MAP? GO!*"

Forgetting her injury, she stomped a paw to emphasize the order. Pain exploded in her flank. A white fog crept from the corners of her vision and blotted out the world. Axel stepped from the mist. Wispy tendrils clung to his hulking form.

She sighed. *Almost over.* Even Jason—stubborn as he was—would surely realize she was finished and would use the opportunity to escape while Axel did…well, whatever he intended to do. The fog burned off as her pain subsided to something tolerable. She threw a glance in the boy's direction, hoping he was already on the move. Instead, he was unscrewing something from a portable generator next to a sidewall.

She growled.

Of course he's not running when he has the chance. That'd make too much sense.

Jason turned from the generator. His torso twisted like a pitcher winding up to throw a baseball.

"Time's up, mutt," said Axel.

Roxxy flinched as the boot sole drove toward her head.

Thwack!

Axel grimaced in pain. A spark plug bounced off his back and hit the concrete with a *ping*.

Roxxy blinked as Axel slowly turned away from her. She was trying to make sense of what had happened as he crooked an arm behind his back and massaged a spot between his shoulder blades. A bright red flush emerged at the base of his neck and crept to cover his bald head like a wash of blood. He bent and retrieved the spark plug, forming a fist with the tapered silver tip of the device protruding like a hole punch.

His gaze settled on Jason. "When I'm finished, your face is going to look like a pile of raw hamburger."

"I'm n-not afraid of you," said Jason, bottom lip trembling. "Just let Roxxy go."

"Is the baby going to cry?" sneered Axel, striding toward the boy.

"*Rarr! Rarr! Rarr! Rarr! Rarr! Rarr! Rarr! Look at me! Look at me!*" Roxxy barked desperately, trying to draw the man's attention, but he ignored her. She staggered after him. Pain flared in her side with each halting step. If she could get close enough, a bite to the back of his ankle would slow him down.

"No, Roxxy!" Jason called out in a panicky voice. "Go the *other* way! Toward the door!"

She struggled on. Her paw crushed a moldy sliver of wood that had fallen from the rafters. A cloud of black spores arose. She sneezed and nearly fainted from the jerky movement.

"*GO, ROXXY!*" Jason flicked the back of his hand to shoo her in the door's direction.

She growled. Had the kid lost his mind? *Shooing* her? And what was with all the yelling for her to leave? He was the one who should get out of here.

"Do you *ever* listen?" wailed Jason.

"*Rarr! Rarr! Rarr! Do you?*" she snarled.

Her breath caught. *Are those* tears *glistening on his cheeks?*

She gave her head an angry shake. *I do* not *have a desire to lick them away.*

"Kid, you can cry like a little punk if you want." Axel unleashed a vicious kick to send a loose rivet bouncing to the building's rear. A rat leaped to avoid the projectile and scurried behind an oil drum. "But it won't help. I'm going to—"

Roxxy's eyes widened as Jason charged Axel. The man was equally astonished because his fist uncurled, and he dropped the spark plug. He recovered and shifted into a fighter's stance.

Jason arrived with legs pumping, clearly intending to smash a shoulder into the man's midsection and drive him toward the door.

Axel waited until the last second before uncoiling and sending a massive uppercut directed at Jason's face. The boy leaned to the side, and the blow connected with his temple, lifting him into the air.

The back of Jason's head bounced off the concrete floor when he landed. He lay still.

"I'm just getting started." A lunatic smile pulled at the corners of Axel's mouth and creased his cheeks. "If anybody ever shows up looking for you, they'd better bring a body bag."

Roxxy's lips skinned back from her teeth. She lunged, but the broken rib brought her down in a writhing heap. She watched helplessly as Axel grabbed a handful of Jason's hair and yanked the thin figure to his feet. A roundhouse slap sent Jason spinning across the floor like an out-of-control ice skater. The gyrations slowed and he crumpled, sprawling next to Roxxy.

As if of its own accord, her foreleg extended, and the pad of her paw settled on Jason's pale, tear-streaked cheek. Her tongue worked, but she was too far away to give the soft skin a proper licking.

The next instant, Axel clutched the boy's t-shirt and hefted Jason like a weightlifter raising a barbell. A massive heave sent the boy flying into the front wall. His body smashed into the same calendar that had cushioned her impact, but Jason hit with enough force to dislodge the curling pages and send them fluttering to the concrete below.

Jason bounced off the wall and fell to the floor. His head mercifully landed on the calendar. His limp form lay framed in the doorway.

"*Rarr! Rarr! Rarr! Rarr! Rarr! Rarr! Rarr! Leave him alone!*" thundered Roxxy.

A grunting heave brought her upright. She took two clumsy steps, but she collapsed into the fan-shaped spread of drying vomit.

"Right about there," murmured Axel, tapping the toe of his boot against Jason's bruised temple.

The man adjusted his weight, and his leg drew back like a soccer player about to kick a ball the length of the field.

"*RARR! RARR! RARR! RARR! RARR! NO!*" Roxxy's hysterical barking reverberated off the metal walls.

Axel's foot snapped forward in a glittering arc as the chains caught the light.

"*RARR! RA—*" Stunned amazement stopped Roxxy in mid-bark.

"What the—?!?" bellowed Axel.

Roxxy stared. *Am I seeing what I'm seeing?*

The kick that'd been sweeping toward Jason's temple was frozen in place, restrained by long, curved teeth embedded in the greasy denim at the rear of the man's ankle. The material was clamped between the jaws of a sturdy, thick-boned form.

"Get him, Toby!" barked Roxxy, thrilled that her friend had recovered from paralyzing shock. "Take him down!"

Toby flung himself back and pulled Axel with him to the middle of the room. The man's arms windmilled as he fought to stay upright.

"Too bright…" mumbled Jason.

Roxxy glanced at the boy, who blinked as if the fluorescent lights were searing his eyes. He levered himself to his elbows but stopped there, panting. A lock of hair was stuck to his damp forehead. Jason lifted a hand to brush it away, but the color drained from his face. The back of his head once again bounced off the concrete. He lay still.

RIIIIIIIPPPPPPPP!

Roxxy turned at the sound.

Axel stumbled backward in one direction while Toby reeled away in the other. A ragged section of denim dangled from the basset's jaws. He slid to a halt, his claws leaving white streaks on the floor. A mighty huff of fluttering lips expelled the spit-soaked material.

"What," roared Axel, crooking his leg to examine the mangled ankle of his jeans, "is going *on* around here?"

Fur bristled along the length of Toby's spine. His eyes fixed on Axel's damaged pant leg, and he charged like a crocodile going after a warthog. Roxxy expected the man to climb onto the nearby worktable, but he held his ground. In fact...Axel's eyes glittered as his hand slid to the rear waistband of his jeans. She recalled the bulge she'd noticed beneath the t-shirt.

"*Watch it, Toby!*" Her cry rang out, but her friend either didn't hear or was beyond caring.

He lunged, jaws wide. Axel's arm whipped forward, and the butt of a pistol struck the bony ridge of Toby's skull. *Crack!* The skin split on the crown of the basset's head. Crimson drops flew from the wound in a rising arc, leaving a trail across Axel's grinning mouth and the white-enameled refrigerator behind him.

Roxxy's breath caught as Toby dropped to the floor with the leaden finality of the dead.

"When you mess with the bull"—Axel kicked the limp form—"you get the horns."

An icy lump settled in Roxxy's chest.

Leo...Toby...Jason...all my fault...

Axel dragged the back of his hand across his lips, leaving a red smear.

He turned to Jason's unconscious form, sprawled just inside the doorway. "Too bad for you, punk. I can't leave any witnesses."

"*RARR! RARR! RARR! RARR! RARR! NO! NO! NO! NO!*" roared Roxxy.

She tried to stand, but her weakened legs wouldn't obey. A frustrated snarl escaped. If she were uninjured, a single leap would've allowed her to tear the gun from Axel's hand. There was only one option now. She extended her trembling front leg and dragged herself toward Jason. The cement provided little purchase for her claws, and her progress was slow. No matter. She'd be near the boy at the end.

Weaker now, she beseeched Axel. "Rarr, rarr, rarr, rarr, please no, please no, please no, *please no*."

"Shut it, mutt," said Axel, throwing a glance her way. "You've been trouble since day one. When I finish with the kid, you're next."

He pressed a catch on the side of the blue-black pistol, polished to a menacing gleam. A cylinder dropped open. He narrowed one eye to inspect the contents. A satisfied grunt followed, and a flick of the wrist resettled the chamber in place.

Axel looked at Jason and extended his arm. The barrel's black opening pointed directly at the boy's forehead. "Punk, I wish you were awake to see it coming."

Roxxy struggled on. The rough concrete tugged at her belly fur as she inched closer. She knew she'd be too late to put her body between Jason and the gun. *But not try?* Not an option.

"Should I pop you *new school,* like they do on TV?" Axel's wrist turned so the gun butt was parallel to the floor. "Or old school?" His wrist rotated back.

Roxxy's labored breathing was now a half pant/half growl. Axel and Jason were both silhouetted in the open doorway, the boy on the floor and Axel looming over him. The man was clearly enjoying himself as he went through some kind of strange pantomime with the pistol, turning it this way and that. Jason's mouth was slack, and his cheek pressed against the concrete.

Roxxy stilled her whimpering by shifting her gaze to the scene beyond the open door. The truck's cargo area was packed from floor to ceiling with cages. Most of the captives were slumped in their pens, weakened by stress and despair. A few watched her alertly. The beagle mix stood balanced on sturdy legs.

The dog's white throat was suddenly revealed when she threw back her head and released an encouraging, "*Woof! Woof! Woof!*"

Bam-Bam added a "*Yip!*" that was a simple "thank you."

Wiggle sent a bark of acknowledgment that Roxxy had indeed done her best.

Shame filled her. She'd wanted to save them so much. Her eyes lifted to the hills beyond the truck. A cobalt ribbon outlined the rolling terrain, and the indigo sky was fading with the onset of dawn.

A lone star hung over the horizon, burning tenaciously like a beacon refusing to die.

Click.

Her attention snapped back to Axel as he cocked the gun's hammer. He squinted down the barrel. "Old school it is."

Roxxy growled and struggled to a standing position, but her body locked in an unyielding spasm of pain.

The flesh dimpled on Axel's trigger finger as he squeezed.

She refused to look away. Doing so would be abandoning Jason. *I wish...I wish...*

A brilliant strobe of light pulsed from the low-hanging star and streaked through the doorway—so bright the metal frame glowed with a diamond-like sparkle. The illumination passed *through* Axel, revealing a skeletal outline of his thick bones. Dust motes glowed throughout the Outpost as if suspended in a phosphorescent sea.

Axel flinched as the gun discharged.

And the light from the star disappeared.

A divot of concrete exploded from the floor next to Jason's head as a thunderous *BOOM!* battered the walls. The acrid scent of gunpowder filled Roxxy's nostrils.

"Can't...see." Axel was doubled over and grinding the heels of his hands against his eyes.

Roxxy blinked. *She* could see fine. In fact, her vision was clear and crisp. She could easily make out the wisp of pale gray smoke curling from the end of the gun clutched in Axel's hand. *Why didn't the light blind me? I wonder…*

An experimental step brought a gasp—not of pain, but of surprise. There was a twinge in her flank, but nothing like the agony of before. In fact, she felt as refreshed as if she'd just woken up from a good nap. *Weird.*

"Weird," muttered Axel, shaking his head, but he appeared to be able to see again.

His shoulders stiffened when he saw the small crater made by the bullet on the floor.

"Can't believe I missed from this distance." He thumbed the hammer back. *Click.* "If at first you don't succeed…"

Roxxy's curls flattened in the wind stream of her leap, and a guttural snarl ripped from her throat—the sound of a she-wolf driving a bear away from her cubs.

Axel whirled, bringing up the gun. The O at the end of the barrel was leveled at her head.

I keep forgetting how quick he is.

She contorted herself into a midair flip, twisting and emerging with a trajectory that changed by a precious few inches. Yellow sparks erupted from the barrel, and a cone of hot air singed the side of her face. Searing pain ran the length of her flank. Dazed, she snapped at the last place she'd seen Axel's gun hand—only it wasn't there. The weapon's discharge had lifted his arm straight up. With nothing to halt her momentum, she crashed into the soft spot at the base of his breastbone. The reek of sweat and gunpowder filled her nose as she bounced from his solar plexus and dropped like a stone.

"Oomph!" Axel toppled backward.

She hit the floor first. Her flank absorbed most of the impact, but the side of her head bounced. The clink of her collar tags was drowned out by the giant bell tolling between her ears. The ringing was interrupted by a sharp sound coming from somewhere nearby.

SNAP!

She hoped the branch had broken near the bottom of the oak's canopy rather than closer to the top. The upper boughs held a bird's nest and a knot of tangled leaves and twigs that was home to a family of squirrels. The long-tailed rodents were pesky at times but kind of cute when…

Where am I?

Groggily, she cracked an eyelid. The overhead lights were *much* too bright. She was resting on her cheek, so she closed her lower eye and let the upper one focus on the rear of the barn. But was it a barn? More like a warehouse or something. And what was behind her? Too much trouble to roll over, and something told her she might not be capable anyway. Her nose quaked. Somebody had been shooting off firecrackers. She was glad she'd slept through *that*. Fireworks and thunder, a dog's worst enemies. And cats. Well, not *all* cats, but most. Muffy was okay at times.

Concentrate!

She pulled her legs beneath her and pushed, but the fur on her chest and belly was stuck to the concrete. Was she sprawled in honey? Carol had knocked a plastic jar of the stuff off the kitchen counter one time. Roxxy had started rolling in it before Carol could scoop her up. Both of them had ended up covered. Bill had walked in the kitchen door, and the two humans had burst out laughing.

Focus!

The gooey substance holding her to the floor didn't smell like honey. Too coppery. Like the box of old pennies Bill kept on a shelf in the garage. She was determined not to let a puddle of wet goo hold *her*. She heaved. Pain ripped from shoulder to hip. Her paw pads slipped in the spreading puddle. A convulsion arched her back and left a crescent-shaped smear across the concrete. A racking cough sent pink foam spraying from her nose. She lay staring into the darkened recesses of the barn. No, not a barn…

Don't fall asleep!

A hacking cough released a new spray—redder now than pink. *Something…something about Jason. And Axel. Protect Jason from Axel! That's it! Where* are *they?*

Her third attempt to roll over was successful but accompanied by a disconcerting *squelch*. When the room stopped spinning, her surroundings popped into focus. She was surprised to see Axel taking a nap. He lay on his back near the door. Even crazier, he was using the corner of the metal toolbox for a pillow. *Why…?*

She swallowed hard. His neck was crooked at an odd angle, and his eyes were open. And blank.

Another coughing fit seized her. Weaker this time. No spray, just a smear coating her lips. Movement caught the corner of her eye, and she whimpered with relief. *Jason!* The boy—no, they were past that—*her* boy, sat up and held his hand to his temple.

She managed a raspy huff and was rewarded when he looked at her. The lock of hair was plastered to his forehead, dark against snow-white skin. His hazel eyes were bright. Glistening, in fact. Her tail attempted a wag but was stuck in the wet stuff. She frowned as Jason's face crumpled and his shoulders shook. How could he be sad when she was so happy? He was safe. That was all that mattered. A new thought brought a soft snort of crimson.

Who would have thought…

Her tongue had somehow gotten too thick to clean her muzzle.

…that I'd turn out to be…

The world grayed to black.

…a good dog.

CHAPTER 40

"I'll be good."

The flycatcher perched atop the oak's branch, curling tiny claws into the bark. The bird's sharp beak combed white chest feathers fading to pale-yellow on its belly. The preening stopped as his beady eyes spotted a jerky, zigzag movement below. He unfolded brown wings with a tiered pattern of white stripes and dove. His flight path flattened a beat above the ground. The twitch of a tail feather bled speed and sent him banking sharply. His beak closed on a brown moth, but he didn't swallow. A series of hard flaps sent him back to the oak, where he braked in midair and stopped net to a rounded nest.

His family's home fit snuggly into the crook of two sturdy limbs, tight to the trunk and high in the tree, creating an almost completely enclosed shelter. Twigs, bits of dried grass, and strands of blond fur intertwined to form the tightly woven haven.

High-pitched cheeping erupted, and three tiny heads popped into view, sporting wisps of dull brown feathers. Mouths opened and closed with frantic insistency. The flycatcher dropped the moth. The largest chick shouldered the others out of the way, but the tiniest of the three hopped on her greedy sibling's back and secured one of the moth's wings. Taking advantage of the melee, the middle-size chick snatched the other wing, and the largest sibling made do with the insect's torso.

"Sis, you're zoning out again," said Lulu. Her tail's black tip twitched nervously across straw-colored grass yielding to fall's cooler temperatures. "What are you looking at?"

"Nothing," replied Roxxy, wondering why the sun wasn't warming the narrow stretch of shaved skin down her flank.

The neat line of stitches hadn't yet begun to itch, but she knew from experience it was only a matter of time. Her gaze returned to the well-sheltered nest. Very late in the season to be raising a family for a flycatcher. Would the chicks fledge before the first frost?

"Roxx?" prompted Lulu.

"Hmmm?" She found it hard to take her eyes from the nest.

The tips of the grass and fur along the rim fluttered in the breeze. A storm might—*rotting beams creaked as wind buffeted corrugated walls.* She shook her head hard enough to spin the tags on her collar to the back of her neck.

Lulu looked at Max, who was lying nearby and gnawing noisily on a red rubber ball. She tilted her head toward Roxxy. He shrugged with a flick of his tail and kept working the chewy. Lulu's gaze flattened into a stare.

Max sighed and released the ball. His big paw flicked it across the lawn. Grass clippings stuck to the wet surface.

"Roxx," he said. "You haven't been acting like yourself. What's up?"

She pointed her muzzle into the quickening wind and was rewarded by the scent of meat cooking on a distant outdoor grill. Steaks. There was no mistaking that special scent of fat rendering around the edge of a juicy slab of beef. She wished she was close enough to hear the sizzle of drippings landing on hot coals. Still, the smell was wonderful and…*the reek of gunpowder seared the back of her throat.*

"Sis!" implored Lulu. "You're shivering."

"A-Am not," replied Roxxy through chattering teeth.

The steady *chuff-chuff-chuff* of a lawn sprinkler echoed from a neighbor's property. She could imagine the rotor throwing water in a glistening arc…*like chains glittering on a boot sweeping toward her head.*

"Roxx," said Max. "You're scaring us! Are you hurting? Is something else the matter?" He ran his nose down her line of stitches. "There's no infection. Are you hurting?"

"I'm fine," said Roxxy.

"You are not fine. You've been acting weird ever since you got home from the hospital."

"And Max knows weird," agreed Lulu.

"Thanks. I—*hey!*"

"Let me try, Maxey," Lulu offered.

"Wait a minute. Are you saying *I'm* weird?"

"Isn't it obvious?" retorted Lulu. "Weirdo!"

"Stop name-calling!"

"Sorry," conceded Lulu. "We need to focus on Roxxy."

Max retrieved the ball and began gnawing. Beneath his breath, he muttered wetly, "*Thishters.*"

"Roxx," said Lulu. "This is one of the rare times Max is right. You've only been home for three days, and I know you're still recovering, but you've been…in a daze or something. Max and I are worried, and I think Momma and Poppa are too."

Max dropped the ball and scooted over so that his rangy frame was at a right angle to Roxxy's. "Sis, tell us what we can we do to help."

She rested her chin on his outstretched foreleg. His tight, wiry curls made a comfy cushion that smelled pleasantly of sage and thyme.

She asked, "Were you in the herb garden earlier?"

"Yes, and don't change the subject. What's up?"

"Nothing."

"Not nothing," insisted Max. "I'm your big brother, and you should let me help. That's my job."

"Here we go," said Lulu, eyes shining.

Roxxy sat up.

"Yes, you're seven minutes older and the size of—Lulu, what's an example of a big, dumb animal?"

"Max."

"Hey!"

Roxxy snorted. "An even bigger, dumber animal?"

"Hippo? Rhino?"

"Right." Roxxy focused on her brother. "You're seven minutes older and the size of one of those big, dumb beasts whose name ends in an O, but that doesn't mean I need you to look after me. I can take care of myself. So stop grilling me." She took a deep breath. "Please."

"*Please*?" repeated Max in disbelief. "That's what I mean. When did *you* become polite? The old Roxxy would've—*OUCH!*"

A nearby chipmunk dropped an acorn at the sound of the loud bark and dove into a tunnel at the base of an oak.

Roxxy spat out the wiry curl that a second before had adorned the tip of Max's ear. "Happy now?"

"Thrilled." He wiggled sideways, removing himself from easy nipping range. The flattened blades of grass where he had sprawled began righting themselves. "Thanks for letting me know you're still you."

"My pleasure." The skin bordering her stitches suddenly felt pleasantly warm under the late-afternoon sun.

"Roxx," said Max. "If you're feeling good enough to take a chunk out of my ear—"

"Hardly a chunk," interjected Lulu.

"A mere speck," agreed Roxxy.

Max plowed on. "Then you should feel up to *finally* telling me and Lulu what happened when you rescued those stolen dogs. We got the basics from Momma and Poppa, but you know how they are. They left out all the good parts. All we heard is that you got hurt and Jason carried you down the hill as the paramedics arrived to help Marcy."

"That about covers it," said Roxxy, feeling the chill return.

The divot in the concrete next to Jason's head...

A wind gust drew a creak from the oak limbs rubbing together overhead. Her eyes lifted to the flycatcher nest. The haven seemed secure but...you never really knew.

"Come on!" Max flicked his tuft-less ear impatiently. "This is the first time Lulu and I have had you to ourselves. Momma and Poppa have been hovering over you since you got home. I want all the grisly details of what happened."

Roxxy flinched. *A snap, a neck at an odd angle, open but sightless eyes...*

"Quit stalling," urged Max. "What—"

"Put a sock in it, Maxey." A frown creased Lulu's snow-white forehead. "I think we should talk about something else. Roxxy looks sort of...uh..."

"Barf-y," supplied Max. He edged close enough to sniff Roxxy's muzzle. "Definitely barf-y."

Lulu snapped, "*No* girl likes to be described as *barf-y*, you dimwit."

"Barf-y isn't an insult. Sometimes you need a good upchuck to clear out the system." Max scooted back and looked expectantly at Roxxy. "Go ahead, Sis. Let it fly."

"*Maxxxx!*" Lulu warned. "You're *not* helping."

"Okay, okay. I'm sorry I brought up barf-y to begin with."

"Change. The. Subject," Lulu ordered.

"Okay! Uh, did you like that new kibble this morning? Crunchy enough for you?"

"Crunch factor was fine," Lulu replied, wrinkling her nose. "But there was too much liver in the blend. The taste made me feel kind of—"

"Barf-y?" suggested Max. "How did we get back on that? In fact, just *saying* barf-y is making me a little queasy right now. Who knew that talking about barf-y could make you feel—☒"

"If you say barf-y one more time," Lulu interrupted calmly, "I will murder you."

Roxxy snorted so loudly her sibs turned to her in alarm. Air stirred from behind. Probably her first tail wag since…since…well, in a while. She suspected the dark memories of Axel and her experience at the Outpost would always linger somewhere inside, but her sibs were drawing her back to a place of light and warmth.

Maybe that's what it takes. Maybe love is what heals us in the end.

"Roxx," huffed Lulu. "How come you seem better all of a sudden?"

"Yeah," Max added. "You don't look so, uh…"

"I give up," said Lulu.

"I wasn't going to say barf-y!"

"Is that even a word?" asked Roxxy.

"Only," explained Lulu, "if you speak 'Max.'"

Roxxy was in mid-snort when the rattle of chain links drew her attention to the opposite side of the yard. Leo squeezed through his customary point of entry and approached in an off-balance, hopping gait. One of his legs extended slightly to the side and was held stiffly by a wrapped splint. Small white bandages speckled his torso. Most of his tawny fur had been shaved, with the notable exception of his mane, which was teased into a short but perfectly round globe.

Roxxy winced as she leaned forward and touched noses with him.

"Wow." Leo examined her stitches, leaning so close his tiny eyelashes tickled her shaved skin. "The last time I saw a row of stitches like that, Helen and I were watching an old monster movie on TV—big dude made up of body parts sewn together."

Roxxy's eyes narrowed. "Meaning?"

Leo ran his nose along the neat line of sutures. "He had the same thing going on. Looked like he'd been attacked by a sewing machine."

"This"—Max nudged Lulu—"is going to be fun."

"I look like a monster?" Roxxy glared at the Pom. "Is *that* what you said?"

"He sure did, Roxx," Lulu woofed. "I heard him clear as anything. Talk about insensitive."

"Wait a minute!" Leo backed up awkwardly as his splinted leg kept getting caught in the lawn. "I didn't mean, uh…what I mean is, uh…I'm sure you'll heal up soon. You're not going to look like a monster *forever*."

Lulu's eyes widened.

"It's like watching a train wreck." She lay down and rested her chin on coal-black paws. "In slow motion."

"Roxx," said Leo in a strangled tone. "I'm trying to pay you a compliment. I can be a bit vain at times—"

"You?" asked Roxxy. "Really?"

"But you're not like me. You're not obsessed with how you look."

"Leo," said Max gently. "You've *got* to stop talking. I have lots of experience getting out of this kind of mess. Trust me."

The Pom took another step back from Roxxy, but the end of the splint caught on an exposed root. His rump hit the ground.

"Roxx, you *know* I didn't mean to insult you. I'm just—"

"Crude and half-witted!" Toby's woof boomed cheerily. "Don't worry about it. Nobody's surprised."

Roxxy whirled. Her stitches protested, and she swallowed a yelp to avoid worrying anyone. Toby was on his deck, sporting a thick padded bandage taped to the top of his head. His claws clattered against the gray planks as he descended the steps in his usual lumbering but sure-pawed fashion. His stocky body rocked from side to side, and his long ears swung like synchronized pendulums. As soon as he reached the lawn, he broke into an ungainly trot.

Leo huffed quietly. "Roxx, don't tell him, but I'm glad to see he's— *What's wrong, Toby?*"

"*Sit down!*" Roxxy yapped at the basset.

Toby's eyelids fluttered, and he staggered sideways into a late-blooming tea olive shrub. Tiny white petals rained down on him. He continued forward on wobbly legs.

"*SIT DOWN!*" commanded Roxxy with so much force that the male flycatcher leaped from a low branch and flew to guard the nestlings.

"Okay, Roxx." Toby's hindquarters hit the grass. He sat wheezing, midway between his house and the fence.

"Take your time and catch your breath."

"I'm worried," Leo whispered to Roxxy. "He looks like he's going pass out."

"Shush! You're going to make him self-conscious."

"I can *hear* you," snapped Toby. "There's nothing wrong with my ears." He stood and approached the fence. "Stop fretting."

"I'm not fretting," yipped Leo. "Who says I'm fretting?"

"Aww, you're worried about me." A traffic helicopter flew low over the house, engine roaring. Toby waited until the noise had passed before adding, "I'm touched."

"Worried?" Leo snorted. "About you? Not likely. In fact, I was just telling Roxxy it's lucky you were hit on the head. Solid bone through and through."

"At least I don't look like a gerbil who was shot out of a cannon."

Roxxy touched noses with him through the chain-link fence and smelled the scrambled eggs Kimberly must've added to his bowl at breakfast. A second later, Leo appeared beside her. He leaned forward carefully on his good front leg and pushed his tiny snout through the chain links. Roxxy caught the sparkle of surprise in Toby's chocolate eyes as he brushed his bulbous nose against Leo's delicate one.

Lulu rose and shook. Her tags still jingled as she huffed to Max. "Come on, big brother. Let's go inside so the walking wounded can get caught up. They haven't seen each other since the night they got hurt."

"No way! I want to stay and hear—*oomph*!"

Lulu straightened after throwing a shoulder into Max's flank. "Get going!"

"But—"

"Besides," insisted Lulu, "we should check on Momma and Poppa. They were both acting strangely earlier."

"Okay."

Max ducked to avoid a ruby-throated hummingbird zipping past one of his triangular ears. Its iridescent wings glittered like emeralds.

"But before we go…" His tail drooped as he looked uncertainly at Roxxy.

"What?" she asked. "More questions?"

"Uh, no." Max pointed his chin at her stitches. "I just hope you've finally learned to stay out of trouble. I…we…worry about you, is all."

She started to reply flippantly, but the remark died under the weight of her brother's earnest cinnamon gaze.

"Sure, Maxey," she replied hoarsely. "I'll be good."

"I'm not asking for miracles. Just stay away from dog-nappers and maniacs."

"Sage advice," agreed Lulu. "Especially when you've encountered a person who qualified as both."

Max frowned. "I'm serious, Lulu. You know how Roxxy is about—"

"I was agreeing, you big softie." Lulu dropped into the *let's play* position by lowering her chest to the ground while keeping her hindquarters raised. "Come on. I'll race you to the back door."

Roxxy watched her sibs dash away. They were trailed by an arching shower of freshly mown grass, flung into the air by their back paws. Roxxy sighed. During the battle with Axel at the Outpost, she had given up hope of ever returning to her forever home. Now, she vowed to appreciate every second of every day with her loved ones. No more adventures for her! She would never leave her property again—except for walks, of course.

"What are you thinking?" asked Toby.

"Just happy to be home." She studied him through her blond bangs. "You looked pretty wobbly on your way over. How long before you're back to normal?"

"Clarify, please," said Leo before Toby could respond. "Normal for a regular dog? Or for a basset hound? How low are you setting the bar?"

"Roxx, did you hear something?" asked Toby. "Sounded like somebody stepped on a squeaky toy."

"Both of you stop it," she ordered.

"What did I do?" asked Leo.

He used his splint to rake an acorn close and began to gnaw. A soft *crack* sounded as its dimpled crown broke.

"Toby," said Roxxy. "Ignore him."

"Who?" asked the basset.

"That's the spirit."

"I'm definitely getting better. The headaches are mostly gone, and I only get dizzy if I run too fast. The vet says I'll be good as new in a week or so." He ran his eye over her flank. "What about *that*?"

"Just a scratch."

The fence bowed inward as Toby shoved his nose through the chain links until his nostrils were an inch away from her wound. He sniffed noisily before giving a satisfied grunt.

"Seems to be healing well. You'll be good as new in no time." Toby leaned back, and the fence resumed its normal shape with a jangling clatter. His eyes settled on Leo's splinted leg and the taped gauze dotting his small torso. "What about you, rodent? Feeling okay?"

The Pom frowned. "See the bandages, genius? Every inch of my body either aches or itches. Some parts ache *and* itch. Each second is a misery."

"Don't sugarcoat it," Toby deadpanned. "Tell me how you *really* feel."

"I *feel* like sinking my teeth into one of those elephant ears, and—"

"You guys behave," said Roxxy, though a following snort belied the order.

Hearing her friends argue was a sure sign they were on the mend. She scooted closer to the fence and directed a questioning tail flick at Toby.

"How's Jason doing? I haven't heard a word about him since"—she swallowed—"that night."

"I haven't seen him, but I've got some news. Susan—"

"Who?" asked Leo.

"Jason's mom. She came over alone last night to check on Marcy's ankle and bring a casserole. They were talking, and—"

"What kind of casserole?" Leo's eyes shone.

"Sort of a beef stew thing with mashed potatoes on top. Kimberly saved me some. Delicious."

"I *do* like a good beef stew," said Leo wistfully, gnawing again on the acorn. "Especially when the meat's tender, and—"

"We were talking," interrupted Roxxy, "about Jason."

The Pom snorted. "Are we following an agenda? I thought we were having a casual conversation, and—"

"*Leo.*"

"Okay, Roxx. Sheesh! Don't be so touchy."

"Go on, Toby," said Roxxy, ears tilting forward.

"Susan told Marcy that Jason's going to be fine. No permanent injuries."

A hard knot of worry loosened in Roxxy's chest. She was about to ask Toby for more details, but the plastic flap on the dog door to her family home clacked open. Her father and mother pushed through, followed by her sibs and even Muffy. Something about the procession was oddly disturbing as they walked stiffly down the deck steps.

"I'd better get going," said Leo, using his splint to lever himself upright.

"Me too." Toby's big tongue made a raspy sweep across his muzzle. "Roxx, just remember that everything will be all right."

She didn't respond. All her attention was on the group heading toward her. Her momma and poppa approached with ears drooping in distress. Their tails bobbed in a failing effort to remain erect. Max and Lulu were close behind, panting and looking as bewildered as she felt.

What could—? Realization dawned.

She gasped and rounded on Toby and Leo. "You both knew!"

"Don't be mad," the basset pleaded in a choked whisper.

He threw Leo a desperate look.

"Roxx," said the Pom, "it wasn't our place to..."

The rest of his words were blotted out by the roar in her head. She barely noticed as the pair crept away in opposite directions, each headed home.

Home...

Her gaze moved jerkily across the yard, bouncing off images...well-loved chew toys...garden paths worn with paw prints...springy clover for napping...a shady area beneath the oak where family meetings had...

Family...

Her eyes traveled back to the approaching figures.

CHAPTER 41

"If you weren't so adorable, you'd be annoying."

"Snuggle up," ordered Roxxy.

Max and Lulu complied, settling close on either side. Their hearts hammered so hard she felt the pounding through the flanks pressed against hers. She gave each sib a reassuring nuzzle before training a hard stare on Jake and Molly.

Her parents sat opposite them, separate from her and the sibs.

Just as it should be. She tasted bitterness on the back of her tongue.

The two groups' shadows stretched across the yard. To the west, the sun was disappearing with alarming speed beneath a red horizon, as if extinguished in a sea of blood.

Molly's dull eyes swept her offspring. "Your father and I thought this day might come."

"*Would* come," Jake corrected, the fur bristling along his spine.

The two older dogs exchanged a look that spoke of a long-standing disagreement.

"*What* day?" asked Lulu.

"Y-Yeah," stuttered Max. "You're s-scaring us!"

Roxxy glared at her parents. "Get it over with!"

"Bill and Carol are moving," blurted Molly.

"Far away," added Jake hoarsely.

"*What?*" Max and Lulu chorused.

"Bill's employer is transferring him to another city," said Molly, beginning to pant. "We—your father and I—are going with them, but you three will be adopted out to new homes before the move."

A line of silver drool slid from the corner of her mouth and settled near a ladybug resting between her paws. The insect's shiny red carapace divided to form two wings. It took flight, leaving a dwindling buzz in its wake.

"But Momma," whimpered Lulu. "That means I'll never see *any* of you again."

"Lulu"—Jake clawed the lawn, and a tuft of brown grass came away to expose the dark earth beneath—"this is the way things have to be. Your mother and I don't have any say in the matter. But I know Bill and Carol will make sure each of you goes to a good home."

"We thought this place *was* home," grated Max. "You should have told us we might be split up. Then we could have…could have…"

His voice broke off in a strangled grunt, and he buried his head against Roxxy's neck.

"I know this is hard," said Molly, running her tongue across her muzzle to clear the drool. "But there is a way for us to always be connected, even though we're separated."

"Connected but separated?" Lulu's scruff bunched. "*What* are you talking about?"

"I'm not saying it properly." Molly glanced at Jake for support, but his face was hidden as he nervously rubbed his front paws across his muzzle.

"Well?" demanded Lulu.

Molly swallowed. "Lulu…all of you…whenever we want to feel connected, we can see…I mean look to the—"

"Star," interrupted Roxxy softly, her gaze on the southwestern sky.

The red horizon had lightened to coral. The sky above was pastel blue darkening to indigo. Above the curvature of the earth shone pinpricks of light. One glowed brighter than the rest.

"Star?" growled Max. "Roxx, we're being split up, and you're talking about a *star*? You're not making any more sense than Momma."

"Just look." She pointed her chin.

"Yeah, yeah. One stands out more than the rest. So what?"

"Hold on a minute, son." Jake turned to Roxxy and said heavily, "I'm disappointed in Leo and Toby. I asked them not to tell you about the Star Legend."

Roxxy's mouth hung open. *Is he talking about* my *star?*

Jake's eyes swept his offspring. "Your mother and I wanted to save the story for the day—well, *this* day—when we had to tell you that you would be adopted into new homes. The tale about the legend will hopefully soften the blow." He paused before adding to Roxxy, "That's why I didn't want Leo and Toby to tell you about it beforehand."

"Don't blame them. Nobody told me anything." She glared. "As usual."

A *whoosh* sounded that all the dogs knew well. A neighbor a few houses down had set a match to charcoal soaked in lighter fuel. The aroma of burning briquettes followed. Conversation stopped as noses twitched.

"Roxxy," said Jake. "If Toby and Leo didn't say anything about the Star Legend, then how do you know it?"

"I didn't know the star was special to *all* dogs. I just thought it was special to me."

"Is *everything* about you?" asked Max.

"Yeah," chimed in Lulu. "I love you, Sis, but you go from one death-defying adventure to another. Every day is a highlight reel."

"What are you two talking about? I'd be perfectly happy just eating and napping. It's not my fault that I keep getting dragged into—"

"Wait a minute," interrupted Jake. "Let's stay on track. Roxxy, how did you know the star was special?"

"Well, I thought I was imagining things at first. Whenever I was trying to decide something important, the star would glow brighter for an instant—like a signal. I think it was telling me to trust my instincts."

"So," growled Max, "the star's an idiot."

Roxxy ignored her brother. "Poppa, when I was at the Outpost, the star showed me how special it really is."

"How?" asked Jake, ears tilted forward.

"Axel kicked me and threw me against a wall—don't whimper, Momma—and I was hurt so badly I couldn't get up. Jason was in even worse shape. Axel had knocked him out." The smell of moldy rafters and the stink of her own vomit coated the back of her throat.

"Roxxy," said Molly softly. "You don't have to say anything more if you don't want to."

"I-I need to finish. Axel aimed a gun at Jason's head."

Roxxy expected the chuffs of surprise from her parents and sibs, but she jumped when Muffy added an outraged hiss. What was it with cats? They had that creepy way of staying dead still so you forget they were there.

She eyed the feline. "How about throwing up a hair ball occasionally to remind me you're hanging around."

"You're just jealous," purred Muffy. "Because you have all the stealth of an avalanche."

"You miserable—"

"Roxxy," prompted Jake. "What were you saying about the Star Legend?"

"I'm not talking about some old legend. I'm describing how the star helped when I was at the Outpost." She took a slow breath and released it. "When Axel fired the gun, the star unleashed the brightest light I've ever seen. It came and went in a second, but it blinded Axel. He flinched, and the shot missed Jason."

"Roxx," asked Lulu, "if you were blinded, how did you—"

"No," interrupted Roxxy. "That's just it. The flash blinded Axel but not me. Somehow, the light even took away my pain…well, most of it. Anyway, when Axel took aim at Jason again, I was ready."

A sudden thought caused her voice to dry up. *Leaving home not only means I'll never see my family again. It means I'll never see Jason.*

She stood and began pacing, hardly feeling the pull of the stitches. She knew why Jason hadn't come to visit her. That dog-hating mother of his—no, Toby had said dog-*fearing*—was undoubtedly keeping him away.

Roxxy's tail drooped. She was going to be whisked off by strangers and would never get to say a proper goodbye to the boy.

"Don't look so sad," consoled Lulu. "Axel *had* to be stopped. No one blames you for what happened to him."

Roxxy's bangs twitched in a frown. Axel? *Oh.* She didn't bother to correct her sister. Better that Lulu think she felt bad about what happened to the man than admitting she was disappointed about never seeing Jason again. She'd had a moment at the Outpost where she had more or less claimed him, but she'd been semi-delirious. It wasn't like she *wanted* to crawl into his lap, put her front paws on his chest, and use her nose to nudge that lock of hair off his forehead. Why didn't the kid have a comb? Was *anyone* looking after him?

"I can hear you grinding your teeth, Roxx," observed Max.

"You're imaging things."

She worked her jaw from side to side before asking her father, "What's the Star Legend about?"

"This is just a wild guess," purred Muffy. "But I'd say it has something to do with a legendary star."

Jake snorted. "Muffy's right. The legend is about *that* star." He nodded toward the southwestern horizon. "The tale's been passed down from one generation of dogs to the next. It all began with a boy finding an orphaned wolf cub."

A twinkle entered Jake's cinnamon eyes. "Come to think of it, the human in the story is about the same age as Roxxy's friend, Jason."

Roxxy huffed, "*I* never said he was my friend. Seems like every time I run into him I get more stitches. The kid's a jinx."

"Duly noted."

Roxxy frowned as Jake wrinkled his muzzle in a way that looked suspiciously like he was suppressing a snort.

"Now," he continued, "back to the legend. Keep in mind all this happened when the only records kept by humans consisted of cave wall drawings. The boy who found the wolf was named Wind Runner. His tribe lived in the foothills bordering vast grassy plains. He stumbled upon the coal-black, half-starved puppy. She lay huddled and sleeping beneath an old log. The ground nearby was torn up and red from blood soaked into the earth. Wind Runner knew how to interpret the signs. The pup's mother had died protecting her from a bear and had then been dragged away to be eaten."

Lulu whimpered, and Max gave her a reassuring nuzzle.

Jake continued. "The pup was asleep and near death when Wind Runner found her. He ran a hand over her sunken flank and was surprised when she opened golden eyes and gazed trustingly at him. The boy was smitten."

"Did he take her home?" asked Lulu.

"No. The only canines in those days were wolves—fierce predators and competitors with humans for the herds of giant elk that roamed the plains. Wind Runner's father had warned him to stay clear of wolves and to kill any young or wounded ones separated from the pack. The boy knew the orphaned pup wouldn't survive contact with his tribal members. He made an instant decision and a moment later was dashing among the rocks with the pup tucked under his arm. He hid her in a clean, dry cave near the village. With great care to avoid being discovered, he snuck away daily to feed her small game."

Roxxy blinked as an itchy sensation rippled down the line of stitches. She rolled to her flank and wiggled. Stiff blades of grass found the strip of skin surrounding the sutures. *Ahhh...*

"Stop scratching," ordered Molly.

"I'm itchy."

"The vet sent you home with a cone," Molly said warningly. "Just in case."

Roxxy stopped wiggling.

"Wind Runner and the pup," resumed Jake, "developed a loving bond as the days passed. A few weeks after finding her, the boy was combing out her coat with a pinecone when a hunting party from his camp stumbled upon the cave. The men shouted for him to move so they could kill the wolf, but Wind Runner wrapped her in his arms and shielded her with his body. The pup was having none of it. *She* tried to squirm free so the hunters wouldn't accidentally spear Wind Runner while trying to get to her." Jake paused. "Do you see? The instant the pup was willing to sacrifice herself for Wind Runner, she stopped being a wild animal and became a..."

His voice trailed off as he watched his offspring expectantly.

"A dog," whispered Roxxy.

"The *first* dog," confirmed Jake.

"Well," said Max. "I didn't see *that* coming."

"Me either," confirmed Lulu.

Roxxy's gaze returned to the star burning brightest in the indigo sky.

"Let's get back to the story." Max sat forward. "What happened when Wind Runner wouldn't let the hunters hurt the pup?"

"The men hauled the boy and wolf back to camp. A tribal council was held, and Wind Runner was able to convince the elders that he could teach her to track game for the hunters." Jake shrugged. "The arrangement worked out so well that she became popular with the tribe."

"That sounds like the short version," said Lulu. "The members of the tribe must've needed a *lot* of convincing to trust her."

Jake flicked an ear in agreement. "Right you are. For now, I'm keeping the story brief, but I do want to share the ending. She and Wind Runner had many adventures together. The years passed, and she grew old even as he became a strong man. Late one night, as she slept at the foot of his blanket, a viper slithered into the grass hut and struck, fangs bared and wedge-shaped head aimed at Wind Runner's ankle. The dog flung herself between her person and the snake. She was bitten on the neck. Wind Runner killed the viper and flung it aside. He pulled the dog close and cradled her shaggy head in his arms. She died tasting his tears as they fell upon her tongue."

Molly added, "The instant her old heart gave out, a dazzling glow appeared above the southwestern horizon. She fulfilled her namesake, and from that day to this, the spirit of the first dog dwells in the brightest light in the evening sky."

Lulu's white forehead creased. "Namesake?"

"I don't get it either," added Max.

"I think I do," said Roxxy slowly.

"Well, of course." Lulu sighed. "You're always one step ahead, Sis. If you weren't so adorable, you'd be annoying."

"In fact," added Max crossly, "I'd say the adorableness and the annoyingness are neck and neck." He fixed Roxxy with a glare. "Spill it."

"Poppa said the pup's eyes were golden." Roxxy flicked her tail in a shrug. "What else is golden? Wind Runner named her Star."

"Right," said Jake.

"So," said Max. "Let me get this straight. Star is the dog's name, and when she dies, her spirit goes to live in the brightest star. That's a lot of star stuff to keep straight. My head is hurting."

"Stop trying to think," said Roxxy kindly. "You'll only make it worse."

"Now, now, Roxx," huffed Lulu. "Max has the ability to think. He just needs practice."

"Thanks, Lulu, I—*wait*, what?"

"You three knock it off and pay attention," said Molly, though her loving tone took the sting from the words. "Focus on what's important. No matter where life takes us—"

"Or how far apart we are," interjected Jake.

"We can look into the night sky, and as long as Star's light shines on us, we'll be in each other's hearts, always connected."

Roxxy and her family turned as one to gaze at the light glowing fiercely against the darkness.

A respectful moment passed before Jake said, "And remember something else. When a person's kind to a dog, or a dog comforts a person, Star's spirit is strengthened. Her light grows stronger. She's proof that the mission of all dogs—Muffy, stop hissing—all *pets* is to love humans and bring out the best in them."

"Hold on!" Roxxy sat up so quickly a bead of blood oozed from a stitch.

"Be careful!" ordered Molly, hurrying over to lick away the crimson drop. She squinted to inspect the almost invisible line of filament sealing the wound. "Roxxy, watch those sudden movements."

"Yes, Momma," replied Roxxy automatically.

Her thoughts were on Axel's plan to send the stolen dogs to some terrible place where they'd never find comfort.

She pinned her father with a stare. "That was a nice story, Poppa, but some pets are forced to live in terrible conditions. They become strays and never find anyone to love them. What does Star's spirit do for *them*?"

"Her light is a promise," replied Jake with calm conviction. "Every pet who longs to bond with a human but didn't have a chance to in this life will find happiness when they cross the bridge and reach a place of lasting love and contentment."

"Bridge?" Lulu asked. "Did I miss something? I thought we were talking about a star. *What* bridge?"

"I'm coming to that," Jake replied. "*The* bridge—the one that takes us from this life to the next. It glows with the most beautiful colors imaginable. The brightest reds and yellows."

"And the richest greens and blues," said Molly. "Like a rainbow sweeping across the sky."

"The bridge reunites pets with all the loved ones they've ever known," explained Jake.

"And if an animal was mistreated in this life," added Molly, "or never found a person to love, then waiting at the end of the bridge is a human with a kind and welcoming heart."

"Wow," observed a wide-eyed Max. "That's some bridge."

"You bet it is," agreed Jake. "But let's wrap it up for now. The three of you can think about things and ask all the questions you want. We still have a few days b-b—" His voice faltered but regained its strength. "Before anyone's going anywhere. Just remember that whenever you want to feel the love that we all share right this minute, simply look into the night sky."

A silence fell that was interrupted by a Hermit thrush's insistent call. *Weeee-ree-ree-ra...weeee-ree-ree-ra.*

Roxxy lifted her hind paw to scratch the line of stitches but noticed her mother's raised eyebrow and instead raked the fur behind an ear. *Stupid cones.*

"There's something else to keep in mind," said Jake while studying Roxxy. "Legend says Star's spirit sometimes take a particular interest in a dog who is, uh…"

"Too stubborn for her own good," interjected Lulu.

"And thinks she's right all the time," chimed in Max.

"And drawn to trouble."

"Like a curly blond moth to a flame."

"Did you two rehearse this?" Roxxy asked her siblings.

Molly snorted. "Let's get back to what your father was saying."

"Thank you, hon," said Jake, giving his mate an affectionate flick of the ear.

He turned his attention to Roxxy. "You said earlier that Star sent a beam of light strong enough to blind Axel?"

"More like a flash. Time seemed to stand still, and I could see every little detail around me like it was frozen in place. Then the flash just disappeared. Axel was blinded for at least a minute. Had his hands over his eyes."

"Hmm… Star's light shines on all dogs, but legend says that once in a great while she'll take a special interest in a dog who's resourceful and dedicated to helping others no matter the danger. When Star takes notice of such a dog, she will glow brighter to offer encouragement. But…" Jake's voice trailed off.

He twitched an ear questioningly at Molly. She shrugged a *me-neither* response.

"What?" asked Roxxy.

"Well," said Jake. "Your mother and I have never heard of Star sending a burst of light that would blind a human—even temporarily. That's powerful stuff. She has taken a *very* special interest in you."

"That must be it," said Max, hiccuping with the effort to hold back a snort. "Star is going all out. She knows that Roxxy is a disaster waiting to happen."

"Poor Star," added Lulu with a sympathetic pout. "She's taken on a project."

"Somebody—*hic*—should've—*hic*—warned her."

"That's right, Maxey. Star doesn't know what she's in for."

The pair collapsed against each other in a fit of giggles.

"I know what you two are in for if you don't put a sock in it," growled Roxxy, secretly pleased at her sibs' amusement. It was an indication they were starting to adjust to the news of the coming separation.

She breathed a sigh. *We might just get through this…*

Jake stood and shook. A burr flew from his wiry coat and landed near a yellow honeysuckle vine. "I heard Carol and Bill discussing their plans. We have a few days before they start interviewing prospective families, so that's enough discussion for now. Besides"—he ran a tongue across his muzzle and withdrew it into his mouth with a wet *smack*—"it's almost dinnertime. Let's see if Bill will slip us some leftover pot roast."

Roxxy rose too quickly and winced when the stitches protested. She paused to catch her breath as her parents and sibs ambled toward the house. Jake's head tilted toward Max. Roxxy heard her father's reassuring tone, even though she couldn't make out the content. Molly walked next to Lulu. They chatted quietly while their tails waved in unison like a car's windshield wipers.

A heaviness filled Roxxy's heart.

"Don't worry."

Roxxy swallowed a startled yip and rounded on Muffy, who had crept up alongside her. "Don't *do* that. Shouldn't you be wearing a bell or something?"

"I'll look after your folks." Muffy brushed her whiskers across her housemate's short muzzle.

"Stop creeping me out," said Roxxy, leaning into the caress despite her protest. She pulled back and studied the cat. Muffy's green eyes were luminous in the light of the full moon hanging above Toby's house. "Look after yourself, Muff. I'll…I'll miss you."

The feline's white paw moved in a blur as claws swept toward Roxxy's startled features. She flinched, but the blow slowed an inch from her cheek. The claws disappeared into their sheaths. A feather-like swipe slid across the side of Roxxy's face.

"You're not a bad sort," purred Muffy, "for a *dog*."

The cat turned and sauntered toward the house without a backward glance.

Roxxy grunted. She should've known the horrible hair ball would have the last word. Her ears lifted as a heavy vehicle braked in the street. Her nose quaked and picked up the familiar scent of diesel fumes from the UPS truck. Early evening deliveries weren't unusual. Her paws itched with the desire to charge to the front section of fence and bark a warning to notify the driver he was on her territory… Then she remembered. The yard and the house—and even Bill and Carol—were no longer hers to protect. Her chest felt as empty as one of the hollow pumpkins Bill discarded after making a pie.

And what would happen to Lulu and Max when the family was split up? Roxxy had no doubt Bill and Carol would take care to find good homes for her and her sibs, but there was always the possibility that something unforeseen might happen afterward. Max and Lulu's new people might become ill or lose their jobs or need to move into a place where dogs weren't allowed. What then? Her sibs might be given away and end up with humans who were uncaring or even cruel. Roxxy shivered as she remembered Basher's poo-filled pen and the crate with the slats missing. The sweet-natured dog was now in his forever home with Vicky, but Roxxy couldn't block out the image of the narrow enclosure where he'd been neglected.

Roxxy looked at the glittering object on the southwestern horizon. Her huff was barely a whisper.

"Watch over Max and Lulu. Keep them safe. In return, if I see a pet or person who needs help, or if I come across another monster like Axel who has to be stopped, I'll take care of it." Her gaze flattened with challenge. "Deal?"

The responding flash came and went in a heartbeat.

"Roxxy!"

She turned. The dog door's flap swung back and forth. Only her mother remained on the deck.

"Yes, Momma?"

"There's something I forgot to mention." Molly's chestnut eyes—the identical shade of Roxxy's—twinkled. "I overheard Carol say Jason's parents are coming over tomorrow. They're thinking of making an offer on the house. Jason will be with them."

"Doesn't matter to me."

"That so?"

Roxxy felt air stir from behind.

Stupid tail!

Author Bio

ROB RONIN HAS BEEN a published author since 2003. He is a psychologist and educator, but doesn't allow those roles to interfere with his duties as personal assistant to his beloved dog, Ginger. She is the inspiration for Roxxy. Rob adopts the philosophy captured by the adage: be the person your dog thinks you are. Please visit: www.RoxxyDog.com.

Illustrator Bio

KIM RONIN IS AN award-winning illustrator and created the original artwork used in *Roxxy to the Rescue*. Kim also produced the drawings used in the interior pages to set the mood for each chapter. Kim has been an active volunteer at the Greenville Humane Society, a no-kill animal shelter in South Carolina, since 2007. Kim has walked thousands of dogs, providing them with exercise and treats to bring them comfort until they are adopted into forever homes.

Muse Bio

THE THIRD MEMBER OF the Ronin household, Ginger, notes that her role in the project was the most demanding. Being adorable is exhausting.

Milton Keynes UK
Ingram Content Group UK Ltd.
UKHW030641191124
451300UK00018B/368/J